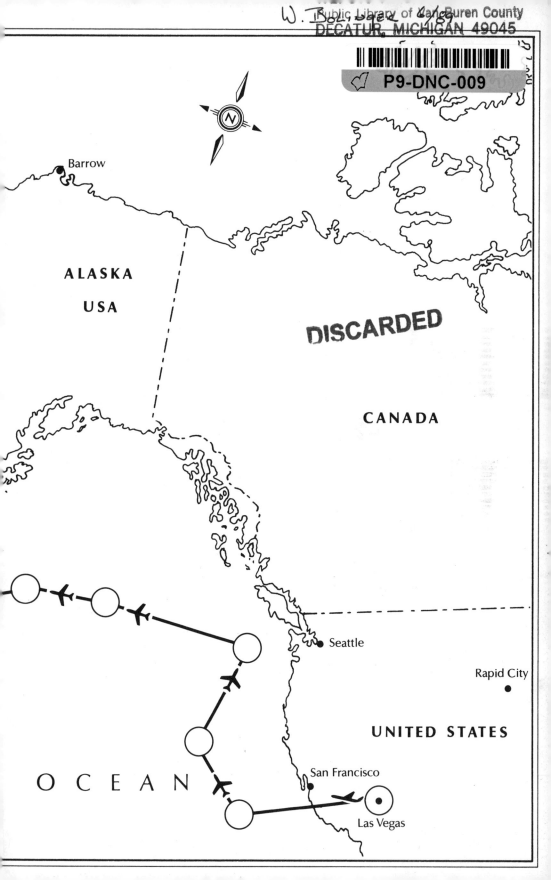

Barrow

ALASKA

USA

CANADA

Seattle

Rapid City

UNITED STATES

OCEAN

San Francisco

Las Vegas

FLIGHT OF THE OLD DOG

FLIGHT OF

A NOVEL BY

THE OLD DOG

DALE BROWN

DŒF

DONALD I. FINE, INC.
NEW YORK

All rights reserved, including the right of reproduction in whole
or in part in any form. Published in the United States of America
by Donald I. Fine, Inc. and in Canada by General Publishing Company Limited.

Library of Congress Catalogue Card Number: 86-46388

Library of Congress Cataloging-in-Publication Data

Brown, Dale, 1956–
   Flight of the old dog.

   I. Title.
PS3552.R68543F5   1987   813'.54   86-46388
ISBN: 1-55611-034-0
Manufactured in the United States of America

10 9 8 7 6 5 4 3 2 1

This book is printed on acid free paper. The paper in this book
meets the guidelines for permanence and durability of the Committee on
Production Guidelines for Book Longevity of the Council on Library Resources.

This book is dedicated to the thousands of men and women of the United States Air Force Strategic Air Command who assure the quality of our nation's strategic deterrent force. I was proud to serve in SAC for seven years, and I know it is a thankless, lonely, sometimes frustrating job. They work in old alert shelters, underground launch centers, dark command posts, and cold hangars—and they are the nation's best. More than any high-tech machine, it is the dedication and professionalism of these men and women that insure the peace and security of the United States.

To all the bomber pukes, tanker toads, missile weenies, sky cops, knuckle-busters, and BB stackers of the Strategic Air Command—this one's for you.

ACKNOWLEDGMENTS

I would like to extend my gratitude to George Wieser and Donald I. Fine, who took a chance on me; to Rick Horgan, senior editor at Donald I. Fine, Inc., with whom I spent many long hours hammering this story into shape; and to my wife Jean, who gave me the support to get the job done. Thanks.

ABOARD A B-52 BOMBER

The Strategic Air Command B-52 was ready to begin its final assault. Though half its bomb load had already been expended, one gravity bomb and four Short-Range Attack Missiles (SRAMs) still stood in the bomb bays. So far, the crew of six had successfully guided their aged bomber through a crucial air refueling; a high-altitude bomb run from thirty-seven thousand feet, with a surprise SA-2 surface-to-air missile attack shortly afterward; and three subsequent bomb runs through a maze of hills and valleys.

Up ahead, closing in on them at a speed of six miles per minute, was the target area—defended by surface-to-air missile sites, radar-guided antiaircraft artillery, and prowling patrols of the most advanced interceptors in the world.

"IP inbound in three minutes, crew," First Lieutenant David Luger announced over the interphone. He was following the B-52's course on a narrow cardboard chart, mentally measuring the distance and computing the time to the IP, or "initial point," the start of a low-altitude nuclear bomb run. Time to start reviewing checklists, Luger thought. The action was going to start soon.

He glanced down at the plastic-covered checklist pages, anticipating each step of the "Before Initial Point" and "Bomb Run (nuclear)" checklists before he came to it. Long years of training had enabled him to fix in his mind the exact details of what he was about to do.

"SRAM missile pre-simulated launch check, completed," he said. "Computer launch programming completed."

No one acknowledged him, but he had not expected a reply. The checklist had been reviewed hours earlier. As Luger reread the checklist items over the interphone to key everyone else that the busiest portion of the ten-hour sortie was about to begin, he found himself squirming in his seat, trying to get comfortable.

"Radios set to RBS frequency," Luger said. He glanced at his chart annotations. "Two seventy-five point three."

"Set," Mark Martin, the copilot replied. "RBS bomb scoring plot is set in both radios. I'll call IP inbound when cleared by the radar."

"Camera on, one-to-four," Luger announced, flicking a small black knob near his right shoulder. A special camera would now record the bomb run and missile launches on thirty-five millimeter film for later study. "E.W., start-countermeasures point in sixty seconds."

"Defense copies," First Lieutenant Hawthorne replied, double-checking his jammer and trackbreaker switch positions. The same age as Luger, Hawthorne was the E.W., or electronic-warfare officer. His job was to defend the B-52 against attack by jamming or decoying enemy surface-to-air missile or artillery-tracking radars, and to warn the crew of missile or aircraft attacks.

"Rog," Luger said. "Checklist complete." He checked the TG meter, an antique gear-and-pulley dial that showed the time in seconds to the next turnpoint. Luger flipped the plastic-covered page over to the "Bomb Run (Synchronous)" checklist, then glanced over at the radar navigator's station beside him. "About one-fifty TG to the IP, radar," Luger said. "Got it together, buddy?"

"Uh huh," Patrick McLanahan said. He was bent over a pile of bomb run charts and radar scope predictions, intently studying his bombing "game plan" as if this was the first time he had seen it. His work area was littered with snippets of paper, drawings and notes. A thermos, which lay underneath several books and papers atop his attack radar set, was leaking coffee over the cathode-ray tube display and the radar controls.

Luger impatiently waited for his partner to begin. The two navigators, representing their SAC bombardment wing in this important competition sortie, were a study in contrasts. Luger was a tall, lanky Texan, with immaculately spit-shined boots, closely cropped black hair, and a penchant for textbook perfection. He was fresh out of B-52 Combat Crew Training after graduating top of his class from both the Air Force Academy and Undergraduate Navigator Training, and was easily the Wing's most conscientious and professional navigator. He studied hard, performed his duties to perfection, and constantly drove himself to higher levels of achievement.

McLanahan . . . was McLanahan. He was of medium height and husky build, a blond and tanned Californian who looked as if he was fresh off the boardwalk at Venice Beach. Despite McLanahan's casual appearance and disdain for authority, he was acknowledged as the best navigator in the Wing, and quite possibly the best in SAC. Together he and Luger combined to make the most effective bomber crew in the United States Air Force. And they were about to go to work.

"Well, let's get this over with," McLanahan said finally.

"Good idea," Luger said. He proceeded to run down the remaining items on the checklist, pausing at intervals to check switch positions with the pilot, Captain Gary Houser. Two minutes later, all switches had been configured and it only remained to activate the bombing system and tie all of the individual components together with the bombing computers.

"Master bomb control switch."

"Good," McLanahan said. "I mean, on, light on."

"Bombing system switch."

"Auto." The bombing computers now had control of everything—the steering, when to release the bomb, even when to open and close the bomb doors. McLanahan had only to position a set of electronic crosshairs precisely on a preselected aiming point on the radar scope, and the bombing computers would do the rest.

The computers would translate the crosshair positioning into range and azimuth data and display the target direction on the Flight Command Indicator (FCI) at the pilot's station. The computers fed altitude, heading, airspeed, groundspeed, and drift through a set of precomputed ballistics data, and derived an exact release point based on that information. Even if the airspeed changed slightly, or if the winds shifted, the computers would recompute the exact point for bomb release.

"Coming up on sixty seconds to the IP, crew," Houser announced. "FCI centered. Sixty TG, ready, ready . . . now!"

"Got it," Luger said, starting a stopwatch as a backup. "Bomb run review."

"Roger," McLanahan replied. "Rocket, rocket, bomb . . . uh, concrete blivet . . . rocket, rocket. This is the live drop over the range. Let's not fuck this one up, ladies. Some joker is going to run out there with a tape measure to see how we score. Nav?" McLanahan said, turning to Luger.

"SRAM fixes will be on the Airport, fix number thirty; target Bravo, fix number thirty-one; and the pumping station, fix number thirty-two. We are running fully synchronous, all computers fully operational, with a drift rate less than—"

"What he means," McLanahan said, "is that the SRAM is tighter than that virgin lieutenant Gary's been seeing."

A conspiratorial snicker could be heard over the interphone.

"Thirty seconds to IP," Houser announced. "Defense?"

"Electronic warfare officer ready for IP inbound, pilot," Mike Hawthorne replied. "India-band radar is searching but hasn't locked onto us yet."

"Gunner has back-up timing, radar," Bob Brake, the crew gunner, replied. "Fire control radar is clear. I'll get back on watch after the bomb run and get set for those Air National Guard fighters they told us about."

"Twenty seconds to IP," McLanahan announced.

"Better stay on watch, guns," Houser said. "Sometimes those Air National Guard guys get a little antsy. Remember last year's Bomb Competition—they didn't wait for the bomb run to finish before they jumped us. The rules committee let them get away with it, too. Realism, you know."

"Okay," Brake said. "I'll still be keeping backup timing until I see something." He flipped some switches and returned to his small five-inch square tail radar display. At the tail of the huge bomber, the turret with four fifty-caliber machine guns slowly came unstowed and began a preprogrammed search pattern.

"Guns unstowed, system capable, radar-search, radar-track," Brake reported.

"Ten seconds to IP," Luger said. "Next heading will be zero-one-zero. Airspeed three-five-zero true. Clearance plane five hundred feet."

He turned to McLanahan. His partner had just removed his helmet and was rubbing his ears, then snapping his neck hard from side to side.

"What the hell are you doing?" Luger said.

"Loosening up, Dave," McLanahan replied. "My brain bucket is killing me." Luger answered calls for his partner until the radar navigator finally put his helmet back on.

Houser's FCI slowly wound down. "Coming up on the IP, crew . . . ready . . . ready . . . now!"

"Right turn, heading zero-one-zero, pilot," Luger said. The huge aircraft banked in response.

"Boy, is it *flat* out there," McLanahan said, studying the radar scope.

"Roger, radar," Houser replied. "I guess that means we're clear of terrain." That information was important to Houser—he was handflying the huge bomber only five hundred feet off the ground at almost six miles per minute. Houser used the EVS, or Electro-optical Viewing System, and terrain-avoidance computer to provide a "profile" of the peaks and valleys ahead, but the best warning was McLanahan's thirty-mile range radar and his experience in guiding the huge bomber around trouble. The "Muck"—McLanahan's less-than-flattering nickname—wasn't always by the book, but he was the best and Houser trusted him with his life. Everyone did.

"Ten degrees to roll-out," Luger reminded the pilot. "Drift is zero, so heading is still zero-one-zero. Radar, I'll correct gyro heading after roll-out. Pilot, don't take the FCI until it's displayed on the EVS scope."

"We're IP inbound, crew," Luger reported. "Pilot, center the FCI and keep it centered. Pat, I'll check your switches when you—"

"Pilot, airborne radar contact at two o'clock!" Hawthorne yelled suddenly over the interphone. "Possibly an F-15. Breaking apart now . . . there's two of them. Search radar on us . . . switching to target track . . . they've seen us."

"Roger, EW," Houser said. The fighter-intercept exercise area was still over eighty miles away, Houser thought. Hawthorne must be picking up signals from some other airplane engaging the fighters. He put the EW's warning out of his mind.

Hawthorne tried to say something else, but he was quickly interrupted as the action of the B-52's bomb run began.

"Copilot, call IP inbound," Luger said. McLanahan had switched offsets and was now peering intently at a radar return that was almost obscured by terrain features around it.

"Pilot," Hawthorne said nervously, "this is not a simulation . . ."

"Glasgow Bomb Plot, Glasgow Bomb Plot, Sabre Three-three, India Papa, Alpha sierra," Martin radioed.

In a small trailer complex located at a municipal airport fifty miles from the ground-hugging bomber, a set of four dish antennas swung southward. In a few seconds, they had found the speeding B-52 and had begun to track its progress toward the target on a mapping board. Other antennas began emitting jamming signals to the B-52's radar, and other transmitters simulated surface-to-air missile site tracking radars and antiaircraft guns. The scoring operator insured that they had positive lock-on, then turned to his radio.

"Sabre Three-three, Glasgow clears you on range and frequency and copies your IP call. India band is restricted. Do not jam India band radar. Range is clear for weapon release." Just then, the scoring operator noticed two extra targets on his tracking display. He immediately called his range supervisor.

"They're at it again, sir," the operator explained, pointing to the two newcomers.

"Those National Guard hot-dogs," the supervisor muttered as he studied the display. He shook his head, then asked, "Has the next competition plane called IP yet?"

"Yes, sir," the operator replied. "Sabre Three-three, a Buff out of Ford."

"Ford, huh." The supervisor smiled at the mention of the B-52's nickname. Once, decades earlier, calling a B-52 a "Buff"—short for Big Ugly

Fat Fucker—was a sign of respect. Not any more. "You got a positive track on the Buff? No chance of the fighters interfering with the bomb scoring?"

"I don't think so, sir."

He thought for a moment, then shrugged. "Let 'em go. I like watching a duck shoot."

"Yes, sir," the operator said.

Mark Martin switched to interphone. "We've been cleared onto the range, crew. Patrick, you're cleared for weapon release."

"Rog, double-M," McLanahan replied. He opened the plastic cover of the release-circuits-disconnect switch and closed the circuit. "Let's go bombin'!" he yelled.

"India band restricted, Mike," Martin called down to Hawthorne over interphone.

"Copy," Hawthorne replied. "Crew, we are under attack. Airborne interceptors at two o'clock and closing fast."

"Mike, are you sure they're on us?" Houser asked.

"Positive."

"Mark, switch radio two to the fighter control frequency and—"

"We can't do that," Luger said. "We need both radios on plot frequency."

"Well, we'll call the site and tell them to chase the fighters off the bomb range," Houser replied, irritation showing in his voice. "They can't do this."

"Bob can take 'em," McLanahan said. "Go get 'em, guns."

"You're crazy, radar," the gunner replied. "It'll mean maneuvering on the bomb run . . ."

"Shoot the bastards down," McLanahan said. "Let's give it a try. If it gets dicey, we'll call a safety-of-flight abort."

"Now you're talkin'," Brake said, turning to his equipment.

"Are you sure, Pat?" Houser asked. "This is your bomb run . . ."

"But it's *our* trophy," McLanahan said. "I say let's stick it to 'em."

"All right," Houser replied, flipping switches on the center instrument console. "I'm taking steering away from the computers."

"The fighters are moving to four o'clock," Hawthorne reported. "They're staying out of cannon range so far."

"Infrared missile attack," Brake said, studying his tracking radar and waiting for the fighters to appear. "Simulated Sidewinders."

"Coming up on the SRAM launch point," Luger said.

"We're going to need to maneuver in a few seconds," Brake warned.

"I've got a safe-in-range light and missiles for launch," Luger said. "We can't maneuver until after these missile launches. Guns, give me a few more seconds . . . Tone!"

"Fighters now four o'clock, three miles and closing rapidly . . ."

Luger pressed the MANUAL LAUNCH button. The missile computer began its five-second countdown. "Missile counting down," Luger called out. "Doors coming open . . ."

It had been hard at first to spot the B-52 down there at low level, the pilot aboard the lead F-15 thought. Radar lock-on had been intermittent at high patrol altitude with all the ground clutter, and then it was nearly impossible because of the heavy jamming from the Buff. Visually, the Buff's camouflage made it difficult to spot and hard to keep in sight if there were any distractions.

Now, though, with its huge white bomb bay doors open, it was like a diamond in a goat's ass. The pilot waved his wingman off to the observation position and began his roll into IR (infrared) missile firing position. At three miles, with the B-52's eight big jet engines spewing out heat, an infrared lock-on would be easy and he'd be out of range of the Buff's little pea-shooter guns. No sweat. An easy kill. On its bomb run, the Buff wouldn't do much jinking, and it had to jam the ground-based threats, too.

"Missile away, missile away for Sabre Three-three," Martin called to the bomb scoring site.

"Acknowledge tone break," the site replied.

"Missile two counting down," Luger began.

"Six o'clock, two miles," Brake said nervously.

"Missile two away," Luger said. "Bomb doors closed. Clear for evasive action."

"Pilot, chop your power!" Brake yelled. "We'll suck this cocky bastard in."

Houser responded immediately, bringing the throttles back to idle. Simultaneously, Martin raised the airbrakes to maximum up and dropped the gear. The airspeed suddenly and rapidly decreased from three hundred and fifty to two hundred knots. On the tail gunner's radar scope, the result was exhilarating and immediate. For the fighter pilot, it was a nightmare come true.

The F-15 fighter chasing them had been flying nearly two hundred miles an hour faster than the B-52 in order to catch up with it from behind and get into an ideal firing position; suddenly, it was as if the huge bomber had just frozen in midair. The fighter pilot was now closing on his target at almost six hundred yards a second. The sight of the massive bomber filling his windscreen froze his trigger finger. The fighter pilot was staring into four fifty-caliber machine gun barrels pointed directly at him.

"Six o'clock, two miles," Brake called out, watching his radar. "Two miles and holding . . . goddamn! One mile, half mile . . . Fox-four! All guns firing! Call Fox-four!"

Up on the attack observation position, well above and to the right of the bomber, the leader's wingman was watching a perfectly executed IR missile run. Suddenly, *something* happened. Spoilers and airbrakes and landing gear doors and landing gears began to spring out of nowhere out of the bomber's huge frame, and the distance between the two planes was chopped to nothing in the blink of an eye. The wingman thought he'd see his first midair collision.

At the last second, his partner ducked under the bomber's belly, flying his F-15 a mere three hundred feet over the hills of Wyoming. The Buff's fifty-caliber guns followed him all the way. The wingman could easily visualize the guns spitting fire, the three-inch-long shells plowing into the fighter's canopy and fuselage, the F-15 exploding into a billion pieces and crashing into the green hills below.

"Fox-Four, Fox-Four for Sabre Three-three, Glasgow," Martin called to the scoring site.

"Roger, Three-three. Will relay Fox-Four." The young operator working the bomb-scoring-site tracking radar looked in amazement at his NCO supervisor.

"Holy shit," the veteran NCO said. "That Buff just shot down a goddamned F-15."

"It's a duck shoot, all right, Sarge," the operator said, chuckling. "But who is shooting who?"

"Dead meat," the F-15's wingman said to himself, peeling off and preparing to start his own run at the B-52, keeping a respectful distance away from the fifty-caliber machine gun turret that, he knew, was now looking for *him.*

Luger and McLanahan could easily hear the wild jubilation of the defensive crew upstairs through the roar of the plane's eight turbojet engines.

"One down, one to go," Brake shouted.

McLanahan manually stepped the automatic offset unit to target Bravo and pushed a small button on a console near his left thigh. Over the interphone, he said, "Pilot, I'm in BOMB mode. Center it up. We're gonna bomb the crap outta them now. Dave, check my switches."

"You got it," Luger said. He compared the bomb computer's countdown to the time remaining on his backup timing watch. "Two minutes to bomb release on my watch."

"Checks with the FCI, nav," Houser confirmed, carefully watching as Martin reconfigured the B-52 for normal flight.

"Pilot, fighter at two o'clock, five miles," Hawthorne said. "Break right!"

"Radar?" Houser asked. "Should I turn? This is your ballgame."

"One second," McLanahan said. "S.O.B.'s are jammin' my scope." He leaned forward so close to the ten-inch radar scope that his oxygen mask almost touched it, then tried to refine his crosshair replacement. Luger couldn't see how his partner could possibly make out any radar returns through all the strobing and clutter. When McLanahan was satisfied, he shouted, "Go for it!"

"Breaking right!" Houser shouted. He put the huge bomber in a thirty-degree bank to the right, turning so suddenly that charts and paperwork flew madly around the navigator's compartment.

"Fighter now at twelve o'clock," Hawthorne said. "Moving rapidly to one o'clock . . . almost two o'clock now . . ."

"We can't hold this turn long, E.W.," Martin, the copilot, reminded him. "The corridor narrows to two miles on this bomb run."

"Fighter now at three o'clock!" Hawthorne shouted. Then, as if in reply to the copilot's warning, he said, "Break left. Guns, stand by for AI at five o'clock."

"Roger, E.W.," Brake replied.

"Center the FCI, pilot," Luger said. "Coming up on one hundred TG."

"Checks," Houser replied.

"Pilot, accelerate if possible," Brake said. Houser began to push the throttles up. "Stand by to chop power again."

"Do it after the bomb run, guns," Luger said. "Pilot, keep the throttles steady."

"Radar?" Houser queried. "This is your run."

"Bring airspeed up as slow as you can," McLanahan said. "Shoving it up too fast will screw the ballistics up, not to mention Dave's precious back-up timing. He might get upset with us."

"Standing by," Luger replied, smirking at McLanahan through his oxygen mask.

"Pilot," Brake yelled, "fighter at seven o'clock, four miles, moving to eight o'clock. Break left!"

"Do it!" McLanahan said. This time, Houser threw the bomber over into about thirty-five degrees of bank. The forty-year-old aircraft shrieked in protest.

"Fighter moving to seven o'clock . . . now six o'clock. Pilot, roll out and center the FCI," Brake said.

The bomber snapped out of the turn and began a slow turn to the right to center the thin white needle in the case of the Flight Command Indicator. Luger, scanning the computer panel before him, pointed to a single glowing red warning light.

"The Doppler is hung up," Luger shouted. The Doppler was the system that provided groundspeed and wind information to the bombing computers—without it, the computers were useless, transmitting false information to the steering and release systems.

Luger tried recycling the Dopper power switches—turning them off and on several times to allow the system to reset itself—but no luck. "Pilot, it looks like the Doppler has gone out. Disregard the FCI. Radar, we need to get out of BOMB mode now!"

"Damned fighters," Martin said.

Luger held up his running stopwatch. "I've got backup timing, radar," he said. "Coming up on seventy seconds to release. Pilot, hold the airspeed right here."

Luger was about to read the Alternate Bombing (Nuclear) checklist to McLanahan, but his partner was already accomplishing the items from memory, disconnecting the computers from aircraft and bombing controls. They were now relying on visual course control, Luger's backup time and heading, and the radar scope to drop the bomb. Instead of the bombing computers sending the release pulse to the bomb racks, McLanahan would send the signal himself with the "pickle," the bombs-away switch.

"Bomb doors coming open, guys," McLanahan said. "Alternate delivery checklist complete. Dave, check my switches when you get a chance. Where's my coffee cup?"

"D-two switch," Luger called out, reminding McLanahan to find the manual bomb release "pickle" switch. Luger's gloved fingers flew over the SRAM computer panel, reprogramming it to take a final position update at the same time the B-52 flew over the bomb target.

"Why did this have to happen to us now," Luger said. "We ought to make a formal complaint about those fighters."

"Relax, nav, relax," McLanahan said. He was sitting back casually in his ejection seat, a contented smile on his face. Then, suddenly, he swept every chart, book, and piece of paper off his desk with a flourish.

"Hey!" Luger yelled across the compartment. "What the hell are you doing."

"Nothing partner, nothing," McLanahan said with a grin. "Everything's great."

"Want me to reset the range-coordinate integrator?" Luger asked excitedly, beginning to pull off his parachute shoulder belts.

"No," McLanahan said, loosening his helmet chin strap. "No sweat. Stay strapped in."

"How 'bout I just give that damned stabilization unit a kick or something? Anything. Damn those fighters. They screwed up our chances for a trophy!"

"Cool out, nav," McLanahan said.

Luger shot him a look. Had he gone off the deep end? Here they were, on a SAC bombing run with the Doppler on the fritz, and McLanahan hadn't even *glanced* at the radar scope since the computers failed.

Finally, McLanahan looked at the radar scope, studying it casually. "Five right, pilot," he said. "Nav, how much time on your watch?"

"Coming up on sixty seconds," Luger said. He was still looking at his partner in disbelief.

"Okay," McLanahan said. "Disregard your timing—it's at least seven seconds off. I'm dropping on release range and bearing. Subtract seven seconds from your timing just in case the radar scope goes out or something crazy like that." He studied the radar scope again. "Four more right, pilot."

"Seven degrees right of planned heading, radar," Luger reminded him.

"Not to worry," McLanahan said. "Check my switch positions and get ready for the overfly fix. Copilot, let me know as soon as you pick up any visual timing points. I know there's not many on this target, but do the best you can."

"I'll try, radar," Martin said. "Nothing so far."

"Okay," McLanahan said. He smiled at Luger. "Ready for the overfly fix, Dave?"

"I'm ready," Luger said. "But you're going . . ."

"Two more right, pilot," McLanahan said. "Bob, my man, where are those fighters?"

Fighters! Luger couldn't believe what he was hearing. His partner probably just had the worst of all possible things happen to him on a Bombing Competition sortie, and he was worried about fighters with less than a minute to bomb release.

"Clear for now," Brake replied.

"AI radar is searching," Hawthorne reported. "They'll be around again in a minute."

"Okay," McLanahan said.

"Pilot, hold your airspeed," Luger said over the interphone. "It's drifting too much."

"Relax, nav," McLanahan said. "We're going to nail this one."

"Nine degrees right of planned heading," Luger said, nervously studying his own five-inch scope. He glanced over at his partner. McLanahan was lounging back in his seat, toying with the pickle switch in his left hand.

"I missed the final visual timing point, radar," Martin said. The crew was suddenly very quiet—everyone but McLanahan.

"Okay, double-M," he said. "Thanks anyway."

"I'm going to bypass this overfly fix, radar," Luger said. They were going farther and farther off course, and McLanahan wasn't doing anything about it.

"Take this fix, nav," McLanahan said, his voice suddenly quiet. He gave Luger the thumbs-up signal.

"But . . ."

"Don't worry, nav," McLanahan said. "I have a feeling about this one."

Luger could do nothing else but comply. He called up the target coordinates, checked them, and prepared for the fix.

"Pilot, I want you to just caress that left rudder," McLanahan said. He leaned forward a bit, staring at one of the seemingly thousands of tiny blips tracking down his scope. "One left. Maybe a half left."

"A half a degree?" Houser said.

"Just touch it," McLanahan urged quietly. "Ever so gently . . . a little more . . . just a touch more . . . hold it. That's it . . . still zero drift, nav?"

"No Doppler," Luger replied. "The winds and drift are out to lunch. So is the ground speed and backup timing. I'm working strictly off true airspeed and last known reliable winds." Luger shook his head, bewildered. What was going on? Was McLanahan doing all this for show? Christ, they were eight degrees off heading!

"Okay. Never mind. I forgot. Coming up on release, nav . . . stand by . . ."

Luger looked over at McLanahan's radar. The cathode-ray tube was a mass of arcs and spokes driving through it from the jamming. How could his partner see anything in that mess?

McLanahan reached down and flicked the frequency-control knob, and the spikes and streaks of jamming cleared for a few seconds. He smiled.

The D-2 switch was nestled gently, casually, between McLanahan's fingers, his thumb nowhere near the recessed button. "Caressing that rudder, Gary?" was all he said.

Suddenly McLanahan's thumb flashed out, too fast for Luger to see it, and the BRIC flashed once as the last bomb fell into space. Luger counted three seconds to himself and pressed the ACQUIRE button on the SRAM computer. Three seconds after bomb release, at their altitude and airspeed, should put them right over the target—if McLanahan had hit the target.

To Luger's immense surprise, the green ACCEPT light illuminated on the SRAM panel.

"It took the fix," Luger said, his voice incredulous.

"We nailed 'em, guys!" McLanahan shouted.

"Sure, sure," Luger said. McLanahan was carrying the act a little too far. They were eight degrees off planned heading and seven seconds short of planned timing—that equated to at least a ten-thousand-foot miss, and probably even a worse missile score. The bad present position update, combined with the bad velocities the SRAM computer would derive from the fix, would nail the lid down on Bomb Comp for crew E-05—with *them* inside the coffin. "Tone!" The high-pitched radio tone came on.

Luger flipped the AUTOMATIC LAUNCH switch down.

"Missile counting down . . . doors are already open . . . missile away. Missile two counting down . . . missile two away. All missiles away. Doors coming closed . . ."

"Missile away, missile away," Martin called to the bomb scoring site.

"Very good, boys," McLanahan said, finally opening his eyes. "Nav, you have navigation. I'll call post-release information, and then I'm going to take a piss. Guns, don't let us get shot down. Not now, after all that work."

"Go take your piss, radar," Brake replied. "You're as safe here as if you were in your mother's arms. Or Catherine's arms. Whichever."

"Wait a minute, radar," Houser said. "Before you unstrap—which, I might add, is illegal as hell while we're low-level but par for the course for you—how about those releases? How far off track were we?"

"Not sure," McLanahan replied. "Might have been two or three hundred feet."

"Keep dreaming," Martin said. "It looked close, but not that close."

"C'mon, really," Houser said.

"I took into account all the turns and the changes in airspeed," McLanahan deadpanned. "I was waiting for the Doppler to go out, you know. I knew it would."

"Case of beer says you pitched it long," Martin said.

"Thanks for the confidence, double-M," McLanahan replied, "but you're on." He turned to Luger. "What do you think, nav?" he asked.

"I think . . . I think you're way off, radar," Luger said.

Martin laughed. "Want to call it off, radar?"

"It was a shack," Luger said. "Zero-zero. Perfect. Better than the others. I don't know why . . . but it was."

Over the skies of Kavaznya, Kamchatka Peninsula, Soviet Union

Two thousand miles to the west of where the Strategic Air Command was holding its annual bombing competition, a drama of a different sort—this one carrying consequences far more serious for the crewmembers involved—was playing itself out. Two types of surveillance machines—one a U.S. Alpha Omega Nine Satellite traveling in a geosynchronous orbit at an altitude of twenty-two thousand three hundred miles, the other a U.S. RC-135 surveillance aircraft flying at an altitude of forty thousand feet—were following courses that would bring them roughly over the same part of the globe in a matter of minutes. The RC-135, with a crew of twelve men and women, had penetrated the Soviet Air Defense Zone to gather data on a strange radar that had begun tracking the aircraft as it passed within a hundred miles of the Soviet coast on its way home from Japan to Alaska.

Suddenly the world got very bright.

The pilots aboard the RC-135 were bathed in an eerie red-orange glow for several seconds, wiping out their night vision. They felt as if they had stepped inside the core of a nuclear reactor—every inch of their bodies felt warm and viscous, as if their skin was about to melt away.

When the red-orange illumination disappeared, the cabin went to black. Several tiny spotlights and some engine gauges operating off the aircraft's batteries could still be seen, but everything else snapped off. The roar of the engines began to subside.

"All of the generators went off-line," the RC 135's co-pilot said.

"We've lost engines two, three and four," the pilot said. "Airstart checklist. *Fast.*"

"Crew, this is the pilot. We are starting engines. Check your oxygen, check your stations, report in by compartment damage and casualties."

20

All departments reported in with only minor equipment malfunctions. The pilot gave an order to code a message to SATCOM. Suddenly the aircraft's reconnaisance officer came on the interphone. "Radar target-tracking signal strength is increasing."

The pilot pushed on the yoke, forcing the RC-135's nose steeply downward. "That last shot was aimed at something else, now it's us . . . We're going down to one thousand feet."

"Pilot," the RSO said, "signal strength increasing . . . blanking out my—"

He never finished his report.

An intense beam of orange-red light slashed across the top and sides of the RC-135. Once it had pierced the aluminum skin of the jet, the beam found little resistance. It tracked precisely along the center of the aircraft, instantly superheating the heavy oxygen atmosphere and creating a huge bubble of plasma. The resulting explosion turned the two hundred million dollar aircraft into flecks of dust in a fraction of a second. The beam ignited the vaporized fuel that erupted from the disintegrated airplane and added the force of fifty thousand pounds of jet fuel to the detonation.

As fast as it had begun, it was over. The fireball grew to three miles in diameter, then hungrily feeding on itself in the intense plasma field, dissolved into the black Siberian night.

WASHINGTON, D.C.

General Wilbur Curtis, Chairman of the Joint Chiefs of Staff, stood at ramrod attention as the President of the United States entered the White House Situation Room, the emergency alternate conference center and shelter. The President was followed closely by Marshall Brent, the Secretary of State, and Kenneth Mitchell, Director of the Central Intelligence Agency. Trailing behind them was a man in civilian clothes but with a short military haircut. He carried a black leather briefcase.

The President, wearing a blue and red athletic warmup suit, glared at Curtis as he sat down at the head of a large oblong table. His thick brown hair was tangled, and beads of sweat dropped from the ends and trickled down his neck. Curtis went over to the steel vaultlike door and checked that it was locked.

The President unzipped the warmup suit half-way and picked up a telephone on the table in front of him.

"Jeff?" he said. "Have some coffee and croissants brought down to the Situation Room right away. And see if you can move the morning Budget Committee meeting to this afternoon. If you can't, let me know and I'll try to shake loose . . . what? No, I don't know how long this will be." He slammed the receiver down on its cradle.

The man with the briefcase set it down at a console in a far corner of the room. He put on a headset and punched a series of numbers into the keyboard. He spoke briefly, then watched the indicators on the console. A few moments later, he nodded and turned to the President.

"Full connectivity, Mr. President," the man said. "Sir, your helicopter is fifty seconds from touchdown on the south lawn. Air Force One is ready for immediate takeoff."

The President said nothing. The man at the communications console was in charge of the "football," a tiny transceiver and several sets of authentication and coding documents packed inside the briefcase. That briefcase was always within arm's reach of the President. In case of a surprise attack or other emergency, the President could instantly direct all of the United States' strategic forces by typing a series of coded instructions into the miniature portable transceiver. Now, in the emergency command post under the White House, the President had instant communications capability with command centers all over the world.

"All right, General," the President said. "This seems to be your little party. Another unscheduled emergency exercise? If so, it couldn't have come at a worse time. I was in the middle of my first workout in a week, and I've got a—"

"It is no exercise, sir," Curtis said. "Exactly fifteen minutes ago, we received confirmation that an Alpha Omega Nine surveillance satellite was lost. It—"

"A satellite?" the President said. "That's all?"

"This particular satellite," Curtis went on, "was this nation's primary missile-launch detection vehicle for eastern Russia and the western Pacific areas. Currently, Mr. President, we have absolutely *no* missile launch detection capability for an estimated one-fifth of the Soviet's ground- and sea-based intercontinental ballistic missiles."

"Surely, you're exaggerating," Kenneth Mitchell said. "We have dozens of surveillance satellites—"

"But only one over eastern Russia," Curtis interrupted, "specifically designed to warn us of an ICBM launch from sea or land. Now we have none—at least, until we can reposition another satellite over that area. That may take some time." Curtis turned back to the President. "Meanwhile, sir, we need to have you available to evacuate Washington in less than ten minutes."

"Why ten minutes?" the President asked, not sure he wanted to hear the answer.

"That Mr. President, is how much warning time we have," Curtis explained. "Ten minutes from when the Soviet ICBMs cross the horizon in the mid-course phase until the warheads impact. We believe none of those missiles would be targeted on Washington, but we can't take the chance."

The President was quiet for a moment. The stillness was broken by the arrival of the President's chief of staff, Jeffrey Hampton, followed by an aide with a tray of coffee and pastries. The aide circled the table, making sure that everyone's coffee cup was filled.

"I couldn't reach all of the Committee members, Mr. President," Hampton said. "I'll keep trying."

"Never mind, Jeff," the President said. "We're going to wrap this up shortly."

General Curtis stiffened. This President, he noted, was never very serious during the few simultions they had held, testing the emergency communications and evacuation plan. Now it was the real thing, and he was already anxious to leave.

"I have more news, sir," Curtis said, not touching his coffee. "We lost an RC-135 reconnaissance plane near Russia sometime this morning."

The President closed his eyes and let his coffee cup clatter back onto its saucer. "How? Where . . . ?"

"It was on a routine training mission from Japan to Eielson Air Force Base in Fairbanks," Curtis said, "when it diverted to investigate some strange signals somewhere between the submarine base at Petropavlovsk and a large research complex north on the peninsula called Kavaznya."

The President nodded. "Any survivors?"

"None so far," Curtis said. "Search teams from Japan are just arriving on the scene. Soviet searchers have been out there, but they haven't found anything."

The President nodded. "How many . . . ?"

"Ten men, two women."

"Damn." The President pressed his fingers of his right hand to his temple and gently began to massage it. "What the hell happened? Why were they over there?"

"A routine radar mapping sortie—a spy mission," Mitchell, the CIA director, chimed in. "They fly off the coast, trying to get the Russians to bring a threat radar up against them. They plot out the radar's location, identify it, see what it does."

"How close to the coast were they?" the President asked. Curtis hesitated. "How *close?*" the President asked again.

"It's closest approach was about thirty-five miles," Curtis replied. "When we lost contact with the plane, they were about ninety miles from the coast."

"Well, dammit," the President said, "I'd be upset if a Russian spy plane was thirty miles from Washington." The President turned to Brent, the Secretary of State, who anticipated the President's next question.

"Technically, Mr. President, they stayed in international airspace as long as they did not overfly Soviet territory," Brent said. "However, the Soviets guard their ADIZ—the air defense identification zone—quite zealously. The ADIZ extends one hundred and twenty miles from shore."

"How did they shoot them down?" the President asked. Again, Curtis hesitated. "General?"

"We . . . we're not sure, Mr. President," Curtis replied. The President looked at the oak-paneled walls around him as if they had begun closing in on him. "Sir, at this time we can't even confirm that the Russians did in fact down the plane."

"You're not sure . . ."

"There was no way we could be sure what happened."

"Goddammit, General," the President said. "We've lost twelve men and women and an unarmed spy plane and you can't tell me what happened?"

"We don't have all the data in yet, sir."

"But you are accusing the Soviets of shooting down that plane?" Marshall Brent asked. "Without evidence?"

"It had to be the Soviets," Curtis shot back. "There was no way—"

"Well, what have you got, General?" the President asked impatiently, pouring himself and Brent more coffee. "From the beginning. And it better be good."

Curtis cleared his throat and began: "Sir, the RC-135 concentrated its patrol on a large research area north of Petropavlovsk—"

"We've received intelligence about secret weapons research activities there," Mitchell interjected. "They've built up defenses there, too. They have an airfield and fixed surface-to-air missile batteries almost as large as at the sub pens at Petropavlovsk. But all we're certain of is a huge nuclear power plant at the facility."

"That may not be all," Curtis said. "We received data from the RC-135 about several new long-range early-warning and surveillance radars in the area, including one of tremendous power. It was powerful enough to disrupt the data coming from the RC-135 in all bands."

"They were jamming us?"

"Not jamming," Curtis said. "Interference. They blotted out a wide frequency spectrum with that one radar."

"So what is it out there?" the President asked everyone in the room. "Are you saying it's a new antiaircraft site? A jammer? What?"

"We have reason to believe, sir," Curtis replied, "that the Soviets have been conducting research into high-energy antisatellite and antiballistic missile lasers at Kavaznya. That radar has enough power and enough capability to find and track objects in Earth orbit. Sir, we believe they may have a laser defense system in operation there."

The President's jaw lowered. He looked quickly at Mitchell and Brent.

"Jesus, Curtis," Mitchell said, giving the General an exasperated look. "Pure speculation. You don't have enough information to—"

"Do you know what they *do* have out there, Mitchell?" Curtis asked.

"Of course," the CIA chief said. "A huge reactor, a large airfield, increased air defense sites—but not some pie-in-the-sky laser defense system. We suspect they have a myriad of weapon experiments being conducted out there—nuclear warhead production, nerve gas, maybe some particle-beam and laser experiments dealing with future antisatellite and ABM devices. But an operational system? Impossible."

"That radar is immensely powerful," Curtis said. "They could easily have constructed a radar with far less power to guide missiles to an atmospheric target. This one can track targets, we estimate, as far as our highest orbiting satellite—as far as thirty thousand miles."

"Suspect. Possibly. Estimate." The President glanced at his watch again. "Is that it? Nothing more definite?"

"We *know* it is a giant research facility," Curtis said, trying to regain his lost credibility. "They have the energy source and a tracking and targeting capability. They've also spent enough money on that complex to achieve spectacular results—"

"We also know," Mitchell interrupted, "that despite the massive amount of money the Soviets have spent on research, they are still at least twenty years from developing a laser sophisticated enough to deploy a credible laser-based ABM system."

"How far are *we*?" Brent asked, his curiosity piqued.

"At least ten years for a laser system," Curtis said. "Turn of the century at most. But we have a working antisatellite system now—the two F-15 anti-satellite groups operational at Andrews and Tacoma. Plus we have the *Ice Fortress* polar missile defense space station project. We can put it up next year on the Shuttle if we want to. We can upgrade it to a rail-gun or kinetic energy ASAT system by—"

"We cancelled *Ice Fortress,* didn't we?" the President asked absently as he sipped his coffee. He turned to Brent. "We cancelled it, right?"

"Absolutely, sir," Brent said. He turned to Curtis. "I hope the fact has merely slipped your mind, General, that launching *Ice Fortress* would be a flagrant violation of the first ratified arms agreement we've had with the Soviets in over twenty years."

"*Ice Fortress* isn't at issue here," Curtis said. "The point is: we can't simply double the estimate of our own technology and apply it to the Soviets. This 'just because we don't have it the Russians can't have it' is nonsense. The Russians play a whole different set of rules than we do. They don't answer to Congress, the press, the public, or the world. They don't cancel projects, close plants, lay off workers, or worry about a budget. If they want a laser defense system *now,* they build one. If they need more money, they buy twenty percent less meat and thirty percent less toilet paper and to hell with public opinion."

"C'mon, General," Mitchell said, "I'm on your side, but our information just doesn't support your theories. The technology involved in creating a laser-based antisatellite system that can hit even a geostationary satellite is tremendous. It is almost mind-boggling to apply that same technique to shooting down warheads a little bigger than a yard in length. The degree of accuracy required is enormous."

"And just because *we* can't do it," Curtis said, "the Russians certainly can't, eh, Mitch?"

"All right, all right," the President said. "Let's stop trying to win debating points." He ran a hand through his sweaty brown hair and tried hard to think. "All I see is two of our country's leading experts arguing and contradicting one another. You say that complex *could* house a Soviet antisatellite or anti-ICBM laser, but then you say they don't have the technology to deploy such a system. Excuse my impertinence, gentlemen, but it sounds like paranoia to me."

"I assure you, Mr. President," Curtis said quickly, "that it's not—"

"Mitch, we need more information on that facility in Siberia," the President said, turning to the CIA director. Can you get it for us?"

"We have some possibilities, sir," Mitchell replied. "At the very least, we should be able to get a more detailed diagram of the complex. I'll give you a complete progress report as soon as possible."

"Good." The President glanced at his watch again. "General, I realize the importance of insuring my fast departure from Washington in case of an emergency, but I simply don't think the world situation warrants this degree of caution. I've got a heavy schedule today and I can't interrupt it."

Curtis looked at the President disbelievingly. Wasn't there any way to convince him of the seriousness of the damage done to the nation's defense?

"I want details of that plane crash as soon as possible. If the Russians aren't cooperating in the search, I want to know about it."

Plane *crash,* Curtis thought. Not *downing.* Not *destruction.* Not *murder.* He's totally disregarded my suspicions.

"We have no evidence of any lack of cooperation, sir," Curtis said quietly.

"Marshall, I think it's time for you to put some feelers out to the Russians," the President said. "Start at the U.N. See if we can get a special Security Council meeting together. We'll hit Karmarov with whatever information we can present there and see how the Russians react. Tell Greg Adams to hit 'em hard—accuse them of everything. See how that polite bastard Karmarov reacts. Maybe we have to jerk off these guys a little to find out what they're up to."

"I'll avoid . . . 'jerking' anyone off, Mr. President," Brent said, blanching at the locker room words as if they had a foul odor.

"Do what you have to," the President said. He turned to Curtis. "Wilbur, I'm truly sorry for the loss of your people. Unfortunately, we don't have enough information to accuse the Russians of foul play. We have to treat it as an accident. There's no sign of survivors, the Russians claim they don't have the bodies or the wreckage, and there was no cockpit voice recorder or flight data recorder even if it was recovered, is that right? A tragic loss."

"Analysis of the signal data from the plane and the destroyed satellite haven't been completed yet, sir," Curtis said. "I'll report to you when that's finished."

"That's fine, General," the President said. "Report to me directly about—"

"I'd also like authorization to develop a response in case we find they do have an ASAT and ABM laser at that complex," Curtis added quickly.

" 'Develop a response?' " the President asked. "That sounds like militarese for an attack plan."

"This is getting quite out of hand, General," Brent said. "I don't feel it's necessary to—"

"Hold on, Marshall," the President said. He looked closely at General Curtis. "Go ahead, Wilbur. What kind of response?"

"I'm talking about what this Administration will do," Curtis said, "*if* it is discovered that my suspicions are correct."

The President glanced at his watch again, seeing his rest time slipping away. "What you're proposing, General—it could stir up a mess of trouble if word were to leak out. You know how close we are to signing that arms-reduction treaty."

"There will be nothing to leak, sir," Curtis said. "I can handle it through my office only. It will consist only of collection and analysis of date on the Kavaznya site, and a compilation of possible options. There will be no military mobilization, no generation of forces, no funding."

The President stood without replying, lost in thought. Everyone in the room jumped to their feet. The President headed for the door, and General Curtis opened it for him.

"Authorized," he said simply as he walked past the four-star general. He stopped and glared at Curtis. "If it leaks, if it damages the negotiations in progress, you'll answer for it. You have my guarantee . . ."

General Curtis caught up to Marshall Brent as they walked toward the underground garage of the White House.

"Drop you somewhere, Mr. Secretary?" Curtis asked, falling into step beside Brent.

Brent hesitated a moment, frowning at the Chairman of the Joint Chiefs. Then, he nodded with a resigned shrug.

"Thanks, General," he replied. "I'm heading out to Andrews to catch the diplomatic shuttle to New York." Curtis, his aide, and Brent climbed into an Army-green Lincoln Continental and headed out into the raw Washington weather. As the driver maneuvered onto the Beltway, Curtis signaled his aide to secure the thick glass separating the driver from his passengers.

"Rough week, eh, General?"

"I've had worse . . . and better," Curtis replied.

"Do you really believe they have this . . . laser of yours?"

"I may be an old stubborn pack-mule, Mr. Secretary," Curtis said, unbuttoning his jacket, "but I listen. Our intelligence sources have been saying for ten years that the Soviets are on the verge of developing the capability to track and hit satellites with lasers. That complex at Kavaznya could easily be the culmination of all that research. I have a feeling in these old bones that some young hotshot in the Pentagon is going to come running to me in the next few days with something from that RC-135's data transmission that says the Russians have *something* big going on over there."

"I find it hard to believe," Brent said, "that the Russians would actually conduct such an attack. The Russians may be a lot of things, but they are not reckless."

"Reckless . . . no. But if they thought they could get away with it, they might just take the chance," Curtis said. "Hell, it wouldn't be the first time they fired on one of our recon planes."

"You're saying they've fired on us before."

"Hell, yes," Curtis said, laughing. "Those sons-of-bitches have brass balls sometimes. They lock onto a RC-135 with fire-control radars, like they're gonna launch a missile at it. They shoot bullets across the aircraft's nose, fly with overlapping wingtips. They even alter their radio navigation beacons to transmit false navigational information to aircraft near their shores, hoping to get a reconnaissance plane to fly into a restricted area. That's why our boys aren't allowed to use outside navigational aids. They transmit false messages or orders on high-frequency radio all the time, or interfere with real messages, or just plain jam the frequencies."

"But what do we do about it?"

"Ignore them, mostly," Curtis said. "As long as we follow the rules and no one gets hurt, we just let them make asses outta themselves. We lodge formal complaints, but they file counter-complaints just as fast and twice as wild as anything they've ever done. After a while, it burns itself out."

"But that Korea Air Lines flight flies near . . ."

"See that? You just can't trust 'em." Sometimes they get serious." Curtis was silent for a moment.

"But that didn't happen with our RC-135," he continued. "No matter how bad the shit hit the fan, the guys aboard her would've stayed cool. If they were under direct attack, or even believed they might soon be under attack, they would have flushed their data."

"Flushed it?"

"As they collect data on Soviet radar and other electromagnetic signals, it's coded and stored in a buffer—a computer storage space. If there's a hint of anything going wrong—airplane problems, attack, equipment problems—the buffer can be transmitted to a Defense Department satellite within seconds. They hit one button and it's gone, all of it. Most operators now have a hair trigger on that button; one engine coughs a bit and the data's gone. The buffer transmits itself periodically after a complicated error-checking routine done between the plane and the satellite.

"If the RC-135 crew knew they were under attack, we would've gotten the rest of their data and an attack or distress code. Even a momentary threat signal from anywhere, especially with that plane so close to shore, would've caused them to flush their data. But they didn't. They never knew what hit them."

"A sneak attack?" Brent suggested. "A fighter could have shot at them without their knowing it, couldn't they?"

Curtis nodded. "At night, a passive infrared missile attack—sure. But it's unlikely. Those RC-135s can monitor hundreds of communications frequencies, especially Soviet Command frequencies. If the crew intercepted any air-to-ground or ground-to-air radio transmissions ordering a fighter to attack, they would have flushed their data, turned tail and run. No Soviet fighter makes a move like that unless it receives an order from the Kremlin itself—unless, of course, the intruder plane actually makes an attack. The Korean Air Lines attack was preceded by two hours of communications, all of which were monitored as far away as Japan. No. Our guys never knew what killed them."

Both men were silent for a long time—Brent searching for an explanation, Curtis simply hopping mad.

"So what can we do about it?" Brent asked.

"There ain't shit we can do about it," Curtis said, sighing. "Unless the Russians try to do something stupid, something really flagrant. If they have a new toy over there, they've had their little fun with it. But if they play with it some more, our young President may go over and kick their little butts for them."

"Something flagrant," Brent said, thinking to himself.

"That's what I like about our boy President," Curtis said, his voice growing suddenly exuberant. "He's a politician and a half, but you can rile him. Just like his ol' football quarterback days—he's all finesse, pretty moves, bobbing and weavin', until he's behind by a touchdown and a field goal. Then he starts throwin' the bomb, goin' for the score."

Brent looked at Curtis and shook his head. "God help us," he said, "if he goes all the way."

THE UNITED NATIONS, NEW YORK

This emergency meeting of the United Nations Security Council is hereby called to order," Ian McCaan, the United Nations Secretary General and ambassador from Ireland, announced. It was almost eleven P.M. in New York. Most of the fifteen delegates and their aides and secretaries held steaming cups of coffee or tea. A few wore angry, tired faces. A few looked anxiously at, it was certain, the two principals for which this meeting was called—Gregory Adams, the ambassador from the United States, and Dmitri Karmarov, the Soviet ambassador.

"Let the record show," McCaan continued, his Irish brogue thick despite two decades spent in the United States, "that this meeting was urgently requested by the government of the United States of American under Provision Nine, unprovoked and excessive use of military force against an unarmed vessel or aircraft near territorial boundaries. The charge of violation of Provision Nine is hereby submitted. The United States delegation has asked that this meeting be closed to all but Security council members, although confidential audio transcripts of this emergency meeting will be made available to all member nations. Ambassador Adams, please proceed with specifications of the charge."

Gregory Adams adjusted his microphone and looked around the table at the other fourteen delegates. This was not a receptive audience. The Russian ambassador looked completely bored. The other delegates looked equally uninterested, and now Adams began to question the wisdom of calling an emergency meeting under these circumstances. Adjusting the dark horn-rimmed glasses that he wore to make himself look older, he cleared his throat and began:

"Thank you, Mr. Secretary-General. On the night of November thirteenth, two nights ago, an unarmed American RC-135 reconnaissance aircraft was making a routine patrol of the eastern shore of the Kamchatka peninsula of the Soviet Union. The aircraft had been on a peaceful training mission—"

"I'm sorry, Mr. Adams," Dmitri Karmarov interrupted, holding his translator earpiece closer to his left hear. He smiled and said in English, "The interpreter has told me that the RC-135 was on a training mission. I wish to be clear on this point—is that the same as a *spy* mission, sir?"

"American aircraft of all types fly near shores all over the world for a variety of reasons, Ambassador," Adams replied. "This particular RC-135 was on a training and routine survey mission, collecting signal coverage data for satellite navigation units for civil and military use."

"Navigation information!" Karmarov's sixty-one-year-old face fairly cracked with suppressed laughter. He made an exaggerated point of hiding his face and choking down a chuckle. "Navigation information . . . very well, Mr. Adams. I apologize for the interruption." Another stifled laugh. The rest of the delegates, although not suppressing any laughter, clearly did not believe for one moment Adams' excuse for the RC-135's mission. Its capabilities were well known.

"That aircraft," Adams said, much louder this time, "was destroyed. Suddenly, without warning and without provocation." Adams looked at the faces of the other delegates, but found nothing in their blank expressions. "This poses a threat to air traffic for all of us, gentlemen. It was not over Soviet airspace—"

"Incorrect, Ambassador Adams," Karmarov said. "I have a report from our air defense radar tracking station at Kommandorskiy Island and Ossora Airbase on Ust-Kamchatka. They report the RC-135 aircraft came within thirty-three miles of our shore . . ."

"Thirty-three miles," Adams retorted, "is hardly over Soviet airspace."

"Not according to the International Civil Aeronautics Organization," Karmarov said. "Article Seventeen, Chapter one-thirty-one, establishes a one-hundred-and-twenty-mile-wide Air Defense Identification Zone around countries that have borders on open ocean. Flight is prohibited in the Zone without permission from the country controlling that Zone. I believe I can safely assume that your RC-135 did not have permission to enter that area . . ."

"Flight is *not* prohibited in an Air Defense Zone," Adams said. He referred to a folder his aide passed to him. "According to paragraph one-thirty-seven of the ICAO regulations, Ambassador, aircraft entering an ADIZ without permission or proper identification risk engagement of a country's sea or air defense forces for the express purpose of positive aircraft identification and precise position, altitude, airspeed, and heading verification only. They can proceed through the area as long as they do not pose a threat to air traffic or national security. They are certainly *not* to be fired on."

"An American military jet the size of the one that intruded into our airspace is most definitely a threat to our security, sir," Karmarov said. "The Article specifies that, if the intruding aircraft is military and has the capability of carrying long-range air-to-air or air-to-ground weapons, it may be turned away from land, challenged, forced to land, or fired on." Karmarov pointed a finger directly at Adams. "It was you who risked disaster, not us."

"The RC-135 has *no* capability of carrying weapons."

"Positive identification of the aircraft was never made until your government contacted us, sir," Karmarov said. "It followed an unusual flight path for a spy plane—not the usual course. Considering the sensitive nature of our activities in that area, I believe the Soviet government acted with considerable restraint."

"Restraint!" Adams said. He contorted his face to display the maximum in indignation. "You destroyed that aircraft. You fired on it without warning, without any consideration of any of the lives on board. You murdered twelve innocent men and women. An unarmed aircraft carrying out a peaceful mission!"

"I caution you to keep your wild accusations in check, Mr. Adams," Karmarov said, louder this time. "We deny any involvement with the missing aircraft except to warn that aircraft out of Soviet airspace. We did not know the exact identity of the aircraft until your Department of Defense notified us of the disaster. We immediately initiated an air and sea search for the aircraft. We do not know what happened to your spy plane. Do not put the blame for your unfortunate disaster on the hands of the innocent Soviet people."

"The RC-135 aircraft reported unusual radar emissions tracking it, just before it was attacked," Adams said. "The crew believed it was target-tracking radar signals from a ground radar installation preparing to attack."

"Show us the data, then," Karmarov said. "You say it was a hostile radar. We say we had nothing but surveillance radars on the aircraft. Show us the data that you say exist, Ambassador Adams. Confront the accused with the evidence—if you can."

"Mr. Adams?" McCaan said, peering over his podium to the American delegate's seat. "Can you at this time provide the Council with this information?"

"The crucial information is being collected for presentation, Mr. Secretary-General."

"You mean decoded, deciphered, edited, and altered," Heinrich Braunmueller, the East German ambassador, said wryly. "Intelligence data takes time to be made presentable."

"We'll bring the data in, you can be sure of it," Adams said. "It clearly shows a tracking radar, one strong enough to steer dozens of nuclear-tipped surface-to-air missiles to it."

"That is a wild, baseless accusation, sir," Karmarov said once again, shaking his head in exasperation. "You'll not get the Soviet Union to admit any culpability in this unfortunate accident."

"Tell the Council, Ambassador Karmarov," Adams said, folding his hands in front of him. "What sort of activities *do* you pursue at Kavaznya? Why is it so important? Why is it so vital that you'd shoot down an unarmed survey aircraft in international airspace?"

"You are beginning to become tiresome, Ambassador Adams," Karmarov said. "I will repeat myself for the last time—we do not know what happened to your aircraft. Kavaznya is the site of an important research facility that I am not permitted, and this council is not entitled, to discuss. Further, your aircraft, by your own admission, was not in international airspace. It was intruding into a Soviet controlled defense zone. It, or, more precisely, the military leaders in your Pentagon that ordered those men and women into violating the airspace of another nation, were the guilty party, not the Soviet Union. The aircraft made no attempt to identify itself, ask for help, state its intentions, or file a flight plan. It was an unidentified aircraft—"

"That you shot down!" Adams said, pointing his finger at Karmarov. He was ready to play one last card. "We *know* you are conducting research into particle-beam weapons, lasers, and other such devices, Ambassador. You may as well admit it. You decided to test your new toy on an unarmed American aircraft."

"And you are on a fishing expedition, Adams," Karamov said. He turned to Ian McCaan. "Mr. Secretary-General, the Soviet Union pleads innocent to the trumped-up charges levied against us by the United States. We demand that the United States shows its evidence against us immediately. If there is no evidence, as I suspect will be the case, or if the evidence is not found to be accurate, reliable, or in clear support of the charges against us, I demand all charges be dropped and a formal apology be delivered by both Ambassador Adams and the President of the United States."

"Ambassador Adams," Ian McCaan said, "are you prepared to present your evidence supporting your charge?"

Adams glared at Karmarov, then studied the faces of those around him. He saw only tiredness, confusion. "The United States will present its evidence to the Council by the end of the week, in a regular session of—"

"Then the delegation from the United States has wasted our time," Karmarov declared. "Ambassador Adams, I feel the need to remind you that an emergency meeting of this Council is not the proper forum for a political diatribe against the Soviet Union. Further, be prepared to confront the accused with evidence if you make such damaging charges. I will ask the Steering Committee of the United Nations to investigate this rash and irresponsible abuse of your privilege and see if charges of impropriety are not warranted against *you*. Mr. Secretary-General, I move for adjournment."

"Seconded," Braunmueller said quickly.

Even McCaan, a long-time supporter of the United States and a friend of Gregory Adams, looked irritated. The rest of the Security Council members were already departing, leaving trails of angry comments behind, when McCaan's gavel tapped the stone.

BARKSDALE AIR FORCE BASE, BOISSIER CITY, LOUISIANA

Lieutenant-General Bradley Elliott, the honorary master of ceremonies, glanced at the typewritten winner's name at the bottom of the five-by-seven card. His shock deepened. In his three years as honorary awards officer for the annual Strategic Air Command Bombing and Navigation Competition, he had never seen anything like it. One organization—one crew, in fact—had blown the doors off the competition as no other crew in history had. The oddsmakers and the crystal-ball gazers were not just wrong about this one—they weren't even in the ballpark.

General Elliott waited until the two stagehands were ready and the audience escorts had moved into position. He straightened his shoulders and smiled. These poor crewdogs, he said to himself. They wait months for the results of the SAC Bombing and Navigation competition, and whoever presents the awards teases them with sly innuendos and hints as to who won. And then, to increase their agony, the escorts walk through the aisles in the audience, stopping in front of a unit's row just long enough for the victory cries to begin, then move on.

A few years ago, Elliott recalled with pride, he stood on stage accepting the trophies for his unit, feeling the applause ripple through the massive hangar. His old unit, the sleek, supersonic FB-111s at Pease Air Force Base in New Hampshire, had been top dog for years. It was different now, though. It wasn't that the modern, super-sophisticated new bombers were taking all the trophies. Rather, crew quality had become the crucial factor.

"The Curtis E. LeMay Bombing Trophy," General Elliott continued, immediately hushing the crowd, "is awarded to the bomber crew—whether from B-52s, FB-111s, or B-1Bs—who compiles the most points competing in both high- and low-level bombing. To give you a little background, this trophy was known simply as the Bombing Trophy from

37

1948 until 1980, then renamed in honor of General Curtis E. LeMay for his contributions to the Strategic Air Command and his support of strategic air power.

"For eight of the ten past competition years, the crews from Pease and Plattsburgh have walked away with the LeMay trophy. It was *thought* by some that the upgraded Offensive Avionics System and the B-1B *Excalibur* would finally bump the FBs out of the running." The General paused, waiting for a reaction from the crews in the audience. Then, he smiled a sly, secretive smile, and glanced at the Eighth Air Force commander and the FB-111 crews beside him.

"With a score of ninety-five point nine percent damage expectancy in low-level bombing and an unbelievable ninety percent effectiveness in high altitude bombing, the 715th Bombardment Squadron 'Eagles' of Pease Air Force Base in New Hampshire set a record in all-purpose bombing—"

At that, a huge roar went up from the audience, and the FB-111 crews from Portsmouth, New Hampshire, began to go berserk. The "fastburner" FB-111 crews had gone through the entire competition in fear and loathing of the "heavies," the B-52s with their spanking-new digital computers and the sleek, deadly B-1s with an even more sophisticated version of the solid-state bombing equipment. A B-52 crew had won the previous year, and the FB crews had felt their superiority in this annual international competition slip.

The FB-111 guys had not done too well in the awards ranking until then, although their performance had been up to their usual near-perfect levels. This, an all-time Bomb Comp record, was their turning point.

Elliott let the celebration continue for a few seconds. *"Sorry, boys, I hate to do this to you . . ."*

He had to raise his voice to make himself heard over the shouts of the FB-111 crews. More effectively than a gunshot or a cannon blast, a single word from Elliott quieted the audience and broke more hearts, including his own:

"But . . .

". . . The winner of the 1987 Curtis E. LeMay Bombing Trophy, with an unprecedented ninety-eight point seven-seven percent damage effectiveness score and an unbelievable one hundred percent score in low-level bombing, is . . . crew E-05, from the 470th Bombardment Squadron."

A massive scream went up from the members and guests of the winning bomb squadron and, as the winning B-52 crew stood and made their way to the stage, an equally noticeable groan went up from the rest of the crews in the huge converted aircraft hangar—now Competition Center at Barksdale Air Force Base in Louisiana. The restlessness was not unlike the reaction of a crowded football stadium when the visiting team has just scored another touchdown and gone ahead by twenty points with only a few minutes remaining in the game. The outcome of the contest, although far from over, was already obvious.

The 470th Bombardment Squadron, and Crew E-05 in particular, had just walked off with five trophies, losing only one trophy to another B-52 unit and three other trophies that could only be awarded to either an FB-111 or B-1B unit. In addition, the 325th Bomb Wing, of which the 470th was a part, had taken three other trophies for their KC-135B tanker unit and also brought home the Doolittle Trophy for the 470th's Numbered Air Force award. Everyone knew the final outcome. If it were not a military formation, the huge converted aircraft hangar may well have been empty by the time the grand prize, the coveted Fairchild Trophy, ever made it into the winner's hands. It was certainly an anticlimatic finish.

Patrick McLanahan, his crew, and officers and invited guests of the 325th Bomb Wing were on stage for a solid hour after the ceremonies, getting pictures taken, holding interviews with military and civilian reporters, and letting the gleam of two long tables full of silver trophies dazzle their eyes. Colonel Edward Wilder, commander of the bomb wing, and Lieutenant-General Ashland, the commander of Fifteenth Air Force and Wilder's boss, then took turns lifting the huge ten-gallon Fairchild Trophy cup over their heads in triumph as a dozen photographers jockeyed for the best positions.

Two men stood away from the jubilant crowd at the front of the hangar, watching the festivities on stage from a deserted projection room overlooking the hangar. Lieutenant-General Elliott had been going over several pages of computer printout and notes as the other man, in civilian clothes, shook his head in amazement.

"A B-52 won Bomb Comp," Colonel Andrew Wyatt exclaimed. "Hard to believe. We've spent megabucks on the B-1, on the Avionics Modernization Program on the FB-111, on the Offensive Avionics System for the B-52's to carry cruise missiles—and an unmodified vacuum-tube B-52 that entered the service when *I* did almost thirty years ago wins the Fairchild Trophy. Incredible."

"Those guys are good. That's all there is to it," Elliott said, closing the classified notes he was reading and handing them back to Wyatt. Wyatt did a fast page-count and locked the folder away in his briefcase.

"I thought the FB-111s were gonna pull it out," Elliott said, "but this was the first year of their AMP weapons delivery system modification and I think they still have some software bugs in it."

Wyatt nodded. "So. What about a tour of your funny-farm in Nevada? The general is brainstorming. He thinks your research and development center might have some toys he can play with."

Elliott smiled and nodded. "Sure—that's why we call it Dreamland." For a few moments both men looked at the celebrations on the floor of the Awards Hangar. Then, General Elliott cleared his throat.

"What's going on, Andy?" he asked. Colonel Wyatt took a fast look around the projection room and decided there was no way the room could be secure.

"Not here, sir," he said in a low voice. "But General Curtis is very anxious to meet with you. *Very* anxious. And not in an . . . official capacity."

Elliott narrowed his eyes and looked sideways at the young aide to the Chairman of the Joint Chiefs of Staff. "Not in an official capacity? What the hell does that mean?"

"It means it's to be a *private* tour," Wyatt said. "He'll be in civvies. He wants to get some ideas, enlist some assistance."

"On what?"

"He'll make that plain to you when he sees you, sir," Wyatt said. Elliott rolled his eyes in frustration.

"More JCS doubletalk," Elliott said. "All right, all right. Day after tomorrow. Staff will be at a minimum—skeleton crew. He'll get the royal tour, but not the royal reception."

"I believe you've got the right idea, General," Wyatt said. He extended a hand. "Very nice to see you again, General."

"Same here, Andy," Elliott said, shaking the aide's hand. "You ever going to get your fighter wing back, or are you content with being a general's patsy?"

Now it was Wyatt's turn to look exasperated. "The old Elliott eloquence," Wyatt said. "Cut right to the heart. No, I'm busier than I'd ever thought I could be, sir. Besides, that fighter stuff is for the young bucks."

Elliott's face darkened. "Well, you're welcome to stay for the rest of the Symposium, Colonel. SAC's biggest bash. The Vice President is showing up in a few hours. The ladies in the Strategic Air Command get better and better looking every year."

"You know General Curtis, sir," Wyatt said. "If I'm not back in Washington before supper, I'll be lucky to get command of a security police kennel. Thank you anyway, sir." Wyatt hurried away.

Elliott made his way downstairs and into the hallway behind the huge Awards ceremony hangar. There, standing alone in front of a huge model of the B-1B *Excalibur,* beer cup in hand, was Captain Patrick McLanahan. He was easy to recognize—the young bombardier had been up on stage receiving trophies for most of the afternoon.

Elliott studied McLanahan for a moment. Why were the good ones always like that? Loners. Too intense. The best bombardier in SAC— probably the best in the world—standing out here, alone, looking at a damn airplane model. Weird.

Elliott studied him closer. Well, maybe not *that* intense. Boots unpolished. No scarf. Flight suit zipped down nearly to his waist. Hair on the long side. Drinking during a military formation. At least a dozen Air Force regulation 35-10 dress and appearance violations. He had to restrain himself from going over there and chewing the guy out.

But he did stroll over to the young officer. "Is that your next conquest, Captain McLanahan?" Elliott said.

McLanahan turned, took a sip of beer, and casually studied Elliott— something that Lieutenant-General Bradley Elliott was very unaccustomed to. The general noticed none of the panic that usually accompanied confronting a three-star general; no stumbling over words, no overly exuberant greeting, no great big macho handshake.

After a moment, McLanahan smiled and extended his hand. "Hello, General Elliott." He glanced back at the B-1B *Excalibur* model. "This thing? No. Too high-tech for me."

"Most young B-52 troops are standing in line for a B-1 assignment," General Elliott remarked.

"Not me," McLanahan said. He nodded toward an old, dusty model of a B-52 hanging in a corner. "There's my baby." He gave an amiable grin and said, "Sorry about Pease. Those guys were tough this year."

"Thanks. The FB-111s will come back next year, I'm sure of it. They were beat out by the best." No reaction from the young radar navigator.

"You say you *want* to stay in B-52s, Patrick?" Elliott asked curiously. "Why? The B-1s will be replacing them by the turn of the century."

McLanahan paused before answering. "I don't know. I guess it's just that people see a new aircraft come on-line and they think all of the older planes are history." He took another sip of beer. "They've condemned the B-52 a little early. She's still got a lot of fight left in her."

Elliott raised his eyebrows. His thoughts exactly. "Old warhorses can still kick ass," he said.

McLanahan smiled. "You know it, sir.

"Well, congratulations again, Patrick. Fairchild Trophy, Bombing Trophy, two years in a row. You're unbeatable, it seems."

"I got the best crew in the business, General," McLanahan said. He drained the last of his beer and crumpled the cup in his hand. "We work hard—and party even harder. Gotta go."

"Stop by the Headquarters Hospitality Room later," Elliott said as he shook hands. "Let's discuss the old monster some more."

"You got it, General," McLanahan said. He hurried off after his crew.

Not much spit and polish to him, Elliott thought. But then he smiled as he recalled a young pilot thirty years before of whom the same could have been said. Had it been that many years? Elliott shook his head. Like the B-52, he was fast becoming a relic. He only hoped that, like the B-52, he had a little fight left in him yet.

The Strategic Air Command *Giant Voice* Bombing and Navigation Competition Center was an immense aircraft hangar, remodeled and converted into the awards and hospitality center that was used only once a year for just this event. Surrounding the hangar itself were dozens of smaller offices and conference centers that, on Hospitality Night, were used by all of the units represented in the competition as specialized drinking and socializing rooms. Each room had a theme, depending on the unit's mission or its geographical location.

The first task at hand, however, was to get inside to visit them. The Competition Center was so crowded, so packed with military men and women in various stages of inebriation, that Gary Houser's crew took ten minutes, once they entered the hangar's immense lobby, to even get near the hospitality rooms. There was a large directory inside the lobby that described where each unit was located, but that defeated the purpose of Hospitality Night. The object was to visit each and every room before the three A.M. closing time.

"I don't believe this," Luger said as he and Patrick moved through the crowd. "This Hospitality Night gets bigger and better every year."

Their first stop was the Texas Contingent, where five rooms had been combined into one long beerhall. The center of attraction in the jam-packed room was a massive Brahma bull lounging in the middle of the beerhall. It had a mural of a B-1B painted on each side. The bull was standing in a huge sandbox. In the back part of the sandbox, already half-covered with bull droppings, was a strip of red sand labeled, "To Russia With Love, From the Excalibur." The bull wore a ten-gallon cowboy hat and was busy eating out of a trough filled with party snacks and corn.

Luger and McLanahan were welcomed by two girls dressed like Dallas Cowboy Cheerleaders, who promptly filled their hands with Lone Star beer and bowls of chili.

"Where y'all from?" one cheerleader asked.

"Amarillo," Luger drawled. "Patty here's from California but he's okay."

"I just love Amarillo," the other cheerleader said, giggling.

"And I just love California," the first one said.

"Well," McLanahan said, slipping an arm around one cheerleader's waist while the other took his arm. "Why don't you two Southern belles show us around your little Texas tearoom here?"

McLanahan weaved unsteadily in a corner of an old-time Western saloon, wearing a toy six-gun at his side and a red felt cowboy hat behind his neck. The place was packed with riotous crewmen, some celebrating, some trying to drown their sorrows with massive amounts of beer and chili. A non-com bartender, a crew chief from the 5th Fighter Interceptor Squadron from Minot, North Dakota, patiently waited on each one of them.

With one hand, McLanahan picked up a huge mug of beer from the end of the bar. He strolled over to a dartboard at the far end of the saloon and looked over the target—five darts, lodged in the exact center of the corkboard.

"Pretty good shootin', huh, Sergeant Berger?" McLanahan said to the bartender. The sergeant, dressed like a Barbary Coast innkeeper, smiled.

"Your Sergeant Brake's the one who can do some shooting," Berger said. "If anyone had told me a B-52 would shoot down an F-15 in broad daylight, I'd have said they were crazy. I was the crew chief on that F-15 that got shot down, but send Bob Brake over here and I'll buy him a beer."

"It would have been different if things were for real," McLanahan said, taking a deep pull of the draft. "You would have nailed us from thirty miles away with one of those new Sidewinders or an AMRAAM, but you don't get any points for a beyond-visual range shot." McLanahan took another swig of beer. That's why it's all just a big game, he thought. Just a game.

As he ambled over to the bar and found himself an empty seat, his thoughts took a depressing turn. He had been in the Air Force, what? Six years now. And he had never dropped a live bomb on a target. Each time that he had pressed his finger down on the pickle switch, it had been a concrete blivet that dropped out the bomb bay doors.

Not that he should complain. The whole point of what he was doing was to defend his country, after all. If defending it meant undergoing exercise after exercise, then so be it. He couldn't help wondering, though, what it would be like to drop a bomb under true "game" conditions. He felt like a fireman who is waiting to be called to his first fire, dreading and welcoming it at the same time.

McLanahan looked up from his beer to find a pretty young brunette in civilian clothes seated next to him. She was talking to another woman who had long blonde hair tied up in a bun. On the blonde's uniform lapel was a lieutenant's insignia.

"Excuse me, ladies," McLanahan said, his voice slurring a bit. "But can I interest either of you in a game of darts?"

The blonde smiled. She looked at her friend. "Wendy," she said, "why don't you give it a try. I never could shoot those things."

The brunette demurred. "I don't think so," she said. "Besides, what chance would I have competing against the King of Bomb Comp himself." She fixed McLanahan with a bemused look, as if all the honors he'd received counted little in her estimation.

McLanahan mistook the look for active interest and charged forward. "Well, if I'm the King of Bomb Comp, then I'm willing to let you be my Queen." He clinked his beer mug against hers and made a toast. "To . . . what was it? Wendy. To Wendy, Queen of Bomb Comp and a credit to the United States Air Force."

Wendy smiled. "Actually, I'm employed by an independent contractor. We build and test ECM gear."

"Well, we won't hold that against you," McLanahan said. He glanced at the blond lieutenant.

Wendy looked at McLanahan for a moment as if deciding something, then rose from her seat and straightened her dress. She reached out her hand. "So nice to have met you, uh—" McLanahan told her his name. "Yes, of course. Patrick. Well, it *was* nice to meet you. But I must be going."

She waved to the blonde. "Catch you later, Cheryl," she said. "Stay out of trouble, okay?"

"I'll try," Cheryl said, but something in her eyes told McLanahan she had no intention of doing any such thing. As Cheryl looked at him over her beer mug, McLanahan thought of the woman who'd just left.

FIGHTER WEAPONS TRAINING RANGE, NELLIS AIR FORCE BASE, LAS VEGAS, NEVADA

Two days after the Bomb Comp festivities ended, Lieutenant-General Elliott rode with General Curtis in a blue Air Force four-wheel drive truck, bouncing and skidding on dark, dusty, pitted desert roads. Elliott was wearing short-sleeved olive-drab fatigues and a blue flight cap. Curtis was wearing a conservative gray suit and tie, even in the dry desert warmth of the early evening. The sun had set a few minutes earlier beyond the beautiful mountain ranges of the high Nevada desert.

"It's incredible," Elliott said, closing the top secret file he held in his hand. "Absolutely incredible."

"And those are the things we're sure of," Curtis said. "Those are the things that'll be presented in the United Nations. I believe—and I'm alone on this so far—that the Russians have an extremely advanced, fully operational laser defense system in place, right now. As a matter of fact, I believe it's been operational for months, ever since the Iceland summit."

"This is amazing. The Russians are further ahead of us in beam defense than anyone ever imagined. So what do we do? Go to the United Nations? Ask them to shut the thing down?"

"That's one option we're pursuing," Curtis replied, loosening his tie against the lingering heat. "But I've been authorized to explore two other possible responses." He paused. *"Ice Fortress* is one of them."

Elliott looked surprised, but nodded thoughtfully. "That certainly will get people's attention," he said. "But it's a sitting duck, if that laser is as capable as you say it is."

"They wouldn't dare shoot down a manned space platform," Curtis declared.

Elliott shook his head. "Tell that to the widows and widowers of that downed RC-135, sir."

Curtis glared at Elliott, but said, *"Ice Fortress* is different."

"You bet, sir," Elliott replied. "It's worse." They rode on in silence. Elliott added: "Besides, wasn't *Ice Fortress* cancelled? I know the Vandenburg control center is closed."

"It *was* cancelled," Curtis said, "but not because it wasn't feasible. We had to cancel it because of that damned treaty we signed. It's frustrating. The Russians can shoot down one of our RC-135s, but we can't violate a treaty. We come out losers both ways." His angry voice seemed loud enough to be heard by the sentries at the guard shack a hundred yards ahead of them.

"I haven't heard anything about the incident," Elliott remarked. "Everything seems very quiet."

"The situation politically has stabilized somewhat," Curtis said. "The White House is hoping this whole thing will just fade away. I'm sure the President will be more than happy to let the matter fizzle out, take the Russians' excuses and minimal reparations. The President is really counting on Secretary of State Brent to defuse the whole affair."

"But the Russians aren't offering excuses or reparations, are they?" Elliott asked, stretching his aching muscles.

"Hell, why should they?" Curtis said. "They're holding all the damn cards. We, the military, whine and bitch that the Russians are shooting down our spy satellites. Half the White House doesn't believe us—and the other half doesn't *want* to believe us." He paused for a moment, then added, "I'm sorry about the RC-135 crew, Brad. I know you worked with them in the past. I'm sorry those crewmembers died."

"I'm sorry, too, Curtis," Elliott said. "Those men and women were doing their job, their *duty,* something they trained hard to perfect. Their murder was senseless—premeditated, cruel, and senseless." Elliott shook his head and tried not to think of the friends he had lost. "So," he said finally, *"Ice Fortress* is one option. And you're out here to see what else we have up our sleeves."

"Putting you in charge out here was the best move the Defense Department ever made, Brad," Curtis said. "What we needed was a guy who never said it can't be done. A guy happy to lock horns with Congress or anyone else who stood in the way of developing new ideas. Now, I need you to find some for me. I want—"

"To take out this . . . this site," Elliott said quickly, glancing sideways at the driver. "Attack it."

Curtis was somewhat taken aback. "No one said anything about 'taking out' anything, especially in goddamned Russia." He smiled. "Jesus, Brad, you're a sonofabitch."

General Elliott smiled back at the Chairman of the Joint Chiefs of Staff, then leaned forward and tapped the driver on the shoulder. "We'll walk from here, Hal. Meet us back at the guard shack in an hour."

The truck ground to a halt, and the driver, a young second lieutenant wearing fatigues and carrying a small Uzi submachine gun, trotted around to General Curtis' door and held it open for him. Both men stepped out.

"You won't get lost from here, will you, General?" the lieutenant asked Elliott in a low enough voice to keep Curtis from hearing. "Straight down the road, about four hundred—"

"This is *my* desert, Hal," Elliott growled. With a smile he said, "Get out of here. Make sure they have fresh coffee at the guard shack, and *don't* drink it all." The young officer saluted, trotted back to the driver's seat, and drove off.

"This, sir, is Dreamland," Elliott said, beaming. He spread his hands out across the desert as he spoke. "Ideas become reality here. Theories become machines. Men like you don't come here just to visit—you come here to get answers." Elliott's mind was racing—it was exhilarating for Curtis just to watch.

"Kavaznya. Heavily defended, I'd say, according to your intel."

"That would be an understatement," General Curtis replied. "They converted their small supply airfield into a full-scale year-round base."

"Rule out a carrier task force, then," Elliott said, nodding. "They'd be blown out of the water thirteen hundred miles north of Japan. The Russians would see a flight of F-15s and their tankers long before they reached Kavaznya, and you might need two squadrons to beat past the defense and take that complex out." He looked at Curtis.

"Bombers. Heavy bombers. B-1s, perhaps?"

"What else would I get from an old SAC warhorse?" Curtis said, smiling.

Elliott went on: "We don't want the Russians to think we just declared war on them. One bomber, launch three, but pick the best for the attack. One lone penetrator, even against heavy defenses, has a chance. Especially a B-1."

"My thoughts exactly."

It was Elliott's turn to smile. "You didn't come here to shop, did you, sir? You came to buy. Cash and carry. Price is no object. All that stuff."

"I wanted to see your little playland here, too," Curtis said, "but I knew you'd have what I'm looking for."

"I don't have a B-1 here," Elliott said as they approached the guard shack. "But I've got something . . . you won't believe."

"I knew you'd put on a show for me," Curtis said. "But where the hell are we?"

"We're in Nevada, sir," Elliott said, scanning the horizon with the corners of his eyes. It was an old Navy seadog trick taught to him by his father: the corners of the eyes can detect motion easier than the center, because of the lesser concentration of light receptors at the edges. "In the middle of nowhere. That's the Groom Mountain range over there," Elliott said, pointing to the twilight-streaked horizon. "You can just barely see Bald Mountain over there. Papoose Range is over there to the south. We are on the northwest corner of Groom Lake."

"Lake?" Curtis said, kicking up a cloud of hard-packed sand and dust.

"Dry lake," Elliott explained. "Properly tested and reinforced. It makes a natural and easily concealed three-mile-long runway." Elliott scanned the horizon, breathing in the fresh, clean, slightly chilling air. "Dreamland."

They walked for a while longer. Suddenly, two streaks of light could be seen several miles in the distance, diving and turning over the nap of the rugged mountains. A moment later, two ear-shattering sonic booms rolled across the desert floor and echoed up and down the valley.

"What the hell was *that,*" Curtis asked.

"Red Flag," Elliott said with a smile. "Probably a couple FB-111s on a night terrain-following sortie out there on range 74. Going max afterburners and supersonic at two hundred feet."

"But that was so close," Curtis said. "What about—"

"Relax, relax," Elliott said. "They were at least fifteen miles away. Besides, those bomber pukes know better than to come any closer to Dreamland. The airspace from ground level to eighty thousand feet is absolutely prohibited from overflight—civilian, military, anybody. It's an instant aircrew violation and a security debriefing they'd not soon forget— *I'd* guarantee that."

Finally, after a few minutes of searching, Elliott spotted the low, dimly lit guardhouse and steered Curtis and himself toward it. "I come out here once a week," Elliott said, "and I still have trouble finding the damn guard shack."

"I don't think your sky-cops would let us wander around out here for too long," Curtis observed.

"True," Elliott said. "They'd send a German shepherd to fetch us back."

A few moments later, they arrived at a small concrete block building. The shack had one large bullet-proof double-paned glass window in front, one door, and numerous gunports around it on the other walls. A twelve-foot-tall fence stretched on either side of the building, and the fence was topped with large, silvery coils of sharp barbed wire. Three fully rigged Air Force security guards emerged from the building and quickly and quietly surrounded Elliott and Curtis. All three were armed with M-16 rifles, one with a mean-looking M-203 grenade launcher attached to the underside of his rifle barrel. A German shepherd dog was led out and began sniffing around the two visitors. The dog took one sniff of Wilbur Curtis and sat down directly in front of him, no more than six inches from the tips of his shoes.

"Don't move, sir," the dog handler said. "Is your identification in your breast pocket?" Curtis nodded, once, very slowly. The guard removed Curtis' wallet while another guard quickly pat-searched him.

"Should I raise my hands?" Curtis asked.

"He means 'don't move,' sir," Elliott said, as his ID was examined. "Bambi there weighs over a hundred and fifty pounds and could probably drag you up a vertical ladder."

"Bambi?" Curtis felt his body stiffen as he looked at the dog.

"I didn't know you were carrying a weapon," Elliott said to Curtis as the guard pulled a nine-millimeter automatic from a shoulder holster.

Curtis grunted, afraid to move his lips any further. The dog was led reluctantly to Elliott for a quick search, and then taken away.

As the two generals drank steaming cups of coffee just outside the guard shack waiting for their ID verification, Curtis surveyed what little visible landscape there was inside the compound. Inside the tall fence, the area was completely dark leading to a row of three hangars. No lights at all were visible anywhere. The large hangars were flanked by several smaller ones. A wide ramp emerged from the opposite side of each hangar, and stretched out over the horizon.

"Why no lights inside the compound, Brad?" Curtis asked after their IDs were rechecked and they were cleared inside the fence.

"Oh, they have lights on, sir," Elliott said. "All infrared. To the guards with their sensors and sniperscopes, it's just as clear as day. The darkness also helps the Dobermans."

Curtis gulped. "Dobermans?"

"Yes, unattended guard dogs. They're more effective if they're allowed to prowl, and they're very shy of lights. They all have laryngectomies, too, poor devils. If they spot you, they won't even give you the courtesy of a warning bark before they go for your throat." Curtis looked around nervously.

"They're not around now," Elliott said. "At least, I *hope* they've recalled them. We'd never know what hit us if they haven't."

They reached the back entrance to the hangar after another hundred-yard walk. "One at a time," Elliott said. They heard a buzzing sound, and Elliott grabbed the doorhandle, pulled the large metallic door open, and stepped inside. A few moments later, Curtis heard the same buzzer and did the same.

Curtis was standing in a long corridor. The walls of the corridor were clear, thick plastic on all sides, even the floor, and Elliott was just stepping out of the second half of the unusual walkway. More security guards studied Curtis carefully as he walked down the corridor and stopped at a plastic door. He was aware of a large cannon-like device tracking him as he walked along, humming like a dentist's X-ray machine. The remote-controlled lock buzzed, and he stepped into the second half of the plastic hallway. Another door later, he joined up with General Elliott.

"Well, that's new even to me," Elliott said. "An X-ray chamber. Must've put it in just in the past few days. It checks for implants. That X-ray device, I'm told, can find microdot transmitters embedded in your teeth, fingernails—even your intestines."

"Hmm. I'm not sure how much good it will do," General Curtis said. "I bet the Russians have Dreamland scoped out from six different angles. A jackrabbit probably can't screw in this desert without some Soviet spy satellite watching him."

"Well," Elliott replied, "they might know about all the activity going on around here, and all the security, and maybe even have snapshots of you and me taking a stroll. But, at least for now, they don't know anything about . . . this!"

They emerged from the security chief's office into the main hangar area. Curtis let out a gasp, and even Elliott, who had seen this plane in nearly every step of its metamorphosis, felt a thrill of pride and anticipation as he studied the immense form before them.

"General Curtis," Elliott said, "meet the Old Dog."

The huge B-52 was completely black, a strange, eerie jet-black that seemed to *absorb* light, totally negating the effect of the hundred maintenance floodlights surrounding it. The surface was absolutely clean and as smooth as a bowling ball. It was as if the B-52, the veteran of over thirty years of service, was in some sort of futuristic, comical costume.

"What the *hell* . . ." Curtis said.

"Don't recognize it, huh?" Elliott laughed. "Officially, the B-52 I-model, although it's only a B-52 H-model with a bunch of modifications. It is without a doubt one of a kind. We use it as a test bed for Stealth-type technology, air-to-air weaponry, weapons mating tests, computer hardware, everything. But she's in top flying condition—she can fly right now if you want. The workers have renamed her from *Stratofortress* to *Megafortress,* and you'll see why. Let me show you around."

Curtis followed Elliott around to the most prominent exterior change on the bomber—a long, needle-sharp nose and sharply angled cockpit windows.

"An SST-style nose, Brad?" Curtis said. "Isn't this going a little too far?"

"We checked out every aspect of this plane's performance," Elliott said. "You'd be surprised how much a long, pointed nose, pointed tip fuel tanks, more streamlined cockpit windows, smoothed and polished skin, and no external TV or infrared cameras help to increase this plane's top speed. The limiting Mach on this plane before modification was point eight-four Mach; now, the limiting Mach speed of this baby is point nine-six without the externals. And it's just as comfortable at low altitude as it is in the stratosphere."

Curtis ran his hand over the skin. "What kind of metal is this?" he asked. "Fiberglass? It's not aluminum. What is it?"

"Radar-absorbing fibersteel," Elliott said. "A composition of fiberglass and carbon steel, stronger than aluminum but as radar-transparent as plastic.

"We can't make it invisible, of course," Elliott said. "It's all a matter of time. If we can get thirty or forty miles closer to the target without being detected, all the expense and trouble is worth it. If an enemy fighter has to come in another ten or twenty miles before he can get a solid missile lock-on, it just improves our chances of getting *him* first and surviving. At night, the special black antisearchlight paint is worth its weight in gold. This plane will be virtually invisible to the naked eye at night. A fighter can be flying side-by-side with the *Megafortress* and he'll never see it." Elliott smiled as they walked around the smooth, pointed nose. "Besides, the black paint and the nose make it look mean as hell."

As they approached the huge bomber, Curtis stopped short.

"You can't . . . Elliott, you really did it this time, dammit." Curtis was staring at a long pylon on each wing, mounted between the fuselage and the inboard engine nacelles. Each pylon carried six long, sleek missiles.

"Beautiful, aren't they?" Elliott said. "Advanced Medium-Range Air-to-Air Missiles. Radar guided, with terminal infrared and home-on-jam guidance. Twenty-five mile range. High-explosive proximity flak warheads. We've modified the main attack radar to act as a guidance radar for these *Scorpions.*"

"*Scorpions,*" Curtis muttered. "Dammit, Elliott. We don't even have *Scorpions* on our front-line fighters yet."

"But I've put them on a SAC bomber, sir," Elliott said. "And they'll go on your B-1s, too.

"Also on each wing we've put two three-thousand gallon external fuel tanks instead of the one normal fifteen-hundred gallon tank. Both the missile pylons and all four external tanks are jettisonable.

"We also have split fibersteel bomb bay doors, which are lighter and more radar-transparent. You'll see why they're split in a moment. There are many places in this beast that radar energy will just *pass through* with zero reflectivity. The radar cross-section of the B-52 used to *double* with the bomb doors open—but not anymore. By applying the same technology to a B-1, which already has half the radar cross-section of a B-52, you can make it practically invisible."

They reached the strange, unrecognizable tail of the airplane. "We eliminated the typical horizontal and vertical stabilizers and replaced them with a short, curved V-tail assembly. We built all of the tail-warning receivers and aft jammer antennas into the tail. We've also included an infrared search and warning system that is designed to detect air-to-air missile launches from the rear."

"You took the tail guns off?" Curtis said, pointing up at the very end of the plane. "No big Gatling multibarrel gun, like on the H-models?"

"Tail guns are antiquated," Elliott said. "Even a radar-guided Gatling gun is not effective enough against the current class of Soviet fighters we're expecting. Hell, some Soviet interceptors can actually outrun a fifty-caliber shell."

Curtis checked the tail end closer. "Well, you've got something up there. A larger fire-control radar, that's for sure. What else? A flame-thrower or something?"

"Land mines," Elliott explained. "Actually, air mines. That enclosed cannon in the back fires twelve-inch-long flak cannister rockets. The aft fire-control radar on the *Megafortress* tracks both the rocket and the enemy fighter, and it transmits steering signals to the rockets. When the range between the fighter and the flak rocket is down to about two hundred yards or so, the fire-control computer detonates the rocket. The explosion sends a pattern of metal chips out a couple hundred yards, which acts like thousands of fifty-caliber bullets being fired all at once. There doesn't have to be a direct hit on the fighter.

"The fire-control radar has an increased detection range of about thirty miles," Elliott continued, as Curtis shook his head. "The rockets have a range of nearly three miles, which is very close to optimum infrared missile firing range."

"Elliott," Curtis said. "This is too much. Way too much. I don't believe you—"

"General," Elliott interrupted, "you haven't seen *nothin'* yet." Elliott waved to a nearby guard standing near the left wing-tip. The guard spoke briefly into a walkie-talkie, received a reply, then waved to the general in response. Crouching below the ebony belly of the plane, Curtis and Elliott went inside the back half of the bomb bay. Once inside, Curtis stopped short.

"What the . . ." Mounted on a large drum-like rotary launcher in the aft portion of the sixty-foot-long bomb bay were fourteen long, sleek missiles.

"Our ace-in-the-hole, sir," Elliott said. "Ten more brand-new AIM-120 *Scorpion* AMRAAM missiles. They can be guided by the fire-control radar, the bombing radar, or they can home-in on an enemy fighter's radar or on the fighter's jamming transmissions. We have them facing aft, but they can attack any threat at any angle. If one of those radars has found a fighter, or if the threat warning receivers can see it, a missile can hit it. The rotary launcher can pump out a missile once every two seconds."

"Unbelievable," Curtis said. "Well, I suppose I should say it's about time, eh, Brad? Nuclear bombers with little machine guns going against Mach one fighters seemed awfully silly to me." He examined the launcher. "I can't wait for you to tell me what the other rockets do."

"Ah, yes. Glad you reminded me," Elliott said. "Four AGM-88B HARM missiles. HARM stands for High-speed Anti-Radiation Missile. They were the stars over Libya in 1985. The missiles home-in on either the radars themselves or, if the radars are turned off, they'll fly the last computed path to the target.

"Twenty-two air-to-air missiles, four air-to-ground missiles, and a total of fifty air mine rockets, all for bomber self-defense," Elliott said, summing up. "Together with the usual chaff and flares and specialized electronic countermeasures packages installed on board, we think we've greatly increased the chances of this *Megafortress* reaching the target. Like I said, sir—a flying battleship."

"Armed to the teeth, all right," Curtis said. He closely examined the long, slender missiles on their launcher and looked forward. "What's this?"

"The only space left for offensive weaponry," Elliott explained. "In using the *Megafortress* as a test-bed we've concentrated mostly on defensive armament for strategic bombers. But she can still carry fifteen thousand pounds of ordnance—nukes, iron bombs, missiles, mines, anything. Or we can put extra fuel, additional defensive missiles, decoys, even personnel up there. How about side gunners, like a B-17 in World War Two? We've already done that with the Old Dog.

"We've been running tests with the new AGM-130 *Striker* TV/infrared guided glide bomb, the biggest non-nuclear bomb in the inventory. The damn thing weighs a ton and a half but can glide twelve miles when released at low altitudes."

"I don't believe it," Curtis said. "This thing is amazing." The two men exited the bomb bay, and several security officers closed the four clamshell bomb bay doors. Elliott then led Curtis to the entrance hatch on the bomber's belly and both men climbed inside.

"Hard to believe," Curtis commented, "that a huge plane like this has so little room inside."

"Believe me, this is *spacious* now compared to a line B-52," Elliott said. "A lot of things have been taken out, miniaturized, or moved to the fuselage area. There's almost room on the lower deck here for a couple airliner seats—in a line Buff, you can't stand side-by-side down here. We've taken out as much extraneous stuff as possible to lighten the plane."

They sat in the navigators' seats downstairs.

"Where's all the navigation and bombing stuff down here?" Curtis asked, examining the blank panels before him. The entire compartment was almost devoid of equipment. There was the radar navigator's ten-inch radar scope and associated controls on the left side, plus a small video monitor beside it with a small typewriter keyboard. Between the left and right sides were three small control panels. The navigator's side had a few flight instruments, but nothing else. All the rest of the equipment slots were covered with blank plastic panels.

"The world's biggest video game," Elliott said with a smile. "Simple, straightforward navigation. The *Megafortress* uses the Satellite Global Positioning System for navigation, along with a ring-laser gyro inertial navigation set. The INS is updated by the satellite, so the radar scope isn't needed for navigation—we've modified it more for threat detection than for navigation.

"The radar nav uses a plug-in cartridge with all the navigation points and computer subroutines in it. The gyro takes three minutes to spin-up to full alignment, and it's accurate to a quarter of a degree per hour just by itself. The satellite system automatically locks onto two of the eight Air Force navigation satellites orbiting the Earth and fixes its position once every five minutes, and it's accurate to a few feet every time. The radar nav also has a combination computer and TV monitor and a keyboard for reprogramming the computer."

Elliott pointed to the ten-inch attack radar scope. "The Old Dog now has a Hughes APG-75 attack radar from the Navy F/A-18 *Hornet* fighter, which can feed targeting and tracking information to any of the *Scorpion* missiles. The radar can also serve as a navigation radar, if necessary, and it can be used as a terrain-avoidance mapping display.

"There's more, sir," Elliott said, "let's go upstairs."

The two men climbed another ladder to the upper deck. "Pilots won't be happy about this," Elliott commented, "but we didn't do much in the pilot's compartment. Their job hasn't changed much. This *Megafortress* has the capability of automatically monitoring its fuel system and electrical panel, so it frees the copilot to help out.

"One major addition is the automatic terrain avoidance system," Elliott explained. "It's an adaptation of the cruise missile's terrain comparison system. We needed a system that could help the Old Dog fly as close to the earth as possible, but without using radar transmissions that would give away the plane's location.

"The satellite navigation system and inertial nav system sends present position, heading, and groundspeed information to a computer, which already has all significant terrain and man-made obstacles for the proposed flight planned region programmed into it. The system finds where it is and figures out what altitude is safe for the proposed flight path. It then sends instructions to the autopilot to fly a set altitude over the terrain. Radar is only used intermittently as a back-up to the system, so electronic emissions that could expose the plane's position are almost eliminated."

They half-walked, half-crawled aft of the cockpit to the defensive crew compartment. "Not many changes at the electronic warfare officer's station, either," Elliott said. "His equipment is more specialized and a bit more automatic. The gunner's station is quite different. He has an eight-inch fire-control radar, the controls and indicators for the defensive missile launcher, and the controls for the air mine cannons and forward-firing missiles. He'll be one busy man back here."

"All off-the-shelf, General?" Curtis asked, finding his tongue.

"If it wasn't, sir, you'd know about it. You didn't."

Elliott led Curtis back down the entranceway ladder. A pair of security guards climbed inside and did a quick inspection of the bomber interior while Curtis and Elliott were watched. After the guards reemerged, the two men were free to leave. Elliott escorted Curtis toward the exit.

"You realize, Brad," Curtis said as they headed for the security gate, "that this whole trip was just a friendly visit. I wasn't asking about any special project or piece of equipment. Just a friendly visit, that's all."

"Perfectly clear, General," Elliott said.

"Good. Now that we understand each other, I want to know—"

"My test bed B-1B arrives in three weeks," Elliott interrupted him. "It's been on the books for months, far earlier than your meeting with the President. No connection could ever be made."

Curtis smiled. Then: "Only one B-1?"

Elliott thought for a moment. "I'm having lunch with the commander of the test and evaluation unit at Edwards in a few days. Colonel Jim Anderson, a real fireball but a great stick. I wanted to invite him in on some of the new Old Dog weapons tests I'm conducting. I think he can supply us with a B-1 A-model the contractors aren't using. We won't be able to bring it here to Dreamland without raising some curiosity, but I think he can arrange to have it . . . at our immediate disposal. We can get it here when . . . the time comes."

Curtis shook his head in disbelief. "And I thought *I* had influence." He smiled. "If I didn't know better, Brad, I'd say you knew what I was thinking all along."

"After Andy Wyatt got hold of me, sir," Elliott said, "I didn't spend time shining my latrines up for your visit." He thought for a moment, then said, "It just so happens that those Old Dog tests will coincide perfectly with the refit of those B-1s. Most of the equipment you've seen here tonight can be put in those B-1s in no time at all."

"All right, all right, Brad. This is starting to get spooky," Curtis said. "Remember, I never asked you for anything, you never saw those intelligence notes, and . . ."

"I understand completely, General." He looked sideways at the Chairman of the Joint Chiefs and said, "Two months."

Curtis shook his head in disbelief. "You mean—?"

"The tests will be completed in two months, sir," Elliott said. "For . . . whatever reason."

"I may need a plane sooner . . . for whatever," Curtis said.

Elliott thought for a moment—but only a moment.

"Then I'll send the Old Dog."

Curtis started to laugh but choked back the urge when he saw that Elliott was serious.

"You're crazy, Elliott . . ." Curtis said. "A thirty-year-old B-52? You've been wandering around this desert too long."

Elliott smiled. "Just a thought, General," he said. "Just a thought . . ."

Andrina Asserni, confidential secretary and aide to Ambassador Dimitri Karmarov, Soviet Ambassador to the United Nations, could scarcely believe it when she was informed by security that Secretary of State Marshall Brent was waiting in the outer reception area of the Ambassador's private residence. "Show him in immediately," she told the guard. And a minute later he appeared.

"Secretary Brent . . . !"

"Zdrastvoayti. Good evening, Miss Asserni," Marshall Brent said in fluent Russian. Asserni's eyes twinkled. How strange and wonderful her language sounded, coming from such a tall, distinguished American.

"May I speak with the Ambassador, please?"

Asserni stammered. "Why, uh, yes . . . of course. My apologies, Mr. Secretary. Please, please come in." She stood in awe as Brent strode into the outer apartment. She had never seen the American Secretary travel like this, alone.

"My sincerest apologies, Mr. Secretary," Asserni said. "I had no idea you would call on us . . ."

"This is a very informal and impromptu visit, Miss Asserni, I assure—"

At that instant, Ambassador Karmarov entered the outer apartment. He wore a simple blue robe in place of a coat, and carrying a can of beer, looked exactly the opposite of his stiff, official persona. "Comrade Asserni, get me the file on—"

"Comrade Ambassador!"

Karmarov looked up from his papers and took a step back. "Marshall . . . Brent . . . I mean, Mr. Secretary . . ."

"I hope I am not intruding, Ambassador Karmarov . . ."

"No . . . no, of course not." He turned to Asserni and handed her the documents he was carrying. "Take the Secretary's coat, Asserni, what possesses you? Why wasn't I notified?" Brent removed his long dark coat with slippery ease, and Asserni took it in her arms like a newborn baby.

"This is an unexpected surprise . . ."

"*Ochin zhal.* I do apologize for any inconvenience this visit has caused, Ambassador," Brent said. "But I was hoping to speak with you on an urgent matter."

"Of . . . of *course.*" Karmarov motioned to his inner apartment. "Do come in." He turned to Asserni. "Bring coffee and brandy immediately. And I will strangle anyone who interrupts us. Is that understood?"

Asserni was too astonished to reply. As she hurried off to the kitchen, Karmarov followed the tall, lean, impeccably dressed American into his inner apartment and closed the door behind him.

The Russian ambassador's apartment resembled a large study, with walls covered mostly with floor-to-ceiling shelves of books of all kinds. The most imposing item in the room was Karmarov's massive desk, a huge, ornately carved antique, well over half the width of the apartment itself. Brent ran a hand over plush leather chairs, noticing that the coffee table in the center of the apartment was genuine Chippendale.

"A most exquisite room, Ambassador Karmarov," Brent said without turning around. Karmarov wrung his hands with impatience as he waved Asserni into the apartment. She set the tray with a silver urn, a long fluted decanter of brandy, china cups, and large snifters onto the Chippendale table and hurried out.

"*Balshoye spasibe.* Thank you," Karmarov said. "Mr. Secretary, we may speak English if you prefer. You need not—"

"I am in Russia now, Mr. Ambassador," Brent said, continuing in urban Muscovite Russian. "It would be a presumption to speak anything but your native tongue."

Brent turned, his hands folded behind his back. The two men observed each other for a moment. Karmarov saw a tall, elegant frame, a silver-maned head; a firm chin thrust defiantly up and outward; a thin silver mustache perfectly symmetrical. The suit was conservative, tailored to razor-sharp perfection, the shoes were polished to a gleaming shine despite the harsh Manhattan streets.

Brent saw a shorter but powerful man, with a full head of gray hair atop broad shoulders. The years of plush living in the most fashionable section of New York had begun to tell on the Ambassador's waistline and chin, but Karmarov's eyes were still as fiery and bright as in his revolutionary youth.

Karmarov finally motioned Brent forward. "*Pazhaloosta saditis.* Please sit down, Mr. Secretary."

Brent took the wide-armed leather chair offered him by the Russian and lightly seated himself. He kept his knees, legs and back perfectly straight as Karmarov joined him. Karmarov reached for the coffee urn but, correctly interpreting a sly grin in Brent's eyes, his hand slipped over to the decanter. He poured a generous amount of brandy for both of them and offered one to the American Secretary of State.

"To your health, Mr. Secretary," Karmarov said in English.

Brent raised his glass. *"Za vasha zdarovye!* And to you and yours, Ambassador," Brent replied.

They let the strong spirits flood their insides, then Brent set his glass down on the table.

Karmarov spoke first. "I am totally embarrassed, Mr. Secretary," he said. "I had no idea . . ."

"It is I who should apologize, sir," Brent said. "This may seem most inappropriate, but I simply felt that I must speak with you immediately."

"By all means," Karmarov said. He took a bigger sip of brandy.

"It concerns the fears some in my government have of the research being down at the Kavaznya complex," Brent began. "They feel—"

"Please, Mr. Secretary," Karmarov said, his eyes serious. "I am not permitted to discuss Kavaznya. It is more than a classified facility, sir. It is a forbidden subject."

"Then permit *me* to speak," Brent said. "Consider this a message from my government to yours—you need not reply." Brent interlaced his fingers and let his arms rest on the chair's wide armrests.

"The Pentagon is convinced, on what I feel is sketchy information, that your government is responsible for the destruction of an American reconnaissance satellite and an American RC-135 aircraft."

Karmarov said immediately, "My government has already categorically denied any involvement—"

"Yes, Ambassador, I know," Brent interrupted. He picked up his brandy snifter, passed his nose over it, letting the palm of his left hand warm the liqueur. He settled back into his chair.

"Allow me to be frank with you, Ambassador," Brent said. Karmarov's eyes widened. "I am not a friend of my country's military hierarchy. I believe it was Montesquieu who once said, 'If our world should ever be ruined, it will be by the warriors.' "

"He referred to Europe, I believe," Karmarov said, his eyes narrowing. Brent nodded.

"It applies to affairs between our nations as well," Brent continued. "Ambassador, we are on the threshold of an historic arms-control agreement. In the two years since those negotiations have been conducted, both sides have managed to keep the uniformed military out of the negotiations.

We have dealt on a level never before attempted—instead of throwing our bloody swords on the table and staring into each other's faces to see who will blink first, like some medieval combat, we have sat down like men and talked true disarmament.

"Ambassador, in our lifetime we can see nuclear weapons eliminated. Not just a phony controlled escalation, not even a numerical reduction. No, I talk of true disarmament."

Brent swirled the brandy in his glass and stared into it. "But there are those who see disarmament as a weakness. They seek to disrupt our efforts at every turn. It is the actions of these 'disrupters' that I wish to warn your government about, Ambassador."

"What . . . actions, Mr. Secretary?" Karmarov asked.

"As I said, there are many in my government who are convinced of your culpability in the loss of our aircraft," Brent said. "They have conjured up a magical laser device, straight out of one of our Hollywood films, and planted it on Ust-Kamchatkskiy, at your research center at Kavaznya. Evidence or not, they have all but convinced the President that this laser exists and that it threatens the security of the United States."

Karmarov could not keep his eyes focused on Brent's. Brent's fingers curled a bit tighter around the brandy snifter as he noticed Karmarov's uneasiness.

Dammit, Brent thought. *Could it be true? Is it possible . . . ?*

"You must convince them, Mr. Secretary," Karmarov said quickly, forcing his eyes back toward Brent's. "I plead with you, my government is deeply and firmly committed to lasting peace and the total elimination of all nuclear weapons from the face of the globe. Nothing must interfere."

"I have come to offer you my guarantee," Brent continued, "that I will make every effort to achieve a workable arms agreement. But I must tell you what is afoot. There is talk of matching the so-called killer laser with a construct of our own. I'm not at liberty to give details, but—"

"Ice Fortress!" Karmarov said suddenly. "The armed space platform! That's what your military means to deploy, isn't it?"

Brent sighed. "Again, I'm not at liberty to discuss—"

"But that's it, isn't it?" Karmarov's face was flushed with anger. "Marshall, you know that deployment of *Ice Fortress* is a clear violation of the 1972 Anti-Ballistic Missile Treaty. It is a violation of the 1982 Space De-Militarization Agreement. It flies in the face of our entire arms elimination negotiations. It is madness."

"Key elements in our military are convinced of the existence of a killer laser," Brent said. "That is also a violation . . ."

"Such a device—should it ever exist in our lifetime—is not a violation of the ABM Treaty," Karmarov interrupted. "The Treaty clearly never mentioned such exotic devices because they exist only in the imagination of a few excitable scientists and physicists. Why write a treaty forbidding something that does not exist?"

Karmarov's rising tone of voice, with the strained chuckle punctuating his last sentence, rang like an echo from the walls of a canyon in Brent's ears. Karmarov continued: "The Space De-Militarization Agreement does not apply, of course, to a ground-based defensive device. It was specifically written to eliminate the placement of weapons of any kind in orbit over the Earth. It was supposed to have averted a madness that swept both our countries. It cannot be possible for your country to deploy *Ice Fortress.* It cannot."

"I have made no admission that such is the case," Brent said. "But I can tell you that many options are being considered."

He looked directly into Karmarov's eyes and paused, as if to lend emphasis to what he was about to say. "The laser is a menace, Dmitri," Brent said. His voice sounded as if it came from the bottom of a deep well. "Find some way to reassure the leaders of my government that their fears about a laser at Kavaznya are groundless. Make some sort of presentation about the research you conduct there, or at least describe the facility in a bit more detail. But put the saber-rattlers to rest . . ."

"I can guarantee little," Karmarov said.

"We must not fail, Dmitri," Brent replied. He got up and took Karmarov's hand in his. "The future—our children's future—may depend on it." Slowly, Brent released his grip on Karmarov's hand. He gave the Ambassador a curt nod and made his way out of the room.

Karmarov watched him leave, then sat down in one of the plush leather chairs. He did not move for a full two minutes. Finally, he rang for Asserni.

"Do they know? Asserni asked.

"They suspect. How could they not suspect?" Karmarov reached down to the table and gripped his snifter with both hands. "What the hell are they doing over there, Asserni? Are they trying to destroy the arms agreement? What do they want the Americans to do?"

Asserni did not reply. Karmarov stared into the brandy for a long time.

"I want the secure line to the Kremlin open all morning," he finally ordered.

"Of course, Comrade Ambassador."

He drained the liqueur and winced—both at the bite of the spirits and from the threats that were now bombarding him from both sides.

"What *are* they doing? What?"

FORD AIR FORCE BASE, CALIFORNIA

Patrick McLanahan was in trouble.

His partner, Dave Luger, had been severely injured by flying glass and metal after his five-inch radar scope exploded from a near-hit by a Soviet SA-4 surface-to-air missile. Their aircraft had just been jumped by a small squadron of four MIG-25s. Climbing out of the low-level bomb run area in broad daylight, the B-52 was a sitting duck for the advanced Soviet interceptors.

Luger, lounging in his ejection seat, watched his partner switch the bomb-nav radar scope from off-center present position mode to station-keeping, bringing the radar antenna up to level with the aircraft's longitudinal axis. The display was now configured from attack mode to scanning mode, with a maximum of five miles range with range marks displayed every half mile. He was trying to save their lives.

"Anything I can do for you, Pat?" Luger asked nonchalantly.

"Watch for the damn fighters," McLanahan said.

"Can't do that, buddy," Luger said. "I've got serious injuries over here, remember?"

As if to emphasize his point, he lolled lifelessly across the aisle, his parachute harness barely keeping him in his ejection seat. He stared up at the overhead circuit breaker panel of the B-52 Ejection and Egress Trainer, his arms flung out awkwardly. McLanahan muttered something about how stupid he looked.

"When did they add *that* into the scenario?" McLanahan asked.

"I don't know," Luger said. "I like it, though."

"You're havin' too much of a fucking good time," McLanahan said.

"I like watchin' you work your butt off, partner."

"Too bad your injuries haven't affected your mouth." McLanahan flipped switches on the instrument panel in front of him and looked over at his partner. "Get strapped in like you're supposed to. Can you still reach your ejection trigger ring, or are your hands blown off too?"

Luger went through the charade of inspecting his hands. "Nope, they look fine." As he reached for his parachute harness straps, he noticed a faint ripple of light in the upper left-hand corner of the radar navigator's ten-inch radar scope.

"Ten o'clock," Luger said, pointing at the scope. "Interference patterns. Could be . . ."

"No cheating now, Luger," the instructor, Paul White, interrupted from the control console outside the trainer. "You're blind, remember? Are you ready for the finale?"

"They've got this place *bugged,*" Luger said, hurriedly pulling on the parachute.

"You'd be dead meat right now if those fighters launched a missile, Dave," White said. "Don't tell me you're going to unstrap yourself like that during the real thing?"

"Only if there aren't any instructors around," Luger said. White did not share in the joke, and Luger quieted up and finished strapping himself into his seat.

"Pilot," McLanahan said, acting as if he was talking to the pilot, "I'm picking up a bogey at ten o'clock, five miles. Moving rapidly to eleven o'clock."

"Roger," White said, acting now as the pilot. Then, switching roles to the crew electronic warfare officer, he shouted, "Pilot, break left now." Simultaneously, he turned a large black knob on the console in front of him, putting the trainer into a sharp left turn. The compartment in which McLanahan and Luger were sitting was mounted on four ten-foot hydraulic legs, enabling it to move in any direction at the instructor's command.

"Bogey at one o'clock, three and a half miles," McLanahan reported. The interference pattern on his radar scope, the telltale sign of the enemy fighter's radar transmissions intermingling with the B-52's radar, disappeared and then hardened into a solid white dot on the upper-right corner of the ten-inch scope. By the time the radar sweep picked up the dot again, it had moved considerably. "Beginning to go off my scope rapidly at three o'clock, three miles. Guns, you should be able to pick him up."

"Pilot," White said, now as the crew gunner, "my fire-control system is broken. All gun barrels are jammed. No radar contact." White switched back to the E.W. "Pilot, the fighter's radar has gone down. Last contact was five o'clock, two miles. Expecting a cannon attack or infrared missile attack. Continue evasive maneuvers." White swung the control knob to the right, and the real-motion simulator responded by slamming both crewmembers into their seats. "Dispensing chaff and flares. Continue evasive maneuvers."

A long pause. The gyro compass and altimeter were both spinning madly as White, striving for maximum realism in his trainer, jerked the "plane" around as quickly as he could without locking up the hydraulically operated moving trainer. Then he leveled the trainer out and said, "Crew, this is the copilot. We've taken a missile hit on number four nacelle. Generators seven and eight are off-line. Pilot, seven and eight engine fire T-handles, pulled."

White studied a hidden closed-circuit TV picture of the inside of the egress trainer—another modification he hadn't told the trainees about. Both McLanahan and Luger were sitting bolt-upright in their seats, heads shoved back, work tables stowed, their hands gripping the ejection trigger rings between their legs. They were fighting to remain upright in the oscillating box. White twisted the controls, and the wildly-bucking box on its hydraulic legs slowly came back to normal. Both navigators were still tense, waiting for the order to eject.

Not yet, boys, White said to himself. He turned and signaled the technicians assisting him to get ready, then clicked on his interphone.

"Okay, gents," White said. "Fun's over. I was just checking out my new full-motion range. What do you think?"

"I'll tell you," McLanahan said, "after I puke on your shirt."

"Thanks," White said. "Okay. You're level at ten thousand feet. Plenty of time to get ready for ejection, right, Luger?"

"No sir," Luger answered. "Last I remember before you blew my radar scope up—and that was a nifty addition to your little chamber of horrors here, by the way—the terrain was mountainous. Some peaks went up to six or seven thousand feet. Maybe more."

"Very good," White said. "Pressure altitude is secondary—it's feet *above ground* you need to worry about. You're still flying over mountains. What else do you have to worry about, McLanahan?"

"The only damn thing I'm going to worry about," McLanahan said, "is how far upwind I can get of that one-point-one megaton bomb I just dropped."

"You guys are sharp, real sharp," White said, beaming. "I guess that's why you picked up eight trophies at Bomb Comp. All right, now, you only dropped your bomb ten minutes ago. We were balls-to-the-wall after bomb release, so we escaped the blast effects, but the fallout is still spreading. So if you were the pilot, Luger, what would you do?"

"Well, we only lost two engines," Luger said after thinking for a few moments. "I'd try to keep this Strato-Pig flying as long as I could toward the coast until she wouldn't stay up any more, then start punchin' people out."

"Even with a squadron of MIGs on your tail?" White prompted.

"Well, *shit,*" McLanahan said. "Our day has already gone to hell. Maybe they'll blow us up, or maybe they'll miss, or maybe they'll go home when they see our right wing on fire. Who knows? I'm bettin' that, even if they hit us again, we'll still have a couple of seconds to get out before the damn plane falls out of the sky. Our goose is cooked either way."

"Okay, Patrick," White said. "Don't get all worked up. This trainer is here primarily to give you practice in using your downward ejection seat, true, but *I* want you guys to get more out of it. Some guys will punch out as soon as they hear the word 'fire.' Others will wait for an order. Some guys will freeze. Some guys will never punch out—they think they're safer in the plane, or that they can ditch it or crash land it. I want you guys to think about what to do. That's all. Ejecting is a traumatic and dangerous thing to do—and I should know, because I've done it three times. I've seen too many guys die unnecessarily because they don't *think* first. Okay?"

"Okay," McLanahan said.

"Well, then," White said, "I, uh . . . listen, I have to use the little boy's room. I'll be back in a few minutes, and we'll just talk about the ejection sequence and finish early. Okay?"

"Sure," McLanahan replied.

"Good. Don't go away."

The interphone clicked dead. Luger turned a puzzled glance toward McLanahan. "Leave early? That's a first."

"I smell a rat," McLanahan said.

"Big deal," Luger said. He placed a hand near the yellow ejection trigger ring, now unstowed on the front of his ejection seat between his legs. "I've punched out of this thing a dozen—"

Luger never finished that sentence.

The trainer suddenly swerved and heeled sharply to the right. Almost immediately afterward, it pitched down so suddenly that both navigators' helmets bumped against their work tables.

The red ABANDON light between the two navigators' seats snapped on. Luger reached for the ejection ring with his free hand, but the cabin rolled over to the left so hard that it appeared it was completely flopped on its side. Not only did Luger's left hand never find the ring, but his right hand was flung away from it.

Swearing softly to himself, McLanahan flicked a small lever on the front left corner of his ejection seat. With his right hand, he grabbed the side of his seat and straightened himself up. The shoulder harness inertial reel took up the slack, anchoring McLanahan's back upright in the seat.

His partner, caught completely unawares, was almost bent in half when the cabin swung over to the left. Straining, McLanahan reached across the narrow aisle and locked Luger's shoulder harness. Luger, propelled by rage that surely could be heard outside on the instructor's control panel, hauled himself upright in his seat.

"C'mon, boys," Major White said, gleefully watching the two navigators struggle on his closed-circuit TV. He glanced over his shoulder to make sure his safety observers and technicians were in place. "Time's a-wastin' . . ."

The lights in the compartment had gone out. The cabin was lit only by the eerie red glow of the ABANDON light, but a few seconds later that too blinked out. The normally quiet hum of the trainer had been replaced by super-amplified sounds of explosions, screeching metal, hissing gas, and more explosions. Smoke began to fill the compartment. White had really laid on the realism this time, McLanahan thought to himself—the smoke began to sting his eyes. The cabin pitched over again, rolling slowly to the right and tipping downward.

Luger swore, louder than ever. He crossed his hands, wrapped his fingers around the trigger ring between his legs, slammed his head back against the headrest, and pulled the ring as if he were doing a biceps curl.

Closing his eyes and grimacing, Luger yelled, "Damn you, Major Whii-iite."

McLanahan saw a rectangle of light appear under Luger's seat, and then his partner was gone, blasted clear of the wildly-pitching trainer by powerful thrusters. Grunting with satisfaction, McLanahan gripped his own trigger ring, braced himself with his legs and feet, and pulled.

Nothing happened.

It was McLanahan's turn to swear, very loudly, but his actions were immediate. With two quick, fluid jerks, he pulled a yellow ring on either side of his ejection seat, freeing himself of the bulky global survival kit underneath him and popping the connections that held him fast. He reached upward, his blind fingers instantly finding the handhold bolted onto the overhead circuit breaker panel, and hauled himself up and out of the malfunctioned seat. The remains of his lap belt and shoulder harness clattered away.

The trainer was now tilted several degrees to the right, and McLanahan had to scramble for a handhold to keep himself clear of the gaping hole where his partner had been sitting a few moments earlier. He clutched the ladder behind Luger's seat and the catapult railing that had shot Luger's seat down into space.

Like a blind man feeling for a chair, McLanahan carefully manuevered himself around the catapult railing, propping his feet against the hatch edge, feeling for the rim of the hatch. The cabin tilted over and down even further, and his helmeted head banged against the side of the open hatch. His parachute felt like a huge concrete block on his back, dragging him closer and closer to the opening. The sounds behind him were deafening.

He was now straddling the open hatch, his feet against the back edge of the opening, his hands on either side, his head staring down through the hatch. There was another terrific explosion inside the cabin. A brilliant white light flashed. With one motion, McLanahan let go of both sides of the hatch. His right hand seized the D-ring ripcord on the harness of his parachute, and his left wrapped around his middle. He tucked his head down and rolled out through the open hatch, curling his knees up to his chest.

He felt a split-second of weightlessness as he somersaulted out. The next instant he was landing with a loud *thump* on the thick nylon safety bag eight feet below. The bag carefully deflated with a loud, relieved sound of gushing air, and McLanahan settled slowly and gently to the floor. The ripcord was in his right hand, and a large green ball that activated his emergency oxygen supply was in his left.

A horn blared somewhere, and several green-uniformed Air Force technicians rushed over to him. McLanahan remained motionless, curled up like an embryo within the mountainous billows of the safety bag.

"Are you okay, Patrick?" White asked as he helped McLanahan off with his helmet. "Hurt anywhere?"

McLanahan uncurled himself and stared at the bottom of the trainer cabin looming over him. "Son of a *bitch!*"

"You're okay," White said with an amused Cheshire-cat smile. He helped McLanahan up to his feet and out of his parachute harness.

"You did great," White said. "It took longer for Luger to punch out on his ejection seat than it did for you to manually bail out after you realized your seat had malfunctioned. Most guys never even make it out. If they don't make it within thirty seconds then they never will, especially at low altitude. You did it in fifteen."

White handed him a beer—fortunately it was their last class of the day—and they walked over to an adjacent classroom. Luger was sprawled on a chair, his flight suit half unzipped, one empty beer can near an elbow and another can in his hand, looking rumpled and angry. He scowled at White.

"No more surprises," he told White. "I'm telling the whole squadron about your tricks."

"No, you won't," White said, chuckling. "I know you, Luger—you'd like me to stick it to your buddies just like I stuck it to you. Besides, if you tell them anything I'll just have to think up some other nasty additions. When was the last time *you* did a manual bailout?"

Luger started to mutter something but then thought better of it.

"Oh, by the way," White said, turning to McLanahan. "You had a phone call from Colonel Wilder's office. Did you get an assignment?"

"Wilder," McLanahan said. He looked puzzled. "No, I didn't get an assignment as far as I know."

"Could be the big time, Muck," Luger said, finishing his beer with a happy belch. "I told you, didn't I? You're going to SAC Headquarters. I can feel it. The wing king wants to tell you himself."

"Any other message, sir?" McLanahan asked White.

"No," White replied. "You've got an appointment to see him, though. Tomorrow morning. Seven-thirty. In his office. What assignment did you put in for?"

The puzzled expression still had not left McLanahan's face. "Hell, the usual wet-dream things a six-year captain puts in for. Air Command and Staff College with a waiver. SAC headquarters. Numbered Air Force job. B-1s to Ellsworth. King of Canada. The usual stuff."

"Well, best of luck," White said. "Always like to see a good man move up."

Outside the trainer building, Luger could hardly contain his enthusiasm as he and McLanahan headed for their cars.

"Man, I knew you'd get your ticket out of here," Luger said. "Hot damn."

"I don't have *anything* yet," McLanahan said. "But why is *Wilder* telling me?"

"Who knows?" Luger said. "But, it *must* be good. If it was bad news he wouldn't wait until tomorrow. Besides, you're Wilder's showpiece, his trophy-producing machine. If Wilder makes general it'll be because of 'Shack' McLanahan."

Luger looked over at his partner and noticed his faraway look. He frowned.

"Man, you don't believe it can happen, do you," he said angrily. "You can't stay here forever, Pat. You've got to decide—"

"I'll decide what I want when I want," McLanahan interrupted. "And I don't need any advice from you."

Luger grabbed McLanahan by the arm. "Maybe you're right. Maybe you don't need my advice. But I'm your friend—and that gives me the right to tell you when I think you're making a mistake. And I think you'll be making a big mistake if you don't grab whatever the big boys decide to give you."

McLanahan sighed and shook his head. "It's not that simple, Dave. You know it isn't. My mom . . . Catherine . . . they're both down on this Air Force thing. Have been for a while. Every since my dad died it's been a real struggle for my mom to keep the bar going. I've had to watch over things. And Catherine—well, you know Catherine. Her idea of the good life has nothing to do with being an Air Force wife. She keeps prodding me to separate from the service and go into business. Lately, it's begun to make some sense."

"Shit," Luger said, "what are you saying to me? That you'd rather be in a three-piece suit shuffling papers, or helping your Mom out with the bar? That doesn't make sense. Here, at Ford, you're the best. Hell, you're probably the best damn navigator in SAC. What would you be outside of the service? Just another guy picking up a paycheck, that's what." Luger shook his head. "It's just not you, Pat. You've got a talent. And you can't turn your back on it."

McLanahan looked out across the airfield at a B-52 taxiing down the runway, then turned back to Luger. "Sometimes," McLanahan said, "I think it might not be bad being a civilian again. At least, I'd be making a difference, getting things done, having an effect. Sometimes it seems as if all we do here is run simulations, conduct exercises." He paused. "Take that trainer session today. A part of me sees the point, and another part sees it as just another game."

"It's a game that could save your life someday," Luger said, "but you don't need me to tell you that."

"No, I guess not," McLanahan said. He gestured toward his car. "Listen, Dave, I . . . I gotta get going. See you tomorrow, okay?"

Lugger nodded. He waited until McLanahan had made his way to the parking lot, then called out. "Hey, Muck!"

McLanahan turned.

"We make a good team, don't we, buddy?"

McLanahan smiled and flashed him the thumbs-up sign.

Thirty minutes later, McLanahan parked his car in front of "The Shamrock," the family restaurant and bar, and made his way through the side entrance upstairs to his third-floor apartment. For some reason, he had no desire to run into his mother or siblings just yet.

An assignment! The more he thought about it, the more confused he became. He knew that this time there weren't going to be any more extensions or delays. If he turned down another important assignment it was probably the end of his Air Force career.

He threw his flight jacket and briefcase in the closet and dropped onto the sleeper sofa with a tired *thud.* Unzipping his flight suit to the waist, he looked around his tiny efficiency apartment and shook his head.

The place was spotless—but not because he was a tidy person. Despite the fact that he lived alone, his mother came by every day at ten o'clock and cleaned and straightened it up. He once tried to discourage her by locking the door and not giving her the key, but his mother, assuming that the lock had broken somehow, had Patrick's brother Paul call a locksmith to open it. She never considered the possibility that her son might just want his privacy.

He got up, kicking his flight boots into a corner of the dining room, and went to the kitchen. He found three six-packs of beer in the refrigerator. Popping open a can, he chuckled to himself. His mother hated to see him drinking anything but milk and water, but she always kept his refrigerator stocked. Without looking, he knew there were fresh towels hanging on the rods in the bathroom and clean dishes in the cupboards.

For a brief second, he felt a pang of guilt. Christ, he thought, what's *wrong* with this setup? Shouldn't he be happy, living with his family, not worrying about cleaning or cooking? Luger would probably give his right nut to have such a life. Around his family, McLanahan was treated as much more than just the oldest sibling. He was the father, the head of the household, the provider and the decision-maker. It was Paul who ran the restaurant and tavern, and it was his mother who cooked and cleaned and served, but Patrick was the oldest, the manager, and therefore got top treatment. That was the way it was supposed to be. That's how Patrick McLanahan, Senior, was treated. That's how things were. Patrick was not even called "Patrick junior" or "Junior" or even "Pat," the way his family used to differentiate between him and his father. Patrick was now Patrick, Senior, even though it was unspoken.

Patrick's father was a city policeman who knew nothing else but work from age twenty to age sixty. After he retired from the force, he took jobs as a security guard and private investigator until Paul was old enough to run "The Shamrock," and even then he slaved over his new enterprise like a teenager. The tavern was everything—not a gold mine, but a family symbol, an heirloom.

Patrick's mother turned immediately to her oldest son after the death of her husband. Selling the tavern, and the apartments that went with the building, was unthinkable. Maureen McLanahan gathered her children around her, told them that selling out would be a dishonor, and charged them with keeping the business open. Because Patrick was the oldest, it was up to him to see they did not fail.

With help from his brothers and sister, and large infusions of his Air Force paycheck for improvements, Patrick kept the old tavern in business. He had been determined to turn that money into the security he wanted for his family, and his mother knew he would succeed. After all, he was the head of the household, and he was a McLanahan. The thought of failure never entered Maureen McLanahan's mind.

Surprisingly, the Air Force had cooperated. They had assigned Patrick to a base close to his family and had extended him a few extra years so that he could finish a master's degree and work on the family business. His success at the annual SAC Bomb Competition two years in a row, plus his knowledge and skill as a navigator, now made him a very valuable commodity.

But that extension was about to run out. His future destination—SAC headquarters in Omaha, Nebraska; the Pentagon in Washington; or a staff position in a B-1 *Excalibur* unit in South Dakota or Texas—meant high-visibility and prestige, but it also meant moving to a location light-years from home. It was a painful thought.

Why is it so painful? McLanahan asked himself. Why is it so difficult?

"Hello there."

McLanahan jumped. "Christ, Cat," he said. "Did you ever hear of knocking?"

Catherine McGraith glided over, took a genteel sniff of him in his hot, sweaty flight suit, and daintily kissed his lips at a maximum distance.

"I thought I'd surprise you," she said. "Evidently I succeeded."

Just seeing Catherine seemed to make things better, he thought. For a moment, he forgot what it was that had been bothering him. Catherine's slender figure-skater body, her tiny upturned nose, her white skin and glistening hair, always made him stop and just *watch* her, study her, take her in.

He reached out, gathered her in his arms, and kissed her full on the lips. "Hmmm. You look very nice," he said. He proceeded to carry her into the living room and fall back with her onto the sofa.

"Patrick!" Catherine said. She pushed him away, but not too hard. "You'd think you were on alert for a whole month."

"You make me crazy all the time," McLanahan said. "it doesn't matter how long I've been on alert."

"It must be the green," Catherine said. "The green flightsuits, the green planes, the green buildings—all that green must make you guys terminally horny."

"*You* make me terminally horny," he said.

Catherine finally managed to push herself away. "C'mon, now," she said, rising to her feet. "I finally succeeded in perfectly timing your arrival home. We have a reservation at the Firehouse in Old Sacramento for seven-thirty. Your mom had your suit cleaned, and you can—"

McLanahan groaned. "Oh, Cat, c'mon. The trainer today was crazy.

I had to manually bail out. Besides, I go on alert tomorrow. I'm really not in the mood for—"

"Alert! Again? You just got back from Bomb Comp. They should give you guys a rest." She paused, looking at him. "Oh, Patrick. Nancy and Margaret from school will be there tonight. Please let's go?"

McLanahan looked up at the ceiling. "I think they are getting rid of me," he said.

"Getting rid of you? What do you mean?"

"I got a call from Colonel Wilder, the wing commander," he said. "I didn't talk to him, but Paul White did. He thinks I got an assignment."

"An assignment. Where?"

"I don't know where. But a few months back Colonel Wilder specifically recommended me to a guy in Plans and Operations at SAC Headquarters. I've got a feeling that's where I'm going."

"SAC Headquarters! In Omaha? Nebraska?" Catherine frowned. "You got an assignment to Nebraska?"

"I'm not certain, Cat," McLanahan said. He could feel the excitement washing away. "That's what I wanted."

"I know, I know," Catherine said. She fiddled with her nails.

"I would be a giant step forward, Cat," McLanahan said, looking at her, trying to read her thoughts. "I think I've worn out my welcome here at Ford. It's time for me to move on."

Catherine's eyes met his. "But you were thinking of getting *out* of the service, Pat," she said. "We were going to get married and settle down and—"

"I'm still thinking of doing it," McLanahan replied. "Especially the marriage part. But . . . I don't know . . . it depends on what the Air Force has to offer. If I get an assignment to SAC Headquarters—it'll be great. A perfect opportunity."

"Patrick, you run a restaurant, the biggest . . ."

"C'mon, Cat, it's not that big," he said. "It's a little neighborhood pub that can't support me or us. And I just watch over things, that's all." He walked over to her and put his arms around her waist.

"You don't have to worry about supporting us," Catherine said. "You know that. You've established yourself in this town. Daddy will—"

"No," McLanahan interrupted. "I don't want your dad to bail me out."

"He wouldn't do that—he doesn't *need* to do that, Pat," she replied, kissing him on the nose. "I want you to be happy. Are you happy in the military? I don't think so."

McLanahan waited a moment before replying. "Sure," he said, "I'd like to get into business—be my own boss someday. But I'm doing a job I like right now, and the Air Force is paying for my education at the same time."

"And tacking two years onto your commitment every time you take a class," she pointed out. "It seems as if *they're* making out better on the deal."

"Maybe," McLanahan said. He sat up on the sofa. "Cat, I don't like to blow my horn, but I'm good at what I do. I *like* being very good at something. It's important to me."

"You can be good for Patrick McLanahan, too," Catherine replied. "The Air Force is pulling your strings like a puppet, Pat. You deserve better than that. Do what you *want* to do, what's *best* for you. Not what's best for the damn Air Force."

She sat down in an armchair in the far corner of the room. "You're not a bridge-burner, Pat," she said. "But I'm not a nomad, either. The thought of moving every two or three years, chasing a carrot held out by some general sitting on his fat behind in the Pentagon . . . well, it sickens me. Those B-52's sicken me, your job sickens me." She rose suddenly from the chair and headed for the kitchen. At the doorway she paused and turned.

"I don't know if I can follow you, Patrick," she said. "Because I'm not sure what you're following. Your own plans and goals—or the damned military's."

She gave him a final look. "Please be ready by seven."

"Hello, Mrs. King. I'm here to see Colonel Wilder."

Colonel Wilder's secretary glanced at her appointment calendar and smiled. "Good morning, Patrick. Colonel Wilder is expecting you in the Command Post. I'll buzz him and tell him you're on your way.

In the Command Post? That was odd—but everything about this meeting was odd. "Thank you, Mrs. King."

"Congratulations again on winning Bomb Comp this year, Patrick," Mrs. King said with a smile. "I know the Colonel is very proud of you and your crew."

"Thanks," McLanahan said. He was about to leave, but paused in the doorway.

"Mrs. King?"

"Yes?"

"Everyone knows that you executive secretaries are pretty powerful persons, working so close to the commander." Mrs. King gave a sly smile.

"Yes, Patrick?"

"Any idea what Colonel Wilder wants to see me about?"

"You *are* a worrywart," she said. "That's probably why you won so many trophies. No, Patrick, this all-important, high-powered secretary has no idea why the commander wants to see you." She smiled at him. "Why? Got a guilty conscience?"

"Me? C'mon."

"Well, then, you'd better get going. I'll tell him you're on your way."

"Thanks."

In his six years at Ford Air Force Base, McLanahan had only been in the Command Post less than a half dozen times. The first time was for his initial Emergency War Order unit mission certification, when every SAC crewmember has to brief the wing commander on the part he will play, from takeoff to landing, if the Klaxon sounded and he should ever go to war. Most of the time, he simply stopped by to drop off some mission paperwork to the command post controllers after a late-night mission, or drop off some classified communications documents for the night. Despite his experience, he was still somewhat awed whenever he had to report to the Command Post.

Part of the aura of the Command Post was the security required to get near it. McLanahan dug his line badge out of his wallet—luckily, he had taken it out of its usual place in a flightsuit pocket—and pinned it to his shirt pocket. He then stood in front of the main entrance to the Command Post, which was a heavy iron grate door. He pushed a buzzer button, and the grate was unlocked for him by someone inside. As he stepped inside the short corridor, called the "entrapment" area, he heard the iron grate door lock behind him.

If there's one thing I hate, McLanahan said to himself, *it's doors locking behind me like that.*

He walked to the other end of the corridor and stood before a door that had a full-length one-way mirror on it. Spotlights were arranged on the mirror to completely flood out the dim images of the men and women working beyond it. McLanahan picked up a red telephone next to the door.

"Yes, sir?" came a voice immediately on the other end.

"Captain McLanahan to see Colonel Wilder."

The door lock buzzed, and McLanahan opened it and stepped inside.

The security didn't stop once he was inside. He was met by Lieutenant Colonel Carl Johannsen. Although McLanahan and Johannsen had crewed together for several months, Johannsen, wearing a revolver strapped to his waist, came up to his old navigator and took a peek at his line badge.

"Morning, sir," McLanahan said, as his badge was quickly checked.

"Hi, Pat," Johannsen said. He looked a bit embarrassed. "I probably taught you everything you know when you were still a wet-behind-the-ears nav. But the boss is here, so we're making it look good. Not under duress or anything?"

"No."

Good. And call the boss 'sir,' okay? I'm still your old pilot to you."

"Yes, sir," McLanahan said. "How do you like the Command Post job?"

"Sometimes I wish I was still flying a Buff low-level in the Grand Tetons," he said. "The boss is in the Battle Staff Situation Room right through there. See you."

On the way to the office, McLanahan passed by the main communications room itself. That was the most fascinating part of the place. It was hard to believe that the wing commander or duty controllers could put themselves in contact with almost anyone else in the world, on the ground or in the air, through that console. They had direct links to SAC Headquarters, the Joint Chiefs of Staff, the perpetually-flying Airborne Command Post, and links to hundreds of other command posts throughout the world. They communicated by telephone, computer, satellite, high-frequency radio, and by coded teletype. In an instant, the SAC Commander in Chief in Omaha, Nebraska, could send a message that could launch all of Ford's bombers and tankers within a matter of minutes. Or, just as easily and just as fast, the President could order those same planes to war.

The Battle Staff Situation Room was the hub of the Command Post during situations, whether real or simulated, where the wing commander and members of his staff met to coordinate the wartime actions of Ford Air Force Base's two thousand men and women, twenty B-52 bombers, and twenty-five KC-135 tankers. McLanahan knocked on the door.

"C'mon in, Patrick."

Colonel Edward Wilder was seated behind the center desk in the Battle Staff office. Colonel Wilder, the commander of all the forces on Ford Air Force Base, looked about as old as a college freshman. He was tall, trim and fit from running marathons a few times a year, and had not a touch of gray in his light brown hair despite being well past forty. He stood, shook McLanahan's hand, and motioned to a thick, cushiony seat marked "Vice Commander."

Wilder poured two cups of coffee. "Black, right, Patrick?" Wilder asked, pushing the cup toward him.

"That's right, sir."

"I should have that memorized by now," the wing commander said. "I watched you put away enough of it during Bomb Comp." As he spoke, he pushed a button on his desk. A curtain over the window separating the Battle Staff Office from the communications center rolled closed on metal tracks. Lt. Colonel Johannsen and the others glanced up at the moving curtain but quickly went back to their duties.

Colonel Wilder had a red-covered folder on his desk in front of him.

"I tried to get hold of you before your trainer began yesterday, but you had already started."

"Yes, sir," McLanahan said. "Major White's egress trainers are getting extremely realistic."

"The guy is a basement inventor. A genius," Wilder said. "The small amount of money we could spare for White's group was the best money we ever spent. We may have created a monster, though."

McLanahan laughed, but it was short and strained. Wilder noticed the atmosphere, took a deep breath, and went on.

"Any idea why you're here this morning?"

I hate when they start out that way! McLanahan thought. "No, sir," he said. "I thought it might have something to do with an assignment."

"It does, Patrick," Wilder said. He paused a bit, looked at his desktop, then said. "Good news. SAC Headquarters wants you. Soonest. Plans and Operations for the B-1 program. Congratulations—that was my first Headquarters job, although I was with the B-52 program when *that* monster was the hot new jet."

McLanahan shook Wilder's proffered hand. "That's great, sir. Great news."

"I hate to lose you, Patrick," Wilder went on. "But they're hustling you out pretty damned quick. Your reporting date is in three months."

McLanahan's smile dimmed a bit. "That soon? For a Headquarters position?"

"It just came open," Wilder explained. "It's a great opportunity." Wilder studied McLanahan's face. "Problems?"

"I need to discuss it with my family," McLanahan said. "It's a big step . . ."

"I need an answer now. It won't wait."

McLanahan averted his eyes, then said, "Sorry, Colonel. I have to discuss it with my family. If an immediate answer's required, I have to say—"

"Hold on, Patrick. Don't say it," Wilder interrupted. "Patrick, I'm not trying to blow smoke in your face, but you're the best navigator I've ever worked with in my eighteen years in the service. You're energetic, intelligent, highly motivated, and you have as much expertise in the inner workings of your profession as anyone else in the command. Your Officer Evaluation Reports have been firewalled to 'Outstanding' every year you've been in the service, and, for the last two years, I've had the unusual honor of being the *lowest* rater on your OERs because they've always gone up to a higher command level. This year it's gone up to Headquarters SAC, and we didn't even request it—the SAC Commander in Chief *asked* for it. Personally. You'd be a real asset to the Plans people."

Wilder punched a fist into an open palm in frustration, then looked at McLanahan. "But you can't balk like this all the time. You have to grab these opportunities when you can."

"Another one will come along . . ."

"Don't count on it, Patrick," Wilder said quickly. He looked into McLanahan's puzzled eyes, then continued. "I meant what I said. You're the best radar nav I've seen. The best. But . . . you need to straighten up a little bit."

McLanahan glared at the wing commander. "Straighten up?"

"C'mon, Patrick," Wilder said. "Gary must've mentioned this to you. Look at yourself. Most guys who go to see the commander polish their shoes, get a haircut, and wear a clean uniform." McLanahan said nothing, but crossed his arms impatiently on his chest.

"Your record outshines everyone else's, Pat . . . but the Air Force wants *officers* nowadays, not just . . . technicians. They want guys who want to be professionals. You've got to look and act like a professional. Real all-around full-time officers, not part-time performers."

Wilder opened a folder—McLanahan's squadron records. "You finished your master's degree, and you're halfway through a second master's degree, but you have hardly any military education. It took you six years to finish a correspondence course that should only take twelve months. No additional duties. Your attitude toward—"

"There's nothing wrong with my attitude, Colonel," McLanahan interrupted. "I wanted to be the best. I worked hard to prove that I am." He paused, then said, "I've been busy at the tavern. I—"

"I don't doubt that, Patrick," Wilder said. "I know your situation at home. But you need to make a commitment."

Wilder stood and walked over to the aircraft status board covering a wall in the Command Post Battle Staff Conference Room. "It's a different Air Force nowadays. You know that. The way things are, Patrick, even just meeting standards won't get you anywhere. You've got to excel at everything . . . and then some. And not just in your field of expertise."

"The so-called 'whole person concept,' " McLanahan said.

"It may sound like b.s. to you, and to a lot of folks," Wilder said, "but it's still true. They want total immersement nowadays. Being good . . . hell, even being above average is the norm. I know you have the raw material to make that commitment, Patrick. You just need to make the decision. Yes or no."

Wilder closed the folder. "Well, that's enough of the party line," he said. "Get back to me as soon as you've made your decision about the assignment. I'll work on keeping it open, but there are no guarantees."

After a long moment, McLanahan got to his feet and said, "Well, I hope that's all, sir, because I've got some thinking to do."

"I've got one more thing," Wilder said, returning to his seat. McLanahan did the same.

"It's the reason why we're meeting here, in the Command Post," Wilder explained, "and another reason why I need your answer to this assignment offer. I received an unusual request for a senior, highly experienced B-52 radar navigator to participate in an exercise. The message was highly classified—I didn't think there was a classification higher than TOP SE-CRET, but there is. I had to receive the message from the communications center personally—in fact, they kicked everyone else out of the place but me. Anyway, naturally I thought of you."

"Sure, why not? I'll do it," McLanahan said. "What is it? What kind of exercise?"

Wilder opened the red-covered file folder in front of him. "I . . . I don't have any idea, Patrick," he said. "I have very simple instructions. Can you be ready to leave in two days?"

"Two days," McLanahan said. He thought for a moment. "Well, it's not much time, but . . . sure I can leave. Leave for where?"

"I don't have that information."

"What . . . I don't understand," McLanahan said.

"Patrick, this is a highly classified exercise. They want you to go to Executive Airport, to the information booth, the day after tomorrow at eight A.M. You show your ID card and this letter." He handed the letter to McLanahan. "You bring nothing else but a change of civilian clothes and toilet articles in one piece of carry-on luggage. They'll give you further instructions when your identity and the letter have been verified." Wilder studied the young radar-navigator for a moment.

"Got all that?"

"Yes, sir," McLanahan replied, shaking off the cloud of confusion. "I understand everything. It just sounds a bit . . . weird, that's all."

"You'll find out, when you've been in as long as I have, Patrick," Wilder said, standing, "that all this hush-hush stuff becomes old hat. Second nature. It may seem like a real exercise in frustration. But they've got to play their games, you know."

McLanahan rose. "Oh, I understand *that,* Colonel," he said.

"Remember, now," Wilder said. "Nobody needs to know about this duty. Keep this letter out of sight. Don't tell anyone else about what you'll be doing or where you're headed, even after you find out at the airport."

"Yes, sir," McLanahan said. "That won't be difficult to do, since I don't know anything about what I'm doing."

"Well, don't tell anyone *that,* either, Pat," Wilder said, smiling.

"Yes, sir." McLanahan turned to leave. Just before he stepped out, he turned to Wilder and said, "Sir, when I get back I need to talk to you about assignments—and the Air Force."

Wilder nodded and folded his hands before him on the desk. "I understand, Pat," Wilder replied. "I'm glad, at least, that you're going to talk before doing anything else. Believe me, I know what you're feeling. We'll talk when you get back, but don't let it spoil this exercise."

"I won't sir," McLanahan said. He turned and left.

Wilder stood, paced the floor for a few moments, then reached into a desk drawer and lit up a cigarette, the first in several years.

" 'You'll find out, my boy, when you've been in as long as I have,' " Wilder said sarcastically, mimicking himself, " 'that this hush-hush stuff becomes old hat.' " What horseshit, Wilder thought. Real horseshit. And he saw right through it all.

Wilder sat there for a long time smoking the cigarette.

I don't understand any of this," she said finally.

McLanahan had just stuffed the last pair of socks in his bulging gym bag when his mother came into the bedroom to watch him pack. She stood, arms crossed impatiently on her slim chest, staring in dismay. He slowly pulled the zipper closed.

"Mom," he said, picking up the bag, "there's nothing to understand."

"Is this some kind of secret mission?" Maureen McLanahan asked, half-jokingly. "Are you a spy? Come *on,* Patrick. Can't you give me a hint?"

"You've been reading too much John LeCarré, Mom," McLanahan said. "I've got orders, just as if I was going to Bomb Comp or off-station training. You know, TDYs, Mom. They come up suddenly."

"But your orders don't say where, or for how long, or for what."

"Mom, c'mon. I don't have written orders. I went into see Colonel Wilder. He gave me all the information."

"Which is?"

"Which I'm not allowed to say." He turned and put his hands on his hips. "C'mon, now. You know better than to pump me for information I can't give."

Maureen McLanahan watched her son for a while. Then: "Catherine said something about the Colonel giving you a new assignment."

Patrick nodded. "I received the assignment I wanted—an excellent position at SAC Headquarters. I had to call them and beg and plead with them to keep the slot open until I get back from this TDY. Any other guy in the Air Force would have packed his bags and been on his way in three days. I may lose that assignment. I may already *have* lost that assignment."

Maureen tried to be soothing. "It sounds like . . . a wonderful opportunity . . ."

"It is," Patrick said. "But Catherine may not follow me to Nebraska—she thinks that the military is manipulating me. And you . . . well, I know what your reaction would be if I moved out."

Patrick slung the bag over his shoulder and hurried past his mother.

"Is that *all* you're taking?" his mother asked as she watched him enter the livingroom.

"This is all they wanted me to take," he replied. "I imagine they'll supply me with whatever else I need."

"Oh, Patrick," his mother said, wringing her hands. "I want to help you make the right decision, but I can't help it. The restaurant is our life. If you move away, I don't know if we could handle it by ourselves."

Patrick walked back to where she was standing and kissed her on the cheek. "I understand, Mom. I really do. But . . . the business is almost running itself now. And you have Paul. You don't need me like before." He gave her a hug. "It will be all right, Mom. Believe me."

Maureen McLanahan buttoned the top button of her son's shirt. "You'll be back, won't you, Patrick?

She hadn't really heard a thing. "Yes," he sighed. "I'll be back."

She brushed back a lock of hair from her forehead and smiled. "I love you, Patrick."

"I love you too, Mom," he said. He gave her a firm reassuring look, turned and walked out.

The ride to the airport in Catherine's Mercedes was fast and very quiet. McLanahan held hands with Catherine right up until she pulled up to the curb in front of the United Airlines terminal, but few words were exchanged. She did not stop the engine, but only put it into neutral and watched as he retrieved his bag and jacket from the back seat.

"I'm going to miss you," he said as he piled his belongings on his lap.

"I'll miss you, too," she replied. There was an uncomfortable pause. Then she added, "I wish you didn't have to go."

"Part of the job, Cat," he said. "It's kind of exciting, all this mystery. A ticket on the Orient Express."

"Well," she said, "*I* don't think it's exciting. It's stupid—sending you off to God knows where and not even telling you when you'll be back."

He stared back at her and said nothing.

"Thank God you won't have to do this much longer," she went on. "This just underscores how the military treats people like you. The best nav in the Air Force, bundled up like a sack of dirty laundry and hustled off to Timbuktu."

"The Air Force has been a good life, Cat. A good job. It's had its ups and downs . . ."

"Oh, Pat, that sounds like you, all right," she said, glaring at him. "Here you are, on your way to some nonsense at a moment's notice, and you're still spouting the ol' party line." She watched him as he opened the car door.

"Got to go, Cat," he said, leaning over and giving her a peck on the cheek. "Thanks for the lift." He started to step out of the car . . .

"Patrick," she said suddenly, "when you . . . get back, we have to talk—about us."

He looked at her for a moment, trying to read her expression, then shrugged. "Okay," he said. "Fine." He stepped out of the car and watched for a few seconds as she drove away.

The information counter handled McLanahan's request as if cryptic orders for tickets were honored every day. He produced his ID card—the only piece of identification he was allowed to bring—and he was promptly given a sealed envelope and directions to the boarding gate.

Curiosity overcame him on the escalator ride to the upper floor, and he opened the envelope. Inside was a round-trip ticket to Spokane, Washington, with an open return date. The office symbol of the ticket purchaser was a strange four-letter military official symbol with no base or office location.

He exchanged one of the tickets for a boarding pass at the gate and sat down to wait. Why all the damn mystery, he asked himself. Spokane was the location of Fairchild Air Force Base, the Air Force's basic survival school. He had already been to basic survival right after undergraduate navigator training, but Fairchild had a number of survival schools and other training courses.

Well, that was it, then. He had been tapped for some exotic survival training school—maybe it was a special school under development. He had heard rumors of a new school in the works that taught survival in environments contaminated by nuclear fallout. Or perhaps it was a new twist on the mock-up prisoner-of-war camp located at Fairchild, a facility complete with interrogation centers, a prison camp, and real Eastern bloc-trained guards and interrogators.

The waiting became much, much easier after McLanahan had sorted it all out for himself. Fairchild. All this lousy secrecy, all the hassles, all the worrying—all for some dumb exercise, some stupid class where CIA or DIA interrogators could get their hands on a *real* crewdog for a while. What a waste.

McLanahan did not have long to wait until his flight was called, and all the passengers were on board in a matter of minutes. Only a handful of people—a few obviously G.I. by the looks of their haircuts, a few civilians—were headed for Spokane. McLanahan scanned an inflight magazine, wishing he'd brought a magazine or a book, wishing the damned military had *let him* bring one.

He was fast asleep, the gentle roar of the engines acting as a narcotic for his settling nerves, long before the plane's wheels ever left the ground.

A waste of time, he nodded to himself just before he dropped off. A complete waste of time.

SPOKANE, WASHINGTON

It was late in the evening when McLanahan finally collected his baggage and stood at the entranceway to Spokane International's central lobby. He put his single carry-on bag down on an empty chair and reread the cryptic, computer-printed instructions he received when he departed:

ARRIVE SPOKANE 2135L. HAVE BAGGAGE IN POSSESSION BY 2200L AND WAIT FOR FURTHER DIRECTIONS.

It was 2345, almost two hours after his scheduled—scheduled *what?* Another classic example of the military's standard "hurry up and wait" procedures. Get to where you're going on time or else, but sit on your butt and wait till *they're* ready.

McLanahan slung his gym bag over a shoulder and went over to a counter with a sign that read SHUTTLE TO FAIRCHILD. The desk was empty, but a sign with two moveable hands on an Air Force recruiting clock face promised that an Airman Willis would be back by twelve o'clock. The hands looked as if they hadn't been moved in months. McLanahan chose a seat near the counter and waited.

A few minutes later, a tall, muscular Air Force enlisted man in a neat pair of combination one double-knits with a few impressive rows of ribbons arrived at the desk. He filled out a line of a clipboard log beneath the counter, turned on a huge portable tape deck, and took a seat on a tall school. McLanahan approached the desk.

"Good evening, sir," Willis said. "Headin' out to the base, sir?"

"I guess so," McLanahan said. "When's the next shuttle?"

"Twelve-oh-five, or thereabouts, sir," Willis replied. He retrieved his clipboard. "Can I see your orders and ID, sir?"

"I don't have orders," McLanahan said. He fished his plastic-coated card out of his jeans pocket. Willis examined the card, made a few entries on his log, and returned it.

"Do you have any quarters arranged sir?"

"No," McLanahan replied. "I left . . . on pretty short notice."

"Do you have someone we can contact at the base? Someone who knows you're coming? Your sponsor perhaps?"

McLanahan pulled out the original message and scanned it. "All I have is a Major Miller, but he only has a Washington office symbol and number. Nobody at Fairchild. I didn't . . . I mean . . . I wasn't sure I'd be coming here . . ."

Willis looked at Patrick McLanahan quizzically, suppressing a slight, "Jesus, another space cadet," remark.

"Well, sir, I can give billeting a call, but without orders or a point of contact you'll be space-available only and that's pretty slim pickins' right now."

McLanahan put the message back in his pocket and said, "The shuttle leaves at five after twelve, right?"

"Yes, sir."

"Okay. Please give billeting a call and see what the room situation is like. My contact, whoever it's supposed to be, was scheduled to meet me by ten. If he doesn't show I might as well get a room and try to contact him in the morning."

"You got it, sir," Airman Willis said cheerfully. He dialed a number, spoke for a few minutes, then hung up with a smile on his face, his head bobbing in time with the beat of the music throbbing from his portable stereo.

"You lucked out, sir," Willis said, filling out his log. "One room at the Qs, ready and waiting. If your Major Miller shows, I'll tell him where you are."

"Thanks," McLanahan said. "I appreciate your help."

"No problem a-tall, sir," he said, maintaining the rhythm with a pencil. "You here for survival school? Got your Odor-Eaters and flea collars ready?"

"I went through all that stuff years ago," McLanahan replied. "I guess they thought I needed a refresher."

"Sure, sir," Willis replied, already tuning himself out now that the goofy lost captain was taken care of. "Everyone needs a little practice bleeding every now and then." McLanahan was going to reply, but Willis was far away in his music and a copy of *Playboy*.

The shuttle arrived not-so-promptly at twelve-fifteen. No one, not even Airman Willis, had talked to him since he made his room reservations.

The entire terminal was almost empty. McLanahan thanked Willis once again and climbed aboard the blue school bus when it beeped outside. Again, he was the only one on the bus as it rattled away.

It was a short drive to Fairchild Air Force base. McLanahan showed his ID to the gate guard and opened his gym bag for the M-16-carrying guard and his huge German shepherd. Fifteen minutes later, McLanahan sprawled sleepily on a queen-sized bed in the Visiting Officer's Quarters.

He undressed, showered, and lay awake on top of his bed for a few confused minutes. It was just after one A.M. Restlessly, he picked up the base phone book and scanned the personnel directory. There were several Millers listed, and even two Major Millers, but neither with a similar office symbol as the one on his printout. McLanahan checked the organizational listings, but there were no organizations on base even resembling the office symbol on the message.

He threw the directory back on the nightstand.

"Screw 'em," he said half-aloud. "If they want me, they should figure out where to find me." He left a six-thirty wake-up call at the front desk and slipped under the coarse olive-drab G.I. horse blankets.

McLanahan awoke with a violent start to the furious sound of impatient knuckles rapping on wood. He felt as if he had been asleep for hours— perhaps it was the billeting clerk pounding on his door because he got no answer on the wake-up call. McLanahan glanced at the clock on the dresser. Nope, he'd only been asleep for an hour.

He slipped on a pair of gym shorts from his bag, smoothed down his blond hair, and opened the door. Two black men, one in a civilian suit and the other an Air Force security guard, were standing impatiently in the doorway.

"Captain McLanahan?" the guy in the suit asked. He did not even look at McLanahan—he was scanning up and down the hallways.

"Yeah," McLanahan replied irritably, scratching his head.

"Patrick McLanahan?"

"Yeah, yeah." McLanahan wasn't in a conversational mood, but his gruff attitude didn't faze these guys.

The guy in the suit looked immensely relieved. He put a finger on the security guard's chest as if driving his commands into the guard's body.

"We got him. Notify the gate guards. Then get an unmarked car and have it sent over here pronto. No Air Force or DOD crap on the doors."

"We got one." The guard trotted away. The guy in the suit pushed his way into McLanahan's room and closed and locked the door.

"I need your ID, Captain McLanahan," he said brusquely.

"Like hell," McLanahan said, finally beginning to wake up. "I want to see *your* ID right now or I'll call back that sky cop you just chased away."

The guy muttered a "Jesus H. Christ" under his breath, but pulled out a wallet and held it up. McLanahan turned on the room light and squinted sleepily at the card and badge.

"Staff Sergeant Jenkins, Air Force Office of Special Investigations," the man said, snapping the wallet closed. "Now, sir, if you don't mind . . ."

"Yeah. Okay." McLanahan fumbled through his jeans and produced the card. Jenkins already had a walkie-talkie in his hand. He studied the card, nodded, and thumbed the mike.

"Control, seven-seven," he said as softly as he could.

"Seven-seven, go," came the reply.

"I've located our subject. I'll be escorting him back to the main rendez-vous point."

"Copy, seven-seven." Jenkins returned the card.

"Captain McLanahan, please get dressed and get your gear together."

"Hey, wait a minute," McLanahan protested. "What's going on?"

Jenkins was frowning impatiently, his fists on his hips. Apparently he didn't like anyone, even officers, asking him "why" and "what."

"Sir, we are going back to meet Major Miller," he said in short, clipped words. He glanced down at his walkie-talkie and clicked it off. "You were supposed to wait at the airport for further instructions, were you not, sir?"

"Yeah," McLanahan said, feeling his ears redden. Shit, he thought. I screwed up. He reached for the jeans, wondering if Jenkins was going to stand there and watch him dress. "Ten o'clock. Nobody showed up. I thought I'd get a room at the base and wait . . ."

"Why the base, sir?" Jenkins interrupted.

"What do you mean, 'why the base'? I get orders to Spokane. It's gotta be . . ."

"Sir." Jenkins was obviously holding in check the massive urge to lash out with a 'you dumb shit officer, who the hell told you to *assume* anything?' but he said instead, "That was an unfortunate . . . *mis*judgment. You were to meet Major Miller at the terminal. He was delayed, but he expected you to sit tight until you received further directions." The spitting emphasis on *mis*judgment was too obvious.

"Okay, okay. Yeah. You're right, sergeant," McLanahan replied. "I'll be ready in a minute."

Obviously, Jenkins had no intention of leaving.

"Where are we going?"

Jenkins did not reply, but he looked more exasperated than ever with every question. McLanahan glared at him as he finished repacking the gym bag and pulling on his jacket. It really did take McLanahan only a minute to get ready because he carried so few items.

McLanahan retrieved his key, stepped out into the hall and turned toward the lobby.

"This way, sir," Jenkins said, grabbing McLanahan's arm and swinging him around toward a dimly lit hallway to the back.

"But my room . . . ?"

"Will be taken care of, sir. This way." Jenkins led him to a side door that opened up to a laundry delivery dock and a dumpster in the rear of the building. A blue sedan, its engine idling, was waiting. As McLanahan headed for the steps leading down from the dock to the pavement below, Jenkins grabbed the gym bag off McLanahan's shoulder.

"I'll take this, sir," he said quietly. "Get in and we'll leave." He trotted down to the sedan, knocked on the window, and trotted around to the trunk just as it popped open. He hid the gym bag under some blankets and then slid quietly in the back seat next to McLanahan.

As they drove out the gate and onto the highway leading back to Spokane International, Jenkins picked up a device from the front seat and clicked it on.

"Bear with me, sir," he said, passing the device quickly over McLanahan's body. He repeated the sweep once more, then clicked it off and set the device next to the driver.

"Now, Sergeant Jenkins," McLanahan said, "can you tell me what the hell's going on?"

"As far as I'm allowed, sir," he replied. "Major Miller was supposed to meet you at ten o'clock at the airport. He was delayed arranging for secure transportation. When he wrote your instructions he assumed that, when your printed instructions left you off at the airport, that *you* would stop at the airport. A bad assumption on *his* part, apparently."

"Well, since we're admitting to poor assumptions tonight, I've got a few more," McLanahan said. "I assumed that my final destination was Fairchild—why else would I be sent to Spokane? Now I'm assuming all this to mean that Fairchild is *not* my final destination."

"I don't know anything about your *final* destination, Captain," Jenkins replied. "You were sent to Spokane for one reason only."

"Which was?"

"Because they only had eight people booked on that flight," Jenkins said, as if that explained *everything.*

"Say again?"

"They needed to know if you were being tailed, Captain McLanahan," Jenkins explained. "They knew who had reservations on your flight, who signed on after you checked in, who arrived at Spokane, and where everyone went and what everyone did when they got off your flight. They could do this because of the small number aboard. They simply picked a time, date, and location with the fewest passengers and had you get on that flight. It just happened to go to Spokane, Washington. It had nothing to do with Fairchild at all—as a matter of fact, it will probably take some fast explaining to someone when the billeting folks find you gone suddenly."

"Tailed! Me? Why would anybody tail *me?*"

Jenkins let out a half laugh, half snort in the car's darkness. "Shee-it," he said, chuckling humorlessly again. "If *you* don't know, Captain, it *must* be *bad* news."

And, at that, the hairs rose on the back of McLanahan's neck. Jenkins' words echoed through his head as the lights of the airport grew larger and brighter.

If you don't know, Captain, it must be bad news.

Jenkins' monotone voice finally penetrated McLanahan's reverie as the car bypassed the main terminal and headed for a row of hangars adjacent to the taxiways, away from the jet parking ramp. The car's driver had already doused the headlights.

"Your bag will catch up with you, Captain, don't worry," he was saying. "Remember now—walk away from the car about ten steps then just stop and . . . *wait.*" McLanahan had to smile at Jenkins' emphasis on the word 'wait,' but apparently Jenkins didn't notice. "Someone will meet you and tell you what to do."

The car pulled to a stop in the middle of a deserted parking ramp, far from the brilliantly lit terminal. The door on McLanahan's side was opened by some dark figure outside. He noticed no interior courtesy lights illuminated—someone had punched holes in the plastic lenses with a knife.

"Sorry for the mixups, Sergeant Jenkins," McLanahan said in a low voice in keeping with the hushed, tense atmosphere.

"No problem, sir," Jenkins said. His walkie-talkie crackled, and he spoke a few words into it. Then, he added, "Good luck," and pulled the door closed. The car moved off and was soon lost in the darkness.

"I don't need luck," McLanahan said to himself, looking around in the gloom. "What I need is *out* of here."

The ramp was completely dark—even the small blue taxiway lights leading from the runway were turned off. McLanahan put the terminal on his right side and stepped forward ten paces, as carefully as if he was following a pirate's treasure map. Somehow, he could *feel* people all around him, lots of eyes watching him, talking about him, but he couldn't see a thing. He could make out a large, seemingly deserted hangar behind him, its huge front bay door open like a dark cave entrance. As his eyes grew accustomed to the dark, he spotted a few light single-engined Cessnas tied down to his left. The parking ramp was breezy and beginning to grow cold.

He made a motion to pull down his jacket sleeve and check his watch, but he suppressed that urge. This time, he was just going to stand and wait. Checking the time would only make him that much more impatient. He zipped his jacket up all the way, shoved his hands in his pockets, and stood watching the runway.

McLanahan guessed that about fifteen minutes had passed since Jenkins dropped him off. His eyes were fully adjusted to the dark now. There were small birds everywhere, jumping and peeping nervously around him. An occasional rabbit scampered down the asphalt, stopping every now and then to test the air and sniff for danger. Once McLanahan thought he heard the static of a walkie-talkie nearby, but he saw no one. He watched every plane that landed—there were only two—expecting it to pull up in front of him any minute, but they never did.

Another ten minutes passed—or was it another fifteen or twenty? The sky was beginning to clear, and the temperature was taking a noticeable dip. Whoever he was supposed to meet out here was going to find a frozen navigator Popsicle because McLanahan was determined not to screw it up again, even if it meant catching pneumonia. He stamped the cold from his sneakers a few times, then removed his hands from the pockets of his light nylon windbreaker and blew warm air on them.

Let's get on with it, boys, McLanahan said to himself. He blew on his palms once again, cursing the air nipping at his uncovered ears, and slapped two chilly palms together irritably.

He never heard the slap. At that exact instant, in the dark hangar directly behind him, a high-pitched whine erupted.

McLanahan jumped an easy six inches and spun quickly toward the noise. As he turned, he was blinded by the glare of a set of four landing and taxi lights aimed directly at him. He had completely misjudged the distance. The lights were less than fifty yards away.

The whine became a low, bellowing roar, and a twin-engined jet taxied rapidly from within the dark hangar, the blinding lights focused directly on the lone figure on the ramp. It seemed to leap out at him, like a tiger springing through a hoop at a circus. McLanahan could not have moved if he had wanted to.

The jet sped up beside him, the wingtip fuel tanks passing a mere five feet from where he stood anchored on the ramp. A curved airstair door was flung open, and a lone man with an Air Force-looking uniform grabbed McLanahan's upper arm with a tight grip and half-guided, half-dragged him to the doorway of the screaming jet.

He was guided with a push onto a hard airliner seat, and a seat belt was quickly yanked around him. The belt was snapped tight around his waist, and McLanahan felt a prickle of panic. They weren't concerned for his safety at all—they wanted him to stay put.

He watched as the man who had pulled him aboard placed a headset over his head and thrust his face forward. He ordered, "I.D. card. Quickly."

McLanahan was startled by the sudden command, and impulsively reached into his right back pocket where the card *always* was. It wasn't there. He squirmed around and felt for the card in his left back pocket. Not there, either.

"Quickly!" the man said again. He pulled a boom mike near his lips and spoke a few clipped words into it. McLanahan glanced at a pair of wild-looking, dark eyes, then turned away as he furiously patted his pockets. Glancing toward the front of the jet, he saw the copilot leaning to his left into the narrow aisle between him and the pilot. The copilot wore a camouflaged helmet and a green flight suit. With a start, McLanahan noticed the copilot half-concealing a stubby, short-barrelled Uzi subma-chine gun behind the cockpit curtain.

"Oh, shit," McLanahan said. His hands flew over his pockets, finally finding the card in his left front pocket. He fished it out and held it up to the man pinning him in the seat, nearly clipping a piece of the man's nose off in the process.

The man snapped on a tiny red-beamed flashlight, examined the card, then swept the tiny beam of light across McLanahan's dumbfounded face. The man's hard features softened a bit, washing clear with an immense sense of relief.

He pulled the mike closer to his lips and leapt to his feet. "Let's roll, pilot," he shouted, dropping the card in McLanahan's lap. The Uzi peek-ing behind the curtain disappeared. The man with the headset scurried back and hauled up the airstair door and dogged it closed. A few short moments later, the jet was screaming skyward.

The guard wearily dropped into a seat across from McLanahan and took a moment or two to take a few deep breaths.

"Sorry about all that, Captain," the man said after the plane was safely on its way. "When you disappeared from the airport terminal, we got a little nervous. We may have overreacted a bit. I'm sorry if we got a little rough."

"I'm the one who should be apologizing, I think," McLanahan said, slowly recovering from his shock. "I've handled this whole thing pretty irresponsibly. Are you Major Miller, the one I was finally supposed to contact?"

The man laughed and nodded toward the epaulets on his shoulders.

"No, Captain. I'm First Lieutenant Harold Briggs. I work for the project coordinator. *We* are Major Miller."

"*We?*"

"Major Miller was a code name for *you,*" Briggs explained. "Whenever you or someone from your unit mentioned Major Miller, my section was notified. I'm in charge of getting you to the project coordinator."

"The project coordinator? Who is he?"

"You'll find that out soon," Briggs replied. "We're on our way, finally, to meet him. Meanwhile, if you need anything, just let me know. Call me Hal, please. I'll be working with you for the entire duration of the project."

"The project?"

"Yes, sir," Briggs said, smiling. "I can't tell you about that. You'll have to see the project coordinator for that. But, I am your aide from now on."

"Aide, huh?" McLanahan said. "Well, I don't know if I can handle that." He extended a hand. "Call me Patrick and can the 'sir' stuff, okay?"

"You got it." They shook hands, and Briggs stowed his headset in an overhead rack and flicked on a light. Hal Briggs was very, very young, with short-cropped black hair on top of a lean, thin face and dark brown eyes. He wore lieutenant epaulets on his blue fatigues, a pair of Army paratrooper's wings, and an Air Force Security Police badge over his left breast pocket. McLanahan noticed he wore a green webbed infantry belt over his blue Air Force trousers, but he couldn't see the weapon holstered there.

"Sergeant Jenkins said something about me being tailed," McLanahan said as Briggs opened a small refrigerator near his seat and pulled out a couple of beers.

"Yeah," Briggs said, popping open his can and handing the other to McLanahan. Briggs tipped his can to McLanahan and took a long swallow.

"Call it youthful exuberance. When you showed up at the terminal, then suddenly disappeared, I got . . . nervous. I called Sergeant Jenkins, who was my backup out there from Fairchild, and I sounded the alarm. Boy, those OSI guys can *move out.*"

"You're not OSI?"

"No." Briggs smiled. "Anyway, Jenkins had a search organized in no time. We were more or less in control of the tactical environment, as we say in the game, at the airport. When you moved to the base, we lost control. Hell, we . . . *I* painted a half-dozen different scenarios about what happened to you. All bad."

"Whoa, whoa!" McLanahan held up a tired hand. "Happened to me? I don't get it. What are you guys so afraid of? What can happen to me? And why *me* in the first place?"

Briggs drained his beer and reached for another.

"Pat, you are very, very hot property right now," he said, watching McLanahan's wide-eyed expression from behind the upturned beer can. "If we lost you, if something happened to you, if you didn't arrive at the project headquarters by tomorrow noon . . ." He finished the beer in a few long, furious gulps, then said, "the vibrations would be felt all the way . . . to the top."

"Hal," McLanahan said, his mouth suddenly very dry, "that's not an explanation." For the second time, the hairs on the back of his neck were catching a breeze from somewhere. "The top? *Top* of *what?*"

"I'm sorry," he said. He reached for the refrigerator door, then stopped, reconsidering, and sat back in his chair and looked at McLanahan. "Listen, there's very little I can tell you. But I do know this. I was authorized to make that fucking little airpatch out there look like Entebbe. I was *authorized,* Patrick. Authorized to do any damned thing . . ."

It was at that moment that McLanahan noticed the Uzi strapped to Briggs' waist.

Nellis Air Force Base, Las Vegas, Nevada

It was late in the evening when Harold Briggs escorted McLanahan from his small, musty billeting room to another building a few hundred yards away. McLanahan realized that all his movements—from the time he landed on that long, long jet flight from Spokane till now—were intended to keep his location a secret.

Why Briggs and the others were trying to keep his location a secret from *him,* he couldn't figure—but they had only partially succeeded. Although he had been taken from the jetport to his room at night through the back door, and although they had apparently tried to erase all traces of his location, he stumbled across the words "NELLIS AUX 5" engraved on the side of a desk in his room. The Learjet they had picked him up with at Spokane, he knew, had a range of about a thousand miles at the speed their pilot was flying—the pilot had kept the engines at full bore the whole way. And if that hadn't been enough, the dry, cold evening and the roar of high-performance jets—not airliners, but military fighters—screaming in the distance gave it away.

Well, so what? He was at Nellis or one of the myriad of airfields, stations, training camps, or ranges in the vicinity. He hoped more answers were on the way when, after an entire day of nothing to do, Briggs knocked on his door and told him they were going to meet the project coordinator . . .

McLanahan and Briggs now sat alone in a small briefing room. They had been sitting in the same room for twenty minutes.

McLanahan was about to turn to Briggs and ask how much longer it would be when the door opened and in stepped . . .

"General Elliott!" McLanahan said. He sprang so quickly to his feet that he felt as though he had left some part of himself back in the chair.

"At ease, Patrick," General Elliott said, smiling. He took McLanahan's hand and shook it. "Welcome to my nightmare."

McLanahan was too stunned to clasp hands. Elliott recognized this and steered him to his chair again.

Elliott wore a flightsuit with three subdued stars on each shoulder and subdued Strategic Air Command insignia on the arms and front. The squadron patch read "3 ACCS," the Airborne Command and Control Squadron from SAC Headquarters. He also wore a .45 automatic pistol strapped to his waist, and carried a large chart-carrying case and three Thermos bottles.

Elliott flipped his wooden chair around and sat down on it with a tired *thud*. He studied McLanahan's still-surprised face. "Relax, Patrick. You'll have your explanation in a moment."

McLanahan blinked at the words. Was his mouth hanging open or something? He took a deep breath and wiped moisture from his palms.

"Coffee?" Elliott asked, extending separate Thermoses to McLanahan and Briggs. "Actually, Hal, there's coke in yours. I know you'd prefer a beer but . . ."

Briggs nodded and smiled. "I understand, sir."

"All right," Elliott said, "here we go. This entire conversation is top secret. It is restricted to just us. No one else at all. I have no assistant, aides, or staffers that need to know what's been discussed. I don't have to ask if the room's secure, because it's my room and my compound and I *know* it's secure. That's the way this project is being run.

"By the way, Hal, you're in on this because I want you to realize all that's happening from here on in. I think you'll be able to operate better when you've got the complete picture. Patrick, Hal here has been on my security staff for a year now. He was assigned to security units for the Pentagon and at SAC until I grabbed him. Now he works for you. He'll make sure that foul-ups like the one we had at Spokane don't happen again."

McLanahan tried to keep his face from reddening but failed.

"This job is very simple, Patrick," Elliott began. "We run a highly classified research and development center here at Dreamland. I'm sure that's little surprise to you; during all the Red Flag sorties you've flown I'm sure you've heard speculation about Dreamland, wondered why you'd get your butt kicked so hard for overflying it. Well, that's why. Most every new design for a fighter, bomber, or missile built in the past ten years probably had its first tryout here at Dreamland."

He paused for a moment, taking a sip of coffee. "We've got another plane that we'd like to test-fly. We'd like you to run it through its paces. Test out the avionics, make some practice bomb runs, wring out the aircraft as much as you can. Much of the equipment you'll be testing will eventually be installed in selected B-1 aircraft."

McLanahan looked puzzled. "That's it?"

"You'll be plenty busy, I assure you, Patrick" the general said. "We're on a very tight schedule. We could be . . . well, let's just say our data might be needed at any time. The more information we have to pass on, the better."

McLanahan shrugged his shoulders. "Sounds fine to me," he said. "But you sure went through some very strange gyrations to get me here. I've got a feeling I still don't know the entire story."

"I hate to sound overly cryptic, Patrick," Elliott said, smiling, "but you know all you're supposed to know right now. You may figure out more as the project progresses. But I must remind you—your location, your duties, everything you see and do, is classified top secret. No one outside this room—I don't care how high their clearance or rank—is to know what goes on here. Understood?"

"Yes, sir," McLanahan said. "One question, though."

"Shoot."

"Why me?"

Elliott smiled, finished his coffee, and stood. "Simple. You're the best. I can't pass up a guy who's won as many Bomb Comp trophies as you."

McLanahan wasn't satisfied with Elliott's answer but nodded anyway.

"Want to see her?" Elliott asked.

McLanahan looked puzzled. "See what?"

"The ship," Elliott said. "*Your* ship. The Old Dog."

"Old Dog?" McLanahan rolled his eyes in exasperation. "Good recruiting technique, General. I'm supposed to get excited about a plane called the Old Dog?"

"You will," he said.

"Is this thing for *real?*" Briggs asked. McLanahan would have posed a similar question had he been able to speak; instead, he stood dumbstruck, staring at the massive form of the *Megafortress.*

They did a walkaround inspection of the airplane. General Elliott let them walk at their own pace, answering all their questions.

"It can't be the same airplane," McLanahan said finally, running his fingers across the slippery skin. "This can't be a B-52."

"A wolf in sheep's clothing," Elliott said. "I assure you."

Briggs entered the bomb bay and McLanahan followed him in a moment later.

"Expecting trouble, General?" McLanahan remarked. He examined the missiles. "*Scorpions!* Eight . . . no, ten of them! On a B-52! They've just come out with these things. They're not even modified for the F-15 yet. And you've got twelve more on the wings. I don't believe it."

Briggs read the lower missiles on the rotary launcher. "HARM. What's HARM?"

"Anti-radiation missiles," McLanahan said. "Homes in on and attacks radar-guided antiaircraft gun and missile sites." He looked at Elliott, and the young man's gaze caused the general's smile to fade a bit. "Trouble and a half, I'd say."

"Nine-tenths of everything on the *Megafortress* is geared toward self-defense and target penetration," Elliott explained. "That has been my number-one priority. This is just a test-bed aircraft. Over the past few years, we've just kept on adding refinements to it. Building a better mouse-trap, I guess." He patted the bomber's smooth skin. "We're going to incorporate the data we get from our test sorties into several other types of aircraft, notably the B-1.

"Let's go inside," Elliott said finally. "The technicians are doing a simulated flight on the avionics right now. It'll give you a chance to see your new gear operate downstairs."

They received clearance from the guards surrounding the huge bomber and climbed inside. Out of instinct, McLanahan immediately climbed into the left seat and scanned the instrument panel before him—his hand even positioned itself on the crosshair tracking handle as if drawn there by magnetism. Briggs, standing behind them near the aft bulkhead door leading to the forward wheel well, merely stood and gaped at the cramped compartment.

"Simple, direct, high-speed, highly accurate navigation equipment," Elliott said. "Satellite global navigation, with position accuracy down to twenty feet, time down to the hundredth of a second, and groundspeed down to the quarter-knot. Plus an inertial navigation system with a ring-laser gyro with heading accuracy to the tenth of a degree after twelve un-updated hours."

McLanahan rested his hands near the computer terminal, studied the keyboard and the video monitor, and then said, "You took the second navigator's seat out. Where's he going to sit?"

"Second navigator?" Elliott was genuinely startled. "Patrick, I just explained to you. This thing has automatic accuracy a navigator only dreams about. You can handle it yourself. Why do you need someone else?"

"What if all this stuff is destroyed? What if it dumps?"

"Dumps? Elliott looked insulted. "You can't dump this stuff. If you turn off all the power, the ring laser gyro has a half-hour backup battery. Once power is restored, the gyro realigns in ninety seconds back to original specifications. And it'll take one satellite cycle—about ten minutes—for the GPS to find itself and start navigating again. It doesn't *dump.* "

"Well, sir," McLanahan said, "I don't know." He studied the controls on the left side and the small rack of relays and boxes behind him. "You kept the original radar set, is that right, sir?"

"Yes," Elliott said, looking puzzled. "It's interfaced with the defensive weapons more, with target tracking modes and—"

"But I still have radar crosshairs?" he interrupted. "Fixtaking capability? Wind runs? Altitude calibrations?"

"Yes, yes," Elliott said impatiently. "You can still update the inertial navigation set with the radar set, and you can put a memory point wind into the system, but you don't need—"

McLanahan didn't let him finish. He simply reached down to the radar controls near his left knee and, with both hands, pushed three buttons simultaneously.

The results were dramatic. Instantly, a relay behind McLanahan's ejection seat smoked and sputtered, every circuit breaker of the few remaining above McLanahan's head popped, and the entire lower deck compartment went completely dark.

"What the *hell* . . ." Elliott shouted.

A technician from the cockpit upstairs dashed over to the hatch connecting the upper and lower decks and shined a flashlight on the enraged three-star general.

"What happened down there?" he asked timidly.

"How the hell should *I* know!" Elliott said. "Get down here and—"

"The BNS a/c exciter power circuit breakers are popped down here," McLanahan said calmly from the darkness. Briggs could be heard breathing in the background. "You'll find the BNS right TR control circuit breaker popped on the right load central panel upstairs, along with the RDPS power supply breakers number one, two, the plus six hundred volt, and the negative three hundred/negative one-fifty volt breakers down here. That smell is the left BNS control system relay. No replacement is usually carried in the spares box.

"Everything tied into the BNS radar is dead, General," McLanahan said. "I can swap around components and bring the radar back, but it won't bring back all the associated equipment including the inertial navigation set and these monitors and keyboard. The satellite system is still operational and it may know where it is, sir, but it can't tell you because there's no screen. I've also erased the navigation waypoints stored in the computer memory, and I'll bet the cartridge reader is dead, also. No automatic navigation."

"God *damn* it!" Elliott said.

"General, may I make a suggestion, sir . . . ?" Briggs said.

"Do it and you'll be guarding a commissary warehouse in Iceland, Briggs!" the general snapped. "Masuroki, get the damn power back on."

"But I don't . . ."

"Reset the power cart first before it drops off the line completely," McLanahan offered. "Then reset the circuit breakers. The ECM and fire-control stuff will need to be turned off and rewarmed up before you do that. That takes thirty minutes—and with all the stuff you've added, probably closer to an hour. I'll need a new relay down here." He made a little pause, then added, "And a right ejection seat. And a sextant. And a nav—"

"That's unrealistic, Patrick," Elliott said as Masuroki scrambled to restore power. "You're not going to hit all those controls all at once like that."

"That simulates about a half-dozen ways to overload the BNS left control relay, general," McLanahan said. "A little moisture, a bad wire, some sort of voltage spike or surge—poof!"

General Elliott thought of the skimpy intelligence data Curtis had shown him—the last words of the crew of the downed RC-135. The awesome power of the strange radar they had encountered . . . the thought made him wince in the cramped darkness of the *Megafortress.*

"All right, all right, hotshot," Elliott said, exasperated. "I guess I got a bit carried away with my toys down here. Let's get out of here. You'll be spending enough time in this beast, anyway."

As they climbed down the ladder, Briggs turned to the general and said, "I think you found the right dude for the job, General."

"Yes," Elliott agreed. He was silent for a moment, then said, "But I'm worried about exactly what the *job* will turn out to be."

It was the largest group of people McLanahan had been with since arriving at Spokane Airport—how many days ago? It had only been three days, and only one since first seeing the *Megafortress,* but it seemed like he had been cooped up in that desert for an eternity. Most of the time since seeing the bomber had been spent in intense study of the handtyped notes and tech orders on the avionics and performance capabilities of the bomber and the *Striker* glide-bomb. It was incredibly simple to operate—highly sophisticated, but simple.

They were in another windowless, stifling, nearly empty office. McLanahan and Hal Briggs had joined a room crowded with eight people already there waiting for General Elliott. The most surprising additions were four women. Two were obviously security guards, but the third was a middle-aged woman in jeans and a safari jacket who stood beside an older gentleman, and the fourth was a much younger woman, perhaps in her late twenties, who stared at the newcomers in surprise. The others took quick glances at the two newcomers and promptly ignored them.

A few moments later, General Elliott entered the room, now wearing civilian slacks and a short-sleeve shirt but still sporting the huge .45-caliber automatic under his left armpit.

"I think it's about time we were introduced to one another," General Elliott said immediately, "although you've all been working with each other for the past few weeks and may in fact have run into each other quite often while working on the Old Dog. Colonel Anderson."

A tall, dark-haired man in a green SAC flightsuit turned and faced the group. He had taken the front and center chair and had leaped to attention when Elliott entered the room.

"Colonel James Anderson," he said in a deep, resonant voice. "Deputy commander of the 4135th Test and Evaluation Center, Strategic Development and Testing, Edwards Air Force Base."

"Colonel Anderson brings a wealth of experience from several different weapon systems to Dreamland," Elliott said. "He has been the single most important source of ideas and our premier trouble-shooter. The Old Dog wouldn't be where it is right now without him."

"Thank you, sir," Anderson said. He returned to his seat and with narrow, piercing eyes scanned the others around him. He looked right past McLanahan, disregarding him.

McLanahan pegged him immediately: the huge silver ring, dwarfing his wedding band; the jump wings beneath his command pilot wings; his thin waist and chin—zoomie. Air Force Academy grad. A Colorado Cuckoo. Not exactly a navigator lover, either.

The man next to Anderson stood. He was a bit shorter, less chiseled and much younger version of Anderson, but he had nodded politely to Briggs and McLanahan earlier and he seemed friendly. "Lieutenant Colonel John Ormack, from the engineering and development section at Wright Patterson Air Force Base.

"The man responsible for a lot of the Old Dog's new tricks in the cockpit," Elliott added. "He's made his job as copilot a million times easier—obviously selfishly motivated. He's released the copilot to help out with bomber defense and crew coordination. He's also racked up a few thousand hours in several aircraft as well. The deputy project officer." Anderson gave Ormack a proud nod and a quick thumbs-up as he sat down.

The younger civilian woman then stood up. Everyone else in the room looked around and past her—everyone but McLanahan and Harold Briggs. She was of average height, with dark hair tied in a scholarly bun atop her head. Her eyes and face were dominated by huge, thick glasses, but, McLanahan thought, she was pretty in a—well, *teacherly* sort of way. She could not have been much older than McLanahan himself. She looked . . . familiar.

"Doctor Wendy Tork," she said briefly, brandishing the word *doctor* like a sword in front of the SAC officers. "Strategic electronic defense engineer, Palmdale, California."

McLanahan nearly bolted out of his seat. No, it couldn't be, he thought. He turned and met the friendly smile of the woman he had met in the hospitality bar back during the Bomb Comp Symposium. He could barely keep his jaw from swinging open.

"One of the country's foremost experts on electronic countermeasures, counter-countermeasures, Stealth technology, and radar," Elliott said. "The electronic warfare operator."

"Holy shit," McLanahan said under his breath. He continued to stare at her, studying her, trying to imagine her in a flight suit. Then out of a flight suit. Both seemed weirdly difficult in their present circumstances . . .

He looked around and noticed Anderson's disgusted, exasperated expression as the colonel studied Tork. Well, McLanahan thought, he likes women even less than navigators, I guess. Heads swiveled around in his direction, so McLanahan decided he was next and sheepishly stood.

"Captain Patrick McLanahan, B-52 radar navigator from Ford Air Force Base," McLanahan said. "This is Lieutenant Harold Briggs."

"Mornin'," Briggs said with a big smile. The icy glare he got from Anderson made him wish he hadn't said that, and he zipped his smile away.

Everyone in the small, stuffy room gave them a cursory nod but little else.

"Thanks for the intro, former buddy," Briggs whispered to McLanahan.

"If I gotta sweat in front of Anderson, so do you," McLanahan whispered back.

"The best in the business," Elliott said proudly. "Without a doubt the most gifted, knowledgeable, and professional bombardier in the United States military. Probably in *anyone's* military. The Old Dog's radar navigator."

"Where's Mentzer, general?" Anderson said sharply.

"I had a problem with Joe's background investigation, James," Elliott replied. Anderson gave Elliott an exasperated, impatient look.

"General, forget that," he said, shaking his head. "I'll vouch for the man, dammit. He modified and tested both the *Striker* TV-guided bomb

and the new sub-atomic munitions. He's the perfect *man* for the job."
Anderson glared at Tork when he said *man.*

"Sorry, James," Elliott said. "Captain McLanahan, however, has recently convinced me of the need for an additional crewmember downstairs. If Mentzer's clearance comes through—well, we'll discuss it."

"Another crewmember?" Anderson said. "A navigator? The Old Dog doesn't need another navigator."

"Patrick has demonstrated otherwise, Colonel."

"What we need, General," Anderson said, "is the man who built the *Striker* and the decoy drones, the man who helped—"

"Colonel Anderson." Elliott had lost all trace of good-naturedness in his voice, although his expression was still light and easy. "Joseph Mentzer is not available at this time. When he is, I'll inform you. Until now, Captain McLanahan is the radar navigator. All right, *Colonel?*"

The emphasis on Anderson's rank suppressed the last spark of resistance, and Anderson fell silent.

"Last but certainly not least," Elliott said, nodding to the last man and the woman beside him.

"Thank you, General," the man said. "I am Doctor Lewis Campos, retired Air Force. This is my assistant, Doctor Angelina Pereira. We are weapons design consultants representing several industries—actually, a mix of several military-industrial complexes."

"And a duo with loads of imagination," Elliott added. "Designers of the defensive armament aboard the Old Dog—the guns, missiles, rockets. Lew Campos will be the gunner in all of the tests we conduct."

"There you have it, ladies and gentlemen," Elliott said. "From now on, you'll be working very closely with one another to gather the information we need. All of you, with the possible exception of Patrick, are intimately familiar with your own devices and equipment—and Captain McLanahan has demonstrated a knowledge of his own systems that would rival anyone here. But it'll be most important that you all learn to work with *each other* to insure the success of these tests."

Elliott was silent for a moment. Then: "Some of you are not military people. You've worked in military centers, designing military weaponry, working closely with other military members, but you never planned on actually flying or participating in operational tests yourselves. We simply don't have the time to train flight test engineers or military personnel to your level of expertise.

"I am heartened by the fact that all of you are volunteers, but that doesn't bind you to a seat aboard the *Megafortress.* If any of you, either now or later on, feel you cannot handle the rigors we'll place on you, see me in private and you'll be released."

There was a sort of relieved nod from everyone—everyone except Anderson.

"Colonel Anderson, the floor is yours."

Anderson nodded thanks to General Elliott, then swung on the rest of his newly assembled crew like a disgusted drill sergeant at an induction.

"The routine is simple, ladies and gentlemen. Our mission is to collect data on avionics, weaponry, hardware, and software aboard the B-52 India model for use in other specialized military aircraft. Very simple.

"To do this, we study. Every waking minute, every free moment, you will spend studying the missions and the scenarios faced in each one. You will not concentrate only on your own specialty. You will be intimately familiar with the duties and responsibilities of every member of this crew.

"When the plane is available to fly, we spend all afternoon, from thirteen hundred hours until eighteen hundred hours, in mission planning. The crew briefing will be three hours prior to takeoff. All of our flights will be night sorties to help insure security, and they will be four hours in duration. There will be three hours debriefing following the sortie, then eight hours crew rest before duty begins the next day.

"When the plane is not available, we will use the simulator. Simulator sessions are five hours long, and there will be five hours for mission planning and briefing and three hours for post-briefing."

Anderson started to pace in front of his assembled crew, staring each one down.

"This is not a scientific laboratory, an office, or a boardroom," he said. "This is a classified tactical unit on an urgent assignment. Because of the need for speed and accuracy, we will consider this field conditions from here on. There will be no leave, no absence, no sick call, no vacation, no days off. You will have no visitors, receive no calls from your other place of employment, or work on any other project save this one. Am I understood?"

No reply.

"You are expected to be familiar with the entire contents of the I-model technical order by noon tomorrow. Then, we will meet here and talk about the plane and its characteristics. Questions?"

Again, no reply.

Anderson turned to Elliott. "General?" Elliott shook his head.

"You will be sorry," Anderson said menacingly, "if you come here tomorrow and you don't know your shit. Dismissed."

The Old Dog's crewmembers filed out, everyone afraid to speak or make any comment with Anderson anywhere within earshot. Elliott, McLanahan, and Briggs were the last to leave.

"That man," Briggs said, "is one intense sonofabitch."

"I can see working with him is going to be a real blast," McLanahan said. "Thanks for the great assignment, General."

"Don't mention it," he replied, smiling. "I hope you've been studying. You're starting out with two strikes against you already."

"I know," McLanahan said. "I'm a nav—and I'm not Mentzer. Who is Mentzer, anyway?"

"An aerospace engineer who has worked closely with Anderson for five years," Briggs replied.

"But he had a clearance problem?"

"Hal here unearthed some . . . discrepancies in Mentzer's background before he came to Dreamland," Elliott said. "Too many overlapping jobs. Our Hal here is the suspicious type—but I haven't gone wrong yet trusting his instincts."

"Why, thanks, General—"

"But, there's always a first time," Elliott said, smiling. "Wait until Anderson hears it was a lowly lieutenant keeping Mentzer out of the project." Briggs groaned. "Anyway, I'm keeping him out of this phase of the project until we get it straightened out."

"Then can I get out of this loony bin?" McLanahan asked, only half jokingly.

"Mentzer only builds them," Elliott said. "He can't drop them. You can. Better than anyone else in the country."

"Great." McLanahan glanced at Briggs. "Hal, my friend, there had better be some beer around this dustbowl, or I'm gonna get real cranky studying tonight."

"You can count on me," Briggs replied.

On the way outside, McLanahan noticed Wendy Tork standing alone between her barracks and the briefing room. He excused himself and walked over.

"I didn't recognize you at first—with the glasses and all."

"How *is* the King of Bomb Comp," Wendy said, placing her hands on her hips.

"Can't complain," McLanahan said, smiling. "Well, actually I can . . . This Colonel Anderson seems to be really bad news. I'd like to drop *him* out of the Old Dog's bomb bay instead of one of those Striker bombs."

"Maybe you'll get your chance," Wendy said, smiling. "But they don't give trophies for that, do they?"

"Not the last I heard," McLanahan said. He shifted his feet uncomfortably, trying to think of what to say next. "So," he said finally, "why didn't you tell me when we met what a crackerjack electronics warfare operator you were? I thought you were some sort of technician."

"You didn't ask," Wendy said. "Besides, you seemed busy basking in your own limelight. I figured you weren't interested."

"But I *was,* " McLanahan said, realizing as he said it that he was much too emphatic. "I mean . . . sure I was interested." God, he was making a mess of this.

Wendy began walking toward the women's barracks and McLanahan fell into step with her. "Hey," he said, "you've got to explain your ECM gear to me. It was the most confusing part of that damn manual. I think I need some expert advice. Tonight . . ."

Wendy stopped a few yards short of the barracks and folded her arms over her chest. "Tonight?"

"If it wouldn't be much trouble," McLanahan said quickly. Wendy hesitated a moment while giving him an appraising look. "All right," she said finally, "tonight it is. See you after dinner."

"Fine," McLanahan said. He waved to her as she disappeared inside the barracks. This may not be a bad TDY after all, McLanahan thought to himself.

The United Nations

Ian McCaan, Secretary-General of the United Nations, had just called the meeting of the United Nations Security Council to order when Gregory Adams spoke:

"Mr. Secretary-General," Adams said, "information has been brought to the attention of the government of the United States concerning the incident described in the specification of charges against the government of the Soviet Union. I have been instructed by my government to allow the ambassador from the Soviet Union to enter a plea in response to the charges in lieu of presenting evidence to the Security Council."

McCaan looked confused. "Am I to understand, Ambassador Adams, that your government is dropping its charges against the Soviet Union?"

"Allow me to explain, Mr. Secretary-General," Dmitri Karmarov interjected. "My government has been in careful negotiations with the American government since the charges were first preferred against us in the emergency session. The charges concern a highly sensitive research and development facility in the Soviet Union, which my government would rather not discuss even in closed Security Council session. Therefore, we have taken steps to enter into negotiations with the United States directly."

"I wish to make it clear," Adams immediately added, staring directly at Karmarov, "that the charges against the Soviet Union still remain. I am prepared at any time to present my evidence against the Soviet Union in this forum."

"That is understood, Ambassador Adams," Karmarov said. "As part of the agreement between our governments, I would like to make the following statement:

"The government of the Soviet Union pleads *nolo contendere* before the

Security Council of the United Nations in response to the charges brought against us by the government of the United States. The Soviet Union acknowledges, incomplete evidence notwithstanding, that activity at the Kvaznya research facility may have caused a situation to develop in which an American aircraft in the vicinity may have experienced difficulties of an unknown type or severity. It is not known for certain if such difficulties resulted in the loss of the aircraft.

"The government of the United States acknowledges that their RC-135 intelligence aircraft was within the Air Defense Identification Zone at the time of question," Karmarov continued, "without proper identification, without a properly filed flight plan, and without clearance from any Soviet controlling agency. The United States has not confirmed that the plane was on a spy mission, which my government condemns, but—"

"But that doesn't mean any—" Adams interrupted.

"I was going to say," Karmarov said, his voice rising, "that the military air defense operators on duty did not take the proper action in the case of such an intrusion, nor did they warn the aircraft of ongoing activity that may have serious effects on aircraft in the area.

"In the spirit of peace and international harmony, therefore, the government of the Soviet Union has agreed to cooperate in the investigation into the causes of the loss of the American spy plane. In return, the United States has consented to let the Soviet Union enter a plea of no contest to its charges until that investigation is completed. As to the matter of possible interference with free-flying aircraft and the alleged negligence of Soviet military operators, we request that the Security Council reserve judgment until a complete analysis of the controller's transcripts and records can be completed."

Karmarov put his head down over his notes and, reading quickly and unemotionally, continued: "The Soviet Union extends its regrets to the family of those lost near our shores. We assure all concerned that we will do everything in our power to resolve the matter. Thank you."

The Russian translator barely was able to spit out the last few sentences trying to keep up with Karmarov. The Russian put his notes down and glanced at the assembled ambassadors.

Ambassador Braunmueller, the representative from East Germany, stood and held out his hands to Karmarov. "Your statement, Comrade Ambassador," he said, "was magnificent. The Soviet Union's willingness to cooperate with the investigation and their openness is to be commended."

"They haven't admitted to anything . . ." Adams said, but he was drowned out by Braunmueller's booming voice.

"Mr. Secretary-General, I move that final judgment be reserved until the full results of the investigation are presented."

"Seconded," another ambassador said.

"I, too," McCaan said, "am impressed and heartened by the spirit of cooperation exhibited by the Soviet Union. I call for a vote."

Adams abstained. As he expected, the vote was unanimous.

"Nemine contradicente," McCaan announced. "Let the record show the vote is unanimous. The plea of *nolo contendere* is to be officially entered. The matter involving the charges against the government of the Soviet Union is hereby suspended indefinitely.

"The government of the United States is hereby requested by the Security Council of the United Nations to respect the spirit of cooperation exhibited by the Soviet Union by cooperating fully with their government in the investigation of the aircraft disaster and not to retaliate or otherwise impose any restrictions or sanctions against the Soviet Union because of this incident."

McLanahan was alone inside the bomber, inside the plastic-skinned, stifling Old Dog. Hal Briggs was with him, watching the activities in the downstairs compartment and taking notes, but effectively McLanahan was alone with the bomber and its equipment.

They were flying three hundred feet above the high desert and looming mountain ranges of Nevada. McLanahan was studying the radar scope, which was now in TTG, or Target Tracking and Guidance mode, searching for attacking fighters. If he spotted any fighters, he would put a circle cursor on it and tell Compos that he was tracking a target. The computer would feed range, azimuth, elevation, direction, and airspeed information to the *Scorpion* air-to-air missiles, and with that information a hit was almost guaranteed.

But the scope was blank and had been for several minutes, and Wendy Tork in the electronic warfare section had reported no airborne interceptor radar signals. McLanahan could feel a cold, prickly sensation on his neck. The mountains were too damn close.

He glanced at his chart. Some of the highest mountain ranges in southern Nevada were right off the nose, and he felt uncomfortable not monitoring their position by radar, even though the automatic terrain-avoidance system had proved its reliability.

Well, damn the fighters, McLanahan thought to himself. If the aircraft hits a mountain, the fighters won't matter.

He punched a button, thinking about the twenty-first century equipment guiding their two-hundred-ton bomber. The blank track-while-scan radar scope changed into a mapping display of the terrain within thirty miles of the Old Dog. Guided by a ring of satellites and by a tiny "game-cartridge" of terrain elevations, the Old Dog was automatically diving and climbing, attempting to hug the ground as close as possible. The satellites, orbiting in geosynchronous orbits twenty-three thousand miles above the Earth, told them exactly where they were; the Inertial Navigation System, INS, told them where they were going; and the computer, ROM, Reading Only Memory, terrain-data cartridge told them how high the terrain was.

A computer fed all this to the autopilot, which told the Old Dog—what a damn stupid name, McLanahan thought—when to climb or dive, and the autopilot would climb or dive in time to keep the plane within a few feet of the selected clearance plane setting. Simple.

Except it wasn't working.

His terrain-mapping scope was almost blank, but for a completely different reason. A five-mile-long ridge loomed ahead, its treelined crest still seven hundred feet *above* the Old Dog's altitude. The ridge cast a dark shadow behind it, as if the radar beam was a headlight being blocked by an oncoming brick wall.

McLanahan knew that if the shadow behind the ridge got larger instead of smaller they'd eventually plow into the ridge. At over seven hundred feet per second, the two-hundred-ton bomber would smear itself right up and over the ridge and scatter pieces of itself for tens of miles beyond. The radar altimeter readout on the video display was flashing, warning that the aircraft was below the desired terrain clearance altitude.

McLanahan glanced at the flight instruments. The vertical-velocity indicator was showing a climb, but it didn't seem like a very steep one. The ridge was now only three miles away, and the shadow beyond blotted out all else right to the edge of the scope.

"High terrain, three miles," McLanahan reported over the interphone.

"I've lost TTG signals, navigator," Campos radioed to McLanahan.

He quickly glanced at the annotations he had placed on the chart the night before. "Elevation eight thousand feet," McLanahan said. "Blank scope. Not painting over it. Also a blinking radar altimeter."

The terrain-avoidance computer was not designed to *follow* the contours of the surrounding hills and valleys as it would in the B-1 *Excalibur* or the FB-111. The B-52 didn't have enough power. The terrain-avoidance system anticipated the terrain ahead of the aircraft's flight path and chose a safe altitude to clear it, as close to the pilot-selected clearance plane setting as possible. Approaching a ridge, the altitude should not be *less* than the selected altitude—it should be more. Much more. And the Old Dog should be climbing a lot faster . . .

"Pilot, climb!" McLanahan ordered. The VVI suddenly jumped, nearly tripling its former climb rate, and the throttles were jammed to full military thrust. The airspeed, however, bled off rapidly as the Old Dog traded altitude for airspeed, crawling skyward.

The radar scope was blank. The ridge was less than one mile off the nose
. . . eight seconds before impact . . .

The radar altimeter indicated less than a hundred feet as the Old Dog
ballooned over the ridge, at near minimum low-level safe airspeed. The
automatic flight control system immediately commanded nose-down as
the ridge line dropped behind them, but McLanahan didn't start to
breathe again until they had regained the two hundred knots lost in the
emergency climb and were safely clear of terrain.

"Clear of terrain for fifteen miles," McLanahan reported.

"Ground position freeze," Colonel Anderson said over the interphone.
The digital readouts and radar images froze on the screen. McLanahan
sat back in the Old Dog's ejection seat, wiping sweat from his forehead
and palms, and took a gulp of Tab.

"What the hell was all that, McLanahan?" Anderson shouted over the
interphone. McLanahan backed the volume of the interphone panel down
a notch in anticipation of yet another yelling match. Harold Briggs, sitting
in the newly installed navigator's seat beside McLanahan, slid off his
headset.

"What was what, sir?"

"All those calls, goddammit! Terrain this, terrain that. That's not your
job."

"What do you mean, it's not my job. My *first* responsibility is to keep
the plane out of the dirt."

Harold Briggs made an obscene gesture directed at Anderson. He felt
fairly safe doing so, because Anderson and Ormack were in a B-52 simulator some two hundred miles away and were tied electronically into the
computer simulation aboard the Old Dog. At the same time, Wendy Tork
was at a research computer terminal twenty miles from Anderson, participating in the same exercise, and Campos and Pereira were sitting at
a fire control test bench elsewhere at Dreamland, also linked to the computer controlling the test. Briggs and McLanahan were inside the Old Dog
itself, still in its hangar at Groom Lake, watching and responding to the
computer-generated battle scenario.

"There's a multimillion dollar computer that can do that faster, easier,
and better than you ever can, McLanahan," Anderson said. "Why do you
need to call out terrain elevation when if I wanted that useless piece of
information I can just call it up on the screen? And I can see the damned
radar altimeter blinking. I don't want you garbaging up the radios with
all that stuff."

"I was calling to your attention, sir," McLanahan said over the voice/
data link, "the fact that we were fifty feet lower than the goddamned set
clearance when we still had seven hundred feet to climb. If the system was

working right, we should have started the climb three miles earlier to *cross* that ridge line *at* two hundred feet. As it was, we barely had enough airspeed to cross the ridge at a hundred feet, and then we ballooned over it another thousand feet and almost hit initial buffet to a stall. The radar altimeter should *never* be blinking, and sure as hell not so close to a mountain."

Anderson had no reply to that, but someone else chimed in:

"Excuse me, Captain," Campos interjected, his voice sounding hollow and metallic over the secure voice-data transmission line, "but please understand the situation here. Right now you have two attackers off the nose, just within radar range. You must spend less time in mapping mode and much, much more time in TTG mode. The *Scorpions* can be launched off threat detection signals from the receiver unit, but without range, elevation and tracking data the chances of a hit at long range are slim. We're relying on using the main radar to guide the *Scorpions.*"

"Besides," Lieutenant Colonel Ormack added from Edwards, "this is only a practice run. The elevation data in this simulation isn't plotted as accurately as the operational cartridge. There's bound to be some belly-scrapers. We're trying to nail down *procedures,* McLanahan—and until we get to the target area, your procedure is to help guide the defensive missiles. Let the computers keep us out of the dirt."

McLanahan rubbed his eyes and took a long, deep breath.

"This is such bullshit," he said to Briggs.

"Hang in there, buddy. You're really running this show, and they all know it."

"Like hell," McLanahan said. "I'm a passenger. Extraneous material."

"You mean 'dead weight,' " Briggs said.

"Thanks for the clarification."

"Okay," Anderson radioed over to the widely separated crew. "We'll back up five minutes and do the leg over again. This time, McLanahan, find the damn fighters before they find us."

McLanahan called up the prerecorded flight plan and waypoint read-outs and watched as the present position coordinates slowly scrolled back to the beginning of the low-level navigation leg.

"You want to see what a collision with the ground looks like, Hal?" McLanahan said. "Just keep watching the scope."

"I saw," a voice behind them said. McLanahan whirled around to see General Elliott sitting in the back of the navigator's compartment, taking notes and listening to the interphone conversations from the instructor nav's station.

"Hello, General Nightmare," McLanahan said. "How are we doing? I think we suck big-time."

"Patrick," the general said, "I don't want to undermine Anderson's authority—he's a great pilot and a genuine asset to the project—but follow your own instincts, your own training. Everyone but you is trusting all this gadgetry with their lives because they don't know any better. Both Anderson and Ormack could see the terrain warning signals in the cockpit and they both ignored them. Keep an eye out for the terrain and for fighters as you see fit."

The general paused, looking around the tiny compartment measuring his words, then said, "I've watched your work, Patrick. You seem to know when the fighters are near before the warning receivers do. You switch in TTG mode before Wendy tells you there are fighters, and you switch into mapping mode and call terrain just in time to avoid a mountain."

"Well, thanks for the encouragement, General," McLanahan said. "My sixth sense or whatever the hell it is tells me to bail out of this project before Colonel Disaster plows us into downtown Las Vegas."

"You'll be doing it some other time, Patrick," the general said. "Or maybe not at all." Elliott flipped the interphone switch. "Colonel Anderson, this is General Elliott. The rest of today's session is canceled. I need to speak to everyone back at the mission center as soon as possible."

"Yes, sir," Anderson said. "Colonel Ormack and myself will be back in two hours. I expect everyone in the mission center when we arrive." Everyone else acknowledged Anderson's instructions, and the data/voice link went dead.

"What's up, General?" Briggs asked. He looked worried and pale in the dim red lights of the downstairs compartment. McLanahan, for some reason, was suddenly very calm, serene. General Elliott seemed to notice the change, and he frowned a bit before continuing.

"You've been shelved, Patrick," Elliott said. "I've been informed that the Old Dog project has been ordered to stand down."

"That means . . ."

"Unfortunately, it doesn't mean going home," Elliott said. "I've managed to get your temporary duty extended here at Dreamland. I can't do the same for the civilians, unfortunately, so it's going to be real quiet around here. But—well, let's call it a slowdown. They don't have the same all-fired need for the Old Dog's data as before. We'll keep busy, I assure you."

McLanahan looked skeptical. "Sorry, my friend," Elliott said, "can't explain it better than that. Let's go and get a cold one while Anderson and the others zoom back."

"I heard *that*," Briggs said happily.

"I meant McLanahan," Elliott said. The three climbed out of the Old Dog's fibersteel belly. Outside, an army of workmen were surrounding the

Old Dog with engine inlet covers and defueling equipment, and weapons dollies were being pushed over to the *Megafortress.*

Elliott stood and watched for a moment as the workmen completed the task of plugging up and taking apart the Old Dog. He then led the group quickly out of the building.

FIFTY MILES EAST OF KAVAZNYA, IN THE NORTH PACIFIC

Alone figure huddled against a steel mast on the wildly-heaving deck of a hundred-foot fishing vessel bobbing in the rough North Pacific seas. The man, wearing layers of fur-lined jackets under his oilskins, braced himself and tried to chop ice from a large winch bolted onto the mast. His mitten-clad hands were covered with freezing rain and ice; only the thick leather thong on the handle kept the rubber mallet he was using from spinning off into the icy sea.

A wall of water crashed against the gunwale and showered the deck. Bits of instantly frozen water penetrated the face mask he wore and cut into his cheeks. He no longer worried about slipping on the pitching deck, unless his boots somehow came off—he was anchored by a quarter-inch of ice to the steel deck.

A deep howl penetrated the roar of the wind and waves around him. He took a better grip on the winch with his mittened right hand and reluctantly turned his eyes seaward. The sting of the wind shot a rod of pain deep into his eyeballs. He squinted against the icy gusts and searched the horizon, trying to follow the howl which was rising in intensity.

There it was. It descended out of the racing clouds and horizontal sheets of freezing rain like a giant bird of prey. It leveled off, seemingly only a few scant feet above the icy foaming waters, and flew directly at the fishing vessel.

The man let the mallet drop on its thong, reached into a pocket of the oilskin, and withdrew a small walkie-talkie. He turned his face away from the wind and the oncoming predator, bent down a bit, lifted his ski mask and keyed the microphone.

"Bridge, Marceaux. Here comes that Bear, full on the port beam." The man heard a feeble voice come over the radio, but couldn't understand it.

No matter. They heard him. He couldn't stand another few seconds with his face uncovered anyway. He dropped the radio back into his pocket, made sure the pocket cover Velcroed closed, and turned to watch the plane.

It was a Russian "Bear" bomber, one of several that had been dogging the fishing vessel in the past few days. This one had the guts—or the poor judgment—to drop below the scuzzy cloud cover and risk direct visual identification of the vessel.

It was truly an imposing sight, especially the turboprop engines. Two massive, ungainly engines hung underneath each huge wing. Each engine had two large four-bladed propellers, an unusual sight on so large an aircraft. The propellers made the aircraft unusually quiet—its low whine did not get louder as it approached. Even in the poor visibility, the large red stars under the wings could easily be seen. This Bear had two radomes on the underside of its fuselage, marking it as a highly modified Bear-F maritime reconnaissance aircraft. Its other notable modification was the addition of two plyons, one on each wing and each loaded with six AS-12 air-to-sea antiship missiles, direct copies of the U.S. Navy's *Harpoon* antiship missiles.

The bomber didn't need that many, the seaman named Marceaux thought. Just one could send this old tub to the bottom.

The Bear flew right over the U.S.S. *Lawrence*'s bow—a violation of international maritime law and a direct warning to the ship. Its size made it look much closer, but Marceaux estimated the bomber was at one thousand feet above the ship, the internationally legislated minimum. Despite the relatively quiet turboprops, the roar of the bomber passing overhead cut through the howl of the storm. It seemed to drive the storm before it, adding to its fury.

"*Cochon,*" Marceaux said, but the curse was lost in the roar of the Bear's engine. A moment later the bomber lumbered skyward and disappeared again into the scuz. Marceaux waited until he was sure the Bear was gone for good, then slowly and carefully made his way along the icy deck toward the midships hatch and the welcoming warmth below.

Sheets of ice dropped off Marceaux's oilskin as he unbuttoned the jacket and stowed it in a locker in the crew's bunkroom. As he peeled off the fur jackets, the ship's chief petty officer passed by and tapped him on the shoulder.

"Intel," he said. "Before anything else."

"*Zut!* I'm freezin', Chief," Marceaux said. "I've been up there for—"

"*Intel,*" the CPO said behind him. "On the goddamned double." Marceaux reluctantly bypassed the galley and the scent of hot coffee and made his way to the ship's hold.

The Intelligence section of the disguised fishing vessel *Lawrence* was formerly the fish processing hold. Indeed, the front one-fifth of the area still held some fish-slicing and freezing equipment—all inoperable, in place for disguise purposes only. The Intel section was now a mass of electronic sensors, radios, maps, computers, and humorless men.

The chief of the Intel section, Commander Markham, passed Marceaux in the doorway. He carried a steaming cup of coffee.

"Well, Marceaux?"

It was obvious to Markham that Marceaux's attention was elsewhere. He passed the cold seaman the cup of coffee. Marceaux drained half of it in one gulp, his breath exhaling as long wisps of steam.

"Now. Fill me in, then fill out a hostile contact log."

"*Merci,* Commander," Marceaux said. "Bear-F, maritime antiship configuration, no numbers that I could make out. Two radomes, one forward, one aft. Observation blisters in the middle and aft, but I couldn't tell if they were manned. K-7 camera door open on the belly. Refueling probe, iced over badly. Useless, I'd say. Twelve total AS-12 missiles, six on each wing, maybe stations for two more on each pylon. Bomb bay closed but not sealed. Ice all over the wings. The pilot had *tres grands bouettes,* I'd say."

"Altitude? Speed?"

"One thousand feet right on the dot, although he flew right over the bow. Speed two hundred knots but no flaps hanging. Low and slow."

"He radioed a warning," Markham said. "Said we were too close to Karanginsky Island."

Marceaux shrugged. "It is a warning he could back up. *Definiment.*"

"Those AS-12s will drop into the sea if he tries to launch 'em," Markham said, heading back to the Intel section's small galley for more coffee. "He might send some naval buddies out after us, but I doubt it. This is the ugliest weather I've seen out here."

"Is he still out there, sir?" Marceaux asked.

"No. He headed home in a hurry. Probably getting iced over pretty bad. Like you said, he had to have king-sized balls to fly around in freezing rain like that."

"Think he made us?"

"They made us as an intel ship days ago," Markham said, filling a mug. "But they're nervous about something. Risking a Bear like that . . . something's going on . . ."

As Marceaux refilled his mug from the pot, Markham wandered over to one of his signal operator's consoles. He studied several oscilloscope-like displays on the console.

His attention focused on a pair of ten-inch signal display scopes, manned by a gray-haired Navy signalman. Markham looked over his shoulder, sipping his coffee. The two signals on the man's scopes, although much different from each other, were perfectly synchronized—when one wave on the scope became active, the other did also. When one stopped, the other stopped.

"Any change, Garrity?" Markham asked the sensor operator. Garrity shook his head.

"They're linked, that's for sure, sir," Garrity replied. He handed Markham a computer printout, then pointed to the left of his two main displays. "That's complete computer verification—frequencies, timing, the works—coded and ready to transmit. Kavaznya is getting stronger. This one"—he pointed to the right oscilloscope—"is still weak but in perfect sync."

"Identification?"

Garrity adjusted some controls on his board, then sat back.

"Wild, wild guess," he said. "A satellite data link."

"A satellite?" Markham whistled. "That radar at Kavaznya is talking to a satellite?"

"Maybe two satellites," Garrity said. "Now this is really wild, I know, but I keep on seeing an embedded data signal in the Kavaznya radar transmission. It's slightly out of sync with these two signals . . ."

"Meaning?"

"Meaning these two, Kavaznya and this second—whatever it is—may be talking." Garrity rubbed at his eyes and went on. "Kavaznya is talking to something else, though. Not a radar signal. A data signal."

"What kind of data?" Markham asked, trying to make some sense of what the operator was telling him.

"Hey, I'm just guessing here," Garrity said, shaking his head.

"Guess some more."

Garrity rubbed once again at his eyes. Then: "Steering signals." As Markham bent forward to study the signals, Garrity pointed at his displays and explained: "Here and here. Kavaznya and Joe Blow satellite. Simple transponder-type signals—interrogate and reply. That means azimuth and elevation . . ."

"Position data," Markham said.

"It has to be," Garrity said. "Kavaznya telling Joe Blow here where he is and vice versa. But then Kavaznya sends this blurb out."

Garrity drew a circle on a sheet of notebook paper. He recreated the Kavaznya oscilloscope signal as best he could. "Right here. I see it every now and then." He drew a squiggle almost parallel to the Kavaznya signal, but much smaller and of a slightly different frequency, or shape.

"The timing is the most critical difference," Garrity explained. "The timing between Kavaznya and the second party is clear, but Kavaznya tells someone else something. And it's not *just* position data. I think it's a steering signal."

"Steering *what?*" Markham asked.

"Don't know," Garrity replied. "I've never seen anything like it—hell, I'm not even sure if I *am* seeing it. A data signal embedded in a radar emission?" He shook his head. "I've been on duty for eighteen hours. I might be seeing beeps and buzzes in my dreams."

"Code it," Markham said.

Garrity looked at him in surprise. "Code what?"

"Exactly what you told me," Markham said. "Everything."

"I told you a fairytale," Garrity said. "A wet dream. I don't have anything concrete. The computer hasn't verified any of my inquiries about the second signal destination."

"That doesn't matter," Markham said. "They told us to report any findings of significance in the Kavaznya area. I heard that request came from *very* high. Code it and send it up for the Old Man's signature, then send it."

"This isn't a finding," Garrity protested. "It's an opinion . . . a guess. It's not really even an educated guess—"

"Listen, Garrity," Markham said, "something screwy is going on. The Russians risk a fifty million ruble bomber in a freezing rainstorm to scare us away. Now Kavaznya is active . . ."

"It's been active for days," Garrity said.

"Then how come you haven't seen these side data signals before?"

Garrity had no answer for that.

"Something's going on, and we're right on top of it," Markham said. "Code exactly what you told me, then send it."

Garrity shook his head. "You're the boss. But do I need to put *my* signature on it? They'll laugh me right outta the Service."

"They might give you a goddamned medal," Markham said. "If you're right."

VANDENBURG AIR FORCE BASE, CALIFORNIA

A single green and gray camouflaged locomotive wound around a curve on a deserted railroad siding. It pulled a quarter-mile-long train of long, six-sided rail cars, moving easily at about twenty miles an hour.

Eight miles away in an underground control center, a group of Air Force officers were being briefed by another group of civilian contractors on the test that was about to take place.

"Range reports ready, Mr. Newcombe," a technician said.

Newcombe, the chief civilian contractor, nodded. "Tell them to stand by. General Taylor, gentlemen, the range has just reported ready. All of the Air Force tracking stations from here to Guam are ready for the first operational test launch of America's newest strategic weapon—the GLM-123 *Javelin* Small Mobile Intercontinental Ballistic Missile, or, as the press has so fondly christened it, 'Midgetman.' "

"What can I tell you about her that you don't already know?" Newcombe searched the faces around him. Taylor shook his head and smiled, lighting a briar pipe. These Air Force generals had been working with him for years. Major-General Taylor, the chief of the Strategic Development Branch, Aerospace Systems Division, Air Force Logistics Command, was an old friend. This test—its success an almost foregone conclusion, after seven previous successful launches—would ensure Taylor's third star and another promotion. Of course, Newcombe's new position as senior vice-president of the *Javelin's* prime contractor was already in the bag.

"The train orbiting the test track is typical of a normal *Javelin* mobile rail deployment," Newcombe said. "Six cars in all—the locomotive, two missile cars, two security cars, and the launch command and control car. Each car is super-hardened against EMP—that's electromagnetic pulse effect, for you neophytes—caused by nearby nuclear explosions."

"The new arms-elimination agreement have you worried, Ed?" one of General Taylor's aides asked Newcombe. "*Javelin* would be the first to lose research and development funding."

"Of course, we all want to see world peace," Newcombe said. "The arms-elimination treaty would be a great breakthrough. But I feel it's just as important to continue with serious research and development. This will mark the culmination of those tests—the birth of a new kind of strategic weapon for the United States.

"The *Javelin* is the most versatile weapon of its kind in the world," Newcombe continued. "Our quick-reaction rail launch test today demonstrates just one possible way it can be deployed; we've done other deployment tests that you won't believe.

"The *Javelin* is small enough to be carried aloft on cargo aircraft, such as a C-5B or even a modified Boeing 747, dropped via parachute, and successfully air-launched—no silo, no launch vehicle or submarine needed. Versions of the *Javelin* have successfully accomplished what we've called 'telephone pole' tests. We've rolled a *Javelin* missile off the deck of a Navy destroyer. In the water, it floated into a perfect upright launch attitude and was successfully fired by remote control.

"Its potential is unlimited. The *Javelin* has an advantage over other small tactical or strategic nuclear vehicles—despite its small size, the *Javelin* carries three warheads, not just one or even two. In addition, the *Javelin* is designed to carry the new maneuverable reentry warhead, which makes the *Javelin's* business end many times more survivable should the Soviets decide to redeploy antiballistic missile defenses in the future. It might be worth it to replace cruise missiles and gravity weapons with *Javelins* if the arms-elimination treaty is ratified." Interested nods from General Taylor—he was already planning on star number four.

Newcombe walked over to a map of the Vandenburg Air Force Base rail test track. "The *Javelin* missile has been riding Vandenburg's track for only a few hours. In a few moments we'll demonstrate the ability of our *Javelin* to launch within sixty seconds of a launch order.

"We've 'leaked' it to the *Javelin* test crew that the launch will be sometime this afternoon. The crew is completely isolated and has no idea that we're about to stage the test.

"When the order is given, the train stops right where it is. A continually-running ring laser gyro navigation unit instantly feeds position and gyro alignment data to the missile guidance system. By the time the rocket is ready for launch, the erector has raised it to firing position and the crew has authenticated the President's launch order."

Newcombe checked the control panel, then studied the map. "General, the crew is right . . . here." He pointed to the map. "Eight miles south of our position. We should be able to see the launch after you transmit the launch command. Sir?"

General Taylor stepped forward and glanced at his watch. "Ten o'clock on the dot," he said. "Let's do it." Newcombe directed the general to a large red button mounted on a box on the master control panel. The Air Force general pressed the button, and Newcombe started a clock. Everyone else glanced at his watch.

"If you'll follow me, gentlemen." General Taylor led the way out of the control room and outside into a large stretch of sand dunes and low scrub trees. Newcombe put the sun on his left shoulder and pointed westward.

"General Taylor's command has alerted the launch crew as well as the tracking and telemetry stations," he explained. "The rest is simple. While the train comes to a complete stop, the doors of the train open and the missile canister begins to erect. The canister is raised rearward, so the exhaust end of the missile is hanging off the end of the railcar.

"Meanwhile, the crew decodes and authenticates the launch order. All of the missile's internal 'housekeeping' functions are automatic. By the time the crew verifies the message and inserts their launch keys, the missile is ready to go."

Newcombe checked his watch; seventy-five seconds had already elapsed. He looked up at his military spectators.

"I told you gents this would be a surprise . . ."

At that instant, a thunderous roar rolled across the dunes. Several of the spectators, Newcombe included, jumped. All looked southward.

The missile itself could not be seen except as a tiny dark speck, but the half-mile-long tail of flame was clearly visible from eight miles away. The pillar of fire rose, accelerating at unbelievable speed. It felt as if the rocket exhaust was blasting at them from directly overhead.

"A few seconds late, gents," Newcombe said over the slowly receding noise. "But spectacular, eh?" Newcombe pulled out a walkie-talkie. "Control, this is Newcombe. Pipe the telemetry narrative outside, please."

"Amazing," General Taylor said. "An intercontinental missile with an eight-thousand-mile range, ready for launch in a little over sixty seconds."

"*Javelin* at sixty nautical miles altitude, seventy-three miles downrange," the voice of the launch controller reported. "Expecting first stage burnout in forty seconds. Speed approaching two thousand miles per hour. Altitude now eighty-three nautical miles, one hundred seven miles downrange . . ."

"Very impressive," General Taylor said. "A most successful launch."

"The *Javelin* hasn't begun to perform, General," Newcombe said. "We'll begin receiving telemetry from Guam and the Marshall Islands soon. They'll tell us the progress of the *Javelin's* warheads. We expect a circular error pattern of not more than a hundred feet."

"One hundred feet!" one of Taylor's aides said. "After an eight thousand mile flight on a *small* ICBM? Why, that's—"

"Unbelievable, I know." Newcombe smiled. "Although the *Javelin* is transportable and deployable in dozens of ways, we haven't just created a mini-ICBM. The *Javelin* is just as accurate as the new MX *Peacekeeper* missile, yet it's one-third the size and one-half the cost."

"*Javelin* at two hundred seventy-three miles altitude, turning further seaward now at three hundred miles downrange," the controller intoned. "Successful first stage burnout and second stage ignition. Velocity seven thousand miles per hour. Inertial systems functioning well."

"We can listen in on the rest of the launch from the visitor's area," Newcombe said. "We have champagne ready."

"Minor inertial course correction," the launch controller said. His voice sounded a bit more strained. Newcombe shot a puzzled glance at the loudspeaker, then wiped his face clean and replaced the puzzlement with a broad smile. No one else had noticed the inflection, or they weren't showing it . . .

"Guam reports tracking *Javelin* on course. *Javelin* at four hundred nautical miles altitude, one thousand one hundred miles downrange," the controller reported. Suddenly his reports were coming faster. "*Javelin* correcting course . . . reestablished on course . . . now correcting course again for premature third-stage ignition . . . Guam reports loss of tracking and telemetry from *Javelin*. Mr. Newcombe, to the control center, please." Newcombe's beeper went off, but he was already running for the command center.

"We have lost the *Javelin*," the monotonous voice continued. "We have lost the *Javelin*."

Aboard the U.S.S. Lawrence

Damage report! All Sections, damage report!"

If anyone could see Commander Markham's hands at that moment, they would see knuckles as white as chalk as they crushed the seatbacks he was gripping for support. Every one of the thousands of lights in the U.S.S. *Lawrence*'s intelligence section had snapped out. A few battery-powered lights automatically came on, but they did little to penetrate the solid darkness of the steel-lined, windowless chamber.

Markham wondered how the order for a damage report was being broadcast. It had to be a battery-operated backup intercom. Hand over hand, he felt his way along the double rows of seats on either side of the aisle toward the front of the intelligence section. He felt a few men rising from their seats, and he risked letting go of the seatbacks to push them back down.

"Keep your seat, Kelly," he ordered. "The damn lights just went out, that's all. Check your station." He heard a timid, "Yes, sir" in reply.

Markham made his way to the ship's radio box mounted on the section's forward bulkhead. The radio was hardly ever used—stray transmissions from the intel section's computers could be picked up for miles through such an antiquated telephone. He picked it up.

The hum he heard in the receiver was deafening, but someone was still trying to use it. "Intel section. Do you read me? Intel section—"

"Intel, Markham here," he shouted into the phone. "Bridge, this is Markham. How do you hear?"

"Very weak," replied the voice—Lieutenant Commander Christopher Watanabe, the first officer, Markham guessed. "Damage report."

"No structural damage noted yet, Chris," Markham said. "All our power is out. All our equipment is shut down."

"Understand no structural damage," Watanabe reported back. "Could not copy the rest. Send a runner forward with a report on the double. The ship is on Condition Yellow. Repeat, Condition Yellow."

"Copy." Markham dropped the phone back on its hook. "All right, now hear this," he called out into the pitch-dark intel section. "The ship is on Condition Yellow. Everyone, one more check of your area for damage and sing out. Kelly!"

"Yes . . . yes, sir?" came the broken, timid voice again.

"You wanna leave so fast, here's your chance. Get up here." The young seaman ran forward. "You're the runner for our section. You don't go topside without a parka, arctic mittens, life vest, and a lifeline—and this time use the damn thing." Markham pushed the youngster aside and peered into the gloom of his now-impotent electronic stateroom. "Listen up. Any damage? Water? Cracks? Gas? Strange sounds? Sing out."

No reply. "Move out, Kelly. Tell Watanabe no damage. Tell him I'll give a report on operational status myself later." Kelly nodded and disappeared through the useless magnetic-lock security door and into the storm beyond.

Markham started to make his way aft through his dark, dead multimillion dollar intelligence section. "Anything?" he asked no one in particular. "Battery backups? Printer buffers? Anything?"

"I've got nothing," one operator said. "That entire battery backup system we had installed is dead. It doesn't work for shit."

"What the hell hit us?" someone else asked. "All my sensors and screens flared, like a huge power surge. Then—*poof.*"

"All right, all right," Markham said, pulling on an orange life vest. "If you don't have anything recoverable, forget it. Pair up and start collecting your hard copy printouts. You'll have to use the hand-crank shredders if Engineering can't get the power back on. If that doesn't work, or if you start to backlog, we'll bag the printouts and start a bonfire in the dumpster on deck. Masters, Lee, suit up and get that dumpster now. No sense in waiting until the Russians start boarding us."

The two men hurried off.

"Printer ribbons, handwritten notes, logbooks, memos, scribbles," Markham recited as he began to pace the aisle, monitoring the destruction preparations. "Astleman, goddamnit, put that life vest on!" Markham made his way over to Garrity's station and knelt down to face the veteran intelligence man.

"What was it, Garrity?"

Garrity ripped the cover off his computer printer's ribbon cartridge and wadded up the ribbon. When he turned toward Markham, there was genuine fear in his eyes.

"I could see it comin'," he whispered. "It was like . . . like a wave of energy. It kept on building up, then everything went dark."

"Kavaznya?" Markham whispered. "Did it come from Kavaznya?"

Garrity nodded, wiping a carbon-blackened hand across his sweating forehead. "Whatever the Russians got out there, Commander, if it didn't blow us out of the Pacific, it at least tagged somethin' else for sure . . ."

WASHINGTON, D.C.

W here the hell is he?" Curtis asked Jack Pledgeman, the President's press secretary, who was trying to ignore the four-star general.

"He's late," Curtis said, loud enough for everyone in the White House Conference Room to hear. Fortunately, the only ones who paid any attention were members of the President's immediate staff and Cabinet who were quite accustomed to Curtis' outbursts. The two dozen cameramen and technicians, putting in final touches to their extensive camera and lighting gear, were too intent on their work to notice. And the members of the White House press corps and other correspondents were outside, hoping to corral the President in the hallway for one-on-one questions before the scheduled morning Cabinet photo session.

Curtis punched a palm in irritation. "When he hears what—"

"Dammit, General, keep it down," Pledgeman interrupted. "Those tapes are rolling over there."

"They won't be—"

"I asked you to—"

Pledgeman didn't get to finish. At that instant, the President strode quickly into the room. The men and women at the large oblong conference table rose to their feet. The President was followed closely by a tight knot of reporters and correspondents. Cameras and lights clicked on and filled the room with a buzz.

The President brushed deep, thick brown hair from his forehead and waved toward the seats. "Thank you, ladies and gentlemen, take your seats." Nobody sat down until the President had stepped over the yards of sound and light cables taped to the rich carpeting and reached his executive's chair.

A bright floodlight snapped on directly in front of the President, right over the Secretary of Health and Human Services' head. "If you don't mind?" the President said, scowling at the light. "You're going to fry one of my people." The light was immediately extinguished. The President nodded his thanks, removed his half-lens Ben Franklin glasses, and wiped them with a handkerchief. Pledgeman quietly admonished the photographer and pointed to a twelve-inch-square opening in a distant corner where he could set up his camera.

"Quite a crowd today, eh, Jack?" the President said to his press secretary. Pledgeman nodded. The President replaced his glasses on his nose and looked over his agenda for the meeting, a shortened and mostly staged version of a formal Cabinet meeting.

A network television anchorwoman, microphone in hand, was stepping quickly into the place vacated by the cameraman. General Curtis steered himself around her, maneuvered around the backs of the chairs occupied by the Secretary of State and the Secretary of Defense, and finally made his way to the President's side. He arrived just as the anchorwoman took one last glance at her notes and smiled at the President. She, not Curtis, had the President's full attention.

"Mr. President, before we get started, I'd like to ask you—"

Simultaneously, Curtis bent down between the Secretary of Defense, Thomas Preston, and the President. He said in a half-whisper, "Mr. President, I have some important developments that can't wait."

The President, eyes drawn to the attractive Oriental newswoman, scarcely noticed Curtis. The general's deep voice interrupted the woman's question.

Pledgeman, on the alert for this sort of embarrassing scene, stepped between the newswoman and the Secretary of Agriculture at the conference table.

"Problem, General?" Pledgeman asked quietly.

General Curtis leaned closer to the President. "Sir, I must speak with you immediately. There are new developments at that . . . power facility we talked about."

"*After* the Cabinet meeting," Pledgeman said.

Curtis hesitated.

"Wilbur, it has to wait," the President finally said. "Is it an *immediate* emergency?"

Everyone watched Curtis. No one knew exactly what an "immediate" emergency was, but it would be plastered all over page one of every newspaper in the country if he said "yes." Coming directly from the chairman of the Joint Chiefs, the classification "immediate emergency" would mean only one thing. He'd have some tough explaining to do.

"It'll have to wait, General," Pledgeman said, repeating the President's words. "We must get started here."

"I'll be in my office as soon as I'm through here, General," the President said as Curtis was ushered out by one of Pledgeman's associates.

As the door to the conference room slammed behind him, Curtis turned on his aide.

"Colonel Wyatt, you will stand here and wait for the President. The instant he comes out of that room, you are to confront him and remind him that I am waiting for him in the Oval Office. Tell him that it is now a matter of national security. Don't speak with anyone else but the President. If Pledgeman or anyone else tells you differently, you have a direct order from me to bust him in the chops. All clear?"

Wyatt, amazed at his boss' behavior, nodded and watched as the general marched down the corridor.

"It's incredible. Absolutely incredible."

The President of the United States stared out the window of the White House Oval Office, making the announcement to the gently falling flakes of snow outside. General Wilbur Curtis collected the sheaves of notes and computer printouts, glanced at the Secretary of Defense, Thomas Preston, and sat down. Secretary of State Marshall Brent stood at the opposite side of the President's cherry desk, looking over copies of the intelligence analysis Kenneth Mitchell, the CIA director, had shown the President. United Nations Ambassador Gregory Adams sat on a couch, seething as he thought of Karmarov's apparent duplicity at the Security Council session.

"Merry goddamn Christmas," the President muttered.

For the first time in months, Curtis felt a huge weight lift off his shoulders. He's finally beginning to believe me, Curtis thought. It had taken the deaths of twelve men and women and the loss of a billion dollars worth of military hardware, plus the new evidence in hand.

"But how can we be sure that this is an orbiting mirror, General?" the President asked over his shoulder, not bothering to turn away from the window. He was holding an eleven-by-fourteen black-and-white enlargement of a large, rectangular object. The object was silvery and slightly curved, with a surface resembling a reflective quilted blanket. A thin web of girders surrounded it, along with several oblong tanks and other vessels.

"Mr. President, the evidence indicates that—"

"The President asked you a specific question, General," Tom Preston interrupted. "How can we be *sure?*"

"We can't be *sure*, Mr. President," Curtis said. "That photo *could* be various things—solar collection panels, solar shielding . . . but look at the facts: Our RC-315 recon plane records massive energy discharge frm the Kavaznya facility. Simultaneously, we record the destruction of a geosynchronous satellite directly over the complex in space. I believe the RC-153 was destroyed by another energy blast to keep it from reporting the data it was gathering.

"Less than two weeks later, the *Lawrence* intelligence vessel we sent over there to monitor the site records another massive energy blast from the Kavaznya site. Seconds later, the third stage of our Midgetman missile prematurely ignites and we are forced to destroy it. Information from the *Lawrence* exactly matches the data on the blast that we received from the RC-153 before we lost contact—"

Secretary of Defense Preston interrupted. "So how does that prove there's an orbiting mirror, General Curtis?"

"Before the energy blast, the *Lawrence* reported unusual data signals being transmitted from the Kavaznya radar," Curtis went on. "Their information is still being analyzed, but the experts on the *Lawrence* have described data transmissions between the radar at Kavaznya and two Soviet satellites in Earth orbit.

"They believe the first satellite was furnishing position data to Kavaznya during the time that the Midgetman missile was in the boost phase. The Kavaznya radar was tracking a second satellite and was also furnishing steering signals to it. Such sophisticated steering signals could be used to align a mirror on the missile.

"After the destruction of the *Javelin* missile was reported, I ordered a simple backtrack. Assuming a lesser blast from Kavaznya—which we didn't know at first since the *Lawrence*'s report hadn't reached us yet— and again assuming an orbiting mirror, we computed all the possible points where a mirror would have to be placed to hit the *Javelin,* and used our Spacetrack optical space tracking telescope at Pulmosan, South Korea to photograph those sections of the sky.

"You have the result, sir," Curtis said, forcing down his anger. To be fair, he told himself, it wasn't that the President did *not* believe him—he didn't *want* to believe him. "The mirror is one hundred and fifty feet long, seventy feet wide. It is attached to the underside of Salyut Nineteen, which has been in orbit for almost a year. The satellite has docking bays, large fuel tanks, and small crew quarters although we do not believe it's manned."

Marshall Brent motioned to the President, who passed the photograph to him. He examined it quickly.

"I assume your experts analyzed this photo for you, General?" Brent asked.

"Yes. Why?"

"Because to the untrained layman's eyes, this could be a photograph of anything," Brent said. "Any satellite. An aircraft."

"But it's not—"

"It could even be faked?" Brent was testing, which he considered his job.

"Do you want me to send a Shuttle full of U.N. members up with Brownies to take snapshots?"

Brent started to reply but was cut off by the President. "General, I think I believe your analysis," the President said unhappily. "But who is going to believe such a thing exists? And we risk much by accusing the Soviet Union of murder . . ."

The President turned to Kenneth Mitchell. "Kenneth, you said you had information on that site. Can you give it to me now?"

"Yes, sir." The Director of the CIA nodded to an aide, who stood nervously and faced the President.

"Analysis of data from the missing RC-135 aircraft as well as information obtained from the *Lawrence* has been completed. Much of it is still speculative, sir."

"Go *on*," the President said irritably.

"Most of our analysis centers around the nuclear power facility, sir. They have built what appears to be a five hundred megawatt facility in the middle of nowhere, without any associated power transmission facilities such as transformers or transmission towers nearby. Therefore, the power plant is at the exclusive disposal of the complex itself. The complex is located on the northeast corner of the Kamchatka peninsula, in what used to be a small fishing village. Its small supply airfield was rebuilt into a full-scale military airfield, originally for construction supply but now used as a headquarters for the site's defenses. About ten thousand people live in the area, civilian and military."

The aide shifted nervously as all eyes focused on him. "The intelligence vessel *Lawrence* has provided valuable data on the energy blasts reported from the complex, and we have concluded that a laser blast of approximately two to three hundred megawatts could have caused the electronic interference reported in the area and could indeed have sufficiently damaged both the Alpha Omega satellite and the *Javelin* missile. The power of the tracking radar could only have come from the nuclear power plant."

"Weren't we watching the construction of the facility?" the President asked. "How could they build something of this magnitude and then spring it on us so suddenly? Why were we so surprised?"

"CIA and DIA have been watching the construction of Kavaznya for four years, sir," Mitchell said, "but . . . well, to tell the truth, sir, we really didn't think too much of their activities there. It has been impossible to get informants anywhere near the complex. We had noticed activity akin to weapons experiments or construction there, so we pegged it simply as a new weapons research facility. The powerful radar wasn't found until the RC-135 mission. We never imagined—we had no idea that the Russians were building an antisatellite or antiballistic-missile laser there."

"Are we really that arrogant," the President said to everyone in the room. "If the Americans can't do it, nobody can. Is that it?"

Mitchell was quiet for a moment, then cleared his throat and nodded to his aide to continue. The President didn't let him.

"So we are decided," the President asked, "that there exists a powerful antiballistic-missile laser device at this Kavaznya complex?"

Mitchell glanced at Preston, then at Curtis. "The data seems all but conclusive, Mr. President."

"Goddamn," the President murmured, then nodded at Mitchell's aide: "Go on."

"As I've said, the Soviets have constructed a huge power plant exclusively for use by the killer laser. They can easily pump over three hundred megawatts into their laser, and they can continue to do so shot after shot. We believe, once they've worked the kinks out—and it won't be long now—that they can fire the laser at full power twice every second. Potentially, over a hundred satellites a minute."

"Or ICBM warheads," the President said.

"That's only a projection, sir," Mitchell interjected. "Hitting a geosynchronous satellite is a relatively easy trick. Besides, the Omega was only blinded—the Air Force had to push it into the atmosphere themselves because it was out of control and they were trying to retrieve it intact if possible. That means the laser is not as powerful as we originally believed.

"And the Midgetman missile was only slightly damaged by the laser. We had to abort it," Mitchell continued. "As a matter of fact, we don't agree with General Curtis that the laser caused the missile to malfunction. There are a number of things that could have caused a premature third stage ignition—"

"The laser *could* easily have caused it to malfunction," Curtis said.

"General, I agree it could," Mitchell said, raising a hand. "But that's your conclusion—not the CIA's. Finding and hitting an ICBM warhead is infinitely more difficult than finding and hitting these other targets we've been talking about. The Omega the Soviets downed is several times larger than an ICBM warhead, and it was stationary. The Midgetman is another huge target, easily tracked and disabled. Besides, it was alone—a retaliatory American ICBM strike would involve hundreds of missiles and thousands of warheads. The laser might tag a few, but not many. Certainly not enough to justify the huge expense of that complex."

"What about the RC-135?" Curtis asked.

"The most vulnerable of all the targets," Mitchell said quickly. "Slow-moving, large, and the closest to the site. And that's *if* the RC-135 was downed by the laser—that hasn't been proved yet." Before Curtis could object, Mitchell quickly added: "Although the CIA believes there's more than enough information to conclude that it was."

The President shook his head. "The nuclear power plant, the laser facility, the radar, and the laser cannon. All in one tiny fishing town on the Kamchatka peninsula . . ."

"Along with two squadrons of MIG-27 Fulcrums, a squadron of MIG-25 Flogger Gs, two SA-10 surface-to-air missile sites, possibly two antiaircraft artillery sites, and early-warning radar picket ships patrolling the coast when the ice breaks up," Mitchell added. "A seagull can't get close to that site without the Soviets spotting it."

The President's frustration was etching deep furrows in his forehead and at the corners of his eyes, and he tried to massage the pain out of both. "Anything else?" he asked.

"Yes, sir," U.N. Ambassador Adams said, standing. "The United Nations Security Council session. When I accused the Soviets of firing a laser at the recon plane, Karmarov lost his usual cool and jumped down my throat denying it. But the official Soviet position remains the same—they maintain the right to protect their shores and deny launching a missile or ordering a fighter to attack the RC-135. They never specifically denied shooting it down with a laser—"

"That's because the idea is so unbelievable," Mitchell said, echoing the President's earlier comment. "Our Strategic Defense Initiative was called Star Wars for a reason—it was meant as a futuristic, long-range plan. We never expected to have an operational system before the turn of the century—it's even more incredible that the Soviets would have one."

"Yet the evidence unfortunately points to the contrary," Marshall Brent said. "Mr. President, I must add my concern to that of Gregory. I have met with Ambassador Karmarov myself—"

"You did?" the President asked, surprised. "When? I never heard anything about it."

"I went to his residence quite unannounced," Brent said. "It had the desired effect—Karmarov lost his famous poker face. He all but admitted . . . he'd deny it, of course . . . that such a defensive laser device existed. I believe our meeting resulted in the Soviet's face-saving decision to enter into a 'mutual' investigation."

"Which has never taken place," Curtis said. "They lied to us from the beginning."

Brent paused, then crossed in front of the President's desk and faced him. "Karmarov mentioned another important point, sir: If it is proven to the world that the anti-satellite laser exists, the Soviets can also prove that such a device does not violate any international treaty or agreement. It is not a space-based system like our *Ice Fortress* system, which violates the 1982 De-Militarization of Space Agreement; nor is it a violation of any ABM treaty, since neither the 1972 agreement or its 1976 amendment mention *ground-based* laser systems—the idea of activating such a site was many times more implausible fifteen years ago than it is today. The orbiting mirror *may* be a violation of the 1982 agreement—if we prove it exists, if we prove it is a mirror, and if we prove that it was used against an atmospheric or orbiting vehicle of another country—"

"But then they are guilty of murder," Curtis said. "They should be convicted of murder. We should demand the dismantling of that laser site as minimal reparation for their crime."

The Secretary of State shook his head. "We could never prove they downed the RC-135 reconnaissance plane, General," Brent said. "Even if we had conclusive evidence that they used their laser system to destroy a satellite and the *Javelin* missile, we could never prove, or convince, that they turned that laser on an unarmed aircraft. It's just too provocative an act to be believed."

There was silence in the President's office for a long time. No one wanted to speak. Each could feel a transition taking place. It was the awful transition from disbelief and even outright denial of what had occurred, to now facing the realization that the weight of damning evidence dictated that something had to be done.

"We need options, gentlemen," the President said finally.

"There is only one option, sir," Adams said. "The Soviets must deactivate that laser complex."

"They have absolutely no reason to do that, Gregory," Brent said quickly. "As I said before, there is no agreement between our countries prohibiting a ground-based defensive laser device."

"It sure as hell isn't just a defensive device, Marshall."

Brent held up a hand. "Please, Gregory. What would you argue if you were in the Soviet's shoes? Tracking error, technical malfunction, even errors in judgment on the part of some obscure bureaucrat. The bureaucrat is fired, heads roll, and the site remains open—"

"And a threat," Curtis put in. "They have already seriously crippled our intercontinental ballistic missile warning capability." He turned to the President. "Sir, the Soviets may claim it's not an offensive weapon, but as long as it's active it can always be used as one. What if they *accidentally* start shooting down satellites all over the hemisphere? They may agree to pay for the ones they accidentally destroy, but we're still out the satellites and the vital surveillance information they provide."

"And if they have the capability to knock down ICBMs as well . . ." the President muttered.

"They can easily neutralize one-third of our land and sea-based missiles," Curtis said. "And when our bombers try to attack, they can take pot shots at them. Hell, even turning on that radar of theirs is enough to scramble the electronics of any aircraft in the area—"

"All right," the President interrupted. "Damn it, you make it sound like a preemptive strike is our only option." He looked angrily at the men around him, settled on the Chairman of the Joint Chiefs.

"General Curtis," the President asked slowly, carefully, "what is the status of your project at Dreamland?"

"Currently deactivated, per your order, Mr. President," Curtis replied. "We wanted to avoid any possible provocation during what seemed a cooling off period."

"But it can be reactivated immediately?"

"Certainly, sir," Curtis replied. "I can see to it that the full team is reassembled."

The President hesitated, then rapped his knuckles on his desk. "Then do it."

General Curtis smiled and nodded, which ignited Marshall Brent.

"The very thought of considering a military option against the Soviets is crazy," he said, his face reddening. "I've told you General—until current treaties and agreements are modified, that complex is perfectly legal. We may demand reparation for the hardware they destroyed—and I have no doubt, when confronted with the evidence, that they will pay a reasonable amount—but we have no legal reason to attack that site."

"Reason? How about the lives of twelve innocent men and women aboard that RC-135, Mr. Brent?" General Curtis shot back. "That's reason enough for me."

"Marshall, I've authorized General Curtis to keep one special military option open—period," the President said. "The time for discussion is rapidly running out. I want you to find a way to force the Soviets to deactivate that laser complex."

If the Secretary of State felt any surprise at the enormity and sheer impossibility of that task, he did not show it—he merely nodded resolutely. "It will be difficult," he said, "but it's our best hope." Maybe our only one, he added to himself.

"We can confront the Soviets with our information," Gregory Adams said. "Present the evidence to the United Nations, as we did during the

Cuban Missile Crisis. Force world opinion to turn against them. Convince the world that the destabilizing force of that laser system is a threat to everyone."

"You've put it well, Gregory," Brent said. "Exactly what we must do."

"All right," the President said hopefully. "I like it. Marshall, Greg, I'm counting on you. This can't go any further. Make sure they know we mean business."

"I have another option that may prod the Russians a bit faster toward a negotiated settlement," Curtis said. The President's smile disappeared. Marshall Brent glared at Curtis.

"*Ice Fortress,*" Secretary of Defense Preston said. "Reactivate *Ice Fortress.*"

"Or at least threaten to reactivate it," Curtis added quickly.

"It's out of the question," Brent said. "The 1986 Arms-Reduction Treaty, which took us two long years to hammer out, strictly forbids *Ice Fortress.* If we bring it back, we are guilty of lying. Our credibility will go down the drain."

"*Ice Fortress* is the only thing we have that can even begin to match up to that laser system," Curtis argued. "Without it, we have nothing to bargain with. Why should the Russians agree to anything we want? Why should they shut down that site? Because we say, 'pretty please?' "

"The Soviets won't ignore us," Brent said. "Gregory and I will confront them in the U.N. We'll present the data you've received and challenge them to deny it. I believe that will be the last we'll hear of any laser defense site."

The President looked grim. "You're right, Marshall," he said slowly. "We hold off with any movement on *Ice Fortress.* It's not an option. Not now."

Marshall Brent looked relieved. "There will be a settlement, sir. We will end this." And at the moment, he had managed to convince himself.

The President nodded, then swiveled around and stared wordlessly out the triple windows of the Oval Office as the others quietly filed out.

THE UNITED NATIONS SECURITY COUNCIL, NEW YORK

Last item on the agenda before the New Year's recess," Ian McCaan announced before a regular meeting of the United Nations Security Council, "is a presentation by the American delegation on the progress of the ongoing investigation of the alleged loss of the American Air Force RC-135 off the east coast of the Soviet Union. We are pleased to have in attendance the distinguished Secretary of State of the United States of America, Mr. Marshall Brent. Mr. Brent, please—"

"Excuse me, Mr. Secretary-General!" Karmarov interrupted, a shocked expression on his face. He half-rose out of his seat as Marshall Brent walked down the center aisle of the closed Security Council chamber. "Mr. Secretary-General, this . . ." he fought for composure, ". . . I was not aware that this matter had been placed on the agenda. No one has consulted my office . . ."

By this time Marshall Brent had reached the floor of the chamber, Greg Adams, the U.N. ambassador, had relinquished his seat to the Secretary of State and now sat behind and to his right. Brent held up a hand a smiled at the Soviet chief delegate.

"I'm afraid I am at fault, Mr. Karmarov," Brent began. Karmarov's protest died in midsentence, and he slowly lowered himself to his seat. "I have taken the liberty of invoking a little-used and rather esoteric regulation in the Security Council's rules of order.

"A 1957 addendum to Article Thirty-nine of the Security Council's Affairs of Conduct allows either side of any dispute before the Security Council to provide periodic progress reports of any council-ordered investigation. I have taken the liberty of putting together a report that I'm sure your fellow delegates will be most interested in—"

"Pardon me, Mr. Brent," Karmarov interrupted again, even more forcibly this time. He bent over to Andrina Asserni, whispered a few words to her, and watched as she rushed out to an anteroom. "That matter is still under investigation. I know that little progress has been made, sir, but it is still fairly early—"

"That's right, Mr. Ambassador," Brent said. "But a status report is still allowed. I'm sorry Miss Asserni was called away to double-check the article, but its validity here has already been examined and approved by the Central Steering Committee." Karmarov looked at Ian McCaan, who nodded.

"Apparently, Mr. Karmarov," McCaan said, "the Soviet secretary on the Steering Committee did not notify you. The request is in order. Of course, you will have an opportunity to add any remarks you wish."

Asserni returned just then with her finger in a thick red leather-bound book. She whispered a few words to Karmarov, who narrowed his gaze and fixed it on Marshall Brent.

"The article you mentioned does not deal with the matter you wish to discuss," Karmarov said, "and apparently gives little authority or justification for such a presentation. It is entirely out of order—"

"The nature of the presentation," McCaan broke in, "and the subject matter convinced the Steering Committee to adapt the rules. Besides, Ambassador Karmarov, it is the last order of business for the Council and no other matters are scheduled until the spring. I'm sure the Council will be interested in the contents of this presentation."

The Russian offered no resistance—in fact, his voice became a bit more apologetic. "The investigation has only been open less than a month . . ."

"And yet it has gone nowhere," Brent said immediately, his tone clipped but steady. "American requests for transcripts, *ordinary* transcripts of your military controllers on duty at the time of the loss of the RC-135 have been ignored. Similar requests by the International Civil Aeronautics Organization have also been ignored. According to ICAO convention, such transcripts are usually submitted to the parties involved in less than twenty-four hours."

Karmarov staged his indignation. "I will personally investigate the incompetence of—"

"My office has already investigated the matter," Brent said. "The Soviet Foreign Ministry advises me that the transcripts were turned over to your United Nations delegation." Karmarov again was about to reply, but Brent held up a hand.

"I understand the situation, Mr. Ambassador," Brent said in a forgiving tone. "The Foreign Ministry did advise me that your office has not had time to fully study the transcripts. Turning the transcript over to us before looking at them yourself wouldn't make sense, I agree."

"I beg the Council's indulgence," Karmarov said. "Pressing matters in my delegation and the last-minute flurry of activity prior to the New Year's recess have delayed my study of those documents."

"Of course, Mr. Ambassador," Brent said. "The Foreign Ministry was kind enough to answer a few questions, though. I hope you at least have had an opportunity to glance at the transcripts so as to enlighten the Security Council on a few points."

"I'm sorry, Mr. Secretary, I—"

"The Foreign Ministry assures me that, although three MIG-29 fighter-interceptor aircraft were launched from Ossora Airfield on the northern Kamchatka peninsula near Kavaznya, they never closed with the so-called intruder aircraft. The RC-135 aircraft was allowed to fly toward the coast without being challenged. Mr. Ambassador, why in the world would the Soviets allow an unidentified aircraft to fly to within thirty-five miles of the coastline, within thirty-five miles of a top secret research installation, without being challenged by three interceptors assigned to pursue it?"

Heads turned toward Karmarov. "Mr. Secretary," Karmarov said through tight lips. "I cannot at this time answer—"

"The Foreign Ministry also reports that no efforts were made to reach the RC-135 on normal, internationally recognized emergency channels. Now, Mr. Ambassador, the Soviet Union launched three advanced interceptors out after an American aircraft it says was intruding into highly sensitive Russian airspace, yet never closed on the intruder. They obviously *saw* the aircraft—yet never tried to raise the aircraft by radio, never tried to warn it away. Why? Perhaps I can offer a reason," Brent hurried on. At his signal, a rear-projection screen began to descend over the mural of "The Rise of the Phoenix" at the head of the Security Council chamber. Ambassador Adams pushed an electronic pointer into his hands and Brent stepped quickly toward the head of the circular Council table.

Flaring to life as Brent stepped up to a small podium at the head of the table, the screen showed several rows of words and numbers on the left and several bar graphs on the right.

"I will show the Council exactly what took place aboard that unarmed reconnaissance plane," Brent began. "This is the exact, unedited position and status data transmitted from the RC-135 aircraft as it approached Kavaznya. It shows summaries of the aircraft's performance and summaries of what the aircraft's sensors were receiving."

Brent hit a button on the console. A second slide appeared beneath the first, this one a map of eastern Asia centered on Kavaznya.

"To better understand the data presented on the left," Brent said, "we will plot the location of the RC-135 aircraft on the map below. The bar graphs are readouts of electromagnetic energy levels outside the RC-135 aircraft. The graphs show levels of heat, visible light, radiation, transmitted energy, and polarized single-frequency light. All of the presentations have been time-synced to show exactly what was happening at each moment."

The screens went into motion. "The RC-135 aircraft is one hundred and forty miles from Kavaznya when surveillance radars from Ossora Airfield north of Kavaznya begin to track it." A circle appeared on the chart. "The circle represents the computer's estimate of the range of the surveillance radar scanning the RC-135—the plane is well within that range." The transmitted energy bar moved upward—all of the other graphs were motionless.

Brent motioned to the scrolling printout. "The RC-135 is now ninety miles from Kavaznya. It is still being tracked by surveillance radar, as shown by this line on the printout—standard India-band surveillance radar. I assume air defense forces have been alerted, but only the missing controller's transcript can tell us this. Here . . ." Brent pointed to the transmitted energy bar graph, "is where a new radar comes on. The plane is still over ten minutes from reaching land.

"See how much the energy level has increased? The printout confirms it . . . here. Frequency, carrier power, modulation—all significantly different, thousands of times more powerful than the ordinary surveillance radars." A new circle appeared on the map, this one several times larger than the first.

"Mr. Secretary-General, I must protest this," Karmarov said.

Brent stopped the scrolling display. "Mr. Karmarov, this presentation has been approved by the Steering Committee for presentation," McCaan said. "What are the grounds for your objection?"

"This appears to be what Mr. Brent says it is," Karmarov said, "but it can also be a clever forgery. Why, I can create such a grand display on my own computer."

"If you are challenging the Steering Committee's judgment," McCaan said, "you must enter a protest with the Steering Committee—"

"But I have not yet had an opportunity to examine any of the evidence being presented."

"The Steering Committee—"

"I *know* about the Steering Committee. But such a . . . jumble of information cannot be brought before the Security Council without—"

"It seems your objection is a procedural one, Mr. Karmarov," McCaan said, "and as such I must overrule it. The admissibility of this data and the manner of its presentation has already been approved by the Security Council as per this body's regulations. Mr. Brent, proceed."

The screen went into motion once again. "The RC-135 is now forty-two miles from shore." Brent pointed at the readout on the left. The map magnified into a much larger scale of the Kavaznya area itself. The red line plotting the course of the RC-135 began to change. "It is here that the plane begins a right turn away from the coastline. As you can see, the transmitted energy scale has greatly increased. At the same time, all other radars in the area have been turned off—all but one. No India-band radars, only the much more powerful Lima band radar at Kavaznya."

Brent turned to Karmarov. "Why, Mr. Ambassador, would your air defense operators turn *off* their radars with an intruder in the area? With three fighters airborne that rely on that radar for vectors to the intruder, why was it deactivated? Where are the fighters?"

Karmarov decided his only response was silence.

The screen froze. The bar graphs had all suddenly pegged themselves at the top of their scales.

"Suddenly, here," Brent said, "there is a massive explosion of transmitted energy, visible light, radiation, and polarized light." The display began to move slowly. "The blast lasts for almost a full second. Gentlemen, the readout for polarized light is a readout of levels of visible light that meets very strict parameters. The light must be pure—one wavelength, one frequency, one direction. Polarized light." He turned and looked at Karmarov. "Laser light. A laser on the order of two hundred megawatts has just been fired from Kavaznya."

The scrolling continued, but the printout display on the left and the movement of the bar graphs halted for several minutes. "The data transmission was interrupted after the laser blast," Brent said. "The tremendous amount of energy disrupts electronic circuits for hundreds of miles. Is that why there are no fighters in the area, Mr. Karmarov? A fighter near that laser blast would fall into the ocean."

No reply from Karmarov.

A few moments later the stream of data returned. "As you can see," Brent went on, "the levels of radiation and transmitted energy are still high. The bar graphs for polarized light and thermal energy have been removed. That is because that data was obtained from an Alpha Omega Nine reconnaissance satellite over Kavaznya. That satellite was destroyed by the laser blast."

"Impossibie," came a voice from the Council table. The rumble of voices increased in volume.

"The crew aboard the RC-135, which is now almost ninety miles from shore, are probably already exposed to lethal doses of radiation, but they are still alive."

One bar graph jumped. "Transmitted energy is increasing again," Brent said. "The radar at Kavaznya is active again—searching for another victim."

"Unfounded accusations," Karmarov protested. "Mr. Secretary-General—"

"The Lima-band radar is at full power again." Brent was no longer looking at the screen but directly at Karmarov, who stared at the data flowing on the screen. "There is a pulse-shift—the radar has locked onto the aircraft, an unarmed reconnaissance aircraft almost fifty miles from shore with ten men and two women aboard."

The screen went blank, and the room went dark. Slowly, the lights were brought back up in the Council chamber.

"Without warning, with malice aforethought," Brent said to Karmarov, "the Soviets disabled a satellite, then, trying to cover their first crime, turned that laser on an unarmed aircraft, killing twelve people."

The chamber was silent. "In America, Mr. Ambassador, we call it murder in the first degree." Brent turned and faced the Council members seated around him.

"Four days ago a test of a new intercontinental missile design was also attacked by the laser at Kavaznya. I will present the data when it becomes available. This time, the data was collected by a vessel anchored offshore from Kavaznya, and not by another satellite. Yet it will prove that not only has the Soviet Union used its new laser to attack another American vehicle, but that it used *this.*" The lights were immediately lowered. Brent clicked a button again, and a magnified, computer-enhanced picture of Salyut Nineteen with the large rectangular mirror attached flashed on the screen.

"Salyut Nineteen, gentlemen," Brent announced, "but with a new and frightening twist—a mirror used to bounce the laser beam to targets over the horizon from Kavaznya!" The murmur in the Council chamber became one of disbelief.

"I know you're not going to respond to any of this, Mr. Ambassador," Brent said, turning back to Karmarov. "You are going to request a video tape of this session, take it back to the Embassy, and talk it over with Moscow. Fine. But the United States requests the reinstatement of charges made back on November fifteenth. We charge the Soviet Union with premeditated murder, conspiracy to commit murder, piracy, perjury, and conspiracy to suppress evidence. We also charge violation of the 1972 Anti-Ballistic Missile Treaty with the deployment of the laser, the Lima-band radar used to steer the laser, and the Salyut Nineteen spacecraft refitted with a mirror for the reflection of laser beams with the purpose of destroying ballistic weapons. We call for the immediate dismantling of the Salyut Nineteen spacecraft and the closure of the entire Kavaznya complex until an on-site United Nations inspection can be made. We are also demanding reparations in the amount of five hundred million American dollars for the death of the American service personnel aboard the RC-135 aircraft and the loss of the RC-135 aircraft, the Alpha Omega Nine satellite, and the *Javelin* missile."

He turned to the Security Council delegates. "I know that, despite our lofty ideals, justice meted by the United Nations is slow and sometimes ineffective. But the government of the United States considers the laser device and the orbiting mirror a major threat to its security, and we cannot, *we will not,* wait long for these devices to be disarmed."

He turned again to Karmarov and raised his voice. "We give the Soviet Union three days to dismantle or render inoperative the Salyut Nineteen spacecraft. If it is not proved to our satisfaction that the Salyut Nineteen's mirror is incapable of steering a laser beam projected from Kavaznya to an atmospheric or ballistic vehicle anywhere on the globe, we will assume that the 1972 Anti-Ballistic Missile Treaty and the 1986 Iceland Summit Arms Reduction Treaty are null and void and take appropriate steps to insure our national security."

"And what steps are those?" Karmarov asked. "Will you go to war to back up your silly rhetoric, Mr. Secretary? Will you destroy civilization because of a baseless, insignificant, pie-in-the-sky threat?"

Brent turned to the Russian ambassador, planting his hands firmly on Karmarov's desk. In a voice so low few could hear except Karmarov himself, Brent said, "Why, Dmitri? Why? We suspected almost from the beginning, and I took a tremendous risk and *told* you of our suspicions. Yet your government continued to use that laser device. Why? It doesn't make sense."

"You were foolish to expose your so-called evidence like this, Brent," Karmarov said softly. "I need not try to explain. But forcing my government into a corner with outlandish grandstanding will not yield the results you want."

"I asked you why, Dmitri," Brent said. "Dammit, I—"

"The device is an instrument of *defense,* of territorial security," Karmarov said between clenched teeth. "It is years ahead of its time, a device that even the most optimistic in your country would not have expected to become operational in another ten years. *It violates no existing treaty.* It affords a defensive umbrella, its existence cannot merely be shouted away with threats."

"You've got a choice," Brent said in a normal voice, stepping away from the Russian ambassador so the rest of the delegates could hear. "Start with the Salyut Nineteen spacecraft. Disarm it, go up there and dismantle the mirror, burn it up in the atmosphere—I don't care. But prove to the United States that you will pledge to use the laser as a defensive device only. Right now it's an offensive weapon, and it's already been used to murder innocent American lives. The other choice is to prepare to accept the consequences of your actions." Brent returned to his seat and slid into it slowly, studying the faces of those around him.

"And what would those consequences be, Mr. Brent?" Karmarov said quietly in English. "Global war? Global death?" He was taunting his American colleague, but Brent folded his hands serenely and returned Karmarov's gaze in silence. Then the memory of their private meeting returned to him. Brent saw that Karmarov had remembered, too. Brent gathered his notes together and nodded to Adams, preparing to leave.

"*Zal Lyot,*" Karmarov said, almost in a whisper. Delegates scrambled for translation earpieces. Brent's gaze narrowed, as if in pain.

"You cannot," Karmarov said. "It will mean the end. You cannot—"

"We can, we will," Marshall Brent said, hoping he sounded more convincing than he felt. He stood, nodded to Ian McCaan, and left the Security Council chambers.

WASHINGTON, D.C.

The scene in the hushed, dimly-lit blast-proof chamber beneath the White House known as the Situation Room could best be described as funereal—and, at that point, the atmosphere exactly matched Secretary of State Marshall Brent's mood.

Brent waited for the President to signal that he was ready, then picked up the sheet of paper that lay in front of him and began:

"Ladies and gentlemen, I have received the reply from the Soviet Premier to our charges concerning the use of the Kavaznya laser installation and the Salyut Nineteen orbiting mirror on the RC-135 aircraft, the Alpha Omega Nine satellite, and the *Javelin* small ICBM. It reads as follows—Quote:

THE GOVERNMENT OF THE UNION OF SOVIET SOCIALIST REPUBLICS CATEGORICALLY DENIES THE CHARGES LEVELED AGAINST IT IN CLOSED SESSION OF THE UNITED NATIONS SECURITY COUNCIL. THE USSR REJECTS THE EVIDENCE PRESENTED IN CLOSED SESSION AS FABRICATION AND INADMISSIBLE. THE USSR DENIES ANY CULPABILITY IN THE ALLEGED LOSS OF ANY AIRCRAFT ON OR ABOUT THE THIRTEENTH OF NOVEMBER, NINETEEN EIGHTY-SEVEN, OR THE ALLEGED LOSS OF AN ILLEGAL SPY SATELLITE ON OR ABOUT THE SAME DATE. WE WILL NOT DIGNIFY THE BASELESS AND LUDICROUS CLAIM OF SHOOTING DOWN A MISSILE OVER THE PACIFIC OCEAN WITH A DENIAL.

"Those sonsof*bitches,*" Curtis muttered.
Brent went on,

THE SOVIET UNION MAINTAINS THAT ANY GROUND-BASED LASER DEVICE IN EXISTENCE IS NOT A VIOLATION OF THE 1972 ANTI-

145

BALLISTIC MISSILE TREATY, SINCE SUCH WEAPONS WERE NEVER ADDRESSED BY THAT TREATY, NOR IS THE PRESENCE OF A SPACE VEHICLE WITH A MIRROR ATTACHED TO IT IN ANY WAY IN VIOLATION OF ANY TREATY.

THE AMERICAN GOVERNMENT'S PROVOCATIVE ULTIMATUM DELIVERED BY THE AMERICAN SECRETARY OF STATE TO THE SOVIET UNITED NATIONS DELEGATION IS GROUNDLESS AND AGGRESSIVE, AND IT IS HEREBY REJECTED. THE UNITED STATES MUST OFFER PROOF, *REAL* PROOF, THAT THE ALLEGED LOSS OF THEIR EQUIPMENT WAS NOT CAUSED BY THEIR OWN INCOMPETENCE OR MALFUNCTION BEFORE THEY CAN BEGIN TO REQUEST ANYTHING FROM THIS SOVEREIGN NATION.

WE FURTHER REJECT THE ATTEMPTS BY THE UNITED STATES GOVERNMENT TO COERCE THE SOVIET UNION BY THREATENING UNILATERALLY TO DISOBEY THE 1972 ANTI-BALLISTIC MISSILE TREATY AND THE UNRATIFIED 1986 ARMS REDUCTION TREATY. A RESPONSIBLE NATION WOULD MAINTAIN THE PATH OF FAIR AND OPEN NEGOTIATIONS TO SOLVE A DISPUTE, AND NOT IMMEDIATELY JEOPARDIZE WORLD PEACE BY OPENLY THREATENING TO CANCEL AND VIOLATE INTERNATIONAL TREATIES.

THE SOVIET UNION, AS ALWAYS, STANDS READY TO REOPEN THE INVESTIGATION OF THE LOSS OF AN AMERICAN AIRCRAFT OFF OUR SHORES, AND TO ENTER INTO TALKS ON ANY OTHER QUESTIONS OR POSSIBLE TREATY VIOLATIONS THAT MAY BE CONNECTED WITH RESEARCH BEING CONDUCTED IN EASTERN SIBERIA. WE PLEDGE OUR FULL AND UNCONDITIONAL COOPERATION IN THE SPIRIT OF PEACE.

"So they've denied everything," Brent summarized. "They're willing to start talks on whether or not the radar violates the ABM treaty, but that's all."

"We're back to where we started," Curtis said. He turned to the President. "Sir, with all due respect, I recommend immediate deployment of *Ice Fortress.*"

Brent shook his head. "And trigger World War Three? The solution would be worse than the problem."

"Mr. Brent, we've had this argument before," Curtis said. "It's time to act." He turned to the President. "Mr. President, if you prefer, we can launch the station itself in two consecutive Shuttle launches, one from Canaveral, one from Vandenburg, in one month. We can delay arming the station until all possible diplomatic avenues are exhausted. If we have no other choice, two follow-on launches can make *Ice Fortress* fully armed and ready two weeks later."

There was a murmur of assent that filled the White House Situation Room. Brent looked around at the assembled advisors.

"We'd be stooping to their level," Brent said. "It would mean an escalation that we might not be able to control."

"Why are they doing this?" the President asked rhetorically, massaging his temples. "Why? They can't be trying to provoke us."

"They've achieved their goal of crippling our strategic warning and surveillance capabilities," Curtis said. "That's why."

Brent sighed. "Dammit, General, you see Russian invasions at every turn. We could launch another spy satellite—we could launch ten of them—and I believe they'd be safe because the Russian's objective has already been met. They've disorganized, confused, and scared this government. Don't you see, General? They *want* us to launch *Ice Fortress.* They *want* us to try to bomb Kavaznya or start a fight somewhere else in the world. No matter what they have already done, *our* response will be seen as much more aggressive in the eyes of the world."

"So what you're saying," Curtis shot back, "is that our best move is to do nothing at all. Make big threats and then wait and wait after they've thumbed their noses at us." He ran fingers through his hair, then slammed down his fist. "No. It's not a matter of being macho. I'm not convinced that the Russians will stop attacking our satellites. I'm not convinced the Russians don't have an attack plan behind this."

Brent said nothing.

"I'm sorry, Marshall," the President said. "I know you tried. I'm thankful to you for your efforts. But it doesn't seem to have worked."

"No, but—"

"We gave them exactly what they needed—more time. They rejected it. Its implication is clear. They'll feel emboldened to do more . . ." The President turned to Curtis. "General, I want a detailed briefing on *Ice Fortress* this afternoon."

"Yes, *sir.*"

"It makes no sense to launch *Ice Fortress,*" Brent continued to argue. The members of the President's Cabinet shifted uncomfortably.

"We've heard all your arguments, Marshall . . ."

"The *Ice Fortress* would be just as vulnerable as the Alpha Omega satellite, wouldn't it, General Curtis? Why launch a seven hundred million dollar target for the Soviets to beat on?"

"Marshall," Ken Mitchell said, "in the case of Omega and the *Javelin,* both vehicles were destroyed by us, not by the laser."

The President looked surprised. "What?"

"Remember, sir, I briefed you on this shortly after the attack on the Midgetman." Mitchell had the look of an impatient schoolmaster. "The

Omega was blinded and damaged, but not destroyed—we lost it when we tried to steer it through the atmosphere in an attempt to recover it intact. The *Javelin* apparently had sustained enough damage to prematurely ignite the third stage booster, but we don't know exactly how much damage was done—it was automatically destroyed when it flew off course."

Brent slapped the table with his hand. "That doesn't answer my—"

"In no case," Curtis cut him off, "was either vehicle shielded against a laser attack. A space station the size of *Ice Fortress,* assembled in space, can be armored to withstand as much direct energy as that nuclear power plant can put out. A beam of laser light, no matter how powerful, is still a beam of light—it can be reflected. I can have the researchers at Wright-Patterson present a more detailed analysis, sir, but *Ice Fortress* can be protected."

"We're betting a lot of money on your analysis, General," Brent said, shaking his head.

"You're worried about the *money,* Mr. Brent—?"

"*No,* dammit," Brent said, exploding. "Mr. President, it's not only the risk of losing the hardware, sir—*Ice Fortress* represents the worst fears about the militarization of space. Can we stand the pressure of world opinion if we launch that thing?"

"I'm more concerned about losing the ability to maintain deterence," Curtis said. "Perhaps you don't understand—we have lost a good percentage of our strategic nuclear deterrent power. Right now, *right this minute,* Mr. Brent, we can't detect a missile launch from eastern Asia. There are twelve submarines docked at Petropavlovsk, each with an average of fifteen sea-launched ballistic missiles. Each of those carry three warheads, maybe more. Mr. Brent, we can't tell if the Russians launch those missiles until they are ten minutes from impact. That's not speculative—that's fact. And the Soviets have demonstrated a capability of destroying *our* missiles in the boost phase. So, if they did launch those missiles, and we retaliated, a good percentage of our missiles wouldn't reach their targets."

Curtis had everyone's attention.

"It may be everyone's image of Armageddon," Curtis concluded, "but we need *Ice Fortress.* The risk of losing it is far outweighed by our need for a bargaining chip."

Brent offered no further argument.

"Marshall, draft a statement of protest to the Kremlin for my signature," the President said. "Get with Karmarov at the U.N. and ask him what the hell is going on. I want the Soviets to *know* they've committed an act of war and that we intend to respond."

"I'd advise against using such language, sir," Brent said.

The President glanced around the Situation Room chamber at the shaking heads. He too shook his head.

"An act of war, Marshall. That's what it is. That's what I said."

The United Nations, Several Weeks Later

It is an act of war!"

Marshall Brent sat back in his seat, turning down the volume of Dmitri Karmarov's tirade on the floor of the United Nations Security Council. Beside him, Gregory Adams took careful notes, penciling in occasional comments.

Karmarov held aloft five books in his hands and waved them in the air for the rest of the Security Council to see. "Five treaties, fellow delegates. The United States has wantonly violated five important treaties with the Soviet Union and with this body. They have wrecked years of vital negotiations that have sought to bring a lasting peace to the world." He threw the books into the aisle in front of him, and the delegate from Rumania quickly reached back to pick them up.

"They are useless. Wasted. Dust." Karmarov waved away the five volumes, pointed a finger at the American delegation. "The militarization of space is not merely a threat to the Soviet Union, fellow representatives. It is a threat to us all. The United States will now continue to build vast machines of destruction orbiting over our heads, over our homes, over our seats of government. This *Ice Fortress* of theirs may now be orbiting over the North Pole, as the Americans claim, but it has the capability to be instantly steered and repositioned anywhere over the Earth. Anywhere. Don't be fooled by comforting assurances. *No one is safe.*

"They say it has no nuclear weapons on board—they even offer to have observers come aboard and examine it, as if it took only a short boatride to get to it. But don't be fooled. They also say their carriers and warships that dock in Japanese ports carry no nuclear weapons, and they are technically correct—until all the critical components are assembled and the weapon is prearmed, no nuclear weapons exist. It is a sham."

150

Karmarov turned toward the American delegation. "I don't care," he said, "what possible reasons the United States could have for launching their *Ice Fortress*. Doubtless, they will blame it on the Soviet Union, as they have blamed so many incidents on us in the past. Doubtless, they will invent another tale of disaster. But there exists no possible reason on this earth for the United States to violate five international agreements and jeopardize the peace and well-being of not only the Soviet Union but of the rest of the world by launching this doomsday device.

"I call upon the United States to immediately deactivate their illegal *Ice Fortress*. Because it appears they cannot be trusted to abide by any agreements between nations, I call upon an independent United Nations team of observers to examine all future Space Shuttle launches to guarantee that they are carrying no weapons of any kind to be used aboard their space platform. I further demand that no corrections be made to the existing platform's orbit so that it may be allowed to reenter the atmosphere and be destroyed."

When Gregory Adams straightened to address the Council, Marshall Brent held his arm. Keeping his hands folded before him on the long, curved table, he glanced around at the assembled delegates and began:

"There comes a time," Brent said, "when international agreements lose meaning. There was a time when the government of the United States felt secure negotiating a lasting peace and true disarmament. Our respective governments hoped against hope that our talks would eventually lead to the elimination of all nuclear weapons from the face of the earth by the year two thousand. I assure you, our government is still willing to continue those negotiations . . . even though we have evidence that the Soviet Union has wantonly attacked American space vehicles, including a satellite, a missile test-firing, and a reconnaissance aircraft with the resultant loss of twelve innocent lives and a billion dollars worth of valuable equipment. We regretfully conclude that the Soviet Union will continue on its reckless course. The evidence is overwhelming, incontrovertible. No treaty of agreement, past, present or future, can oblige us to give up our ability to defend ourselves.

"Our original charges and the evidence we presented to support those charges stand. Absent the desired approval of this body, we must use our own resources to protect ourselves.

"The antiballistic missile space platform will remain until it is demonstrated to our satisfaction that the Soviet Union will cease all attacks against our reconnaissance satellites and aircraft. We ask again that the Soviet Union show its good will by deactivating the Salyut Nineteen orbiting mirror spacecraft immediately. We can wait no longer." He bowed his head, trying to summon additional strength. "I am very sorry, we can wait no longer."

He then stood and quickly left the Security Council, with Gregory Adams following close behind.

The Space Shuttle *Atlantis*

They were in business again.

Navy Commander Richard Seedeck prepared his spacesuit for his upcoming EVA, extravehicular activity—his spacewalk. The forty-two-year-old veteran astronaut, now on his second Shuttle mission, was having the time of his life.

Seedeck had just returned from *Atlantis'* flight deck, where he had been pre-breathing pure oxygen for the past hour. He was now in the airlock, smoothly but quickly putting on his equipment. Jerrod Bates, a civilian defense contractor on board *Atlantis* as an expert advisor and engineer, watched Seedeck put on his suit, marveling at the speed with which he dressed. It always took Bates twice as long to accomplish the same task.

There was nothing like being in space, Seedeck thought, and nothing like being on board the Space Shuttle. No one on board was a passenger—everyone was a crewman, a necessity. Each was busy seventeen hours a day.

And there were fewer "mice and monkey" research flights, too. Like this one. This one was top secret all the way, all heavy-duty military hardware. Even the usual press speculation about the payload was nonexistent—or it had been effectively quashed.

"What are you smiling about, Commander?" Bates finally asked.

"I'm smiling at how good this feels, Bates," Seedeck said, talking through the clear plastic facemask he was wearing. He finished donning the lower torso part of his spacesuit and unbuckled the upper part from a holder in the airlock. Bates reached out to hold the bulky suit for Seedeck to climb into, but that was unnecessary—Seedeck merely let go and weightlessness held the suit exactly where Seedeck had left it.

"I've been doing that for four days now," Bates said through his faceplate. "I forget—nothing falls up here."

"I still do it sometimes," Seedeck admitted. "But I've learned to use it." And he did—Seedeck had his helmet, gloves, his "Snoopy's hat" communication headset and his POS, his portable oxygen system, all floating around the airlock within easy reach.

In one fluid motion, Seedeck held his breath, removed his POS face mask, and slipped into the upper torso part of his suit. If Seedeck started breathing cabin air, he would reintroduce deadly nitrogen into his bloodstream and risk dysbarism, nitrogen narcosis, the "bends"—Bates had also been pre-breathing oxygen for the same reason. Still holding his breath, he attached several umbilicals from the huge life support backpack to his suit and connected the two halves of his suit together, nodding as both he and Bates heard a distinct series of clicks as the unions and interlinks joined.

Bates couldn't believe the brush-cut veteran he was watching. It had been well over two minutes, and Seedeck was still holding his breath and still acting like a kid in a candy store. Seedeck locked on both gloves, put on his "Snoopy's hat" communications headset, locked his helmet in place, and watched the pressure gauge on his chest indicators as the suit pressure gradually increased to 28 kilopascals. When the suit was pressurized and Seedeck had double-checked that there were no leaks, he finally released his breath with a *whoosh*.

"I don't believe it," Bates said as he put on a mid-deck cabin headset to talk to Seedeck. "You went nearly six minutes without breathing."

"You'd be surprised how easy it is after pre-breathing oxygen for an hour," Seedeck said. "Besides, I've done this once or twice before. Check my backpack, please?"

"Sure," Bates said, and double-checked the connections and gauges on Seedeck's suit and gave him a thumbs-up. "It's good."

"Thanks. Clear the airlock. Admiral, this is Seedeck. Preparing to depressurize airlock."

"Copy, Dick," the *Atlantis*' mission commander, Admiral Ben Woods, replied. "Clear any time." Woods repeated the message to Mission Control in Houston five hundred nautical miles below them.

Seedeck turned to the airlock control panel and moved the "AIRLOCK DEPRESS SWITCH" to 5, then to 0, and waited for air to be released outside. Three minutes later, Seedeck was exiting the airlock.

It was a sight he would never get used to—the mind-boggling sight of the Earth spinning above him, the colors, the detail, the sheer size and spectacular beauty of Planet Earth five hundred miles away. *Atlantis* was "parked" right over the North Pole, and Seedeck could see the entire

Northern Hemisphere—the continents of North America, Europe, and Asia, as well as the North Arctic region and the Atlantic and Pacific oceans. Clouds swirled around the globe like gentle strokes of a painter's brush, occasionally knotting and pulsing as a storm brewed below. Because of the Shuttle's normal upside-down orientation, Earth would actually be his "sky" during the entire EVA.

Seedeck closed and locked the airlock hatch, clipped a safety line onto a bracket near the hatch and began working his way hand-over-hand along steel handholds to where *Atlantis'* three MMUs, manned maneuvering units, were attached inside the forward bulkhead of the cargo bay. He inspected one of the bulky, contoured devices, then unclipped it from its mounting harness.

Turning around so his backpack was against the MMU, Seedeck guided himself back against it. He felt his way back with his knees and sides until he heard four distant clicks as the MMU locked itself in place on his backpack.

"MMU in place, *Atlantis.*"

"Copy."

With his safety line still attached, Seedeck made a few test shots from the MMU's thrusters, then unclipped his safety line and moved himself out of the MMU's holder. Pushing gently, he propelled himself away from *Atlantis'* cargo bay and out into space.

"Clear cargo bay, *Atlantis.* Beginning MMU tests."

Seedeck knew that Admiral Woods, who would be watching him from one of the eight cameras installed in the cargo bay and remote manipulator arm, was choking down a protest, but Seedeck had an urge he couldn't ignore and this was his time.

A normal MMU maneuverability test consisted of short distances, short-duration movements, all with a safety tether connected. He was supposed to go up a few feet, stop, do a few side-to-side turns and try some mild pitch-ups, all within a few feet of the airlock hatch and manipulator arm in case of trouble.

Not Seedeck. With his safety line disconnected, Seedeck nudged his thruster controls and performed several loops, barrel rolls, full twists, and lazy-eight maneuvers several meters above the open cargo bay doors.

"MMU maneuvering tests complete," he finally reported as he expertly righted himself above *Atlantis'* cargo bay.

"Very pretty," Woods said. "Too bad NASA isn't broadcasting your performance in prime time."

Seedeck didn't care. There was only one word to describe this feeling—ecstasy. Without a tether line, he was another planetary body in the solar system, orbiting the Sun just like the planets, asteroids, comets, and other satellites around him. He was subject to the same laws, the same divine guiding force as they were.

Seedeck floated for a few moments before bringing his thoughts back to the business at hand. He spotted his objective immediately.

"Inventory in sight, *Atlantis*. Beginning translation."

They weren't allowed to call it anything but "the inventory" on an open radio channel. The *Atlantis* had been parked about six hundred meters away from the huge object, the closest they were allowed to approach it—it would be a short translation, jargon for space-walk, over to it. Seedeck opened a bin in the center of the right side of the cargo bay and extracted the end of a steel cable from its reel mounted on the cargo bay walls, attached the cable to a ring on the left side of his MMU, then maneuvered back into open space and headed for the object floating in the distance.

It was the first time Seedeck had seen it, except of course for photographs and mock-ups. It was a huge steel square, resembling some sort of massive pop-art decoration suspended in space. Each side of the square was a hundred-foot-long, fifteen-foot-square tube. One large rectangular radar antenna, two thousand square feet in area, was mounted on each of two opposite sides of the square, pointing earthward. Mounted on one of the other two sides of the square were two smaller data-transmission dish antennas, one pointing earthward, the other pointing spaceward. On the remaining side was an eighteen-inch diameter cylinder twelve feet long with a large glass eye at one end, also pointing to Earth. Enclosed within heavily armored containers on the four sides of the square were fuel cells, rocket fuel tanks, fuel lines, and other connectors and control units running throughout the steel frame.

Mounted in the center of the square was a huge cylinder, seventy feet in diameter and thirty feet long, armored and covered in shiny aluminum—*Atlantis* had to move its position now and then to keep the brilliant reflection of the sun from ruining its cameras. The spaceward end was closed, but the earthward side had a removable armor cover that revealed five fifteen-foot-diameter tubes, earthlight reflecting around the shining, polished walls inside, all empty.

This was *Ice Fortress*.

In all the articles, presentations, and drawings, it looked like a Rube Goldberg tinker-toy contraption, but out here in position it looked awesome and as mean as hell. The two large radar antennas, Seedeck knew, were target-tracking radars searching for sea- or land-launched intercontinental ballistic missiles. The smaller dish antennas were data-link antennas, one for transmitting steering signals from the platform, the other for receiving target tracking data from surveillance satellites at higher orbits around earth. The large cylinder with the glass eye was an infrared detector and tracker designed to search and follow the exhaust of an ICBM in the boost phase. The radars could track warhead carriers, "busses," in the midphase or even individual reentering warheads as they plunged through the atmosphere, and it could even differentiate between decoy warheads and the real thing.

The large center cylinder was the "projectile" container, which housed the launch tubes for *Ice Fortress'* weapons. The entire station was armored in heat-resistant carbon-carbon steel, and smooth surfaces and critical components like the missile cylinder covers and fuel tanks were also covered in reflective aluminum film. Seedeck had heard rumors about all these strange additions to *Ice Fortress,* but that wasn't his concern.

Seedeck's job today was to make *Ice Fortress* operational for the first time.

The station was almost a military unit unto itself, Seedeck thought as he completed his inspection of *Ice Fortress.* The station received missile-launch detection information from orbiting surveillance satellites that would tell *Ice Fortress* where to look for the missiles. The station could use either its radars or its heat-sensing infrared detectors to locate and track the rockets as they rose through the atmosphere. *Ice Fortress* would then launch its "projectiles" against ICBMs heading toward North America.

Projectiles. Weird name for *Ice Fortress* weapons, Seedeck thought. *Ice Fortress* carried five X-ray laser satellites. The satellites consisted of a main reaction chamber and fifteen lead pulse rods encasing a zinc lasing wire surrounding it, like knitting needles in a ball of yarn. The reaction chamber was, in essence, a twenty kiloton uranium bomb—roughly equal to the destructive power of the first atom bomb that exploded over Hiroshima.

Ice Fortress sensors would track any attacking intercontinental ballistic missiles and eject the X-ray laser satellites toward them. When the satellite approached the missiles, *Ice Fortress* would detonate the nuclear warhead within the satellite. The nuclear explosion would create a massive wave of X-rays that would be focused and concentrated through the pulse rods. The X-ray energy would create an extremely powerful laser burst that would travel down the rods and out in all directions. Any object within a hundred miles of the satellite would be bombarded into oblivion in milliseconds. The explosion, would, of course, destroy the satellite, but the awesome power of the X-ray laser blast would decimate dozens, perhaps hundreds, of ICBMs or warheads at one time—a very potent and, if nothing else, cost-effective device.

Seedeck knew a lot about the X-ray laser satellites that would be used with *Ice Fortress*—the *Atlantis* carried five of them in her cargo bay, and it would be Seedeck's job to load them into the launch cylinder on *Ice Fortress.*

Seedeck now attached the cable to the front of the central launch cylinder and turned back toward *Atlantis.* While Seedeck had been inspecting *Ice Fortress,* Bates had been putting on his own spacesuit and was just emerging from the airlock when Seedeck completed his inspection.

"Seedeck to *Atlantis.* The inventory appears OK. No damage. We'll be ready to proceed at any time."

"Copy," Woods replied.

"This is Bates. I copy." Bates had moved into *Atlantis'* cargo bay and had begun to unlock the canisters containing the partially disassembled *Ice Fortress* satellites. His job would be to remove the mountains of packing material from the satellites, then reassemble the component parts. It would not become an actual nuclear device until reassembly, and it would not even be possible to arm it until it was installed in its launch tube on *Ice Fortress.*

Meanwhile, Seedeck had returned to *Atlantis.* He maneuvered over to the cable reel and activated its motor, tightening the cable. He double-checked the controls. To avoid breaking the cable, a friction clutch device would keep the cable tight during small shifts in distance or motion between *Atlantis* and *Ice Fortress* and an emergency disconnect button would open the pawl on *Ice Fortress* and release the cable. The release could be activated by Bates from the cargo bay, by Seedeck from *Ice Fortress,* or by Woods inside *Atlantis.* Seedeck then attached a plastic saddle onto the cable that rode along it on a Teflon track.

"Guide ready, *Atlantis,* " Seedeck reported. He carefully maneuvered closer above Bates, who was putting the finishing touches on the first X-ray laser satellite. The satellite, its lead-zinc rods folded along its sides, was well over ten feet in diameter and, at least on earth, weighed over a ton; Bates handled the massive object like a beachball.

"Ready," Bates said, and unhooked the remaining strap holding the huge satellite from its stowage cradle in the cargo bay. Using a hydraulic lift on the cradle, Bates raised the cradle a few inches, then suddenly stopped it. The satellite continued to float up out of the cargo bay and right into Seedeck's waiting arms.

Seedeck grabbed a handhold on the satellite and steered it easily toward the saddle. As if he had been doing this procedure all his life, he expertly clamped the cylindrical satellite onto the saddle and steadied it along the cable. Although the satellite was weightless, Seedeck was careful not to forget that the thing still had two thousand pounds' worth of mass to corral—it was hard to get it to stop moving once it got going. He attached a safety line between the saddle and the satellite, and the satellite was secured.

"Heading toward the inventory with number one," Seedeck reported. Despite himself, Bates had to chuckle at the sight. Seedeck had maneuvered over the satellite and had sat down on top of it, as if he were sitting on a huge tom-tom drum. He was gripping the satellite with his boots and knees, riding atop five hundred pounds of high explosives and ninety-eight pounds of uranium. One tiny nudge on his right-hand MMU control, and he and the satellite slid along the two-thousand-foot-long cable toward *Ice Fortress.*

It turned out to be a very efficient way of getting the X-ray laser satellite to the platform. In two minutes, Seedeck and his mount eased their way toward *Ice Fortress,* carefully slowing to a stop with gradual spurts of the MMU's nitrogen-gas thrusters. As Woods and the crew of *Atlantis* watched through telephoto closed-circuit cameras, Seedeck jetted away from the satellite, maneuvered underneath it, unhooked the safety strap and latch, and slid the satellite away from the saddle. Seedeck gave the saddle a push, and it skittered back down the cable to *Atlantis.*

Using a set of utility arms mounted on the MMU, Seedeck guided the satellite toward the open center launcher. With the ease acquired from several days practicing the maneuver in the huge NASA training pool in Texas, Seedeck guided the device straight into the launcher. Once the laser satellite was inserted a few feet into the tube, a pair of fingerlike clips latched onto the satellite and pulled it back into the tube. Seedeck waited until he felt a faint CLICK as the unobtrusive yet frightening device seated itself against the arming plate at the back of the tube.

"*Atlantis,* this is Seedeck. Confirm number one latched into position."

"Stand by," Woods told him. He relayed the request to Mission Control. The answer came back a few moments later.

"Seedeck, this is *Atlantis.* Control confirms number one in position."

"Roger, *Atlantis.* Returning to Orbiter."

It took Seedeck two minutes to return to *Atlantis'* cargo bay, where Bates had another satellite ready for him. The saddle had slid the two thousand feet all the way back to *Atlantis* with Seedeck's one little push.

"Seedeck is back in the bay, Admiral," Bates reported.

"Copy. Stand by." Woods relayed to Houston that no one was near *Ice Fortress.*

A few minutes later Woods reported: "Control reports full connectivity. The inventory is on-line. Good job, Rich. You're hustling out there."

Seedeck nodded as Bates gave him a thumbs-up. The *Ice Fortress* was now operational. It was America's first strategic defense device, the first of the "Star Wars" weapons—and the first time nuclear weapons had been placed in orbit around the Earth.

"Forty-five minutes from start to finish each," Seedeck said. "should be done by dinnertime."

"It's my turn to cook," Admiral Woods said. "Thermostabilized beef with barbecue sauce, rehydratable cauliflower with cheese, irradiated green beans with mushrooms. Yum."

"I ordered the quarter-pounder with cheese, Admiral," Seedeck protested. Bates was smiling as he watched the navy commander maneuver the second X-ray laser satellite onto the saddle. Moments later, Seedeck was riding along the cable toward the menacing latticework square in the distance.

"That's the one thing I miss up here," Bates said as he turned back toward unpacking and reassembling the next satellite.

Bates noticed the first light, a bright deep flash of orange that illuminated everything. It got brighter and brighter until it flooded out his eyesight, then turned to bright white. It was as if Seedeck had come back and pushed him in the side, rolling him over, or as if Seedeck had slid the saddle back along the cable and it had come back and hit him in the backpack. Bates wasn't wearing a MMU, but he was secured to the forward bulkhead of *Atlantis* above the airlock hatch by his tether. There was no sound, no trace of anything actually *wrong*. It felt . . . playful, in a way. It was easy to forget you were in space. The work was so easy, everything was so quiet. It felt *playful—*

Bates spun upside down and slammed against the left forward corner of the cargo bay. Some invisible hand held him pinned against the bulkhead. The only sound he heard was a hiss over his headset. He tried to blink away the stars that squeezed across his vision.

He opened his eyes. Seedeck and the second X-ray laser satellite were gone.

"*Atlantis,* this is Bates . . ." Nothing. Only a hiss. He found it hard to breathe. The pressure wasn't hurting him, only squeezing him tight—like a strong hug . . .

"*Atlantis . . . ?*"

"Seedeck. Rich, answer." It was Woods. The hiss had subsided, replaced by Admiral Woods on the command radio.

"*Atlantis,* this is Bates. What's wrong? What—?"

An even brighter flash of light, a massive globe of red-orange light that seemed to dull even the brilliant glow of the Earth itself. Bates opened his eyes, and a cry forced itself to his lips.

A brilliant shaft of light a dozen feet in diameter appeared from nowhere. It was as if someone had drawn a thick line of light from Earth across to *Ice Fortress.* The silvery surface of *Ice Fortress'* armor seemed to take on the same weird red-orange glow, then the beam of light disappeared.

A split-second later a terrific explosion erupted from the open end of the launch cylinder aboard *Ice Fortress.* A tongue of fire several yards long spit from the earthward side of the station. Sparks and arcs of electricity sputtered from one of the spindly sides, and *Ice Fortress* started a slow, lazy roll backward, sending showers of sparks and debris flying in all directions. Bates ducked as the cable connecting *Atlantis* to the space station snapped back and hit the forward bulkhead of the cargo bay.

Bates' voice was a scream. "Commander Seedeck. Oh, God . . ."

"Mission Control, this is *Atlantis* . . ." Bates heard Admiral Woods' report. "We have lost *Ice Fortress.* Repeat, we have lost *Ice Fortress.* Bright orange light, then massive explosion. One crewman missing."

"This is Bates. What's—?"

"Bates, this is Admiral Woods. Where are you? You all right?"

Bates reached up with his left hand for one of the handholds on the forward bulkhead, found that the pressure was all but gone.

"I fell into the cargo bay. I'm okay—" Just then a sword of pain stabbed into his skull and he cried out into the open communications panel.

"Bates . . . ?"

Bates looked down. The lower part of his left leg was sticking out at a peculiar angle from his body.

"Oh God . . . I think I broke my leg."

"Can you make it to the airlock?"

"Admiral, this is Connors. I can suit up and—"

"Not if you haven't been pre-breathing," Woods told him. "Everyone, make a fast station check, report any damage, then get on the cameras. Find Seedeck. Connors, Matsumo, get a POS and start pre-breathing. Bates, can you make it back to the airlock?"

Bates grabbed the handhold. He expected a tough time hauling himself upright but suddenly found he had to keep from flinging himself up out of the cargo bay in his weightless condition. Slowly, he began to haul himself back toward the airlock hatch.

"Bates, what happened out there?"

"God, it looked like . . . like one of the damn *projectiles* detonated," Bates said as he crawled for the airlock. The X-ray laser satellites had numerous safety devices to prevent an accidental nuclear detonation, but the reaction chamber needed a big explosion to start the atomic chain reaction, and those explosives had no safety devices. Something, some massive burst of energy, had set off the five hundred pounds of high explosives in the satellite's reaction chamber.

Just as he safely reached the airlock, Bates looked back to *Ice Fortress*. It took him a moment to spot it again, several hundred yards from where it had been a few moments before. It was lazily, almost playfully spinning away, its radars and antennae and electronic eyes and spindly arms flopping about as if it was waving goodbye. Occasionally a shower of sparks erupted from its surface. And a trail of debris hovered in its wake, as if it were dropping crumbs on the trail to help find its way back . . .

Commander Richard Seedeck left nothing. Nothing was left of him.

WASHINGTON, D.C.

The President examined a large wall-sized chart projected on the rear wall of the White House Situation Room. He ran a finger over the black line, making sure it ran right through Kavaznya. The line wasn't quite straight—drawn by a computer, the Great Circle course was a series of straight lines representing dozens of heading changes. But it was the shortest distance, the President knew, to an encounter that now seemed unavoidable.

General Wilbur Curtis and his aide stood behind their chairs watching the President. Curtis knew that the President was looking at something no other American president had ever seen—a chart of an actual peacetime attack plan against the Soviet Union. Even though hundreds of such plans existed, none had ever been presented to the President for his direct approval.

After quickly examining the chart, the President took his seat at the head of the oval table. Curtis kept watching the President as the other advisers all took their seats after him. Dark rings had formed around the President's eyes, he was noticeably thinner, and his shoulders drooped.

Well, it was a terrible strain on all of them, because this young President relied so heavily on his advisors in foreign affairs. He was extremely effective when it came to domestic problems and he was immensely popular at home, but overseas it was a different matter. He and his Cabinet had tried to convince the world that the Soviet Union was threatening the United States, *trying* to provoke a conflict—but few believed him, mostly because they were afraid to find out it was the truth. The consequences of that were too scary. The war of words had reduced Secretary of State Marshall Brent as well. His usual polish and spirit were noticeably dimmed.

Now, the laser had taken another life, and the President was looking at what he feared most—a direct assault against Kavaznya. In the U.S.S.R. . . .

Assembled were his National Security Council, his Cabinet and the Joint Chiefs of Staff. They had already held a hastily formed meeting of their own. Now it was time for them to present the plan they had come up with.

"Let's have it, General," the President said, prompting the chairman of the Joint Chiefs. Wilbur Curtis nodded and stood.

"Yes, sir," the general began. "Two B-1B *Excaliburs* from the new Tenth Bombardment Wing at Ellsworth Air Force Base will execute this mission. Yesterday they were flown from Dreamland, where they were undergoing design modification, to Ellsworth, where each was armed with two AGM-130 *Striker* TV-infrared-guided bombs. Per your order, sir. It's the largest non-nuclear standoff weapon in our arsenal. It uses a small strap-on rocket motor to glide as far as fifteen miles from a low-altitude release, and it has the explosive power of one ton of TNT. The bombardier can steer it to its target using a TV eye in the nose, or it can lock-on to a target with an infrared seeker."

"Two *Strikers*, General?"

"An added insurance factor, sir. Two weapons targeted for the same point. If the first weapon fails to detonate, the second, impacting five seconds later, will take out the target. If the first works, the second bomb will be destroyed in the blast. The second aircraft insures destruction of the primary target and has the additional task of air defense suppression."

There was a rustle of uneasiness, even from those who had been in on the entire Kavaznya crisis from the start. This was not an exercise or simulation Curtis was talking about.

"The bombers have been equipped with the standard coded switch and permissive-action-link security arrangements," Curtis continued. "Those are the electronic switches between the weapons and the bombardiers' control panels. We're treating the *Strikers* just like nuclear weapons—no prearming or launch possible without a coded strike message from you, sir, transmitted via satellite communications or normal UHF traffic and entered into those switches. Two of the most experienced *Excalibur* crews will fly the missions—both senior Standardization-Evaluation crews. They've been briefed and are standing by.

"The aircraft will follow the routing as shown," Curtis said, pointing to the large computer-drawn chart. "From Ellsworth, they'll fly through Canada and then through Alaska. They'll be refueled by two KC-10 tankers out of Eielson Air Force Base, then proceed northward to the Arctic Ocean. They'll orbit just north of Point Barrow, in their SNOW-

TIME exercise orbit area, and wait for your first authorization message. The SAC Green Pine communications center at Point Barrow will relay the message.

"They will not be allowed to prearm the weapons at this point. If they are ordered to remain in this orbit area, it will appear to any outside observers as just another SNOWTIME arctic defense exercise. SAC holds them several times a year. Both the Russians and the Canadians are accustomed to our bombers orbiting the Arctic Ocean on training missions.

"If they receive the first strike authorization, the aircraft will continue southwest to approximately sixty-seven degrees north latitude, escorted by the second group of KC-10 tankers. They will orbit in open airspace over the Chukchi Sea, north of Siberia, and wait for the second strike authorization message—if we haven't transmitted both messages at the same time. If they receive the second authorization, they finish their final refueling and head toward the target."

"How accustomed are outside observers to bombers orbiting so close to Russia?" Secretary of Defense Thomas Preston asked. "That's not one of our usual operating areas."

"True, sir," Curtis replied. "But the B-1s will still be well outside Russian radar coverage and still well within international airspace. It's unlikely they will even be spotted. If the Russians do detect them, they may be suspicious, but we feel it's unlikely they will mount any counterforce. Air defense forces are extremely light this far north."

"Any chance of that laser attacking the B-1s?" the President asked. He still could not believe the explanation he had been given for why the laser had managed to knock out *Ice Fortress.* By timing their attack when they did, the Russians had managed to hit the space platform when the X-ray satellite launch cylinder was open and exposed. Had they waited only a few hours later, all the X-ray satellites would have been armed and the cylinder would have been closed.

"No chance, sir." The President looked skeptical.

"The Soviets have to find a target before they can hit it, sir. The B-1s won't be in range of the main tracking radar at Kavaznya until much later, within twenty or thirty miles of the target—they'll be terrain-masking in the mountains along the Kamchatka peninsula until then—and by the time the radar does spot them they'll be within range of the *Striker* glide-bomb."

"But the orbiting mirror?"

"They used the orbiting mirror against an ICBM four hundred miles up," Curtis said. "An ICBM with its motors running and red-hot climbing through the atmosphere is an easy target to be tracked by infrared-seeking satellites, and the Soviets have a data-link setup with the laser to attack ICBMs tracked by satellite. An aircraft flying only seven miles high can't be tracked accurately by an enemy satellite. They can't hit what they can't see. But if they somehow *did* fire the laser against the B-1s, we feel the dissipation of heat from shooting through the atmosphere, then reflecting the beam down through the atmosphere again would dilute the energy sufficiently for the aircraft to escape. No, sir, the B-1s are safe from the laser until close to Kavaznya. Then, the standoff range of the *Strikers* will keep them away from the laser. The laser should be destroyed before it can get a shot off."

Curtis now moved his pointer down into Asia. "Our people encounter little resistance or even chance of detection until fairly close to the target. They drop to low altitude just prior to crossing the north coast of Sibera, just before entering high-altitude warning radar coverage around the town of Ust-Chaun, but they can return to high altitude all across eastern Siberia to save fuel until approaching the northern edge of the Kamchatka peninsula. They drop to terrain-following altitudes down the Korakskiy and Sredinny mountain ranges to the target."

Curtis changed the slide, showing a greatly enlarged overhead photograph. "This is the latest satellite reconnaissance photo we have of Kavaznya, Mr. President, taken early last year. The B-1's primary target is here." Curtis switched to an even more highly magnified view.

"This is the mirror housing, a large dome maybe forty feet in diameter from which, the CIA believes, the laser beam is projected into space. Two *Strikers* will be programmed to impact here. Another glide-bomb is programmed for the main laser tracking radar, and another is programmed for Ossora Airfield north and east of Kavaznya.

"As you can see, sir, the mirror housing is very isolated—the rest of the complex, except for the nuclear power plant, is underground. The nuclear power plant is considered an alternate target. If the crew experiences—"

"*No,*" the President said. "Not the power plant, for God's sake. We might as well drop a nuke on them if we destroy a nuclear power plant. I won't be blamed for another Chernobyl. No alternative target. If the B-1s can't attack the mirror dome, they don't go."

Curtis, not altogether happy with that, nodded, then again switched to a map of the North Pacific. "After their attack, the B-1s get back into the mountains and stay there at terrain-following altitudes until they exit low altitude radar coverage, then cross the water toward Alaska. Possible landing sites are Attu, Shemya, Elmendorf, and Eielson.

"After landing, they'll refuel and return to Ellsworth . . . undoubtedly they will be regenerated and put on hard SIOP strategic nuclear alert."

"If the base still exists," someone muttered.

The President stared at the sortie chart. "It seems too . . . easy," the President muttered.

"I beg your pardon, Mr. President?"

"It seems too simple," the President said, not much louder. Curtis strained to hear. "Where are the defenses? You've told me for years about stiff Russian air defenses. Here . . . there's no threat?"

"The target area is still heavily defended, the defenses include—"

"The *Excaliburs* can make it, General?" the President interrupted. "They can get in?"

Curtis turned to Lieutenant-General Bradley James Elliott, who stood and faced the President.

"General Elliott," the President said. "Good to see you again. Well, what's your opinion, Brad? Can they make it?"

"I think so, sir. With the new equipment we've tested at Dreamland and built into these B-1s, they should stand a hell of a chance. At low altitude, the Russians won't even see the *Excaliburs* until forty, fifty, maybe sixty nautical miles from the target. At nine miles a minute, the *Excaliburs* will be on top of them before fighters could ever launch—and at two hundred feet in the mountains it'll be impossible to find them. If they are attacked the *Excaliburs* have the fuel reserves for a supersonic sprint across the target, and they have specialized jammers, antiradar missiles, and even flying decoys to handle surface-to-air missiles. But the *Strikers* will be launched fifteen miles from the laser facility, so the B-1's can stay in the mountains all the way."

The President looked away and stared at the enlarged photograph of Kavaznya, then turned back to his advisers.

"I know what you're thinking. This attack, the last thing any of us have wanted even to consider, now looks as if it will happen . . . our repeated attempts in the past few days to move the Soviets from their inflexible position have failed. Diplomatic channels remain open and it's still my hope that Secretary Brent will somehow get a commitment from the Soviets that will let me order these B-1s to scrub their mission. But if he doesn't and I am forced to give the strike order, I want it very clear to everyone that what we will be conducting is, in a real sense, a police action. Every effort has been made to control and contain the scope of this mission. We do *not* want war with the Soviets. We do *not* want a nuclear exchange. But we must face the fact that the existence of the laser facility and the Soviet Union's policy of a peacetime quarantine of Asia will eventually cripple our ability to defend ourselves against attack or to mount a second strike in reprisal. We must, it seems, take this action now, with its inherent risks, to avoid the certainty of far greater risks later . . . General Curtis, go over the fail-safe procedures again."

The Chairman of the Joint Chiefs stood. "Sir, we need a direct order from you to launch the two bombers, a second one to allow them to proceed past the established SNOWTIME arctic exercise orbit area they usually operate in, and we need a third, separate order to allow the bombers to cross the fail-safe point and prearm their missiles. The third message is their authorization to strike.

"Bombers will continuously monitor SATCOM and HF radios for coded recall or termination instructions, and they can be recalled at any time. They cannot proceed on their missions unless they have two one-hundred-percent operable missiles and an aircraft that meets their tactical doctrine specifications. Our communications satellites will be programmed to automatically transmit a recall message every half hour *unless* we instruct them *not* to. So if communications are disrupted the mission will automatically terminate."

The President nodded, looked around the room. No one else offered any comment or suggestion. After an unendurably long moment, the President reached down and opened the red-covered folder prepared for him the day before. He broke the seal and reviewed the document inside authorizing the first step of Curtis' plan.

DREAMLAND

Patrick McLanahan was sitting alone in the semidarkness of his cramped, rickety wooden barracks room when he heard a faint knock on the door. He smiled and opened it.

Standing in the doorway, wearing a dark gray flight jacket, flight suit, and insulated winter flying boots just like his own, was his partner, Dave Luger. Luger had his hands thrust in his pockets and was scuffling the sand around with his toes.

"Ready to go, Muck?" he said, still poking around in the dirt.

McLanahan glanced at his watch and looked at the sky. "Oh-seven-hundred hours," he said. "You're a bit late, aren't you?" Luger checked his watch and shrugged.

"What difference does it make?" Last two days, there hasn't been any reason to be on time. All we've been doing is sitting on our behinds."

McLanahan had turned to pick up his jacket, which was slung over the bedpost behind him. "Wait a minute," he said, glancing over his shoulder. "What am I hearing? Is this the same guy who has been bitching for the past two months about the hours we've been putting in? The same guy who every night for three weeks threatened to strangle me for arranging it so he'd be brought here to Dreamland?"

Luger fell into his ever-familiar gunfighter's slouch. "Yeah, well, I still don't have fond memories of Lieutenant Briggs barging in on me while I was with Sharon to say that I was going to be taking a little trip. And having that prima donna Anderson on my ass fourteen hours a day hasn't been any picnic either. But ever since those B-1s lit out for Ellsworth two days ago, it's been boring as hell. I mean, what the hell is there to do if you're not in the simulator or out on a training jaunt?"

"Not a damn thing," McLanahan said as he closed the door to his room and locked it. Actually, that wasn't true, he thought. He *had* been able to spend more time with Wendy these past couple days, and was thankful for that. It was the first real chance he'd had since she came back with the other civilians working on the project to get past that stony facade she put up and find out what she was about. Before these past two days, even in their late-night study sessions together, she had stayed detached. Now, after spending some relaxed hours with her, he understood better the reason for her detachment. She wanted first and foremost to be accepted as a professional, as someone who could step into *any* man's role and perform with maximum efficiency. He guessed she'd had a tough time in this male-dominated Air Force world, and that concealing a part of herself—the part that was soft and feminine—had after a while become an automatic defense. He couldn't help comparing her to Catherine, whose privileged upbringing had made her much more self-assured and outgoing and yet . . . well, less interesting . . .

"Hey, Pat," Luger said as they walked to the briefing shack, "why do you suppose Elliott called a meeting this morning? Think he's going to give us our walking papers?"

"Maybe it's more than that."

"What do you mean?"

McLanahan continued walking. They were nearing the women's barracks. "Well, it seems to me that we wouldn't have spent all that time testing out that equipment on the Old Dog, and then installing equivalent systems in those B-1s, if the B-1s weren't being used for *something.* Maybe something big. Take that terrain cartridge we were testing before the B-1s left. Well, Bill Dalton, the nav for Zero-Six-Four, said something about it corresponding to an area over the Sarir Calanscio Desert in Libya. That's complete bull. Those planes will be flying through the mountains."

Both men were silent for a moment, lost in their own thoughts. "Hey, there's Wendy and Angelina," Luger said, spotting the two coming out of the women's barracks. He waved to them and the four joined up a few yards short of the briefing shack.

"I see we're not the only ones who're late," Angelina Pereira said with a smile. She was the only one of them not wearing a flight suit.

Nice lady, McLanahan thought to himself. Nice *and* tough. She reminded him a little bit of his mother. He nodded toward Luger. "Dave here had to get his beauty sleep. Good buddy that I am, I decided to wait for him."

Wendy looked worried. "Pat," she said, "do you have any idea why General Elliott called us together?"

McLanahan shrugged. "I expect we'll find out soon enough," he said as he opened the door to the shack.

***

General Bradley Elliott removed a pair of sunglasses and looked out over his captive audience. He wore a thick green nylon winter-weight flight jacket over a set of standard starched Air Force fatigues with subdued green and black name tags, a subdued Strategic Air Command patch, and subdued black stars on his collar. He propped himself on a desk at the front of the room and twirled his sunglasses absently.

"Well, I'm glad that all of you have seen fit to put in an appearance," Elliott said. "Even if a bit late." He looked at the four stragglers who had just entered the room.

"I've called all of you here," he said, "to provide some explanation for the events of the past two days, and of the past few months. As most of you have surmised, the improvements and modifications we made in those two *Excaliburs* were not implemented on the off chance that they might prove of use at some future date. They were carried out with a definite purpose in mind."

Elliott paused to stare at the faces around the room. Directly in front of him, Colonel James Anderson sat straight in his chair. To his immediate left was Lewis Campos, his forehead shiny with sweat. At the back of the room, Patrick McLanahan sat staring at the floor, his legs straight out.

"Ladies and gentlemen," Elliott said, "approximately twenty-five minutes ago two B-1s—the B-1s you've worked on these past few months—took off from Ellsworth Air Force Base. They are launching as part of a possible strike force on an area in the Soviet Union."

There was a collective gasp from those in the room. McLanahan felt suddenly sick to his stomach. He looked over at Luger and shook his head.

"I said *possible.* They'll orbit in narrowing circles near Russia while the politicians still work for a negotiated solution. If there isn't one, the B-1s go in . . ."

"A negotiated solution to *what?*" Lewis Campos asked, his voice rising above other whispered comments.

"Quiet down, people," Elliott said, opened his locked briefcase, extracted a series of photographs and handed them to Colonel John Ormack, who passed each to his left.

"The photographs that are being circulated," Elliott went on, "show a facility that has been built in the Soviet Union in a small fishing village called Kavaznya. The Soviets have built an actual anti-satellite and anti-ballistic missile laser there. In the past few months they've been *using* it."

"On what?" Dave Luger asked as McLanahan studied the satellite reconnaissance photographs. "There hasn't been anything in the news—"

"And there won't be," General Elliott interrupted. "Injecting public sentiment into the situation could make it more volatile than it already is. The fact of the matter is that the Kavaznya laser has proved very effective. Although the Russians haven't even admitted the presence of the weapon, it has destroyed over five billion dollars worth of American equipment and has taken thirteen lives."

"My God," Luger said, reflecting the collective sentiment.

"Our job is nearly finished here," Elliott continued. "I'll want all of you to stand by for the next few hours in the unlikely event SAC command needs your input on some aspect of the B-1s' gear that may not be functioning correctly, but after that you'll be free to go. I've already had the Transportation office arrange your flights back. You also are ordered not to reveal a word of what I have just told you. You all have top-security clearance, and I felt you were entitled to know what you've been a part of. Knowing should also make you acutely aware of the necessity of not revealing to anyone ever what you have been doing here."

Suddenly the door to the briefing shack was thrown open and Lieutenant Harold Briggs hurried into the room. He halted two steps away from Elliott. "General," Briggs said, "we've got a problem."

Elliott's face turned pale. He noticed that Briggs was wearing his short-barreled Uzi submachine pistol mounted on a shoulder harness, and that the harness had three hand grenades clipped into it. "Hal?"

"Got a report of a light airplane that dropped off radar coverage into the area a few minutes ago, General," Briggs said. "Ridge-hopped in from Vegas, we think. We've got security patrolling the area from Dreamland on out."

"Did it make it into Dreamland?" Elliott asked. The odds against it were tremendous—any kind of aircraft over a few hundred pounds in weight would be picked up by a dozen different sensors patrolling the desert.

"We're anticipating the worst."

Luger and McLanahan were already out of their chairs. Anderson was leaning forward, ready to move on Elliott's order.

"James," he said, "get your people over to the Old Dog's hangar right away. They'll be safer there."

Anderson nodded and turned to the others. "All right, you heard the General. Let's get moving."

As McLanahan hurriedly led Wendy out of the briefing shack and over to the Old Dog's black hangar, he heard the sound of gunfire and explosions. Looking to his left, he noticed a billowing cloud of smoke at the entrance to the compound.

"Holy shit," Luger said behind him, "we're under attack!"

In less than half a minute each member of the Old Dog test team was in the hangar and McLanahan was bolting the door. He had just turned away from the door and was heading into the bowels of the hangar when he heard a pounding outside and Elliott's voice. He opened the door for General Elliott and Briggs.

"It's more serious than we thought," Elliott told Anderson, who had moved forward to join them. "You must—"

He never finished. The first explosion was felt rather than seen. Its impact point was on the far corner of the black hangar, on the roof. To Elliott, it felt as if the entire four-acre roof above their heads was vibrating like a sheet of tin.

Elliott and Ormack were thrown off their feet by the shock wave. Anderson tumbled against the Old Dog's front wheels, landing on his head and shoulders.

Briggs managed to stay on his feet. Still gripping his Uzi, he helped Elliott up off the hangar floor.

"Take cover, General," Briggs said as the second explosion came, three times more powerful than the first. A fifty-foot hole was blown into the roof a hundred feet from the Old Dog's left wingtip, showering the wing with bits of metal and concrete. The wall beneath the hole ripped open as if someone had pulled a giant zipper down the side of the black hangar all the way to the ground. An acetylene line burst and flames shot skyward. Automatic gunfire erupted outside the open mouth of the hangar. The opening was filled with running workers and armed security police trying to spot the attackers and dodge the stampede of terrified workers. Bodies began to fall.

Elliott shook debris out of his hair and struggled to clear his eyes and throat of dust and gas. He turned and saw the first impact point on the far corner, the second right beside the bomber, and the gunfire outside the hangar. He did not need to be a general to realize that the next mortar round was going to be right over their heads and that more bodies were going to pile up outside.

"John." He grabbed Ormack and put his mouth next to his ear. "Get aboard. Start 'em up."

"What?"

"The engines. Start 'em up. Get this thing *moving.*"

"Moving?"

"Taxi the goddamn plane out of here, they're going to blow this place apart. *Move.*" He shoved Ormack toward the hatch. Ormack tumbled to the polished concrete floor, and for a split second Elliott thought he wasn't going to get up. Then Ormack scrambled up on his hands and knees, found the boarding hatch, and climbed inside.

"Campos, Pereira." He found the defensive systems operator and his assistant stumbling around the bomber's right wing, bumping into the

Scorpion pylon, not sure which way to turn or run. Elliott grabbed them both by the necks, ducked them under the bomber's belly. "Get aboard."

Angelina reacted instantly, scrambling up the ladder. Campos, confused, watched as his assistant disappeared inside. He turned to Elliott.

"No, I can't—"

"Get up there, goddammit."

"I won't get into that thing." Campos used his bony elbows and fists and broke free, bolted toward the open hangar door, ignoring bursts of gunfire erupting all around him. He crashed against the edge of the hangar opening and paused, then turned and took one last look at the black bomber.

"Campos," Elliott ordered, "take cover . . ."

Too late. Just as Elliott called out Campos turned and ran outside. As he turned, a third explosion tore into the front of the black hangar, ripping out the entire left side of the building, and Campos disappeared in a blinding flash of light and a screech of burning, shattering metal. The left side of the hangar opening sagged and crashed to the floor.

Elliott could only watch and duck as the hangar opening crashed down and bullets whistled around him. He turned and saw Anderson just getting to his feet at the front of the plane, his head and face bleeding.

Elliott hurried over to help Anderson climb aboard the bomber. He felt a sting on his right calf, reached down and his hand came back covered with blood. He put his right leg down to stop himself and see what was wrong. It refused to support his weight and he sagged helplessly to the floor.

"General," Anderson said, crawling over to where Elliott lay bleeding, "we've got to get out . . ." One of Anderson's eyes refused to stay steady, rolling from side to side.

"Get on board," Elliott ordered. A high-pitched scream issued from the number four engine. Anderson turned and saw exhaust fumes bellowing from the nacelle.

"The engines . . . they're starting . . ."

"Ormack's on board. Get going." Elliott noticed a huge gash on Anderson's head, struggled to push himself off the floor to help Anderson get to the hatch. The scream of the engine changed to a roar, and soon the number five engine sounded.

"Jim . . . hurry . . ." Elliott managed to rise to his left leg. As he did a line of six red holes, big as quarters, appeared on Anderson's gray flight suit from his collar bone to right thigh. Anderson did not seem to notice. He continued to walk toward the open hatch, then stumbled into the bomber's sleek black side and crashed to the floor, leaving a red streak on the Old Dog's polished surface.

Suddenly Hall Briggs was beside Elliott, firing his automatic pistol one-handed at whatever moved outside. Again he dragged the general to his feet, the Uzi smoking in his right fist. "We've got to get you on the plane, General—"

"No, I've got—"

"Get on that plane."

"Chocks . . . got to disconnect the—"

"I've done all that, General. Chocks, air, power, pins, streamers. Now get your ass on board."

Briggs fired at a running figure in the doorway, then hauled the resisting general up into the hatch, where a pair of hands—McLanahan's—grabbed the general by the lapels of his fatigues and hauled his feet clear of the hatch.

"Briggs," Elliott yelled. "Get up here, *now.*"

McLanahan put Elliott's hands on the ladder, and the general realized what he had and pulled himself painfully up to the upper deck. McLanahan then turned back to the open hatch and extended a hand to Briggs, who was on one knee, firing into the distance.

"Get on board, you jerk," McLanahan said.

"Not my plane, my friend," he said as a loud ringing started in McLanahan's ears. *"Adios."*

Briggs was gone, and a second later the hatch snapped shut and the outside latch locked into position.

McLanahan was about to open the hatch, but the *Megafortress* made an incredible lurch and he was thrown toward the back of the offensive crew compartment.

"We're movin'," Luger said in amazement.

"Either that or they just blew half the fucking plane away," McLanahan said, got back to his feet and went for the ladder to the upper deck.

What McLanahan saw on the upper deck made his guts turn.

Wendy Tork and Angelina Periera were standing over a dazed and bleeding Bradley Elliott. Periera had been knocked off her feet by the sudden motion of the bomber and was just regaining her balance, her jeans and blue workshirt covered with blood.

Elliott looked as if he had been wading in red dye. His right leg was covered with dark, clotted blood. Blood was everywhere—on Periera, on Tork, on Elliott, on the deck, on the circuit breaker panels—everywhere. Wendy was trying to wrap an arm of her flight jacket around the two large openings in Elliott's calf. Elliott himself was hovering just above consciousness; awake enough to feel the intense pain, groggy enough to be unable to move or help anyone. Sweat poured down his face.

"McLanahan." Ormack swung around in his seat. "Get up here."

Ormack was in the copilot's seat, checking the gauges. McLanahan half-ran, half-crawled up front and knelt between the pilot and copilot's seats. He stared out through the sleek cockpit windows over the drooping needle nose of the Old Dog.

"We're moving."

"Damn right," Ormack said. "Sit down. Help me."

McLanahan stared at Ormack.

"Well, sit *down.*" Ormack grabbed McLanahan by the jacket and yanked him forward into the pilot's seat. He grabbed Anderson's headset and slapped it over his head.

"We taking off?"

"If we can," Ormack said.

"We have clearance?"

"I got an order. From him." Ormack jerked a thumb toward Elliott. "He owns the six thousand square miles were sitting on, not to mention this plane. And this hangar, which they're about to blow up on top of us. Now listen. Just watch the gauges—RPMs, fuel flow, EGTs. If anything looks like it's winding down, yell. Watch me on the left." Ormack pushed the throttled forward, and the huge plane rushed toward the hangar opening.

"The door's down, we won't make it. Cut it right—"

Ormack gripped the wheel, moved the steering ratio lever on the center console from TAKEOFF LAND to TAXI, nudged the right rudder pedal. The bomber swung gently to the right. Ormack reached down to the center console and moved the steering ratio lever back to TAKEOFF LAND. "That's all the room I got."

"I don't think it'll make it . . ."

McLanahan watched as the hangar door came toward them. Before they reached the opening he saw Hal Briggs kneeling at the door opening, trying to take cover behind a fallen steel beam. He saw the wngtip rushing toward him. Letting the Uzi drop onto its neck strap, Briggs held his hands out and apart as far as he could, gave McLanahan a thumbs-up, then took off at a dead run outside the hangar.

"How're we looking?"

"Hal said four feet."

"Four feet what?"

His question was a head-pounding, wrenching scream of metal that thundered from the left wingtip. The Old Dog veered sharply to the left. A less painful but still frightening crunch of metal exploded from the right wingtip.

Ormack looked at the fuel gauges. "We lost the left tiptank. Maybe both of them."

McLanahan didn't want to look back. All he could see were dozens of bodies littering the road ahead of them, a burning fuel truck and over-turned security police trucks. There was still a handful of cops firing into the wooden barracks outside the fence surrounding the black hangar.

"Lucky this whole dry lake is a runway," McLanahan said.

Ormack nodded. "Just watch the gauges, I hope they can get the fence open—"

A Jeep pulled up beside them, sped ahead of the bomber easily—although Ormack had jammed the Old Dog's eight throttles up as far as they could go, the half-million-pound bomber accelerated slowly.

"It's Hal!"

In the distance McLanahan could see Briggs' Jeep speed toward the closed gates. He could tell brakes were being applied, but the Jeep crashed headlong into the right side of the gate going at least fifty miles an hour. Intentionally or not, it did the trick. The right side of the wide gate burst open. The Jeep did two full donuts in the sand-covered concrete, then came to a stop. Steam poured out of the radiator. The right side of the gate was half-open, the Jeep was stalled on the runway-driveway, and the left side of the gate was free but still closed.

"C'mon, buddy," McLanahan murmured, "you can do it."

The distance between the bomber and the gate was decreasing rapidly. Briggs was trying to get the Jeep restarted. He gave it a few seconds, then jumped out and started pushing.

Ormack brought the throttles back to idle, which seemed to make no difference.

"We gotta slow down."

As if in reply, three mortar shells exploded in front of the bomber. Briggs tripped and sprawled in the sand. Another explosion crated a huge waterspout of sand off the right wing, and Briggs and his Jeep were lost in the rolling cloud.

The explosions rocked the bomber as if it were caught in a typhoon. Ormack checked the airspeed. "Seventy knots. If we hit the brakes at this speed, they'll explode. We can't stop in time anyway. Briggs . . ."

Briggs had managed to get the Jeep cleared off the runway behind the fence. He ran over and hauled on the right side of the gate. The heavy wide fence slowly opened. Briggs sprinted through the sandstorm and pulled on the left gate. A securing pole was dragging in the sand, and Briggs had to throw his entire skinny body against the fence to move it.

"It's stuck," Ormack said.

"This is going to be a real short flight if he doesn't open that gate," McLanahan said.

But the fence wasn't moving. Briggs' legs were pumping, his once spit-shined boots scraping against the sand, but it wasn't helping.

The fence was half-open when Briggs slipped and slumped to the sand, then rolled to his right to jump back to his feet. As he did he saw the Old Dog.

The aircraft looked like a gigantic pterodactyl coming toward him. And the pencil nose of the bomber, tilted down for takeoff, was aimed right at his heart.

Briggs jumped up, his eyes on the monster with wings speeding toward him, and body-tackled the fence. The fence jumped a few feet, but Briggs kept on going, his legs didn't stop pumping until the blast of eight turbofan jet engines swept him off his feet and into the fence.

"He *did* it," McLanahan said.

"We aren't out of it yet." Ormack slowly throttled up to full power, then reached down and hit the flap switch. "After the fence we got three miles of concrete left. It'll take another minute to get the flaps down, another minute to accelerate this pig to rotate speed. We run out of hard surface in less than a minute."

McLanahan finally found the flap indicator. "It's not moving . . ."

"It probably jammed during one of those explosions," Ormack said, holding tight to the wheel. "It might take them longer to come down—or the flap motors will burn out. One of the other."

The indicator moved to ten percent. Twenty percent. A pause—then a longer pause. Thirty percent. The bomber began to rattle.

"Forty percent." McLanahan scanned the instruments, then looked out the window. Through the dim morning light he saw the glitter of steel on the horizon. He stared harder. Perched directly in front of them was a large, boxy aircraft, with some men scattered around it.

"What the hell is that?" Ormack was staring into the distance.

"It's an airplane on the concrete," McLanahan said. "They're blocking our path." He glanced down at the flap indicator again. Still forty percent. "The flaps stopped."

"We can't do it. We need the whole dry lake now." Ormack reached down and shut off the flap switch, freezing them at forty percent down.

"Can we rotate with the flaps stopped?"

"We'll run out of time before we hit that plane. We'll have to stop . . . pull the 'chute—"

"*Wait.*" McLanahan searched the control panel near his left arm, finding a switch marked "DEFENSE CONSENT." He flipped the switch from SAFE to CONSENT.

"Angelina." He arched around in his seat. "Angelina. Turn on the missiles. The forward missiles."

"What?"

"The *Scorpions.* Turn 'em on."

Pereira scrambled forward, clutching onto the pilot's ejection seat. "Turn them on? We can't. They need to align, lock onto a target—"

"I don't need them to align." McLanahan looked out the sloped windows. Angelina followed his gaze, finally spotting the aircraft sitting on the runway. They could now see the attackers trying to level a bazooka at them. *"Do* it," McLanahan ordered.

Angelina hurried back to her station. To McLanahan, the wait was excruciating. He glanced backward a few times, but as the plane rushed forward he focused on the camouflaged attackers. There were four of them—two firing rifles from behind the plane, two others loading the bazooka. *"Angelina . . ."*

"Ready," she called behind him.

"Fire." McLanahan threw his arms up in front of his face as he said it.

He never saw the results—but then, no human could see the advanced AMRAAM air-to-air missile as it fired off the left pylon at Mach two. The missile leapt forward on a stream of fire. The primary solid-fuel engine had just barely reached full impulse burn when it plowed into the plane less than a half-mile in front of the Old Dog.

What McLanahan did see was a blinding flash of light and a massive black cloud of smoke and dust. A split second later, the needlelike nose of the Old Dog plunged through the chaos.

Nothing happened—no crunch of metal, no explosion of the windscreen in front of him. A moment later the cockpit windows cleared, revealing a barrier infinitely larger than the plane they had just blown away—the seven-thousand-feet of granite called Groom Mountain.

"Go for it," McLanahan called out to Ormack.

Far behind the *Megafortress,* Hal Briggs had been pinned to the fence, his face mashed into the chain link by the force of the jet blast. He heard an explosion a few moments later, expecting the crash, the sound of exploding fuel, waiting for the fireball to engulf him. It didn't happen. It was an eternity until he could clear the stinging sand out of his face and eyes and look toward the horizon.

What he saw was the Old Dog lifting off through a cloud of gray and black dust over the morning Nevada desert. A lump of burning metal lay several yards from the sand-covered runway, with smoking bodies flung hundreds of feet away.

The Old Dog hovered perhaps fifty feet above the high desert floor, nearly obscured by the cloud of dust. He could barely see the huge wheels retract into the huge body—and then the aircraft rose like a winged rocket into the clear morning air.

"Jesus H. Christ," Briggs muttered, sitting in a three-foot drift of sand and tumbleweeds. "They did it. They *did* it."

Ormack flipped a switch on the overhead console beneath the cabin altitude indicator. Slowly the long, black needle nose moved upward and snapped into position. Half the windscreen was now obscured by the long SST nose, the windows blending in with its sleek lines.

"Watch the instruments," Ormack said cross-cockpit. Despite the noise inside the bomber, he and McLanahan were still talking loud enough to be heard without the interphone. "Gear coming up. I hope someone got all the ground locks." He reached across and moved the gear lever up. The red light in the handle snapped on.

"Instruments are okay," McLanahan said. He found the gear indicators on the front panel beside the gear level. One by one, the little wheel depictions on the indicators changed to crosshatch and then to the word UP, and the bumping and screeching of tires stowing in the wheel wells could be heard. "Right tip gear up . . . forward mains up . . . aft mains up . . . the left tip gear is still showing crosshatch."

Ormack cross-checked the indicator with the TIP GEAR NOT IN TRAIL caution light—it was showing unsafe too. "It might be hanging there, or it could be part-way up. We probably ripped out the whole left wingtip." He did some experimental turns left and right. "Steering feels okay. The spoilers seem like they're still working." He glanced down and double-checked that he had shut off the fuel valves from the left externals. "We can try emergency retraction later."

He ran a hand over his sweating face and scanned instruments, left and right, as the *Megafortress* cleared the snow-covered Groom Mountain ridge line. "Looks like we lost all the eighteen thousand pounds in the left external A tank—probably lost the whole tank. The left external B is still with us but it's feeding too fast, faster than the right externals. It's probably dumping all that fuel overboard." He shut off the fuel transfer switch to the left external B. tank. "That means we're short about forty thousand pounds."

He looked over at McLanahan, who was still staring at the mountain ridges sliding under the Old Dog's sleek black nose. "Pat, check the hydraulics."

McLanahan scanned the quarter-sized hydraulic gauges on the left control panel. At first he was diverted by the fancy schematics added on to the panel showing the direction and metering of hydraulic power from the six engine-driven hydraulic pumps.

"Well?"

McLanahan then noticed it. "Pressure on the left outboard spoiler-tip gear is low."

Ormack shook his head. "Well, we're going to lose the left outboard system pretty soon. Make sure the standby pump switch is off."

"It's off."

"We're not going to try to emergency raise the tip gear," Ormack said. "The entire wingtip is probably smashed. We'd deplete the hydraulic system for nothing." He checked airspeed and altitude. "Okay. We're airborne. Flaps coming up."

McLanahan watched the gauge closely. A half-minute later they indicated full-up.

"Well, something's finally working okay," Ormack said.

"Good job," General Elliott said above the noise in the cockpit. Ormack and McLanahan turned in surprise. The general was standing between the two ejection seats, nodding approval. McLanahan looked at his leg. There was a large bandage and elastic cloth wrapped around the calf and thigh.

"How's your leg, General?"

"Hurts like hell, Patrick. Feels like something took a bite out of it. But Wendy and Angelina did a fine job. Lucky we had so many first aid kits on board."

"What the hell *happened,* General? Who were those guys that attacked us?"

"I'm not sure, Patrick. I was advised by intelligence of certain rumors, but I never thought . . . It looks like maybe there was a leak somewhere. My hunch is that whoever authorized that attack expected those B-1s to be still at Dreamland." Elliott cleared his throat. "I'll take it now, Patrick."

"You sure you feel up to it, General? Your leg—"

"I'll let John push on the rudder pedal if I need to. Otherwise I can handle this beast. Get everyone else on helmet and oxygen and stand by for a climb check." So saying, Elliott moved himself aside and let McLanahan climb out of the seat and pass around him to go downstairs. Then with help from Ormack, he settled himself into the pilot's ejection seat and fastened the parachute harness.

"All right," he said, readjusting the headset and placing his hands around the yoke. "I've got the aircraft."

"Roger, you have the aircraft," Ormack acknowledged, assuring positive transfer of control with a slight shake of the control column.

"Let's clean up the after takeoff checklist. Landing gear."

"Gear up, indicating five up," Ormack replied. "Left tip gear is reading crosshatch. Left outboard hydraulic system is low and will probably fail soon."

"Confirmed." Elliott rechecked the hydraulic gauges. "It'll be okay for the time being. Flaps."

"Lever up and off, flaps up."

"Throttles."

"Set for MRT climb. Nav, you up?"

"Nav's up," Luger replied immediately.

"Outside air temp zero, anti-ice off."

"MRT EPR two point one seven."

"Throttles set," Ormack said, checking the gauges.

"Start switches."

"Off and FLIGHT."

"Air conditioning master switch."

"Seven point four-five PSI, radar and defense, normal cooling air available," Ormack said as conditioned air rushed from the cabin vents.

"Offense copies," Luger replied as McLanahan buckled his parachute harness and rechecked his equipment.

"Defense copies," Pereira said mechanically, watching as Wendy Tork secured herself into her seat. Angelina scanned her instrument panels, then opened her checklist and began to bring up her array of armament equipment.

"Slipway doors, open then closed." Ormack reached up and flipped the SLIPWAY DOOR switch to OPEN on the overhead panel. The green CLOSED AND LOCKED light went on. He flipped the switch to NORMAL CLOSED and the indicator came on again.

"Open then closed, check closed."

"This beast climbs like an angel," Elliott said. "We're past twelve thousand already. Crew, oxygen check." He glanced around his seat. His helmet was nowhere in sight.

"Go ahead and check them in, John," he said. "I'll check mine when I get leveled off." Ormack looked slightly embarrassed. He pulled the boom mike closer and said, "Defense?"

"Uh . . . defense is not complete."

"Neither is offense."

Elliott looked in surprise at his copilot. "We don't . . . ?"

"Nobody," Ormack said.

"*Nobody* has an oxygen mask? No helmet?" Elliott said over the interphone.

"We didn't exactly have time to pack a lunch, General," McLanahan said.

"God*damn* it," Elliott said. He checked the cabin altimeter on the eyebrow panel; it held steady at seven thousand feet. "Cabin altitude is steady at seven thousand. How about any masks at all? Emergency masks? Anything?"

Ormack checked behind his seat. "The firefighter's mask is in place," he said, pulling the bag around and examining the mask. It was a full-face mask with a bayonet clip for the ship's oxygen system, designed for a crew member to plug into a portable oxygen "walkaround" bottle and battle a cabin fire.

"One oxygen mask," Elliott said. "No helmets."

"We'll just have to stay below ten thousand feet," Ormack said. "We can't risk a higher altitude. A subtle loss of cabin altitude, the entire crew gets hypoxic—we'd be dead before we knew it."

"We can't do that," Elliott said. "This aircraft is top secret. We've got to get to a higher altitude and isolate ourselves until my staff or *someone* comes up with a suitable landing base. Under ten thousand feet, too many air and ground eyes can watch us."

"Then I'll just keep this thing on until we land, sir," Ormack said. "A few hours at best. I can handle it."

"No," Elliott said. "The mask restricts your vision too much, and there's no communications hookup. Okay, ladies and gents, listen up. Until we get back on the ground, we're all in jeopardy. No one has any oxygen, at least not a safe supply. You can stick your oxygen hose in your face and go to 'EMER' to get a shot of oxygen—as a matter of fact, we'll do that—but it's a real danger. We'll do station and compartment checks every fifteen minutes. Check around more often. Keep alert for signs of hypoxia. The copilot and I will take turns with the fire mask. Check around your stations to see what else we're missing."

"Does it matter, General?" Wendy asked. "We're going to land soon, aren't we?"

"When it gets dark, and when we find a base that can take us. Obviously, Dreamland is out. Tonopah or Indian Springs might be alternates. Angelina, Wendy, get in contact with mission control and—"

"Problem, General," Angelina interrupted. "No secrets."

"No communications documents? No encoding tables? IFF?"

"I'm afraid not."

"What *do* we have on board?"

"The whole world will know about us in no time, General," Ormack said. "The attack on Dreamland, this plane, the whole thing. They can't keep all this secret. When this plane lands, the whole world will be on hand to see it."

Elliott pushed on the yoke to level off at seventeen thousand feet, staring straight ahead over the long, sleek nose of the *Megafortress*. "I suppose you're right," he said. "Level-off checks, John. Angelina, get a UHF phone patch through Nellis to Cobalt Control. That's my section in Washington. Advise them that we're okay and request a secure radio setup and frequency as soon as possible."

"Roger."

Just then a loud voice over all the UHF radios on board interrupted them. "This is Los Angeles Center on guard. Aircraft heading two-eight-five, altitude seventeen thousand feet, squawk five-two-one-nine and ident if you can hear me."

"That's us," Ormack said. Elliott reached down to his side panel, set the IFF frequency, turned the transmitter to ON, and hit the IDENT button.

"Aircraft is radar contact," the air traffic controller replied. "Change to frequency two-nine-seven point eight."

Elliott changed the frequency. "Los Angeles Center, this is Genesis on two-nine-seven point eight."

"Genesis, ident and spell full call sign," Los Angeles came back. Elliott spelled the name.

"Genesis?" Ormack said. "What's that?"

"It's an old classified collective call sign for military experimental aircraft from Edwards," Elliott told him. "We used it when we wanted to go to the high-altitude structure but didn't want anyone, even the military airspace controllers, to know who we were. Dreamland has launched a lot of aircraft without flight plans all over this area. I hope the guy asks someone else about it instead of me."

"Genesis . . ." the confusion in the controller's voice was apparent. ". . . Genesis, we show no flight plan for you. Say your departure point."

"Unable, Los Angeles."

There was a longer pause. Then: "Genesis, your primary target is very weak. Say type of aircraft, intentions and destination."

"This guy is trying to gut it out even if he doesn't know what he's doing," Elliott said to Ormack. He switched to the radio. "Los Angeles, Genesis is requesting direct Friant, direct Talon intersection and holding at Talon within fifty nautical miles at flight level three-niner zero."

"Unable your request through valley traffic without a flight plan, Genesis . . ."

"Request you contact our command post on military AUTOVON or Department of Defense DTS nine-eight-one, one-four-two-four, for our flight plan if it isn't in your system in the next two minutes. Meanwhile, request direct Friant, direct Talon at the three-niner zero."

"Genesis . . ." the controller, not accustomed to pilots telling *him* what to do, was clearly agitated. "Unable. Enter standard holding north of the Coaldale two-five-three degree radial between twenty and thirty DME, right hand turns, at one-seven thousand five hundred until we straighten this out."

"Genesis is proceeding VFR at this time, Los Angeles," Elliott said. "Maintaining sixteen thousand five hundred feet, proceeding direct Talon. We'll file a VFR flight plan with Coaldale Flight Service."

"Genesis, you have your instructions," the controller called back. "Enter holding as directed."

"Passing over the Coaldale VORTAC, General," Ormack said.

"Nuts to that," Elliott said, and switched the mode 3 IFF to 7600, the radio-out IFF advisory. "Climbing to three-nine zero, crew," he said over interphone. "John, dial up Friant."

"He's gonna be pissed," Ormack said as he changed the TACAN frequency to steer themselves to the next navigation point.

"If he never gets our flight plan, he'll never know who we are unless he scrambles interceptors against us," Elliott said. "If he gets our flight plan, it won't matter. If he scrambles fighters . . . well, we don't have a tail number. We don't even look much like a real B-52."

"Genesis, this is Los Angeles Center"—the controller's voice was ragged—"you are violated at this time. Turn left to heading—"

Elliott switched off the radio. "I'll keep the emergency and radio-out squawks going until we're out over water," Elliott said. "He may be pissed but he'll clear the airspace for us."

"Not the best way to begin," Luger said to McLanahan in the downstairs compartment.

McLanahan gave a shrug. He opened his checklist and began to activate the radar, satellite navigation system, and the ring-laser gyro. A few minutes later the radar was warmed up and ready for use.

Luger meanwhile was plotting a fix on a high-altitude airways chart he found in a flight publications bag behind his seat.

"Any jet charts in there? GNC charts? Anything?" McLanahan asked.

"No, standard FLIP bag," Luger told him.

"Great. Just great. Well, we do have a flight plan. There should be Red Flag bomb range training data in here." McLanahan checked that the correct mission cartridge was inserted into the reader, then flipped the READ lever. Twenty seconds later the flight plan, target coordinates, fixpoints, weapon coefficients, and terrain elevations for the entire southwest United States were resident in the master computer. He then checked the gyro, nav computer, and satellite global positioning systems.

"The ring-laser gyro and satellite systems are ready to go," McLanahan said. He turned the satellite navigator to SYNCHRONIZE. "We need a present position fix to align the gyro and start the nav computer. After that it'll take a minute to start navigating on its own."

As Luger took radar fixes and began a rough DR log on the margins of the enroute charts, McLanahan waited for the satellite to lock on. After two minutes the SYNC ERROR advisory light was still lit.

"Okay," Luger said, putting his plotter down. "We're on a pretty good heading to Talon intersection. How's it going over there?"

"Bad to worse," McLanahan said. "I just realized why. The satellite GPS needs a synchronizer code."

"And naturally we don't have one."

"Naturally," McLanahan said. He punched the *Scorpion* missile radar on to TRANSMIT and switched it to its original navigation radar mode. He looked into the scope, watching the Pacific coastline come into view in one hundred mile range, then in frustration switched it back to STANDBY.

"It's hard to take a radar fix without a radar chart or description of the fixpoints," he said. "The ring-laser gyro will probably align with an overfly fix or a DR position, but I don't know how accurate the heading will be."

"Bottom line—Luger to the rescue!" Dave said. "You were a psychic, partner. You needed a nav right from the beginning."

McLanahan flipped his interphone switch. "Want an update on the situation down here, General?"

"I'm afraid to guess. Well, if we don't have a satellite communications channel or IFF mission squawk, we certainly don't have a GPS code. No GPS, no reliable gyro. What else?"

"How about no charts and no target and fixpoint descriptions?"

The interphone clicked dead for a moment. Then: "Well, do the best you can."

"You bet," McLanahan said. "We're deaf, dumb, blind, and lost, but we'll do the best we can."

Washington, D.C.

"All right. Let's have it," the President said, wearily.

General Curtis nodded and continued, pointing to a map of the California coast that was projected on the rear-wall-screen in the White House Situation Room. "Yes, sir." He pointed to the Dreamland area. "As you know, an attack was staged on the project base. Approximately a dozen individuals were involved."

"Good lord, things are going to hell already." He turned to Jack Pledgeman, his press secretary. "What about the press?"

"They know about it, of course," Pledgeman told him. "The Air Force comment was standard 'no comment.' It's no secret in southern Nevada that Dreamland is a highly classified research area. Speculation runs rampant, of course, but the press has no inkling of the projects we're conducting there. I'm sure they don't know about the Old Dog or the runway at Groom Lake. The biggest problem, in my estimation, will be the casualties. Eight military and three civilians."

"Put a clamp on that, too," the President said. "I'll write a letter to the families regarding the sensitivity of the project they were working on and the importance of secrecy. The families must know that their family members were involved in highly classified work for the government. They'll be notified of what happened in due time. Clear, Wilbur?"

"Yes, sir," Curtis replied.

"This is not a formerly classified project," the President emphasized. "We keep a clamp on things right now. Control of this project starts right here." He turned again to Curtis. "General, what's the status of the Old Dog test team?"

All eyes turned to the Chairman of the Joint Chiefs of Staff. "Colonel Anderson, the chief operational designer of the Old Dog, was killed in the attack . . ."

The President's shoulders slumped.

"Lewis Campos, the civilian designer of the *Scorpion* defensive armament interface and the airmine tail defense system, was also killed."

"Well, who the hell is flying that B-52?" Secretary of Defense Thomas Preston asked.

"The aircraft commander is now Lieutenant-General Bradley Elliott, the Old Dog project director."

"Elliott?" the President said. "How did *he* get on board?"

"General Elliott was there when the attack started," Curtis told him. "When Colonel Anderson was killed he got on board and he and Lieutenant Colonel John Ormack, the crew copilot, taxied the bomber out of the hangar and launched it."

Curtis checked his notes: "General Elliott's aide, Lieutenant Harold Briggs, reported that Elliott was wounded in the right leg during the attack. All of the other members of the test team are aboard. He also reported that the bomber suffered damage taxiing out of the hangar—lost four feet of the left wingtip and one external fuel tank."

"Are we in contact with the plane?" the President asked.

"Yes, sir," Curtis said. "So far, only nonsecure UHF contact. They launched without any classified coding documents. What we are trying to do right now is code a message to the crew to get them to set a three-digit address code into their satellite transceiver. Once we're hooked up that way, we can transmit instructions."

"Where are they now?"

"They're orbiting one hundred and twenty miles off the coast of Big Sur at high altitude, as far off the jet airways as possible. Elliott is obviously trying to hide his plane as best he can."

"Why is he still in the air?" asked Thomas Preston. "It's loaded down with weaponry, modified to the hilt—it should be back on the ground immediately."

"I believe General Elliott feels that in broad daylight there's nowhere the plane can land without attracting attention. The Dreamland runway is usable but the hangar was destroyed and there are newspeople all over the place."

"Any alternate landing sites for the plane?" the President asked.

"There are several possibilities," Curtis said, "and the Old Dog still has eight hours of fuel. Two airfields on the Red Flag restricted area are prime sites, although they're not nearly as secure as Dreamland. A few possibilities in Seattle, Washington, and Alaska."

The President leaned back in his chair. "We can't send the Old Dog instructions without risking eavesdropping or discovery. Meanwhile, we have two other fully armed bombers on their way to Russia . . . If Elliott isn't in danger, then he can wait until tonight and land the plane somewhere where it can be concealed. Preferably back in Dreamland or Southern Nevada." The President closed his eyes and said to his press secretary: "Jack. Ideas on how to call this?"

"We'll call it a terrorist attack on a deactivated Air Force research facility. The base was being dismantled by military and civilian workers, a shadowy terrorist group with ties to Qaddafi struck the facility, believing it still to be active."

"We may never know the real truth about where the attackers came from or how they managed to slip through the base defenses," Curtis said. "We've established that they were flying an American-made cargo plane, but so far the wreckage has yielded few clues as to its ownership. All of the bodies have been shipped to DIA labs in Washington for dental and fingerprint analysis and examination of personal effects, but whoever the hell organized the attack was damn careful to cover his tracks. There were Caucasian as well as Orientals, and all of them wore American-made clothes. Except for a piece of metal we found, that appears to have come from a Soviet-made bazooka, there's really nothing to suggest, let alone prove, Soviet involvement . . ."

"Who else would want to attack that base?" Preston asked.

"I've asked myself the same question, Mr. Secretary, but so far the evidence against the Russians is almost entirely circumstantial—"

The President cut him off. "We'll go with the terrorist story for now and revise it if we have to." He turned again to his press secretary. "Jack, don't forget those letters to the families. I want them on my desk A.S.A.P."

"Half-hour, Mr. President," Pledgeman said, and left the room.

From behind closed eyes the President asked, "Anything else, gentlemen?" No reply. "Any Soviet reaction?"

"Nothing, Mr. President," Marshall Brent said. "Probably waiting for us to accuse them. I'll be meeting with Karmarov shortly."

The President turned to General Curtis. "Status of the B-1s, General?"

"Dead on time, sir. They'll be getting their first refueling over Canada right about now."

The President was silent for a moment. Curtis was positive the President was going to cancel the B-1 sorties when he finally said: "I'll be upstairs in my office. Keep me advised of their progress every half hour. I'll monitor the mission from there."

"Yes, Mr. President."

"And get Elliott and his . . . his Old Dog on the ground. Have them keep their plane hidden as best as possible. They can wait for a night landing, but that's all. I've got three planes too many flying already."

"We'll send the Old Dog up to Seattle, sir," Curtis offered as he headed for the door. "They've got the room and the right people to disarm it—"

"Dis*arm* it?" the President said. Everyone in the Situation Room froze. "Disarm it? What the hell is it armed with, General?"

"Sir, General Elliott's plane, if you remember, was a test-bed experimental aircraft. It . . . it probably has all of the weaponry the *Excaliburs* have—the air-to-air missiles, the—"

"They don't have any nuclear weapons on board, do they, General?" Tom Preston, the Secretary of Defense, said. "No one authorized—"

"No, sir," Curtis said quickly. He turned to the President. "General Elliott's B-52 was conducting tests on the *Striker* TV-guided glide bomb. He is probably carrying one of them."

"Well, make damn sure that plane is disarmed as soon as it lands," the President said. "We don't need another screw-up."

The President didn't wait for Curtis' muted "Yes, sir," but stormed past the Marine guards and headed for the elevator.

Curtis waited until the others had left, then headed for the Situation Room communications center, where communications experts were working out a transmission routine for the Satellite Communications code, SATCOM. Once Elliott had the code and had set it into his SATCOM receiver aboard the Old Dog, Curtis could talk to the crew. But first he had to figure out how to give the code to the crew without compromising the code itself.

He walked into the communications center. "Well?"

"Transmitting now, General," the chief of the center reported. "It'll be picked up by the SAC Emergency Action Network in a few minutes, and it'll continue until ordered to stop."

"Good. You know that the crew has no decoding documents, no secrets."

"Yes, sir. They shouldn't need any. We have direct voice backup routines being put together if necessary."

Curtis nodded. "Word from the *Excaliburs?*"

"Ops normal message three minutes ago from both birds," the chief said. "Still hadn't finished refueling."

Curtis accepted the full printout of the *Excalibur* crew's messages and put it in his briefcase. He sighed, louder than he intended.

"Keep me informed." And wondered what next could go wrong.

"Genesis, this is Los Angeles Center."

General Elliott put down the can of water Dave Luger had found in a rations container downstairs and readjusted his microphone. "Go ahead, Los Angeles."

"Your emergency flight plan has been received," the controller said. "Your call sign is now Dog Zero-One Fox. You are cleared to orbit as required. Acknowledge."

Elliott looked quizzically at Ormack. "Strange call sign," Elliott said.

"Dog Zero-One Fox acknowledges, center," Elliott replied over the radio. "Any other messages, Los Angeles?"

"Negative, Zero-One," the controller replied. "Radar service terminated, cleared to contact oceanic flight following."

"Zero-One Fox, thank you." Elliott picked up the olive-drab can of water from the crew survival kit and took a sip as he stared out of the cockpit windows.

"Well," Elliott said, "we're cleared—but to where? How? For how long?"

"They'll try to contact us—somehow," Ormack said. "We're monitoring all the SAC Command Post frequencies, SATCOM, all the emergency frequencies, and the SAC Emergency Action Alpha monitor periods on high-frequency radio. Maybe they haven't decided what to do yet."

"Well, I've decided," Elliott said, rubbing at the pain spreading in his right calf. "We've got to land this beast tonight. If they don't tell us where, we'll pick the place. Tonapah, Indian Springs—wherever we need to go." Over the ship's interphone, he said, "Crew, we've received notification from Center that our call sign is now Dog Zero-One Fox."

McLanahan said: "Any word on what we're supposed to do?"

"Not yet," Elliott said. "Just keep monitoring your assigned frequencies. We should hear something soon."

"Can someone take HF for a while?" Luger said. "The static is driving me nuts."

"I'll take it," McLanahan said, reached across and took the high-altitude general aviation chart that Luger was using to copy the high-frequency radio messages on. He glanced at his watch. "Three more minutes until Alpha monitor." He switched his interphone panel waver switch to the HF setting and winced as he turned the switch on. He fumbled for the volume knob. "Sorry I volunteered. You got three-eleven, remember. Here's the log I made up."

Luger looked over the mountain of radio messages on the UHF alternate SAC command post frequency. "Just routine messages," he said. "What are we looking for?"

"Anything," McLanahan said. "A clue. Something unusual."

"Can't they just say, 'Hey you guys, set A-B-C in the SATCOM'?"

"Then everyone who hears the message sets it in their printers. It's not secure anymore."

"Or, 'Hey, Dog, land at Tonopah'? Oh, never mind. Same reason."

"Real smart boy," McLanahan said. "Alpha monitor period." He shut off all the radio switches except HF and pressed the headset pads closer to his head to hear better the Strategic Air Command emergency action message broadcasts. Alpha monitor was the primary time period for worldwide Strategic Air Command messages over the high-frequency radio spectrum.

"How's the fuel look, John?" Elliott asked Ormack.

"Still about seven hours at this throttle setting," Ormack said, checking his homemade flight plan filled out on the back of a piece of cardboard. "We can still fly across the country twice if we need to."

"My butt won't hang in there that long," Elliott said.

"How about your leg?"

"Still smarts," Elliott said, gently touching his calf.

Ormack reached into a flight publications holder behind his seat and pulled out the North America IFR supplement. "I've got the frequency for McClellan Global Command Control," he told Elliott. "I'll give them a call, tell them we're exiting the ADIZ." Over the interphone he asked, "Anyone using the HF?"

"The Muck's copying a message," Luger replied. He glanced over at McLanahan, who was intently listening to the static-charged radio message, occasionally tapping a pencil on the characters he was transcribing.

"Let me know when he's finished," Ormack said. "Any problem with keeping up with our position?"

"No, sir."

"I'll need some more endurance figures in a minute. I'll probably need an ETA to a fix somewhere when I call McClellan."

"Ask and ye shall receive," Luger said, and looked over again at McLanahan, who had just switched his interphone knobs to their normal positions.

"HF is yours, Colonel," Luger said. "Nav clearing off to the sextant. Hey, Muck, I gotta take a sun shot. You wanna do the honors or count me down?"

"I've done the last three shots on the sextant," he said. "Gimme the watch." As Luger got up to head to the upper deck to take the sextant positions, McLanahan grabbed his arm. "Anything unusual about any of these HF messages you copied, Dave?" He tapped his pencil on the long lines of numbers and letters, together with the time of transmission and the call sign of the command post that made the transmission.

"No, the usual number of characters, no special order or anything. Of course, we can't decode the messages."

"Something in the messages . . . Dave, did the message say 'fox' or 'foxtrot'?"

"What? Oh, the phonetic spelling for the 'Fs,' you mean?" He thought for a moment. "Yeah, you're right. 'Fox'! Not 'foxtrot'! But it's the same thing, right?"

"Maybe, maybe not." McLanahan pulled the mike closer. "Angelina? Any luck?"

Angelina made an obscene gesture at the row of buttons on the SAT-COM printer, which were used to set the address enable codes into the printer-receiver. "My finger's getting numb setting codes."

"I think I might have something," McLanahan said. "We just got HF traffic. They're using 'fox' in their messages instead of 'foxtrot.' It's the same as that strange suffix on our call sign."

" 'Fox'? Sure, why not? I've tried dozens of other codes." In the gunner's compartment, Angelina set the address enable switch on the SAT-COM printer to DISENABLE. She then set the address code windows to 'F-O-X' and changed the address switch to ENABLE. "Nothing," she said.

"Try those characters backwards," McLanahan told her. "That has to be the key."

Angelina entered 'X-O-F' into the printer address code and switched the receiver to 'ENABLE.' Instantly, the SATCOM printer rumbled to life. "It worked!"

"Great," Elliott said. "Read out any messages you get as soon as possible."

"Just a stream message with our call sign in it so far," Angelina said. "I'll get an acknowledgment message out right away." She unstowed the SATCOM keyboard and began to type out an acknowledgment message. Fifteen minutes later she keyed the mike again.

"Message, General," she announced.

"Go ahead."

"It reads, 'Orbit at SHARK intersection for recovery at Boeing Auxillary Eleven at zero-eight-hundred hours Zulu. Insure weapons safe for recovery. JCS.' That's it. I got the codes for the satellite navigation system, too. I'll pass down the GPS code to the nav in a minute."

"Well, that's it," Elliott said. "We'll have this beast down on the tarmac in a few hours." He turned to Ormack. "Sure was nice getting behind these controls again, John. I'm just sorry about the circumstances."

Elliott stared out the windowscreen and watched the Old Dog's nose as it veered into the sun. The pain continued to throb in his right leg as he thought about the two *Excaliburs* headed toward Russia.

Disconnect, seven-seven."

The boom operator hit a trigger on his control stick, and the nozzle of the KC-10 *Extender*'s refueling boom popped out of the receptacle, a small white cloud of JP-4 jet fuel vapor streaming away in the slipstream of the B-1B *Excalibur* below. The boomer pulled on the stick, and the boom moved quickly away from the black shape hovering below his panoramic window beneath his toes. He hit another switch, and the boom motored up and automatically stowed itself under the modified McDonnell-Douglas DC-10's tail.

"Clear One-Three to the wing," the pilot aboard the B-1 requested.

"Clear to the right wing, One-Three," the lead B-1 replied. The B-1 that had just completed its refueling slowed, dipped its right wing, and slid out of view of the KC-10 boom operator. Just as he cruised out of view, the boom operator got another glimpse of the pylon full of missiles slung under the *Excalibur's* wings.

"Refueling complete," the boom operator radioed to the copilot. He swiveled his headphone microphone away from his lips and wiped sweat from his face and neck. Refueling a B-1 was always hard—even though they were steady platforms, their dark NATO camouflage made it hard to find their open receptacles, even during the daytime.

But these two B-1s were different—very different. Their dark gray coloring was gone, replaced by dull jet-black surfaces. Even with the electrofluorescent aiming grid on the *Excalibur's* nose, the boomer had been very reluctant to extend the nozzle into that dark, shapeless void. He knew he had only about a six-foot margin for error before he stuck the nozzle into the bomber's radome—or, worse, through its windscreen. Even though he had been a boom operator for fifteen years and six feet was a lot of free space to work with, there was always the possibility of error. Two planes flying twelve feet away from each other, traveling at almost three hundred and eighty miles an hour—well, it was easy to screw up.

The copilot was giving the offload report to the two bombers: "Kelly One-Two flight, you received a total of one hundred and seventy thousand pounds, about equally divided. Clear to tactical frequency. Clear us for a right climbing turn."

The lead B-1 aircraft commander, Colonel Bruce Canaday, checked his left window. "See One-Three out there, Bill?" Canady's copilot checked his right window. At that moment, the second B-1 slipped into fingertip position about twenty feet from his leader's right wingtip, its position lights and anticollision beacon popping on.

"Got him. He's in fingertip."

"Gascap flight, clear for a right climbing turn. Thanks for the gas."

"Gascap flight copies. Good luck, you guys." Canady watched as the huge KC-10 tankers banked to the right and flew above and out of sight of the B-1s.

"Kelly flight, post-refueling checks," Canady radioed to his wingman.

"Two," came the reply.

"Ed, got the post-refueling message ready?" Canady asked his offensive systems operator. The radar navigator had just finished composing the coded message for transmission via AFSATCOM, notifying the Joint Chiefs of Staff that they had received their last scheduled refueling before approaching the continent of Asia.

"Ready to go."

"Send it. Did we get our hourly 'go' message?"

"Received the last one five minutes ago," the navigator replied. "I'm expecting the first fail-safe message any minute."

Just then his Air Force Satellite Communications printer clattered to life. The navigator transcribed the phonetically coded message into a codebook, then passed it to the defensive systems operator, the DSO, across the narrow aisle from him.

Together, the officers carefully decoded the message, then rechecked it.

"We got it," the navigator said. "Cleared to proceed on course to the second fail-safe point. We can expect the 'strike' message within the hour."

"Confirmed," the defensive systems officer added.

Canady didn't reply. He did a quick station check of his instrument panel, then was silent.

"I'm still betting we get terminated," the copilot said.

"I'm hoping so," Canady said. He switched to interplane radio. "One-two flight, cleared to route formation when post-AR checks are complete."

"Post-AR checks complete, moving to route." The second *Excalibur* banked slightly right, moving out to approximately a half-mile beside his leader. It was much less strenuous on the pilot to move away from the leader then stay in close formation for long periods of time.

"Confirm receipt of Golf, Tango, Sierra, Oscar, Pappa," the navigator radioed to the wingman's nav, checking to be sure the other aircraft had received and decoded the same 'go' message.

"Copied and confirmed," from the second nav.

"Status, One-Three?"

"One-Three is in the green," from the second *Excalibur.*

"One-Two is in the green too," Canady replied. Both bombers were one hundred percent ready—no malfunctions, no abnormal readings, no fuel shortages. The mission would be canceled if either bomber had a serious malfunction.

"Copy." To the crew Canady said: "Two good bombers, guys. So far we're a go. Nav, I'm ready to do a TFR check whenever you are."

"Rog." The nav opened his checklist to the INFLIGHT TERRAIN-FOLLOWING RADAR SYSTEM CHECK section, running the automatic terrain-following autopilot self-test.

As the two pilots and the navigator began the systems check, the defensive systems operator began another electronic countermeasures equipment check while listening to the high-frequency radio. As he flipped through transmitters and receivers, running self-tests on the mostly automatic equipment, an "S" symbol blinked on at the top of his computer-generated threat receiver scope.

The intermittent signal caught his eye, but he ignored it—the symbol did not return, and it wasn't accompanied by an audio warning tone. Probably a glitch or a stray signal from the second B-1. He continued his checks.

A few minutes later the "S" reappeared—this time with a fast, high-pitched warning warble. The defensive systems officer put away his checklist and took all of his electronic gear out of their "self-test" modes back into STANDBY.

"Pilot," the DSO called over the interphone, "where's the wingman?"

The pilots were beginning to check the second TFR channel. "On our wing," the copilot answered irritably. "We're doing a TFR check. Can it—"

The DSO flipped over to the interplane frequency on his radio panel. "One-Three, say your position."

"Route," came the terse reply.

"Behind us?"

"That's where 'route' usually is."

"Do you have us in sight?" asked the DSO, his voice betraying excitement. He hesitated, then switched all of his transmitters from STANDBY to TRANSMIT.

"Affirmative," the pilot of the second B-1 replied.

"I see him too, Jeff." That was from the second *Excalibur's* DSO. *Something* was out there . . .

"Pilot, defense has search radar, twelve o'clock, extreme range but closing slowly."

"Roger." Canady wasn't too concerned. The nearest land at twelve o'clock, other than pack ice, was six hundred miles away. "Probably a glitch. Did you say closing, Jeff?"

"His signal is getting stronger," the DSO reported. "I can count a twelve-second antenna sweep now. Moving just to the left of the nose."

"Moving? Jeff, recycle your equipment and see if it—"

"The other DSO sees it, too, Colonel. Either we both got the same glitch, or it's a—"

At that instant the computer verified the signal, changing the symbol on the threat scope from "S" to a batwing-like symbol with a circle inside it.

"Airborne early warning aircraft," the DSO said. "Right off our nose."

"A *what?*"

"A radar plane. Long-range airborne surveillance."

"Well, what the hell is it doing up over the goddamned North Pole?" the copilot asked. "We're thousands of miles from any military base."

"It's locked onto us," came from the DSO. "He's got us."

"Maybe it's one of ours," the copilot said. "It can't be Russian—we're only a hundred miles north of Barrow. Maybe we should cruise toward him and take a look, or try to raise him on—"

"Like hell." Canady reached down to the center control console and flicked the running lights on and off, signaling his wingman to rejoin him without using the radios. His copilot watched his signal, then searched the sky out of his right window. A moment later the second *Excalibur* bomber appeared out of the semi-darkness and rejoined on Canady's right wingtip, tucked in so close the copilot was sure their wingtips were overlapping.

"Two's in," the copilot said.

"Jeff, could he have seen both planes?"

"Probably. Depends on his range, but I'd say yes."

"Those S.O.B.s found us. Out here a thousand miles north of nowhere, we run smack into a surveillance plane . . . well, we don't have to let him get a visual identification on us."

Canady pushed his stick right and inched the throttle up. The copilot immediately checked that their wingman was turning with them.

"He must've anticipated you'd be turning," the copilot said. "He's right with us."

"The signal's turning left toward us." Canady moved the throttles up to full military power.

"Approaching Mach One," from the copilot. "Wing sweep." Canady pulled the wingsweep handle aft, and the *Excalibur's* long, graceful wings disappeared from view, sweeping back until they nearly merged with the B-1's dark, sleek fuselage.

"Are we putting any distance betwen him and us?" Canady asked.

"No," the DSO said. "He's got the cutoff on us."

"Mach One," the copilot reported. There was no difference in the feel of the plane; only the airspeed and Mach indicator tapes told them they were flying faster than the speed of sound. Canady's copilot checked for the wingman out his window.

"One-Three's moved out a little to get out of the shock barrier," he said, "but he's still with us."

"Signal is moving to ten o'clock," the DSO said. "We're getting some space between us, but he's heading perpendicular to our course. He'll get a solid visual on us."

"Mach one point five."

"If he didn't know who we were before, he can take a good guess now," Canady said.

"One-Three's still with us."

"Signal almost abeam us now."

Canady looked out his left cockpit window. There, about ten miles off their left side, was a large white transport-like aircraft with a big disk-like radome mounted on top of its fuselage.

"I can see it. Ten o'clock," Canady said. "It looks like an E-3 AWACS. Can it be one of ours?"

"Look at the tail," the DSO said. "T-tail or conventional?" Canady had to strain to see it as the *Excalibur* whisked past.

"T-tail," he said. "And . . . escorts. He's got escorts, two fighters on his wings."

"Russian *Mainstay* surveillance plane," the DSO said, his voice cracking. "Looks like a C-141 with a radome on top, right? It's the Russian version of our AWACS. It pulls double-duty as a tanker, too."

"He's going to pull his double-duty right on our ass," Canady said. "Nav, cleartext a message over SATCOM. Tell them we have a Russian AWACS and two fighter escorts behind us. Give our position and flight data and ask for instructions."

"Already sent."

"We can't keep this up for long, Colonel," the copilot put in. "We're behind on the fuel curve and we don't have authorization to cross the second fail-safe point. If we start a second orbit, that *Mainstay* will catch up to us with its fighters."

Canady unbuckled his oxygen mask and pounded his instrument panel in frustration. "DSO, can you see those fighters behind us?"

"No. All I see is the AWACS—but the fighters won't need to turn on their radars to find *us*. If the AWAC can see us it can vector in the fighters better than the fighter pilots."

"Can you jam that AWACS' radar?"

"At this range, yes, barely."

"If we ducked down to low altitude, could he follow us?"

"The *Mainstay* has good look-down capability," the DSO said. "We might lose him if we combine jamming and a hard, fast descent . . ."

"But then what?" the copilot interrupted. "We're still an hour from landfall and we're still not authorized to cross the second fail-safe point. He's got two fighters to look for us, and the fighters have plenty of fuel. We're behind the fuel curve as it it is."

"To hell with the fuel and the second fail-safe point," Canady said. "I won't risk being caught or shot up by those fighters. I'll keep it at Mach one point five until we reach land, then throttle back and hide in the terrain radar ground clutter."

"Or we can engage those fighters and the AWACS," the radar nav said. Everyone else grew quiet. He had voiced the unthinkable—attempt a dogfight with the Russian fighters. The *Excaliburs* were the first American strategic bombers to be fitted with air-to-air missiles—the attack would be completely unexpected.

"If we have to, we will," Canady said. "Arm the *Scorpion* missiles, DSO. Let's have them ready . . ."

Canady looked out his left cockpit window. Illuminated by the faint glow of the sun just below the horizon was a Russian fighter, cruising directly cockpit-to-cockpit across from Canady, so close to the *Excalibur* that the Russian pilot and his back-seat weapons officer could clearly be seen. Canady noted the red star on the MiG-31 *Foxhound's* vertical stabilizer and the four air-to-air missiles slung under its wing. Even traveling over a thousand miles per hour, the massive Russian fighter kept up easily with the *Excalibur*, flying in perfect side-by-side formation.

"A MiG-31," the copilot said. "Right beside us." He turned and looked out his right-side window. "The other one is off One-Three's right wing."

"Nav . . ."

"I'm sending it now," the radar navigator said, typing in a new uncoded emergency message into the satellite communications terminal.

"They got us," Canady said quietly. Silence from the crew, which felt naked, vulnerable. Nowhere to hide, nowhere to run. Their protective camouflage, their weaponry, their terrain-following capability, even their speed was useless.

"Priority messages from the B-1s, sir." Jeff Hampton rushed into the Oval Office with a long computer printout strip. At a stern glance from General Curtis, Hampton gave the message to him.

"Well, General?" the President said irritably, taking a sip of coffee.

"First message is a coded post-refueling message, sir. They completed their last refueling successfully. Next message acknowledges the first fail-safe order, authorizing them to proceed to—"

The President saw the color drain from Curtis' face. "What is it?"

"Seven minutes ago . . . oh, goddamn . . . two more messages transmitted in the clear—they didn't code them. First message indicates the formation was spotted by a Russian *Mainstay* airborne warning and control aircraft one hundred three miles north-north-west of Point Barrow, Alaska."

"Spotted by a *what?*"

"A Russian radar plane." Curtis walked over to a map of the Northern Hemisphere. "Here—just a few miles away from the first orbit point. That *Mainstay* is a copy of our E-3A AWAC surveillance plane. It can scan hundreds of miles around itself, track planes at high or low altitude, vector fighters—"

"Did the Russians actually *see* the B-1s?"

"They . . . yes, visual sighting was made." Curtis began to read the last message, then reached out his hand and held onto the back of a chair.

"I don't believe it," the President said. "General, you told me there wouldn't be any Russian planes within two thousand miles of that orbit point."

"Mr. President . . ."

"What? There's more?"

"Yes sir, the . . ." General Curtis didn't know if he could read it. ". . . the *Excaliburs* were intercepted by two Russian MiG-31 *Foxhound* fighters."

"What!"

". . . shortly after being spotted." Curtis' face had turned even whiter. The President dropped back into his leather seat.

"Did the fighters attack?"

"No." Curtis looked again at the message. "This last report says the fighters were shadowing the bombers. The B-1s tried to outrun them but couldn't. Last reported speed was Mach one point five, still four hundred miles from the second fail-safe point. The fighters are still with them."

The President bent over his desk. "General, how can those fighters be so far from Asia?"

"The *Mainstay* is a tanker, too," Curtis said. "It can sustain two fighters like that for five thousand miles." He paused, then turned and walked back to the President's wide cherry desk.

"Sir, there *has* to be a leak somewhere. First, the timing of the attack on *Ice Fortress,* then the attack on Dreamland, and now these B-1s being spotted so fast. It can't be coincidence—"

"Yes, I agree, but that's not the problem now. We've got two bombers up there headed for Russia, and two fighters alongside them ready to blow them out of the sky."

"Sir, I've got an—"

"We have to recall the bombers. Those fighters could take them out any time—"

"Yes, sir, but if they were ordered to do so they would have done it already."

"They could be waiting for orders from Moscow."

"That's possible, but Canady and Komanski, the commanders aboard those *Excaliburs,* are the best in the business. They just won't let the fighters take them out. The *Excaliburs* have the new *Scorpion* air-to-air missiles, advanced jammers, and better camouflage, plus they're just as fast as a *Foxhound* at high altitude and faster at low altitude."

"Curtis," the President said, shaking his head in disbelief, "you're not suggesting that the *Excaliburs* fight off those MiGs and continue."

"No, sir, but . . . they shouldn't be recalled, either."

"For God's sake, why?"

"Sir, the objective is still the neutralization of that laser site—"

"*Without* starting a war, may I remind you."

"Yes, sir. Like we agreed, limited resources, precision bombing, little or no collateral damage. The B-1s are now essentially neutralized. They probably *could* escape the *Foxhounds,* but they wouldn't have the fuel reserves to continue their mission. Plus the Russian air defenses are alerted. All the Russians need to do is draw a straight line from the bombers present position to Kavaznya and look along that line to find two B-1s."

"So?"

"Sir," Curtis said, leaning toward the President, "there is only one aircraft in our inventory more heavily armed, more capable, and more prepared to accomplish this mission than even those two *Excaliburs*—the Old Dog."

"The Old . . . you mean that B-52 test airplane? The one that almost got blown up in Nevada?"

"The Old Dog has more defensive weapons, more power, better range and better countermeasures than the B-1s. That plane is manned by the experts that designed all the gear aboard the *Excaliburs.* And they have the best bombardier in the Strategic Air Command aboard."

"Curtis, that's out of the damned question." The President began to pace the office, then abruptly, stopped and faced Curtis.

"How the hell could a B-52 get in when two B-1s got caught?"

Curtis took a deep breath to hide his excitement. He didn't want to blow this. "The Old Dog wouldn't go in the same way." He walked over to the large map, found the President had come along with him. "The Russian air defenses will be swarming over the north area, waiting for more attackers—they'll probably be expecting a mass of bombers. General Elliott could pick his way in from the south—"

"How would he know what route to take to avoid being spotted?"

"Sir, General Elliott, who's now in command of the Old Dog, has spent months studying the defenses of the Kavaznya area and the Kamchatka peninsula. He knows them much better than I do. I'm betting he can find a gap in the radar coverage and get in without giving away his position. And once he gets in the mountainous terrain of the Kamchatka peninsula, a whole air wing of fighters couldn't find him."

The President shook his head, turned his back to Curtis.

"Sir, the Old Dog is already airborne," Curtis reminded him. "It doesn't have a flight plan—it's a non-mission. The Russians may even believe it was destroyed in the attack—we can leak that it was destroyed. It can be diverted easily."

"What about the damage, the injuries?"

"I'll check on its operational status," Curtis said. "Get a report from General Elliott, have him make a decision whether or not he can accept this assignment."

"Would Elliott say no? I know him. He's gung-ho as they come—"

"But he wouldn't risk the lives of his crew unless he knew there was a chance of success. That *I* know."

To Curtis' surprise, and relief, the President said: "Get Elliott's decision."

"Yes, sir." Curtis turned to leave the room, then hesitated a moment. "The Old Dog is vulnerable to the same security leak that has compromised us all along. Under the circumstances it would be wise to take certain steps—"

"Such as?"

"Well, sir, such as keeping knowledge of the Old Dog's involvement between just the two of us."

"No way," the President said. "I rely on the support of my advisers, and I've no doubt about their integrity. We'll restrict knowledge of this to the Cabinet, but the Cabinet *must* be involved."

"Very well, but I would like to suggest one more thing. If the Old Dog is to get through this, it will have to play it by ear. A set of recall options can't be reliably built into the mission plan without compromising it. And there's always the possibility of a leak if the crew had to radio back for a go-ahead."

"What I think I'm hearing, General, is that you want me to give the strike order now, even with negotiations going on?" The President shook his head.

"Sir, right from the beginning the Soviets have failed to negotiate in anything like good faith. They've kept us at the bargaining table under false pretenses while they've carried out their own hidden agenda. The loss of the *Midgetman* and *Ice Fortress* both happened while so-called negotiations were going on. They've demonstrated that they've never intended to do anything but stall for time. Negotiations are in name only."

There was a long silence as the President considered Curtis' words. "There's truth in what you're saying. And I'm not unaware of history . . . FDR thought that Secretary of State Cordell Hull could work out an agreement with the Japanese just before they attacked Pearl Harbor. He underestimated their duplicity. It seems I've made the same mistake, and for the same reasons. We both wanted a result so much we lost sight of realities . . ."

For a moment all that could be heard was the ticking of the brass clock on the President's desk and the muted sound of trees swaying in the wind outside.

"All right, General . . . you ask Elliott if he's up to this. If he is, there'll be no turning back . . ."

McLanahan and Luger were dozing in the downstairs offensive crew compartment when Elliott came over the radio: "Crew, listen up. We have received orders from the Joint Chiefs. It was why I had you accomplish a thorough equipment check a few minutes ago. Now, I want to make another check—a people check. You all remember earlier today when I told you about the planned B-1 sorties that launched early this morning. Well, it seems those B-1s were discovered and intercepted just north of Point Barrow about fifteen minutes ago."

"Intercepted?" Ormack asked.

"Somehow the Russians knew where the B-1s would be coming from. They had a *Mainstay* early-warning and control radar plane waiting for them, dragging two MiG-31 *Foxhound* fighters with it. The B-1s didn't have a chance to evade."

"Did . . . the B-1s get shot down?" Wendy asked.

"No, but the fighters are dogging them. They've been ordered to hold at a fail-safe orbit point over the Chukchi Sea just outside Soviet airspace. It's presumed the MiGs will follow."

"But why are the B-1s continuing?" Luger asked. There was a long moment of silence.

"Don't you get it?" McLanahan said. "They want *us* to do it."

"How the hell are *we* supposed to make it if two B-1s couldn't?"

Elliott took over. "It'll be risky trying to get past their early-warning radar net, much less flying over the Soviet Union, I agree. I need your thoughts, people. We've got some left wing damage but our offensive and defensive weapons and systems are all operational. We don't have proper military charts but we have general aviation charts plus, fortunately, a terrain cartridge for the Kavaznya site. We'll also get refueling support going in and fighter coverage coming out."

Elliott hoped it was sinking in, hoping his crew was buying it . . . *his* crew? It hadn't been *his* crew until a few short hours ago when they were close to death in that hangar in the high Nevada desert.

"I won't go on unless I have everyone's support," he said. "I know none of you thought you'd be part of an actual mission, much less a raid against an installation in the Soviet Union. We've only flown together a few times—hell, I wasn't even a part of the crew. John and I are the only ones who have ever flown in combat. If we aren't one hundred percent agreed, we land in Seattle and that's that. But consider the situation. The Russians have continued to use their laser at Kavaznya in spite of all our diplomatic protests. They have, literally, crippled our ability to detect ballistic-missile launches over the Pacific or the Pole. If they decide to launch an attack we have only a few minutes' warning before the warheads impact. I believe that if the B-1 mission has failed—and it has—the next step is either a cruise missile attack from long range, a naval strike force, or an intercontinental ballistic missile attack on Kavaznya. The laser site can probably protect itself against all those threats. And the sight of cruise missiles or an ICBM heading toward Asia could well result in someone pushing an even bigger button and triggering a thermonuclear exchange . . ." Was he laying it on too thick? No, dammit, he was laying out the awful option. Speaking the unspeakable . . . "I truly believe this crew and this plane is the one answer left. I believe we have a very good chance of getting past

Russian radar, avoiding their air defense, neutralizing that laser facility, *and* getting back."

It was the longest speech he had ever given. The throbbing in his right leg that had stopped over the past hour now was returning full force.

"If you like the odds, say so. If you don't say so. Without everyone pulling together, we for sure won't make it."

Ten minutes later Elliott sat back in his seat, drained. He no longer had feeling in his right heel, and the throbbing pain had reached his knee. He thought again of what Curtis had told him. So far the Russians had been one step ahead. Curtis was obviously afraid that they might be tipped off to the Old Dog's mission too. Well, that wasn't going to happen, the odds were too damn long. Seattle seemed as good a place as any to stage his protective aerial sleight of hand . . .

"Seattle coastline in sight," McLanahan reported, returning his ten-inch radar display to the two hundred mile range. "One o'clock, one hundred miles."

These were the first words anyone in the crew had spoken since their decision. Elliott turned to Ormack.

"Get us clearance into Seattle Center airspace, John. Wendy, see if you can raise Boeing Field on HF. Get us permission to land."

"Seattle Center, Dog Zero-One Fox is with you at two-five thousand."

The Seattle Air Route Traffic Control Center controller checked his radar display. He had already received a call from McClellan Air Base's Global Command Control radio operator that Dog Zero-One Fox would be appearing in his sector. And there he was—right where McClellan said he would be.

"Dog Zero-One Fox, good evening, radar contact at two-five thousand feet."

Earlier the Seattle controller had passed along a Mode 3 "Squawk" identification code to McClellan for the airplane to set in its IFF, its Identification Friend or Foe system. The IFF would transmit the four-digit code to the controller's computer, which would display a data block near the airplane's radar dot with the plane's call sign, altitude, ground-speed, and a computer ID number. The Seattle controller checked the area from which McClellan said the aircraft would be coming and, as advertised, the data block and beacon target symbols appeared at the extreme outer edge of his one hundred and fifty-mile range scope. There was no primary target return—a smaller symbol superimposed on the larger beacon target symbol—but that wasn't unusual at extreme ranges.

"Dog Zero-One Fox, confirm your destination is Seattle-Boeing Field."

"That's affirmative, Seattle. We'll be requesting permission for a visual to an auxillary field when within ten miles. Boeing has been notified."

That was very strange, but the controller had heard of it before. To avoid attention some experimental or classified planes used one of Boeing's numerous auxiliary fields scattered around Seattle instead of the main corporate terminal. When they did, they didn't tell the controller which one until in the vicinity of all of them. The approach controller would have to clear the airspace and grant clearance to make an approach to a very wide area, which really complicated air traffic control in the already super-congested Seattle-Vancouver-Portland area, but at this time of day it wasn't too much of a hassle. The procedure wasn't limited to military flights, either—the private aircraft firms guarded their newest developments almost as zealously as the military.

"I've been advised, Zero-One Fox," the controller replied. "I'll pass it along to Seattle Approach in—"

The Controller saw something that made him blanche—a beacon code being changed to 7700, the emergency code. The plane's data block was instantly surrounded by a flashing border, and the letter "EMRG" began to flash above the beacon target.

It was the newcomer—Dog Zero-One Fox.

"Mayday, mayday! Seattle Center, Dog Zero-One Fox!"

"Zero-One Fox, I copy your emergency code." The controller buzzed his shift supervisor, who hurried over and plugged his headset into a jack on the console.

"Shift supervisor A. Watt on console seven, ID number S-one—one-three-one, time two-three-one-seven local time." That was for the benefit of the continuously running tape that was monitoring all communications—the tape that would be used in an accident investigation.

"Dog Zero-One Fox is declaring an inflight emergency at this time," came the hurried transmission. The voice—presumably the pilot, the one who had made the initial call-in to Seattle—was nearly drowned out by a thunderous noise in the background.

"It sounds like . . . water? A waterfall?" the controller murmured.

"He's depressurized, Ed," the supervisor said. "It's windblast. A big one, too. If it's a depressurization, the noise should stop. If it's glass panel failure, it won't . . ."

The shift supervisor switched to a Center-wide intercom. "This is Watt to all controllers. Clear airspace from radials two-six-zero to three-two zero from Hoquiam VORTAC for inbound emergency aircraft in ten minutes. Advise Boeing, McChord, Bowerman, and Portland of possible diverting emergency aircraft, type unknown. Advise McChord and Coast

Guard search-and-rescue. Aircraft is currently on the two-eight-two de-gree radial from Hoquiam at one hundred and thirty nautical miles, flight level two-five zero, groundspeed four-twenty knots."

Meanwhile, the first controller watched transfixed as the altitude read-out of the emergency aircraft began to wind down. "Zero-One Fox, are you encountering difficulty maintaining altitude?"

Through the roar in the background the pilot said, "Seattle, descending below ten thousand feet . . . lost pressurization . . . fire on board . . . emergency! Emergency! Mayday! Mayday!"

"Understand, Zero-One Fox. We are clearing the airspace for you. If possible, turn left, heading two-eight-zero, vectors for emergency landing at Boeing Field, cleared to descend and maintain ten thousand feet."

No reply. The altitude readout was winding down, faster and faster.

"Twenty thousand . . . eighteen thousand . . . fifteen thousand . . . Andy, rate of descent increasing . . . passing through ten thousand feet . . ." Over the radio he said, "Dog Zero-One Fox, climb and maintain ten thousand feet. Acknowledge."

The noise of the windblast over the frequency all but drowned out any reply.

"Passing eight thousand . . . rate of descent slowing but he's still going down . . . passing five thousand . . . low altitude warning!" Over the channel the controller said, "Zero-One Fox, *climb*. Pull up, pull *up*. If you're in a spin release your controls. Acknowledge . . ."

"Beacon target lost," the supervisor said. "This is A. Watt plugged into console seven, local time two-three-two-zero, Seattle ARTCC. We have lost Dog Zero-One Fox on radar. Last report from the pilot said he was descending to ten thousand feet due to inflight emergency, fire, and loss of pressurization. Rate of descent from flight level two-five-zero estimated at fifteen thousand feet per minute, slowing to approximately ten thousand feet per minute but mishap aircraft never regained altitude or appeared to level off. No primary or secondary targets visible at this time. No flight data visible. No aircraft within sixty nautical miles of mishap aircraft noted. No emergency locator beacon transmissions yet received. Coast Guard and Air Force search-and-rescue forces have been alerted."

Several minutes later the President, still in the Oval Office with General Wilbur Curtis, took the message from Jeff Hampton that the FAA had lost Dog Zero-One Fox from radar, that the plane had experienced a major emergency and had plummeted twenty-five thousand feet into the ocean in less than two minutes.

The President forced his left hand steady as he replaced the phone receiver on its cradle. He looked at Curtis. "Dog Zero-One Fox has disappeared. Presumed lost a hundred and thirty miles off the west coast."

Curtis said nothing. Apparently too shocked, the President decided.

"How long can the *Excaliburs* stay in their orbit, General?"

Curtis checked his watch, made a fast calculation. "They must leave in six hours to have enough fuel to reach Eielson with the necessary reserves. We'll have a tanker back in the first orbit area to give them extra fuel, but six hours is the most."

"Order them to depart the orbit area in five," the President said. "I know it doesn't make much sense keeping them out there. They'd be sitting ducks if they tried anything, but at least it will make the Soviets nervous having two B-1s heading toward their backyard. We may even be able to bluff them into thinking those *Excaliburs* have more fuel and firepower on-board then than they thought. It might even get them to negotiate for real . . ." The President's voice was flat. Who could blame him? He was still thinking of the Old Dog—thinking of another plan that had failed, and of the crew that would never come back.

He swiveled his seat around and stared, unseeing, into the gray, snow-covered world outside the Oval Office.

Dave Luger checked the master computer's clock on his TV display. Weird, he thought. Watching a machine doing his navigation for him. Playing a big "video game" in the belly of a B-52 somewhere over the north Pacific.

Well, not exactly "somewhere." With the GPS up and running, he knew within sixty feet where they were at any given moment—and the GPS measured those moments within one-hundredth of a second.

Luger plugged his nose and blew against the pressure—a "valsalva," designed to clear his ears after their hair-raising dive to "disappear" from Seattle Center radar. "General?"

"Go ahead, Dave," Elliott said.

"Fifteen minutes to the decision point." Luger quickly called up a fuel reading on his video display. "I've got us right on your updated fuel curve, Colonel."

"Checks up here," Ormack acknowledged.

"So we're not leaking fuel?" Wendy asked.

"Negative," Ormack said. "At least there's some good news."

"Well, it's time we talked about the bad news," Elliott said. "This is what we're looking at. According to Patrick and Dave, and courtesy of those twelve navigation satellites feeding our computers information, we're fifteen minutes from a major decision point.

"We now have about thirty-four thousand pounds of fuel left. Thanks to that phony screaming-ass descent back there that had all those air traffic controllers buffaloed, and the hour-long cruise at five hundred feet above the water, we'll soon be running on fumes. From our decision point ahead we can divert to Elmendorf Air Force Base in Anchorage and have about fifteen thousand pounds of fuel. That's the absolute minimum amount of landing fuel for a normal B-52. With this plastic monster of ours we can overfly Elmendorf and with favorable winds and a lot of luck divert again to Eielson Air Force Base in Fairbanks with about three thousand pounds remaining. That figure is significant because that's the normal tolerance of the fuel gauges we have—we can have six thousand at Eielson—"

"Or we can have zero," Angelina said.

"Exactly. But that plan does give us two available airfields to set this beast down on."

"Is there another option?" McLanahan asked.

"Yes, Patrick. We can continue on our flight planned route. The only available airfield with a halfway decent runway for us becomes Shemya in the Aleutians. Fuel reserve over Shemya would be about five thousand pounds."

"Five thousand pounds?" Wendy said. "That's cutting it close. Are they any—?"

"There are other airfields nearby," Elliott said, anticipating her question. "All of them are shorter and narrower than Shemya, but we should be able to put down on any one of them. I bring up this option because Shemya has two things that we could use—a fairly isolated runway and fuel. We need the isolation if we ever hope to keep this plane and this mission secret. The decision becomes this—head toward Elmendorf with one good option but an end to our mission, or head toward Shemya with only a few poor options but an outside chance of continuing on."

"I don't see there's an option, General," Ormack said. "We've come this far . . ."

Elliott nodded at Ormack, silently thanking him. To the crew he said, "I guess I'm bringing all this up to give each of you another out, another chance to put this bird down."

"We've given you our answer, General," Wendy said.

"I know, and I thank you. But you've had a few hours to think about it. I'm putting the question again."

"I've got a different question," McLanahan said. "How's your leg, General? We can't complete this mission with less than a one hundred percent effort from *everybody*—you said so yourself. Are you one hundred percent, General?"

"Of course I am." Elliott turned and found Ormack looking at him carefully.

"I can handle it, John."

"He has a point, General. You're worried about us not having the commitment—but do you have the capacity?"

Elliott paused, then spoke into the interphone. "I won't deny it, crew. My leg hurts like a sonofabitch. But if I didn't think I could get this beast to Kavaznya and back again, well, I would have said so back there when we were over Seattle."

Silence. Then McLanahan spoke. "All right, General. That's good enough for me."

"Me, too," Angelina said.

"And me," Luger added.

The entire crew voiced their assent.

"All right, then," Elliott said, "do any of you have any brilliant ideas about how we can get enough gas to finish this mission?"

Downstairs in the lower offensive crew compartment McLanahan gave his partner Luger the thumbs-up sign and spoke into the interphone.

"I have an idea, General," McLanahan said. "But it may involve breaking some rules."

"If there was ever a time to break rules, Patrick, this is it. Let's hear it."

"Well, we'll have to call you General Jean Lafitte after this one," McLanahan said, "but here's what I had in mind . . ."

Elliott flipped his radio over to HF TRANSMIT, took a deep breath: "Skybird, Skybird, this is Genesis on Quebec. Emergency. Over."

The command post senior controller on duty in the tiny SAC Command post on the tiny island of Shemya, perched nearly at the tip of the Aleutians, had to restrain himself from spilling his coffee as the emergency call blared through his speaker. Calls over HF, especially emergency calls, were few and far between up here at the extreme northwestern tip of the United States of America. He whipped out a grease pencil and noted the time on the slate of glass covering his desktop.

He switched his radio to HF and keyed his microphone. "Calling Skybird on HF, this is Icepack on Quebec. Spell your call sign phonetically and go ahead with information."

"We got him," Elliott said over interphone. Over the high-frequency radio, he said, "Copy you, Icepack. I spell golf, echo, november, echo, sierra, india, sierra, SAC Special Operations. We are one-eight-zero miles east-south-east of your station. We have declared an emergency for a double engine fire and fire in the crew compartment. Massive fuel leaks. Request emergency random refueling with strip alert tanker and emergency recovery at Shemya."

The deputy controller was furiously writing the information down on a logbook. He opened the classified call signs book.

"Checks," the controller said to his partner. "Special ops out of Edwards."

"So what's he doing way the hell up here?" the senior controller said. "Call the commander." He checked the weather forecast printout on his console, then turned back to his radio.

"Understand your request, Genesis," the controller replied. "Shemya is reporting marginal conditions. Can you divert to Anchorage? Repeat, can you divert to Anchorage?"

"Negative, negative," Elliott replied. "Less than one-five minutes of fuel at present rate of loss. No navigation equipment. Magnetic instruments only. We are only estimating our present position."

"Understand, Genesis," the senior controller said and looked over to his NCO partner.

"Got the boss on the line, sir," the NCO said. The senior controller grabbed the phone.

"Colonel Sands here."

"Major Falls in the Command Post, sir. Inbound inflight emergency requesting a strip alert tanker."

"How far out is he?" Sands asked.

"He estimates about one hundred and seventy miles now, sir. He said less than fifteen minutes of fuel."

"Hell, we might not make it even if we launched right now. Who is it?"

"They're using a strange call sign, sir," Falls said. "Genesis. It's a special ops call sign out of Edwards."

Sands swore under his breath. Special Operations. An experimental or highly classified mission. But from Edwards? "How's the runway now?"

"Slick as owl shit, sir. RCR still about ten. Fifty feet either side of centerline is free of ice to about twelve RCR. Taxiways are about eight RCR."

"Status of the strip alert bird?"

"In the green, sir," Falls said, glancing over at his assistant. The NCO cupped his hand over the telephone he was using.

"The crew's being recalled to the pad, sir," the NCO reported.

"Have them report directly to their plane," Falls said. He turned to his telephone. "Crews are responding to their planes, sir."

"Get an authentication from this Genesis," Sands said. "I'm on my way."

"Command post clear." Falls opened the communications code book, checked that the date and time were good and turned to his radio. "Genesis, this is Icepack control. Authenticate Alpha Echo."

Elliott turned to Ormack. "They want me to authenticate."

"We don't have any code documents."

"Unable to authenticate, Icepack," Elliott replied quickly.

Falls winced. What the hell was going on?

"Genesis, we cannot provide strip alert support without authentication."

"Icepack, this is the senior controller aboard Genesis," Elliott said over the high-frequency radio. "The communications compartment has been severely damaged. Half the crew is dead or injured. We have no means to authenticate."

A few moments later Colonel Sands was wriggling his chubby desk-bound body out of his parka. "Status?"

"He said he was unable to authenticate, sir," Falls said. "Fire inside their crew compartment and communications center, injuries. The senior controller seems to be the one in command."

"Senior controller? Communications center? Sounds like an AWACS or EC-135—but it's an Edwards call sign?" Sands picked up the microphone.

"Genesis, this is Icepack. Over." He bent toward the speaker.

"Go ahead, Icepack. Urgently need strip alert support."

Sands searched his memory. "I recognize that voice. Where?" He keyed the microphone. "Genesis, say type of aircraft and souls on board."

"Unable, Icepack."

"Son of a bitch," Sands said half-aloud. "What's going on? Damn . . . that voice." He thought quickly . . . "Get hold of Anchorage Center, find out where this guy came from."

"Already did that, Colonel," the NCO told him. "Nothing. No squawk. Not even radar contact. He's been outside the ADIZ until now."

"Then screw him," Sands said. "This sounds too fishy. We due for an air defense test or something?" Falls shook his head. Sands grimmaced and keyed the microphone. "Genesis, strip alert support is not authorized without proper authorization. Unless you identify yourself, you'll have to swim back."

Elliott looked preoccupied as Ormack said, "What do we do now, we've only got—"

"Sands!" Elliott suddenly blurted out. "Eddie Sands! That sorry son of a bitch. They stuck his ass in Shemya." Elliott keyed his microphone.

"We are unable to authenticate . . . *scum-maggot.*"

Sands paled as if he had seen a ghost. Slowly he brought the microphone to his lips.

Falls glared at his wing commander as if he had been slapped in the face. Sands angrily jammed the mike button down. "Say again, Genesis."

"You heard me, slime-worm," Elliott shot back. "Unable to authenticate."

To Falls' immense surprise, a hint of a smile began to creep across Sands' face.

"Genesis," Sands said carefully, the smile still working its way across the pudgy face of the Shemya wing commander. "Once more. Is this for real?"

"Affirmative . . . dirt bag."

Aboard the *Megafortress,* Ormack looked befuddled. "What . . . ?"

"He'll have the tanker airborne in five minutes," Elliott told Ormack, relaxing in his ejection seat. "Crew, prepare for refueling."

Sands dropped the microphone into Falls' lap.

"Has the strip alert crew called in?"

"No, sir, I expect them any—"

"Call the vice commander," Sands said, zipping up his parka. "Tell him he's got the store. Put me on the strip alert flight orders. Notify Reynolds that I'm coming aboard for his emergency refueling."

Faster than any of his men had ever seen the pudgy commander move, Sands was out the door. Falls' partner looked baffled as the full-bird colonel sped down the hallway and into the subzero cold outside.

"What the hell?"

"Don't ask me, Bill," Falls said.

"What about the old standard operating procedures?"

Falls thought a moment. "We follow them, even if the colonel doesn't. Notify the interceptor squadron on alert. Tell them the KC-10 is taking off in support of emergency refueling, but that the aircraft they'll be rendezvousing with is unidentified. The unidentified aircraft is not considered hostile but it has refused or is somehow unable to establish contact with any civilian or military agency."

"Got it." The NCO picked up the phone and dialed as rapidly as he could.

McLanahan was announcing: "Eleven o'clock, seventy miles." Over the newly assigned UHF command post frequency they were using as the air refueling frequency, he said, "Icepack one-oh-one, Genesis has radar contact at seventy miles at your two o'clock position."

The pilot of Icepack 101, the KC-10 tanker from Shemya, looked to Colonel Sands, who was sitting in the IP jumpseat between himself and his KC-10's copilot.

"A new voice," the pilot, Joe Reynolds remarked. "Sounds like a nav if I ever heard one. I thought there was only one survivor on board?"

"Radar contact at seventy miles?" Sands echoed. "Maybe not as helpless as they said they were."

"Do we keep on going?" Reynolds asked.

"We keep on going," Sands told him. "I recognize a voice on board."

"Precontract check complete," Ormack said aboard the Old Dog. "All external lights are off right now."

"Good," Elliott said.

Just then Wendy Tork reported, "I've got search radar contact at eleven o'clock."

"That's the tanker," McLanahan said. Wendy checked the oscilloscope-like frequency pattern on the frequency video display.

"Confirmed," she said.

McLanahan flipped on a switch marked BEACON on his radar control panel, checking that the radar manual tuning frequency remained on the preset "doghouse" beacon frequency range. The tiny dot representing the tanker on his radar changed into a line of six tiny rectangles in a one-two-three dot pattern. "I've got his beacon." He switched to interplane. "One-oh-one, contact on your beacon. Beacon to standby."

The six-dot pattern disappeared. "Go back to operate." The pattern reappeared.

"Positive ID, our eleven o'clock, sixty-five miles."

"Check on air-to-air TACAN," the copilot aboard Icepack 101 acknowledged. The mileage on the air-to-air TACAN receiver, which gave the distance between the two aircraft, slowly clicked down.

"What do you hope to find, sir?" Reynolds asked the wing commander alongside him.

"I don't know," Sands told him, "but I wouldn't want to miss whatever it is."

"But who are these guys? They don't sound like they're in trouble to me—"

Sands shook his head. "They sound like they're in trouble, but not like they've told us. We had to launch—but we don't have to rendezvous with them."

"Then what—"

"I'm up here to investigate, Joe. Gather information. But I'd be breaking a dozen rules if I allowed this aircraft to join with an unidentified aircraft. If we'd refused to launch they'd have disappeared forever. No, we'll head toward them. But instead of turning we're going to buzz right past this joker."

"And then?"

"And then we'll let the Nineteenth escort them back to Shemya."

"The interceptors? Are they up there?"

"If I know Falls it's the first thing he did after we took off," Sands said.

"But what about their gas? They said fifteen minutes."

"It's been fifteen minutes right about now," Sands said, checking his watch. "Do those guys sound like they're about to fall into the ocean? Someone's screwing with us, Joe. Nobody does that with me. We'll lead these guys back to the base, then find out what the hell's going on."

***

"Inside sixty miles," McLanahan reported, switching his radar back into search-while-track mode.

"Copy," Elliott said. "Ready, Wendy? Angelina?"

"Ready," Angelina said.

"All set, General," Wendy told him, "but I don't see the other ones yet."

"Believe me, they're coming," Elliott said. "Hit 'em with just a little at first. When he switches over, blot 'em out."

"Will do."

"Sixty miles," McLanahan called out to the tanker. Part of his transmission was interrupted by a high-pitched squeal.

Sands winced and fumbled for his volume control knob.

"Genesis, you have a loud squeal on your radio," Ashley, the KC-10's copilot, called out.

"Copy," McLanahan replied. His transmission was almost completely blotted out by noise. "Switching radios." McLanahan waited a few moments, then said, "How do you copy now, Icepack?"

The noise was almost unbearable. "Genesis, this is Icepack. Your radios seem to be malfunctioning. Do you have FM or VHF capability?"

"Roger," Elliott said. "Switching to VHF now." On interphone he said, "Okay, Wendy. Shut 'em out."

Wendy smiled and flicked a transmitter switch to MAX, carefully checking the frequency video display.

"This is Icepack on VHF air refueling freq," Ashley said. "How copy?"

"Too high, General," Wendy said, studying the new VHF frequency range on her video display. "Lower. To at least one-twenty megahertz."

"Icepack, take it over to one-one-two point one-five," Elliott said.

Sands, aboard the KC-10, looked curiously at Ashley who along with Reynolds shared his confusion. Ashley switched frequencies.

"How do you copy, Genesis?"

"Loud and clear, Icepack," Elliott said. Over interphone he said, "Okay, I got him, Wendy. Take 'em all down."

"Will do, General."

"Range, Patrick?"

"Fifty-five miles, General," McLanahan told him. "And I've got additional radar contact at twelve o'clock, eighty miles, fast-moving. You were right."

"He's only following SOP," Ormack said.

"He's still a snake," Elliott said. "He was a snake at the Academy, and he's still one. Patrick, I've got it."

"Go get 'em, General."

"Icepack, this is Genesis," Elliott said over the new VHF frequency.

"Go ahead, Genesis."

"The name is Elliott, Eddie," the general began, staring into the twilight. "We're at fifty-five miles at your one o'clock. You launched without proper authentication, leaving me to believe that you have no intention of rendezvousing with us. You're going to turn the opposite direction, or fly past us. Either way, it'd be a mistake."

"Why, General Elliott," Sands said, grinning. "I figured it was you. What's a big SAC cheese like you doing in a hell-hole like this?"

"You're going to make this rendezvous, Colonel—"

"Or else, were you going to say? We're getting pretty feisty in our old age, aren't we? Well, I've got news for you, *sir*—we're heading back to Shemya, and we're going to—"

"Just watch your one o'clock, Icepack."

"Now listen, Elliott—"

As Sands was posturing aboard the KC-10 tanker, Wendy ejected four bundles of chaff from the wings of the *Megafortress*. Angelina locked her airmine radar onto the cloud of metallic tinsel behind them, and when they moved about a mile behnd the bomber fired a single airmine rocket at the cloud.

From the cockpit of the KC-10 *Extender* tanker it resembled a giant flower-like fireworks display, even at their extreme range. The airmine rocket plowed into the cloud of chaff and exploded, mixing thousands of chips of metal into the explosion and fire caused by the exploding rocket. The detonation ignited the chaff and the shrapnel from the rocket, creating a fiery cloud that spread rapidly across the evening sky.

"Turn range is twenty-two, Eddie," Elliott said over interplane. "Left turn. Or we'll make another little fireworks display on your tail."

"Switch radio two back to command post," Sands said sharply. "The fighter'll be on three-eleven. Have them get their asses up here." He stared at the slowly dissipating cloud of fire ahead and clenched his fists. "Screw you," he muttered, "I'm running this show, General."

As Ashley switched frequencies from VHF to UHF range and keyed the microphone, an ear-splitting squeal drowned out his call.

"He's trying to transmit on three-eleven," Wendy said, studying her emitter video display.

"We're jamming UHF and VHF too," Elliott said to the KC-10. "So forget about calling those fighters. We're jamming IFF and we'll squeal out HF, too."

"Thirty-five miles, General," McLanahan said.

"One more convincer, Eddie," Elliott told him. "I understand you folks have threat-warning receivers now. Well, check it out."

On the interphone he called down. "Lock onto him Patrick."

McLanahan hit his TRACK switch, pressed the ENABLE lever on his tracking handle, and guided a circle cursor over the radar skin-paint of the KC-10 tanker. When he released the ENABLE lever the circle remained on the return and a green numeral "one" lighted on McLanahan's TV screen.

"Got him," McLanahan announced. On board the KC-10 the results were a bit more dramatic. On the threat-warning receiver on the instrument panel between the pilots, Elliott's plane had been showing as an "S," for search radar. The "friendly" symbol on the threat radar video display suddenly changed into a hostile "bat-wing" threat symbol. Moments later a red MISSILE ALERT illuminated as the threat receiver's internal computer interpreted the steady "lock-on" signal from the unknown aircraft as a missile tracking signal—indicating a missile ready to launch.

"We gotta get out of here," from Ashley.

"Easy, copilot, easy," from Reynolds.

"How do we know who he is?"

"The S.O.B. is bluffing," Reynolds said. "He's a goddamned friendly. He won't shoot. Set the IFF to EMER. Get on GUARD and call those fighters."

Sands waited a few moments while Reynolds directed his crew. The anticipated results came a few second later.

"IFF's faulted," Ashley said. "No interrogate indication."

"Heavy jamming on all emergency frequencies," the flight engineer reported.

"Okay, okay," Sands said. "Tie the autopilot back into the rendezvous computer. Make the turn."

"But we can't—"

"Yes, we can. Someone's either playing a very big joke . . . or is very serious. It doesn't matter—we're committed," he said, and flipped over to the interplane channel.

"Okay, Genesis, you convinced us," Sands said. "Or should I say, General Elliott? Don't worry, we'll make the turn. Are we going to have to listen to that missile alert bull all through the refueling?"

Elliott smiled. "Take it down, Patrick." McLanahan deselected the TRACK switch and punched in "one" on his keyboard, and his circle cursor went to the "home" position in the upper left corner of the radar scope.

"Icepack turning left heading two-seven-one," Ashley said nervously on the radio.

On board the Old Dog, McLanahan watched the radar return carefully for a few moments, then said, "He looks fine, General, normal turn rate, correct direction. He should roll out two miles ahead of us."

"Good. Get back on long range radar and get a fix on those fighters. I've got a visual on his lights."

McLanahan switched from thirty to eighty mile range and immediately a large bright return appeared, just passing the thirty-five-mile range mark.

"Thirty-five miles, General. Closing fast."

"Genesis has visual contact," Ormack said. He pointed out the cockpit windows into the growing blackness.

"So, General," Sands said, "last I heard you were in the Looking Glass unit in Omaha. You're a long long way from Nebraska, *sir.*" He paused, then: "I thought the missile alert stuff was sort of childish, General. You wouldn't fire a missile at one of our own. Now let's cut the crap—"

"Not now, Eddie," Elliott broke in. "Now, I know you have a code-word that sends those F-15s home. We'll release your fighter frequency so you can tell them they're not needed."

"Then you also know, General, that I got a word that'll have those trigger-happy jocks blow you into atoms."

Elliott looked at Ormack. "He's right."

"Game's over. If I say nothing—or if you keep jamming and I'm not *allowed* to say anything—those boys come in hellbent for blood and with itchy trigger fingers on real Sidewinders. It may be too late already, sir, what with their interplane frequency being jammed like that. If this is some sort of exercise, it's gone *way* too far—but I'm not yelling uncle. *You* are. Right now. What'll it be?"

"I'll tell you what, Eddie—"

"Go ahead, General, I've got plenty of gas—and firepower."

"I've got more than a code-word, Eddie, I've got a story. A story about a certain wing commander at a conference in Omaha. About a certain air division commander's wife. A story about a blond kid in an Italian family . . ."

"Stop crappin' around, Elliott—"

"My mission is no crap, Sands. I may not be doing it by the book but I'm Special Ops. We both get to tell our stories to headquarters when we land." Elliott quickly switched to interphone. "Patrick. Range to the interceptors?"

"Twenty-five miles."

"Well I've got a story about a certain hot-shot one-button in the Philippines that should prove entertaining," Sands hit back.

"I had dinner with the Secretary two weeks ago, Eddie. While you were chipping ice cubes out of your undies I told him that story. He bought me a martini afterwards. Look, we're running out of time, I don't want those fighters any closer." On interphone he said, "Frequency clear?"

"Yes, sir," from Wendy. "The interceptors are contacting their command post for engagement authorization."

"You're on, Eddie," Elliott said.

"*Cutlass* flight, this is Alpha aboard Icepack one-oh-one on channel nine."

"Copy you loud and clear now, Icepack," the lead pilot of the F-15 *Eagle* two-ship formation replied. "We have visual contact on you but not on your receiver. Heavy MIJIing on all frequencies. Permission to join on your receiver's wing for positive ID."

"Negative," Sands told him wearily. "Positive ID already established. Status is Red Aurora. Red Aurora. Alpha out."

"Patrick?"

"Fighters are turning," McLanahan reported. "Heading back toward the coast."

"Shut down UHF again, Wendy," Elliott said. His order was instantly confirmed by a loud crackle of static on the radio he was monitoring.

"That won't be necessary, Genesis," Sands said over the VHF refueling frequency. "We'll play ball, damn you. But the fighters and my command post will just get nervous if they can't talk to us."

"I'm counting on you, Eddie."

"Open a window and we'll shake on it, *General.*"

"Wendy, open up three-eleven again," Elliott said. "Leave everything else shut down."

Sands unplugged his interphone and oxygen connections and cleared off to the air refueling pod in the back of the converted DC-10 airliner. He strapped himself into the long wide boom operator's bench and stared out the window beneath their feet.

"What's his range?" Sands asked the boom operator.

"Almost two miles. Still can't see him. And it's not even completely dark yet."

"Genesis, this is Icepack. You guys are either very small, very dark, or both. Turn your lights back on or we'll be up here a long time trying to plug you."

"Who's in the pod, Eddie?" Elliott asked.

"Just me and the boomer."

"No other spectators, Eddie. Deal?"

"I got a feeling I don't want to see this," Sands muttered over VHF. "*Okay,* agreed. Let's see what's such a big goddamned deal."

"Lights are coming on."

The formation lights revealed the size of the unknown receiver, but nothing else. It appeared like a group of stars flying in formation behind the KC-10 tanker.

"We're also going to need fuselage lights, Genesis," the boomer said. "I've got your receptacle light okay but no azimuth or elevation references."

"Give 'em the fuselage lights, John," Elliott said. He was busy adjusting his seat down and forward for the best position for refueling.

"Roger," from Ormack. Just then the Old Dog began to slide to the right, Ormack pressed on the left rudder pedal and looked anxiously at Elliott.

"General? You okay?"

"Sure, I've got it."

"We're yawing to the right. Straighten her out. Let up on the right rudder." The Old Dog slowly straightened out.

"You've got the refueling, John," Elliott said, relaxing his grip on the yoke. His head rested on the headrest on the back of the ejection seat, his chest heaved.

"But—"

"I was testing out the rudders," Elliott told Ormack. "I pushed on the right pedal but didn't feel anything happen so I pressed harder. I still can't feel anything . . . I think I've lost my right leg."

"Goddamn," Ormack said, grabbing the yoke and putting his feet on the rudder pedals. "I've got the aircraft."

"You've got the aircraft," Elliott responded, shaking the yoke. Ormack gave it a shake to confirm he had control. Elliott slid a hand down his right leg and over the calf. A few hours earlier such an exploration would have caused almost excruciating pain. Now, nothing. He could see his finger pressing on the muscle beneath his knee, but he felt *nothing*. It was an eerie feeling, like touching a hunk of salami . . .

Ormack looked anxiously at the huge KC-10 looming before them, its boom extended, waiting.

"General," Ormack said firmly, "I'm aborting this mission—"

"*No*"

"McLanahan had a point, sir. It's not worth your leg—"

"Refuel this aircraft, Colonel," Elliott said firmly. "We're not stopping now."

"But, General, I—"

"I said refuel this bomber. Two men have already sacrificed *their* lives for this mission." He grabbed the yoke, gave it an angry shake and put a gloved hand back on the throttle cluster between them. "And if I have to refuel this plane without your help I will. Understood?"

Ormack slowly nodded. "All right, General, all right . . . I've got the airplane . . . but I need a pilot, General. A one-hundred percent combat ready pilot. Do I have one?"

"Well, my right calf is about twenty-five percent, John. But your pilot who also happens to be commander of the Old Dog is one hundred percent. Refuel this plane."

Ormack nodded in surrender, looked at the air-to-air TACAN distance readout. "Icepack, Genesis is approaching one-half mile."

The boom operator gripped his fly-by-wire digital boom controls and stared into the darkness below. The wingtip position lights of the mysterious receiver were just barely visible, as were some fuselage and upper-position lights. The slipway-door light danced eerily in the gloom before him, and he had to close his eyes to avoid getting the "leans," a loss of equilibrium caused by the moving light without any horizon references. There were lights out there, but even at a half-mile he couldn't see any airplane body to go with them.

"Genesis," the boom operator said, "be advised I have your lights but have insufficient vertical, horizontal, and depth references for a safe call to precontact position."

"We have a good tally on you," Ormack told him. "Clear us to precontact and we'll give you range countdown to contact. If you can't see us that way . . ." He looked to Elliott.

"Clear us to precontact," Elliott said, filling in for Ormack. "Stick the boom out there, booms. We'll put this plane underneath it and you plug us."

"Roger, Genesis," the boomer said uneasily. "You are cleared to precontact position, with caution."

"Roger. Moving in."

Sands and the boom operator stared anxiously as the slipway door light moved toward them.

"One hundred feet," Ormack reported as his own depth perception finally snapped in. Before, he had merely aimed the top of the Old Dog toward the nozzle light ahead; now he could better gauge the actual distance involved.

"Still no—" The boom operator paused. For an instant he could discern an object passing just on the edges of his wide pod window. He tried to piece that glimpse into a whole airplane, but it was impossible.

"Stabilized precontact," Ormack reported.

"What?" from the boom operator.

Nothing. The boom operator saw nothing below him except a single light. Everything else melted completely into the space around it. The precontact position on most large aircraft was twenty feet behind and ten feet below the nozzle, less than sixty feet from where he and Colonel Sands sat in the boom pod. They were looking directly below the nozzle, in the glow of the small nozzle light, and there was nothing. In the depths of the growing twilight, Mason *thought* he could see the outline of a large aircraft—but it could just as easily be his imagination playing tricks on him. "Genesis, I'm going to turn on the belly lights."

"Who's in the pod?" Elliott asked quickly.

"Colonel Sands and Tech Sergeant Mason," the boom operator replied.

"Okay. Eddie, make sure that's all that goes in there."

"Hell, I'm not sure if *I* want to be here."

"Clear on the belly lights," Ormack said, taking a firm grip on the yoke. The boom operator reached above him and flicked a switch.

And suddenly there it was. The long, pointed nose stretched underneath the boom pod. Just on the edge of the pod window the outline of the eleven missiles were visible on their gray pylons. In the direct glare of the tanker's light the forward fuselage could now be seen, but the rest of the plane, aft of the training edge wing roots and beyond, was invisible. Through the sleek, sharp, Oriental-like angles of the strange-looking cockpit windows, the pilot and copilot, without helmets or oxygen masks, could barely be made out.

"What the . . ." The boom operator's words stuck in his throat.

"You got him, booms?" Reynolds asked over the tanker's interphone. "What is it?"

"It's . . . it's a B-52 . . . I think," Mason stammered over interphone.

"You *think?* What the hell is it?"

"It's a damned spaceship. It's . . ."

"Acknowledge, Icepack," Ormack repeated. "Stabilized precontact and ready."

"Elliott, what the hell are you flying?" Sands demanded.

"Gas first, Eddie. Questions later."

"Forward ten," the boomer said. "Cleared to contact position. Icepack is ready." Ormack expertly slid the *Megafortress* ahead. His practice and experience made for a steady platform, so all the boomer had to do was extend the nozzle a few feet.

"Genesis showing contact," Ormack said. "Nice job, boom."

"Icepack has contact," Mason reported. He started the fuel pumps. "Taking fuel, no leaks."

"Taking fuel," Ormack acknowledged.

"All right, Genesis," Sands said. "How about some answers?"

"Eddie, you don't want to know," Elliott told him, glanced over at John Ormack and managed a smile. The *Megafortress* was so smooth and steady that it was easy for Ormack to keep the huge bomber in the boom's refueling envelope—it seemed he was scarcely touching the controls. "You don't want to know where we've been, where we're going, or what we're doing."

"Where you're *going?* There's no question about where, General. You know—hell, you knew about my code words so you *must* know—that I can only give you enough fuel to make it to Shemya or a suitable alternate. I can't fill you up."

"You've got to, Colonel. We need as close to full tanks as possible."

"General, I've busted more rules in the past twenty minutes than I've done in two years. And that's a lot, even for me. I can't give you that much—"

"This isn't a strip alert refueling any more, Eddie," Elliott said. "This is now an unscheduled, alternate tactical refueling. We had tanker support from Eielson and Fairchild scheduled but they didn't launch. Now you're it."

"You had *two* tankers?" Sands said. "What the hell you going with two—?" And then Sands stopped, looked in disblief at Reynolds and Ashley. They arrived at the answer simultaneously. Missiles on the strange B-52's wings . . .

"Elliott," Sands finally said. "What the *hell* is going on?"

No reply.

"Jesus Christ," Sands said. He rubbed the bridge of his nose and stared at the bomber below them.

"Ashley?"

"Computing max offload now, Colonel," the copilot replied, pulling out his performance manuals, charts, and flight plans.

"Give us enough to land at Anchorage with ten thousand over the high fix," Sands told the copilot. "We may need it if runway conditions at Shemya deteriorate. God *damn.*"

Under the close eye of Mason on board the KC-10 and Elliott aboard the Old Dog, it was nearly an hour later when Ashley nodded to the flight engineer, who radioed back to the boompod on the tanker's interphone.

Elliott looked across the cockpit and rechecked the fuel distribution system's indicators. Ormack had taken it off "automatic" to avoid putting fuel into the left outboard wing tank in case it sustained any damage when the tip tank ripped off at Dreamland, and now the system required careful monitoring.

"Showing no flow down here," he radioed to the tanker.

"That's it, Genesis," Ashley said. "We've got enough to return to Shemya, shoot one approach, go missed approach, and arrive at Anchorage with ten thousand over the fix."

Elliott totaled up the gauges and checked it against the fuel totalizer. It would have to do.

"I'll take a disconnect, Icepack," Ormack said. In the refueling pod

Mason gave a short countdown and punched the nozzle out of the Old Dog's receptacle. Ormack reached up and closed the slipway door.

"Descending to two-seven zero," Ormack reported.

"Eddie, I want to thank you for your cooperation," Elliott said as the Old Dog began its descent away frm the KC-10 tanker. "I assure you, I'll take full responsibility for any heat you might take."

"I'm counting on that, General," Sands said. "I guess this makes us even."

"We were always even."

"Maybe . . . You know I have to file a report about this. The refueling, the comm jamming, the expended munitions. Everything."

"Of course. No offense intended, Eddie, but I know you'll file the report in your usual complete, timely, thorough manner."

"Anything *else* you need, General?" Sands asked, biting out the words.

"A name, Eddie," Elliott said. "A tanker, a deployment, a large aircraft from Anchorage that passed by within the past twelve hours."

"Sure, why not?" Sands turned to the interphone, asked the copilot for the communications kit, then said over the radio, "Might as well set an all-time record for breaking the rules in one glorious day."

" 'Bag' was a KC-10 fighter drag from Elmendorf to Nellis," Ashley said, checking his classified call sign booklet. " 'Crow' was an AWACS from Eielson to Sapporo. 'Lantern' was a KC-10 from Elmendorf to Kadena."

"I'm not going to ask why you needed that," Sands said. "Can we turn around now? How much further toward never-never land do we have to follow you?"

"Clear to turn, Eddie—and thanks."

"See you . . ." Sands watched as the descending bomber melted into the darkness.

"Genesis is clear," Elliott reported to him. Then, silence. The lights on the huge aircraft blinked out, and it disappeared completely.

The boom operator looked wearily at Colonel Sands.

"Reynolds, are the radios clear?"

"Negative," the pilot told Sands. "Still heavy jamming."

"Well, he can't jam SATCOM," Sands replied angrily. "Transmit a post-refueling report directly to SAC. Label it URGENT. Report the receiver's call sign, direction of flight, onload, everything. As soon as we're out of range of their jammers, direct command post to make a transcript of the radio transmissions." Sands stared out the boom window into the inky blackness. "I'll file it in my 'usual timely, efficient manner,' you old bastard," Sands muttered. "And I'll be there to watch you roast on a spit."

***

"So what's the news?" Elliott asked Ormack. The copilot had just got off the interphone with McLanahan, coordinating the distances, altitudes, and fuel flows. Elliott had just finished a five-minute stint on the firefighting oxygen mask and had done a station check of the cockpit and left and right load central circuit breaker panels, the two massive walls of circuit breakers and fuses lining the pressure cabin between the pilot's and defensive operator's compartments. He had also checked for fuel leaks around the air refueling valve in the upper deck walkway.

"Want the good news or bad news first?" McLanahan asked him.

"Better give me the bad news first."

"We are some sixty thousand pounds short of fuel," Ormack said.

Elliott had no answer to that one. The enormous quantity involved . . .

"Eighteen thousand of that, of course, was the left outboard drop tank," Ormack went on. "I put some fuel in the left inboard drop and left outboard wing tanks during refueling, but there's a serious leak in both those tanks and it's almost gone—about fifteen thousand pounds. I transferred the rest into the mains to keep from losing it all. There might also be a small leak in the right outboard tank, which happened when we hit the hangar. Our automatic fuel management system is now out the porthole until the right drop tank and outboards are dry. That's why we have so much rudder trim in—the right wing is twenty-one tons heavier than the left."

"Sixty thousand pounds short," Elliott muttered. "Two hours fuel. Well, what's the *good* news?" He looked to Ormack, who nodded to McLanahan.

"I've been looking at the aeronautical charts on board," McLanahan began. "There are some civil aviation airways from Alaska to Japan that cross very close to the Kamchatka peninsula."

"Sure," Elliott said, as Ormack pulled out his copy of the high-altitude navigation chart from his publications bin. "The Russians can't completely close off their airspace, even their air defense identification zone. But we'd need a flight plan to enter that airway. If we just appear out of nowhere we'll get intercepted for sure."

"But they won't see us," Wendy Tork said.

Ormack asked, "How can they miss us? That airway is only . . . ." he measured the distance with a pencil ". . . about a hundred and twenty miles from their radar."

"Well, Seattle Center couldn't see us at that same distance. Remember, they only had a secondary beacon target on us, on our transponder. And I'd guess that Seattle's radar is better than a Siberian one. Our fibersteel skin has already proved itself—Los Angeles Center couldn't see us after we launched out of Dreamland, and we were right in the middle of their airspace."

"But we've somehow got to jump into their coastline," Ormack said. "How do we do that?"

"Dave and I have been doing some wagging on the computer down here," McLanahan said, "and here's what we've come up with . . . there's an island off the east coast of the Kamchatka peninsula, midway between Kavaznya to the north and the sub pens at Petropavlovsk to the south. It's pretty big and has an airfield—if I'm not mistaken they've got sub communications gear there."

"Beringa," Dave said, pointing to his high-altitude map. "They've got a circle around it that looks like surveillance radar only. No high-altitude coverage." He went back to his work on the computer terminal.

"Beringa Island," McLanahan took it up, "is right in a gap in high-altitude radar coverage between Ossora Airfield near Kavaznya and Petropavlovski. It's also only a few miles off the high-altitude airway between Anchorage and Japan. We can head toward that gap, cut just to the south of surveillance radar coverage at Beringa, and still be at high altitude all the way. Once we get inside high-altitude radar coverage, we'll only be about seventeen minutes from the coast. We duck under high-altitude radar and then get into the mountains along the spine of the Kamchatka peninsula. If we stay away from Beringa radar, the lowest we'll have to go is about five thousand feet until we get into Kavaznya low-altitude surveillance radar coverage."

"Did you work out the fuel for a plan like that?" Elliott asked.

"Yes," Luger told him, "and it's close. We'd never make it back to Eielson, that's for sure. We'd barely make it back across the Bering Strait, but we'd do it." I hope, he added to himself.

Ormack looked at Elliott, who shrugged. "Looks like one of those ice-bound alternates will have to do," he said.

"We do have another problem," Luger said, checking the computer display again. "The computer doesn't have elevation data for any of the Kamchatka peninsula except for about a hundred miles around Kavaznya. That means that most of the ride up the mountain ranges would be either at safe-clearance altitudes or manual terrain-avoidance. That's a pretty wild ride even for our experienced crew. We're good, but good enough for two hours of manual terrain-following? We have no detailed charts, no terrain elevations. We'd be relying on radar the whole way until the computer could start driving the boat."

"Well," Elliott said, "now I know why we brought two navigators along. Do you think you could have come up with all that so fast, John?"

Ormack shook his head. "Not with all the computers in Japan, General."

"Well, we've got the gas, and now we've got a plan. Patrick, Dave, how long will it take you to reenter your new flight plan in the computer?"

In reply, the steering bug on the pilot's Attitude-Directional Indicator swung around until it was pointing about twenty degrees left of their present heading. "Steering is good to intercept the airway," Luger said. "The new flight plan is entered and active."

"Are we clear of Attu airspace?" Elliott asked.

"Affirmative," McLanahan said, checking his chart and the satellite navigator's present position readout. "Attu is off our four o'clock, just over a hundred miles. We're in international airspace."

"Second-station computer control coming in," Elliott said. He engaged the autopilot to the navigation computers, and the Old Dog banked left in response to the new turning signals. Soon the heading bug was centered at the top of the heading indicator case.

"We'll be within high radar coverage of Ossora Airfield in about an hour," Luger reported.

"Good," Elliott said. He forced himself to relax and found that his grip on the yoke was that much tighter. "If there are any last-minute equipment checks to do, now's the time to do them. If not, try to get some rest."

Ormack looked across at the three-star general beside him, and they exchanged smiles.

"Well, at least try to *relax*," Elliott corrected himself.

Luger checked the position and heading readouts and marked a fix point on his chart. " 'Relax,' he says. Better said than done. Less than an hour from low level, about two hours to the target—a target in goddamned *Russia*—and he wants us to—"

He glanced over at McLanahan. His partner had his arms wrapped around his body, his head awkwardly lying back on the headrest of his ejection seat. His snoring could be clearly heard over the roar of the Old Dog's eight turbofan engines.

"Amazing," he said, shaking his head in disbelief. "Absolutely fuckin' amazing."

"Ten minutes from horizon crossing," Luger announced.

McLanahan had just caught Luger's last announcement as he plugged into the defense instructor's interphone cord once again. He handed Wendy and Angelina two cans of water each and a green packet of freeze-dried food. "Leave one can out for now, and stick the rest in the pockets in the liner of your jackets." He watched as both women unbuckled their parachute harnesses. They were now wearing life preservers, small green pouches on a harness on their waists, and had to buckle those to unzip their jackets and stuff the water and food into the jacket pockets.

Angelina's water and food rations stuck out in bulky bulges from her denim jacket. With McLanahan's help she refastened her parachute harness and slipped on the silver firefighting gloves she was using as flight gloves. Wendy had already given Angelina her thermal underwear tops and was drinking hot soup made in the hot cup downstairs. Angelina, however, still shivered in the chill of the Old Dog's upper cabin.

"Comfy?" McLanahan said to Angelina. "I hope you ladies don't have to go potty now."

Angelina turned on him. "Are we supposed to eat this stuff in a life raft bobbing in the North Pacific Ocean? What's the point?"

McLanahan looked at Wendy—that scenario had never occurred to her.

He cleared his throat and said quickly, "Nah. Down low level the aircraft shakes around a bit. Things tend to roll around. You don't want to have to unstrap to look for your water." It was a lame excuse, but Angelina, noticing Wendy's thin-lipped expression, nodded and turned again to her equipment.

Wendy was staring blankly at her threat receiver display. "I wonder if we're kidding ourselves . . . about what we're doing . . ."

"The thought has crossed my mind," McLanahan said. "It's impossible to be certain about that. I think that . . . well, you have to listen to your gut . . . I keep seeing Hal Briggs trying to open that fence for us back at Dreamland, I wonder if he's okay . . ."

General Elliott came over the interphone. "Patrick, get strapped in. Time, Dave?"

"Two minutes to horizon passage," Luger reported.

McLanahan gave Wendy what he hoped was a reassuring squeeze on the arm, then turned and climbed downstairs back to his seat.

"Horizon passage," Luger announced, marking a fixpoint on the high-altitude airways chart he was using. "Two hundred and seventy miles to Kavaznya."

"Scope's clear," Wendy reported quietly, still thinking about what McLanahan had said. Her voice recovered its strength, though, as she brought her attention back to business. "We're still at extreme detection range. With our fibersteel body and anti-radar enhancements they might not get a radar return from us until we're about one hundred miles out. If then."

"Will you be able to tell if they can see us?" Elliott asked.

"I'll be able to see their transmission signal when it comes up," she replied. "I've got an idea from Seattle Center's radar and from the Shemya tanker and the fighters Colonel Sands chased us with what signal strength it takes to get a solid skin-paint on us, so I can tell you when we're getting close to that. I can also see if they search or try to lock onto us with any height-finding or missile-guidance radars."

"And nothing so far?"

"Nothing. Not even search radar. But being so close to the horizon does strange things to electronic transmissions. They could've spotted us even before we crossed the plane of their horizon without my knowing, or they might not see us until we're well above the horizon. It's hard to predict—radar bounces off the ionosphere in weird ways. Like I said, they may already have detected us."

Elliott checked the IFF controls to make sure they were all off. "Crew, double-check around your stations to be sure you're not transmitting on anything. Radars, radios, jammers, anything. Switch your wafer switches to INTERPHONE to keep from accidentally talking over the radios."

McLanahan double checked his interphone switches, also checked to make sure the circuit breakers controlling the bomb bay walkway lights were off—if they had to open the bomb doors the walkway lights could easily give the bomber away at night.

"Offensive checks," McLanahan reported.

"How far are we from—"

"Search radar at two o'clock," Wendy suddenly called out. The announcement shook up McLanahan and Luger in the lower offensive crew compartment.

"Here we go," Luger said. He was bundled up with his jacket zipped up to his chin, collars pulled up. He had long ago cleared off his retractable work desk. Only the high-altitude chart remained.

"It feels so weird," McLanahan said. "They can see us now. It feels a lot different."

"Yeah," Luger said. "Kind of a joy ride—until now."

"Two o'clock?" Elliott said. "What's at two o'clock? Korf Airfield? Anadyr? It can't be Ossora or Kavaznya—unless we're off course—they should be at twelve o'clock."

Wendy studied her frequency video. "It's a different frequency than a ground-based radar, and it's stronger than the radar should be so far away."

"Could it be the laser's tracking radar?"

"No, this one has a very low frequency—an old system. I think this is an airborne search radar."

"Airborne?" Ormack said in surprise. "Maritime reconnaissance or some sort of patrol—"

"Or a chance encounter," Elliott said. "Let's wait to see what—"

"He's got us," Wendy announced, studying the frequency shift and listening to the radar's real audio. "Change from a slow scan to lock-on. No height-finder or uplink—just a faster scan."

"Like station-keeping?" McLanahan asked. "Like a mapping radar switched to narrow sector?"

"That would explain it," Wendy said. "He's transmitting on UHF."

"Can you get a frequency?" Elliott asked her.

"Only a wide frequency range. High UHF. I can't tell if he's getting a response."

"Let me try to get him on attack radar," McLanahan said. "At least confirm if he's airborne."

"Go ahead," Elliott said. "No more than a few seconds, though."

McLanahan adjusted the antenna controls to point his large attack radar at two o'clock, set the range for a hundred miles, then greased the TRANSMIT button. After three full sweeps he turned the radar back to STANDBY. "Looks like he's airborne, all right. Two o'clock, sixty miles. With my antenna tilt two degrees below level I'd estimate his altitude at thirty-three thousand feet—"

And then came the challenge: "Unknown aircraft, two hundred and forty kilometers northeast of Ostrov Kommandorskiy, respond." Followed by another message, which sounded like the same request, this time in Russian.

"That's us," Luger confirmed. "About a hundred and thirty miles northeast of Beringa."

"Sounded like he was on GUARD channel," Ormack said, monitoring the emergency UHF channel. "Do we answer him?"

"You're sure he's tracking us, Wendy?" Elliott asked.

"He can see us, all right, but I don't think he's tracking us. Just following us with his radar. There's no guidance-type tracking signal."

"How far are we from the Alaska-Japan airway?"

Luger checked his chart against the computer's present-position readout. "Just a few minutes ahead—"

"Unknown aircraft, please respond. *Pazhaloosta.*"

"Please?" General Elliott smiled. "Sounds like a kid. A *polite* kid."

Ormack looked at his pilot with surprise. "I didn't know you understood Russian."

"I learned just enough to get my head blown off," Elliott said. He thought for a moment. "If we tried to duck down to low-level now—"

"He might lose us if we pushed it over hard enough," Ormack said. "We might make it."

"I don't think he could follow us with his radar," Wendy added. "It doesn't seem to be a sophisticated system, but he'd report losing us. He's also in contact with someone out there. It might be Ossora . . ."

"Or it might be a wingman," Lanahan put in. "Maybe an escort."

"Can you jam his transmissions, Wendy?" Elliott asked.

"Yes, but that would be a dead giveaway."

"All right. Let's get on the airway and see what this guy does." He turned the wheel, and the bomber banked steeply to the left. "If he intercepts us, we'll have to—try to down him. No other choice. Copy, Angelina?"

"I'm ready, General," she said, checking her weapon-status indications.

"We'll be just outside radar range of Beringa on this heading," Luger reported as the Old Dog completed its steep turn.

"Permission to use the tail radar to pick him up, General," Angelina called.

"Not yet." Elliott took a deep breath, pulled the microphone closer to his lips, then switched his radio switch to GUARD.

"Calling unknown aircraft, this is Lantern four-five Fox on GUARD. Say your call sign. Over."

"Lantern four-five Fox, this is Besarina two-two-one on GUARD. I read you loud and clear." The Soviet pilot then said something in Russian.

"Besarina two-two-one, I read you, but I don't understand Russian." Elliott paused, then said, *"Ya in gavaryoo na vashim yizikye kharasho.* Say again."

"Prastiti. I am sorry, four-five Fox. You . . . you are United States aircraft?"

"Da."

"Amirikanskaya," the Soviet pilot said excitedly. Then, more officially, reported, "Four-five Fox, you are at our twelve o'clock position, seven-six kilometers." A slight pause. "I . . . I never talk to United States before."

Ormack let out a long breath of air. "Looks like you may have made a friend, General."

"Two-two-one, you are Soviet military plane?" Elliott asked.

"Yes!" came an enthusiastic reply. *"Pay Vay Oh Strangy.* Far East Command." Elliott translated to the crew, as he did all the Russian.

"PVO Strany," Elliott said over interphone. "Air Defense unit. Could be a Bear or Backfire recon plane."

"Or a fighter," Angelina said.

"Gyda vi zhivyoti—excuse, *pazhaloosta.* Where you from, four-five Fox?" the Soviet pilot asked. "New York? Los Angeles? I know San Francisco."

"Butte, Montana," Elliott said. Let him chew on that.

"Mon-tanya? My English not very good. They teach English but we do not use much. Difficult."

A pause, then: "Four-five Fox, contact Kommandorskiye Approach on two-six-five decimal five. Immediately." The new voice was clipped, military, authoritative.

"Da, tovarisch," Elliott replied.

"I report . . . I report you on course okay, commander," the Russian pilot said in a low, almost secretive voice. "You correcting back. Not okay to come closer. Okay, commander?"

"Balshoya spasiba, tovarisch," Elliott replied. "Thank you."

"Pazhaloosta. Nice to talk English to you, Montanya."

"Two-six-five decimal five, roger," Elliott repeated. Just before he changed channels he asked, *"Atkooda vi?* Where are you from, two-two-one?"

"Ya iz—er, I from Kevitz," the Soviet pilot said with hometown pride. "Big fisherman. Nice to talk, Montanya. *Dasfidaniya, mnyabileochin priyatna!"*

Ormack shook his head as he changed the radio frequency. "Nice son of a bitch, wasn't he?"

"Kevitz," Elliott said. "That's what Kavaznya was known as before they built the laser there."

"He gave us a break," Luger said. "I'll bet he plotted our position. He must've noticed us because we were so far outside the airway."

"He's not scanning us on radar anymore," Wendy reported.

Elliott reset the frequency on the number one radio.

"You're not going to contact Kommandorskiye, are you General?" Ormack said.

"We don't have any choice, John. If we don't contact them, our friendly Bolshevik back there comes back and blows Montanya and his friends away."

Elliott keyed the microphone. "Kommandorskiye Approach, Lantern four-five Fox is with you at flight level four-five zero."

"Lantern four-five Fox, roger, at flight level four-five zero," the Russian air traffic controller replied in hesitant English. "Say your heading, please."

"Sto shizfisyat. Heading is one-six-zero, Approach."

"Roger, four-five Fox. *Spasiba."* There was a slight pause, then: "I do not have a flight plan for you, Lantern four-five Fox."

"No shit," Ormack said over interphone.

"We are on a military flight plan from Alaska to Japan," Elliott said.

"I show no flight plan," the controller repeated. "Please relay type of aircraft, departure base, destination base, time enroute, hours of fuel on board, and persons on board, please."

"No way," Ormack said. "I haven't done an international flight plan in years, but at least I know it's never relayed to a Soviet controller."

"Yes," Elliott said, "you're right. This guy's just fishing for information." On the radio Elliott said, "Kommandorskiye, we will ask Kadena overwater flight following to relay our flight plan to you."

"I will be happy to take the information, sir," the controller said . . . "as a convenience."

Nice try, Ivan, Elliott said to himself. Over the radio: "Thank you Kommandorskiye. We will notify Kadena. Stand by."

"Very well," the controller replied coldly. "Lantern four-five Fox, squawk three-seven-seven-one and ident."

"Shit," Ormack said. "Now he wants us to get a squawk."

"Looks like we're digging a hole for ourselves," Elliott said, reached down and set the four-digit IFF identification and tracking code, leaving the altitude encoding and modes one, two, and four switches off. He then switched the IFF to ON and hit the IDENT button.

"Four-five Fox squawking," Elliott said.

"Radar identified, Lantern four-five Fox," the Soviet controller replied. "I am not reading your altitude. Please recycle mode C."

"Recycling," Elliott said. He turned the mode C altitude encoder on.

"I am reading your altitude—" Elliott switched him off.

"I have lost your altitude again, four-five Fox. Recycle again, please."

Elliott repeated his "failed" mode C routine.

"Your mode C appears to be intermittent, four-five Fox," the controller at Beringa finally said.

"Roger, we'll write it up, sir."

"I cannot allow you to cross into Petropavlovsk airspace without a fully operable identification encoder, four-five Fox," the controller said. "Please turn twenty degrees left, vectors clear of Soviet airpsace. Maintain heading for one-five minutes, then resume own navigation. *Ochin zhal.* Sorry."

"How far does that put us off the airway?" Elliott asked Luger.

"We're almost on the airway now. We'd end up seventy, eighty miles west."

Elliott turned the Old Dog to the new heading.

"How long are we going to be in Beringa's radar coverage?"

"We're only on the edge of it now," Luger said.

"Their radar signal is very weak," Wendy said. "No guarantee—but I don't think they've got a primary target on us."

"Meaning . . ." Ormack began.

"If we shut the IFF off, we disappear," Elliott said. "Just like Seattle. Patrick, how far are we from your next planned turn-point inland?"

"We'll never hit it on this heading."

"Call it up," Elliott said, taking manual control of the Old Dog. The computer heading bug swung almost fifty degrees to the right.

"About twenty minutes," Elliott estimated. "That puts us between both Beringa and Petropavlovsk radars."

"And as close to the coast as we can get between the two radars," McLanahan added.

"I don't think it'll take Beringa that long to discover we don't have a flight plan," Elliott said. "Things are going to get hairy pretty soon. Wendy, you're sure he can't see us?"

"As sure as I can be."

"Can you jam their radar in case he spots us?"

"Yes, I'm positive of *that.*"

Elliott adjusted his parachute harness. "This means we're close to the penetration descent, crew. Wendy, prepare to take the Center radar down. We'll be making a power-off descent in a few seconds. When everyone's ready to go, we'll start a gradual turn toward the gap in the radar coverage. When Beringa notices us off-course we'll engage the terrain-avoidance computers, make a rapid descent to five thousand feet and a quick turn toward the gap. Once we go coast-in we'll stay at five thousand unless the navigators tell us differently. We'll rely on the shorter-range mapping radar to stay down just low enough to clear the terrain until the computer enters the altitude-plotted region, then put it on the deck when we get within range of Kavaznya's radars—or if we get chased down beforehand. Questions? Okay, how much time to the gap?"

"About fifteen minutes, General," Luger said.

"Anyone looking at us, Wendy?"

Wendy was studying her scope, cross-checking some of the signals present with a frequency comparison chart in her checklist. "I can see Beringa looking for us, but I'm sure they can't get a primary target on us—their signal is very weak. No airborne radars up. There's . . ."

"What?"

"Another search radar comes up only every few minutes or so," she said, puzzled. "It's not a Soviet radar, at least not one I've seen before. It's extremely weak and intermittent—like it's being turned on and off at random."

"Can it see us?" Elliott asked her. "Could it spot us if we were at low altitude?"

"I don't think so. It doesn't come up long enough for me to analyze, but the signal is so intermittent that I don't think they could plot us even if they could see us. It could be nothing more than a trawler or cargo ship with a weather radar."

"Well," Elliott said, unclenching his hands from the yoke, trying to relax, "it seems we've got more than enough to think about."

Gently he eased the wheel to the right and pointed the sleek nose of the Old Dog toward the Soviet Union.

"Here we go . . ."

The Chief of Intellitence aboard the U.S.S. *Lawrence* ran down the metal hallway to the radio room, where a small knot of officers, enlisted personnel and civilian technicians clustered around one bank of radio scanners.

"What the hell is going on?" Markham asked as he pulled off his orange fur-lined jacket.

"An American aircraft, Commander Markham," Lieutenant J.G. Beech, the senior controller, reported hastily, cocking one earpiece of his headset to the side—but not enough to keep him from listening to the channels he was monitoring. A seaman came up to him with a short message. The senior controller read it quickly, swearing softly to himself.

"Well, what the hell is it, Beech?"

"An American aircraft, Commander," Beech said. "Came over UHF GUARD emergency channel a few minutes ago." He shook his head. "The aircraft is in Soviet airspace, being controlled by a Soviet controller—"

"An *American* aircraft?" Markham grabbed the note out of Beech's hand.

"Lantern four-five Fox," Markham read. "Lantern. That sounds familiar."

"It should," Beech said. "We monitored four Lanterns from Elmendorf dragging a bunch of F-4s to Japan yesterday. Those were KC-10s with an international flight plan—coordinated days in advance. Lantern two-one through two-four."

"Did you get this guy's flight plan?"

"There's no Lantern four-five Fox," Beech said. "Never was. It didn't come out of Elmendorf."

"Where, then?"

"We're double-checking," Beech said. "But this guy has no flight plan. We're trying to get confirmation from Elmendorf but so far we have nothing."

"Did you get *anything?*" Markham asked. "Type aircraft? Anything?"

"Nothing. I'll get the tape for the staff meeting, but there was nothing. A Soviet controller on Beringa Island in the Kommandorskiyes asked him all that when he looked up his flight plan, but he didn't tell him anything . . . Here's how it went, sir . . . a PVO Strany jet out of Petropavlosk picks up a Lantern four-five Fox on airborne radar and calls for him in the blind on GUARD. When he started to call we got on the radar and looked for him, too. We had the PVO jet all the way but we couldn't find the other guy until the PVO jet called out his range and bearing. We plotted him forty miles east of the airway—and then we got a track on him. This four-five Fox plane looked like he was heading toward Russia—"

"*Toward* Russia?" Markham swiveled in the navy-gray seat. "From *where?* Didn't we see him before?"

"He just sort of appeared out of nowhere. We weren't really scanning for aircraft but we should have spotted him before the PVO-Strany surveillance plane did. I don't know how we—"

"Where is he now?"

"We lost contact with four-five Fox right after he crossed back onto the airway," Beech said. "Apparently he was crossing south of the Kommandorskiyes, and that's just about the limit of our coverage.

"But get this—when we picked him up on radar he wasn't squawking anything. When he contacted Beringa they assigned him a mode three squawk, but his mode C altitude readout was out. Then Beringa kicks him out of their airspace and gives him a vector out around Petropavlovsk airspace."

"Jesus," Markhan said, wiping his forehead. "Someone's screwing up but bad here." He thought for a moment. "No mode one? Mode two? Four?" Those were U.S. military-only identification codes.

"Nothing—not even after Beringa talked to him."

"An aircraft with a military call sign," Markham said, "but with nothing but mode 3—and *that* assigned by a Soviet controller."

"He was speaking Russian to him, too, sir," a technician said from a nearby radio console.

"Russian?" Markham said. "What the hell was he saying?"

"Conversational. Please, thank you, that sort of thing. Asked the PVO Strany recon jet pilot where he was from."

"Did the Lantern pilot sound Russian?"

"No, sounded like maybe he used to speak it in the past, but he was definitely American. Even said he was from Butte, Montana."

"We have no further contact with this guy?"

"Radio contact only," Beech said, "but he hasn't talked to Beringa for some time so we couldn't get an updated DF steer on him." He motioned over to a large glass plotting board near the communications center, which he and Markham walked over to.

"Here's our position," Beech told the intelligence chief, pointing to a tiny ship sticker, "a hundred and fifty miles west northeast of the Kommandorskiyes. Here's the airway—we're sitting almost directly under it. We first plotted the unknown aircraft here, northwest of us and forty miles east of the airway, heading southeast. He intersected the airway here and flew along it for a few minutes until Beringa chased him further away from Petropavlosk airspace, which he'd run into in about twenty to thirty minutes. Our last DF steer put him south of the Kommandorskiyes, a little bit west of the airway. But Beringa control had confirmed him on a mag heading of one four-zero, which would put him well outside Petropavlosk airspace. Even if he went direct to Sapporo or Tokyo he'd never get close enough to worry anyone."

"Is there *any* chance this could be a Soviet aircraft?" Markham asked. "How do we know it's American?"

Beech looked puzzled. "Well . . . except for his call sign, we don't, sir."

"But you've said there's no Lantern four-five Fox from anywhere."

"We haven't received confirmation from Elmendorf," Beech said. "They won't talk about their aircraft on unsecure radios. All we know is that no flight plan has been filed on a Lantern four-five Fox. It could've been dropped, or filed late . . . It's unusual but it can happen. And . . . well, he *sounded* American, sounded military."

"Enlightened speculation goes down okay here, Beech," Markham said, trying to smile but not managing it. "But how do we account for this?" Markham pointed to the projected trackline of the unknown aircraft. "What's he doing way the hell over *here?*"

Beech shrugged. "Maybe he got lost. *Really* lost. Maybe he's sightseeing. Joyriding. Some jet jockey with a fake call sign playing fucking Red Rover with the Russians?"

"Well, we'll leave that one to the CIA or the Air Force," Markham said. He stood and stretched. "Send a report to headquarters about this guy. Advise to obtain positive identification before allowing him into Japanese airspace. Suggest a navy or DIA investigation on him when he lands." He ran his hands over his expanding belly. "I'm going to see if they've dreamed up anything new to do with hamburger in the mess. I'll be upstairs."

"Lieutenant Beech," one of the radio operators suddenly called out, "Channel seventeen, sir."

Beech replaced his headset. After a moment he said urgently, "Jonesy, put it on speakers. Sir, listen to this."

The operator flipped a few switches, and soon the room was filled with static. A few moments later a Russian accent boomed, "Lantern four-five Fox, acknowledge."

"It's Beringa," Beech said to Markham.

"Lantern four-five Fox, this is Kommandorskiye Approach Control on GUARD frequency. Urgent. You are violating Soviet airspace. Lantern four-five Fox, turn thirty degrees left immediately and ident. Repeat. You are one-zero-zero kilometers off course and in violation of Soviet airspace.

Turn left thirty degrees immediately and ident." The warning was then repeated in Russian and in clumsy Chinese.

"One hundred kilometers," Beech said. "What the hell is that guy up to?"

"Whatever," Markham said, "he's in deep shit now."

"Lantern four-five Fox, this is Kommandorskiye Approach on GUARD. I have lost your beacon. Repeat, I have lost your beacon. Check your IFF is in NORMAL and squawk ident immediately. You are in violation of Soviet airspace. Identify yourself immediately."

"That's it," Markham said. "Cancel that last report. Prepare a priority One message for Pacific Fleet headquarters. Say that an unidentified aircraft, presumed American military, has violated Soviet airspace. Give our position and the last reported and estimated position of the aircraft. Soviet intentions are unknown but we expect them to search, intercept and destroy. We do not have any reason to believe that the unknown aircraft has an emergency, but tell them that he may be having navigational difficulties. More details to follow. I'll have the Captain sign it immediately. And get a report ready for the Old Man," Markham told Beech. "He's gonna want one fast. I'm going to get permission to send up a radar balloon."

"We may be able to move closer to his last reported position," Beech suggested. "Get on the other side of the Kommandorskiyes. If this guy's in trouble we can—"

"We haven't even established if the son of a bitch is American," Markham cut in. "He could be part of some elaborate Russian scheme to pull us away from monitoring Kavaznya. I'll suggest it, Beech, but I won't recommend it. Besides, he'd be too far inside Soviet territory for us to do anything."

As his intelligence people hurried to execute his orders, Markham studied the plotting board. In front of him a technician made a series of computations and drew another line, plotting the unknown aircraft's possible location.

"I don't know who you are," Markham said under his breath, "but, buddy, you just stirred up one hell of a hornet's nest."

"Call up the next point," Elliott said. His arms were extended almost straight out from his body, straining to hold the control yoke forward, forcing the Old Dog down toward the dark waters of the north Pacific. The heading bug swung twenty degrees to the right. As the Old Dog started a right turn to the new computerized heading, Elliott spun the large trim wheel by his right knee forward to help him hold the bomber's nose down—at the current rate of descent and high airspeed, the *Megafortress* wanted nothing except to zoom skyward.

As he reached for the trim wheel Elliott touched his right knee. The feeling—a tingling sensation, like it was asleep—had still been there a few hours ago, but it was gone now. A ring of pain encircled his thigh midway between his knee and hip like a clamp. A muscle twitched involuntarily on his right buttock. He looked over and saw Ormack carefully watching him.

"Bad?"

"Just watch your damn instruments, John."

Ormack nodded, not reassured.

Nearly forty years earlier, Elliott recalled, he had hurt that knee falling out of a hayloft on his father's farm. While sitting in the school library, sidelined from the football team, he had read all the books printed on the subject of knee injuries, vitamins to help mending ligaments, special exercises to strengthen muscles. After the cast came off he nursed the weakened knee back to health in only a few weeks, just in time for baseball season. The year his school won the state championship. He remembered the pride he felt at the time. Would he be as proud when this was over?

"Will that heading keep us clear of Beringa's radar?"

"It should," Luger said. "It'll take us around on a one hundred and twenty-mile arc." He checked the altimeter on his front instrument panel. It was spinning down faster than he'd ever seen, like a clock gone haywire. He was so light in his seat that he had to snatch his charts and pencil in midair to keep them from floating away in the negative Gs. "Passing twenty-five thousand for five thousand," he called out. He remembered Major White's egress trainers back at Ford, the way White made his huge mechanical beast dance on its ten-foot hydraulic legs. Well, this was for real—and it was much more than White could ever dream up . . . "Passing twenty thousand." Ford Air Force Base seemed very, very far away.

"How far were we from your start-descent point, McLanahan?" Ormack asked.

"Still about six minutes."

"I'm surprised," Luger said, "that they took that long to catch us. Hell, we were almost seventy miles off-course before they called us."

"Coming up on fifteen thousand," McLanahan sang out.

"Both radar altimeter channels are ready," Ormack repeated. "Clearance plane is set to five thousand feet. Autopilot pitch command mode slaved to radar altimeter."

"Good." Elliott flipped switches on his left panel beside his ejection seat. "Okay, crew, listen up. You now have full authorization for all defensive measures. Angelina, you have *Scorpion* missile consent. *Scorpion* bay doors are at your command. Keep your radar transmissions to an absolute minimum. Wendy, you have full jamming authority. If any tracking or guidance signals come up that you think are strong enough to paint us, jam the piss out of them. Patrick, you're now on interceptor watch. Leave navigation to Dave unless he needs help in the mountains. If Wendy sees any fighters that look like they're trying to track us, you've got authority to transmit and lock onto them."

"Passing ten thousand, General," Luger said. "Five thousand to go."

Elliott slowly began to pull back on the yoke and bring the throttles forward from idle to cruise thrust. The roller-coaster descent began to subside. As Luger counted the altitude down, Elliott decreased the descent rate until the Old Dog was leveled off.

"Radar altimeter lock-on," Ormack announced. He flipped a switch, double-checking the readouts. "Both radar altimeter channels are ready."

"Autopilot coming on," Elliott said. He flipped the autopilot switch on. The Old Dog remained rock-steady at five thousand feet. Now a pitch computer, slaved to signals from the radar altimeter, would work to keep the Old Dog at a mere five thousand feet above the water.

"Autopilot's engaged," Elliott confirmed. "Setting four thousand for a system check." He turned the clearance-plane knob down one notch, and the Old Dog started a gentle dive, settling to precisely four thousand feet above the water.

"Resetting five thousand." He turned the knob clockwise and the huge bomber started a slow climb back to five thousand feet.

"Anybody looking for us, Wendy?" Elliott asked.

"Very low-power radar signals. Much too low to see us. Nothing from Petropavlovsk radar. Lots of UHF and VHF radio transmissions, though."

"But none of it on GUARD anymore, I'll bet," Ormack said. "They know we can monitor GUARD."

"Which means they're no longer interested in rescue," Elliott said. "No more Mister Nice-Guy." He thought for a moment. "Time to the coast, Dave?"

"Twelve minutes," Luger said, checking the computer readouts.

"I feel exposed down here," Elliott said. "I feel everyone can see us. I can't wait to get back into the dirt."

"I'd expect company long before that," Ormack said. "I'd expect a fighter sweep of the area along our projected track line, then a second flight on the landward side."

"What altitude you figure the fighters will come in?" Elliott asked.

"If they have the resources—and I'll bet they do—it'll be a high-cap, low-cap arrangement. The lowest might be five thousand feet. More likely, eight to ten thousand. High-cap will be up around thirty thousand."

"How's the fuel situation?"

"Worse than I thought," Ormack told him. "I've just put the fuel management system back to automatic. The early descent had little effect on the curve, but the tip gear we're dragging is just sucking our gas up. I have us at least five thousand below the revised fuel curve."

"Every pound of gas is critical now," Elliot said. "Patrick, can we cut off any points on your flight plan? Cut this corner a bit?"

"Risky," McLanahan said, studying his chart. "We can head for the next point on the flight plan. It'll save us about five minutes or so, but it'll put us closer to a small town on the coastline. I wanted to avoid this town by at least ten miles. If we cut the corner, we almost overfly it."

"At high altitude, ten minutes worth of fuel is a drop in the bucket," Ormack said. "Down here . . ."

"Is that town defended?" Elliott asked. "Any airfields there? Naval docks?"

"I don't know," McLanahan said. "There's no detail like that on the charts I'm using."

"We'll have to risk it," Elliott said. "The faster we get back over land, the better I'll feel. Call up the next point, Patrick."

McLanahan punched up the new destination number on his keyboard, verified the coordinates with his penciled notes on the margin of his makeshift chart and displayed the destination. The pilot's heading bug shifted thirty degrees more to the right. The Old Dog banked right in response.

"Landfall in six minutes," Luger said.

"Stay on watch, everyone," Elliott said. "Stay on watch . . ."

"They're launching the whole goddamned Russian Eastern Air Defense Command," Beech said. He was sitting in direct command of the intelligence section; Markham and Captain Jacobs, captain of the *Lawrence,* were on the bridge.

"The son of a bitch couldn't have picked a worse place this side of the Caspian Sea to disappear off Russian radar," Markham told Jacobs. "Directly between Petropavlovsk and seven nuclear submarines in the pens to the south, and Kavaznya to the north."

"But how did he go off their radar?" Jacobs asked, studying the slides Markham's group had prepared of the situation. "I thought a mosquito couldn't get through their radar coverage."

"We're not sure, Captain. More than likely, the guy crashed or ditched. Right from the beginning it sounded like the guy was having navigation problems."

"Navigation problems don't make planes ditch," Jacobs said. "If he had a catastrophic emergency, enough to cause navigation or flight control problems, why the hell didn't he declare an emergency? The Russians would've helped him—I've seen them do it before."

"I don't know, sir. He may have panicked." Markham got up and pointed at the chart. "Radar coverage is sort of skimpy around here, too," he said, as much to himself as to Jacobs. "Petropavlovsk radar coverage doesn't quite extend this far north, but Beringa's radar does cover this entire gap."

Jacobs was about to say something but was interrupted by Beech on the intercom.

"Captain, message from PVO Strany, Far East Command headquarters, to all units. In the clear. Uncoded."

"I'm surprised they didn't read part of it in English," Jacobs said. "What are they saying?"

"Air Defense Emergency declared for the area. General orders for deploying searching fighters in the area. Complete closing of Soviet airspace."

"Send it," Markham said. "Direct CINCPAC via JCS. Priority One."

"Yes, sir."

Jacobs studied the chart closer, finally picked up a pair of dividers lying on the console near his seat. "We use two hundred and fifty nautical miles for Center radars, right?"

"Yes, sir," Markham said. "Standard line-of-sight-ranging. A bit more, depending on altitude."

"But you don't have a big circle around Beringa," Jacobs noted, measuring the lines around the islands that composed the Russian members of the Aleutian chain.

"They don't have a Center radar," Markham said, his excitement rising. "They have shorter-range, low-altitude capable radar. Approach control radar."

Jacobs measured a two hundred and fifty mile circle from Petropavlovsk. The circle barely intersected the radar circle from Beringa.

"They overlap . . ."

"But there's a gap," Markham said, pointing at the chart. "They overlap, but there's still incomplete coverage. If you avoid this circle—"

"—he's out of range." Jacobs stabbed the chart excitedly and looked at Markham. "And Petropavlovsk won't see him if—"

"If he's low level. Below five or six thousand feet, he gets lost in the background radar clutter, even over water."

"Wait a minute." Jacobs held up a hand. "You said this guy was a tanker."

"He had a tanker call sign," Markham said, checking his notes. "Lantern four-five Fox. Out of Elmendorf. But he had no flight plan, and Elmendorf reports no four-five Fox."

"So he's not a tanker. Then what?"

"A low-altitude penetrator?" Markham muttered. "A . . . a *bomber?*"

"It seems he knew exactly where to go. Exactly. How else would he know about the gaps in radar coverage?"

Markham nodded. "But . . . he surprised that recon jet."

"Got his fingers caught in the cookie jar, maybe?"

Markham shook his head. "Spotted by a recon plane, he . . . he turns around before they figure out he's headed inland—"

"*Toward Kavaznya,*" Jacobs said.

"And he's disappeared again, going in the back way."

"Goddamn," Jacobs muttered. "Why me? Why now?"

"None of our communications on this entire boat are completely secure, sir," Markham reminded the captain, second-guessing him. "If we blow the whistle—"

"Why the hell doesn't anybody tell us what's going on? Well, it's too late now anyway. The whole Far East Command is after him. He won't get far."

"So what do we do?"

Jacobs shook his head. "We do nothing. Nothing we *can* do. That guy, whoever he is, is all on his own."

"Four minutes to coast-in," Dave Luger announced.

Elliott jerked himself out of his reverie. He hadn't been sleeping—he couldn't really remember the last time he had—but he had been in some sort of daydream ever since descending to low level. Now his eyes were locked onto the dim glow of the small Russian town they were approaching.

The tiny town, too small to have a name on Luger's general-purpose navigation chart, appeared as a scattering of lights off in the distance. Just one small blob of lights, with a small string of lights trailing away— probably a lighted path down to the docks for the fishermen, or the main road in and out of town.

It wasn't the first Russian town he'd seen, but this one seemed different. Innocent. Peaceful. Moscow, the last time he was there as an Embassy adviser back in the seventies, was menacing. Even during the newlywed years of detente, he felt its choking, suffocating presence. Here, over the cold rough pioneer-like badlands of eastern Siberia, it *seemed* different . . .

Elliott unconsciously gripped the yoke tighter. The sight of the long SST nose of the Old Dog reminded him where he was, what they were doing. He readjusted his microphone.

"Wendy?"

"Nothing, General," Wendy replied, nervously anticipating his query. "Random, low-power VHF." Her voice was a clipped monotone.

"Distance to the coastal mountains, Dave?"

"General, I don't know for sure. My enroute chart doesn't show any detail of the Kamchatka peninsula. I'll need a few radar sweeps to range them out."

Elliott considered that. He couldn't wait to get within the safety of the mountains, but still . . . "All right—authorized. But no more than a few seconds."

"Better let me take a look," McLanahan said, readjusting his attack radar controls. "I can look out eighty miles in full-scan, Dave's limited to thirty in a small cone."

"Do it," Elliott told him. "Dave, can you draw a picture of the terrain? Give yourself a little topographic map?"

Luger blocked out a section of his high-altitude chart and measured out a rough eighty-mile-range radar-scope diagram, then loosened his parachute and ejection seat straps and leaned over as far as possible to look at McLanahan's ten-inch display.

"Ready."

"Here we go." McLanahan finished reconfiguring and pretuning his scope, then pressed the RADIATE button. The radar image of the eastern shore of the Kamchatka peninsula appeared—the first radar picture, McLanahan thought, from an American bomber about to make an attack on an installation of the Soviet Union. Don't dwell on it, he told himself . . . "Gently rising terrain in the next forty miles."

Luger was furiously shadow-graphing the scope presentation on his chart. "Navigation looks good—we're about thirty miles from the coast on radar, our heading looks good to avoid overflying that town. It should pass about two miles to our left. High terrain starts in about thirty-seven miles, but so far nothing is above us. Some high stuff at sixty miles but still no big shadows."

"Which means," Ormack said, "that five thousand feet might be a safe altitude for us."

"Got all you need, Dave?" McLanahan asked.

Luger shook his head as he added some detail of some long-range peaks to his bastardized terrain chart. "Few more seconds . . ." he muttered.

McLanahan nodded and continued studying the scope. "That town looks pretty big," he said over interphone as he studied the display, adjusting the video and receiver gain controls to eliminate the terrain returns, then turned to his partner. "Done with the long range, Dave?" Luger nodded. "I'm checking that town in thirty-mile range. It looks funny." He moved the range selector to thirty-mile range. The small town was now magnified in good detail at the top of his scope.

"Make it quick," Elliott warned.

"Funny?" Ormack asked. "How funny?"

"Funny as in bad news Real bad news," McLanahan said. He stared at the magnified scene for a few more sweeps, then quickly put his radar scope to STANDBY.

"General, we gotta turn. Now. At least twenty degrees right."

Why . . . ?"

"*Ships,*" McLanahan said. "One dock full of big mother ships . . ."

"Search radar at twelve o'clock," Wendy suddenly called out.

Elliott shoved the eight throttles forward and banked the *Megafortress* hard to the right.

"Give me COLA on the clearance-plane setting, John," Elliott ordered. Ormack reached across and turned the clearance plane knob down to its lowest setting. COLA—Computer-generated Lowest Altitude. Now the terrain-avoidance computer would select the lowest altitude possible for the *Megafortress* based on a small error factor of the radar altimeter or terrain-avoidance computer, plus aircraft bank angle and terrain elevation.

The computer, starting at a COLA altitude of about a hundred feet, would then evaluate itself and readjust its minimum COLA altitude, continuously striving for the lowest possible altitude. Since the Old Dog's terrain-avoidance computer was slaved only to the radar altimeter, the new lowest altitude would equate to the highest error tolerance of the radar altimeter—a scant thirty feet—plus a few feet for the normal rolling oscillations of any autopilot.

The huge bomber plunged its nose toward the inky blackness of the Russian Pacific, then slowly back to level as it quickly reached its commanded altitude. Now, nearly four hundred thousand pounds of man and machine, guided by a single thin radar beam from the bomber's belly, were skimming only a few dozen yards from the surface of the water at over four hundred miles an hour.

"Still only search radar," Wendy reported, leaning forward intently toward her TV-like threat display. "High power but still scan mode. They're . . ." A chill worked its way up McLanahan's spine even before Wendy finished her analysis of the new signals being transmitted.

"New signal coming up," Wendy said suddenly. "Narrow-scan search . . . height-finder coming up . . . they've got us, General. They've found us, surface-to-air missile signals coming up . . ."

Jeff Hampton's voice sounded strained and excited as the President picked up the telephone near his chair.

"Say that again, Jeff?" the President said, rubbing interrupted fitful sleep from his eyes. He massaged a knotted muscle in his neck and forced himself to concentrate.

"An Air Defense alert was called about fifteen minutes ago over the

Kamchatka peninsula," Hampton repeated, gulping for air. "In Russia."

"I know where the goddamned Kamchatka peninsula is, Jeff. Go on."

"An unidentified aircraft, presumed to be American, disappeared off their radar. Real close-in. Violated airspace. It . . . it had a call sign similar to . . . to the one General Elliott was using."

"Elliott? Brad Elliott? My God!"

"Not confirmed sir, but—"

"I'll be right down. Alert General Curtis. Have him meet me in the Situation Room on the double."

The President hurried out of the parlor, quickly dressed and went downstairs.

Brad Elliott, you old devil . . . You got in. You son of a bitch—you made it in.

Wendy could only focus on the video threat-display. Millions of watts of energy, directed along specific frequency and power ranges, were at her command, yet she stared transfixed at two erratic waves along one line of the threat display. Her hands were flat on her thighs, palms down, despite the Old Dog's steep bank turn which usually made her grab onto her ejection seat armrests.

The audio pickup of the two radars was hypnotizing. The first radar emitted a scratchy bleeping sound, like a seal's bark. It had begun as an intermittent signal but was now coming over twice as fast—India-band narrow-scan search radar, aimed directly at them. The second radar gave off a higher-pitched squeal, like a rusty hinge. It signaled the presence of a Golf-band height-finder, supplying altitude information to a surface-to-air missile's guidance computer.

The computer-controlled threat analyzer apparently couldn't make up its mind—it was switching its analysis symbol from "2" to "3," indicating SA-2 or SA-3 strategic missiles, which were usually designed for high-altitude penetrators. Some SA-2 systems on ships or in remote deployment areas carried nuclear warheads. The missiles . . . they called them "telephone poles" in Vietnam . . . were barely capable against low-altitude penetrators—but the Old Dog was well within the missile's lethal range.

"All radars in standby," Luger announced, double-checking both his and McLanahan's controls. He blinked in surprise at his pressure altimeter—it read minus sixty feet. He checked the radar altimeter readout on McLanahan's video screen and saw that it was pegged at a hundred feet. One hundred feet! If the COLA computer didn't compensate properly, at this altitude with only twenty degrees of bank they'd drag a wingtip in the water.

With an unsteady hand he reset the Kollsmann window on his pressure altimeter until it read a hundred feet. He could almost see the water skimming below him at over six hundred feet a second. He could do nothing else but monitor the instruments, watch and wait.

"Wendy?"

"Yes?"

"Wendy," McLanahan shouted over the intercom. "Wendy. Answer me."

"Patrick, I . . ." She closed her eyes, focusing on his voice. She opened her eyes, took a deep breath, became aware again of the threat analyzer in front of her.

"Steady tracking and surveillance signals," she reported, her voice stronger. "Tracking us, but no guidance or uplink."

Elliott watched the tiny blob of lights in the distance. Suddenly he saw a small shaft of light flare brightly, erupting from the outskirts of the town.

"Missile launch! SA-2!" from Wendy.

"I've got it, I can see it," Elliott said.

"I've got the uplink shut down." Wendy carefully adjusted the jammer's frequencies, as if she were adjusting the focus on a microscope. She glanced up at her radar altimeter repeater. "How does it look?"

"It's heading right for us," Ormack said.

"Make a hard turn into it," Wendy ordered.

"*Into* it? That will—"

"*Do* it, General," Wendy said over the interphone. The Old Dog rolled into a steep bank to the left.

"I can still see it . . . wait." Elliott's voice was suddenly less strained. "I can see the whole tail of the missile . . . it's gone. It went behind us . . ."

"Come back to the right, maximum bank, military thrust," Wendy said. Elliott immediately did it.

"SA-2 signal coming back up," Wendy said suddenly. Her hands flew over the High-speed Anti-Radiation Missile control panel. "Anti-radar missile one programmed and ready for launch."

Angelina checked her switches, watching her indicators as a HARM missile on the aft bomb bay's rotating launcher was pulled into the lower launch position. "Ready."

Wendy hit the LAUNCH button. The fibersteel bomb-bay doors swung open, and the first HARM missile was ejected into the slipstream. The launcher automatically rotated another HARM into launch position.

"HARM has a good lock-on," Wendy reported. "SA-2 missile alert . . . HARM still locked on . . . SA-2 solid missile alert." Suddenly both the MISSILE ALERT threat signal and the HARM missiles's lock-on status indication blinked off.

"SA-2 radar down," Wendy said, her breath coming back. Angelina sat back in her seat, her body relaxing. "They've switched back to wide-area search," Wendy said, monitoring the threat audio from her receivers. "No other missile tracking signals. They've lost us."

The town was passing out of view. Elliott watched the distant lights, now almost obscured by the horizon so close beneath them, as it slid past the left cockpit windows.

"Good shooting, people." He didn't say "ladies." There were no "ladies" aboard. "Call up the next point," Elliott told the navigators. "I don't want to head back to the same point. If they look for us, they'll plot our track and find us along that path." McLanahan punched instructions into the computer, the bomber made a slight turn back to the left. A few minutes later Luger announced they were crossing the coast.

"Hey, Tork. What the hell were you doing back there?" Ormack said. Wendy was waiting for him.

"Colonel Ormack," Wendy said, "the next time I give an evasion command, I don't want it second-guessed. An SA-2 leaves the rails three times faster than any speed this plane could hope to reach. At our range it gives us only a few seconds to react. Our best defense is to acquire the missile visually. Once we see it, our chances of evading it go way up. If you're unsure of the right defensive maneuvers it would be best to keep quiet and do as you're told."

Ormack closed his mouth. She was right.

"He got the message," Elliott said. "Crew, that was only the first test. There'll be a lot more before we're through with this. Dave, how long until Kavazyna?"

Luger looked at his chart. "I'd say we'll be overflying it in forty minutes, General."

Forty minutes. The thought was like a damp chill permeating the pressurized interior of the Old Dog.

THE WHITE HOUSE SITUATION ROOM

G ive it to me right now," the President ordered.

"Yes, *sir,*" General Curtis said enthusiastically. The President and the JCS Chairman were alone with the President's aide Jeff Hampton and several Marine guards and military communications technicians in the White House Situation Room. Curtis looked as spit-shined and polished as always, even in these early-morning hours and in spite of the short notice. The President, in sharp contrast, had pulled on a football warm-up suit after receiving the notification and then ran down to the Situation Room.

Curtis walked rapidly to the rear of the chamber.

Here, Curtis thought, was a President who wanted *action.* Quite a switch from the political animal he'd always known. He went over to a large projection chart on the rear wall that depicted the State of Alaska and most of Asia. The Kavaznya laser complex was highlighted with a large triangle—a target symbol. Several circles were drawn: large circles around radar sites clustered all along the Russian coastline and near cities; smaller circles representing defensive surface-to-air-missile sites.

A very large circle was centered over the north Pacific, midway between Hawaii and the Aleutians—the kill zone of the Soviet's new orbiting steerable mirror. The circle encompassed the entire north Pacific, the State of Alaska, all of the arctic and even large parts of Canada.

One black-lined route was depicted—the attack route of the B-1B *Excaliburs,* which were still orbiting over the Chukchi Sea six hundred miles west of Alaska. "The alert was called because of an unknown aircraft that disappeared from Soviet radar here a hundred and fifty miles south of the Kommandorskiye Islands. It was under radar control from Kommandorskiye Center."

The President looked at him. "Elliott? General *Elliott's* plane?"

"We know its call sign," Curtis said. "Lantern. Lantern Four-Five Fox—"

"Fox. The same as Elliott's . . ."

"I believe so, sir. It seems he made it."

"Son of a bitch," the President said, not knowing whether he should be elated or worried—he was happy that the Old Dog had done what the B-1s had failed to do, but now it too had been discovered. "What about the Lantern part?"

"Lantern was yesterday's Zulu call sign of SAC's Sixth Strategic Wing at Elmendorf Air Force Base in Anchorage," Curtis said. "The Sixth has several KC-135 and KC-10 tankers, plus RC-135 reconnaissance planes."

"So it *wasn't* Elliott?"

"Well, sir," Curtis said, hesitating, his Kansas drawl leaking through, "we called the Sixth. They had no Lantern Four-Five Fox at all that day. They had a fighter drag earlier—some tankers escorting F-15s—that flew fairly close to Soviet airspace on its way to Kadena, but no four-five call sign. Right now, we're checking our some possibilities. Kommandorskiye Center apparently had no flight plan on file for Lantern Four-Five Fox. Kommandorskiye was told by Lantern that they would have Kadena Global Command Control relay their flight plan. That's standard procedure for military flight plans. Meanwhile Kommandorskiye assigned Lantern an identification code and allowed it to continue southward. A few minutes later Kommandorskiye kicked Lantern out of its airspace because of a malfunctioning identification signal. It was given a heading well clear of Soviet airspace. A half-hour after that Kommandorskiye calls Lantern and says they are seventy miles *inside* Soviet airspace."

"Inside their airspace? How did that happen?"

"We're not sure but I'm operating under the assumption that Lantern Four-Five *is* Elliott and his crew. I haven't figured out how he got the fuel—he didn't have nearly enough to fly all the way across the north Pacific Ocean. I should receive some word soon . . ."

"Then our game is on—for real," the President said. He looked up at Curtis. "Your plan seems to have worked, General."

"Yes, sir. When that Russian Air Defense emergency was called, those B-1s were tying up three quarters of the Soviet fighters in the area. The intelligence ship *Lawrence* didn't report any fighter activity further south. If it is Elliott, and I'm betting it is, he's got quite a head start."

The President absorbed that, then: "General, recall the B-1s immediately. If the Russians find Elliott over the Kamchataka peninsula they'll shoot down the *Excaliburs* for sure."

"Yes, sir. And if I know those bomber crews they'll put the pedal to the metal getting back here."

"So that shrewd old bastard *made* it." The President shook his head, still finding it difficult to believe what had happened. He turned to Hampton. "Eight A.M., Jeff. I want the National Security Advisors, JCS, House Speaker, minority and majority leaders of both houses of Congress and Armed Services Committee chairman of both houses. Request a secure videophone connection with the prime ministers of the NATO countries and the attendance of all available NATO ambassadors. Those who can't meet in the Oval Office will confer via secure videophone."

The President nodded his head decisively. "That's when I will inform them of the strike against the laser complex at Kavaznya." He turned to Curtis. "General, I want you airborne, right away, to direct Elliott's sortie and withdrawal."

Curtis nodded, saluted his Commander-in-Chief, turned and exited the White House Situation Room. As he did so his step was firmer, his eyes brighter than at any time in the past few months.

As the Old Dog streaked across the skies of the Kamchatka peninsula in eastern Russia, one of its electronic eyes looked straight ahead and kept the crew of six from crashing into the rugged mountains of the Kamchatka, while other eyes scanned the skies for electromagnetic signals aimed at it, looking for enemies who were looking for them.

It was Dave Luger who controlled the first "eye"—a beam of radar energy that swept in a forty-five degree cone on either side of the Old Dog's sleek nose. If there was an obstacle along the beam's path it would reflect the radar energy directly back to be displayed on Luger's scope.

The other eyes—the sensors and antennas of the electronic countermeasures system—were mostly computer-controlled. A computer would instantly analyze a signal, identify it, determine its danger level and jam it if necessary. Luger's "eye" was different. He constantly had to adjust the radar presentation, search the scope for tiny peaks or ridge lines, be able instantly to evaluate the terrain around them and determine a safe altitude. . . .

Luger suppressed a yawn and directed the stream of cool air from a vent right into his face. He had been leaning forward, intently studying the scope, for the past thirty minutes. The parachute he wore felt like a boot resting on each of his kidneys, but he was afraid to take his eyes off the scope to readjust it. He knew the pilots upstairs were blind—all they could see were some jagged peaks in the gray starlit horizon, which just made them all the more nervous.

Without the terrain-avoidance computer, it was his radar against the mountains. When the scope was clear he would direct a shallow descent until terrain appeared, then climb again until it disappeared. It was like terrain-avoidance in the G- and H-model B-52s—except there was no TV screen for the pilots to watch, no terrain-avoidance trace that gave the pilots an exact picture of the disasters waiting for them. *He* was their eyes now.

At the moment Luger was watching one particular reflection on his SITUATION scope. It had a range of thirty miles, but for some reason he hadn't seen this large ridge line until it was much closer. Quickly he pressed the interphone button under his left boot.

"High terrain, thirteen miles, twelve o'clock."

Elliott and Ormack both sat up, and Ormack instinctively pushed on the throttles, preparing to pull the Old Dog's nose skyward. "Thirteen miles," he said. "How come you didn't see it before?"

"Climb first, ask questions later, Colonel."

Ormack gritted his teeth and pulled back on the yoke as soon as he noted a definite increase in airspeed, added five hundred feet to the Old Dog's altitude and leveled off.

"Clear of terrain for thirty miles," Luger reported. Ormack reengaged the low-altitude autopilot and Elliott checked the switch positions.

"I repeat, why the hell didn't you see that terrain earlier, Luger," Ormack said. "The most critical phase of this mission so far and you're asleep down there—"

"That's bullshit, Colonel," McLanahan said. "There's a dozen reasons why terrain won't show until it's closer in—snow, trees, fog. It *sure* as hell isn't because anyone's sleeping down here. Maybe you ought to come down here for a while, Colonel, and you keep this hunk of metal out of the dirt—"

"*Enough.*" Elliott told them. He had been quiet ever since they evaded the SA-2 missile but was furious now. He glared at Ormack. "This is no goddamn time for squabbling." Cross-cockpit, he said, "John, what the hell is it? Those guys down there sure as hell aren't sleeping and you know it."

"Ah . . ." Ormack rubbed his eyes, stared straight ahead into the inky blackness all around them. "I'm sorry, I guess I'm just beat." He took a deep breath and tried to rub a kink out of his left shoulder. "I guess I've been on the edge ever since—"

He glanced over at Elliott. The General was slumped forward in his seat, his hands looped over the control yoke, his head awkwardly dangling to one side.

"*General.*" He reached across and shook Elliott's right shoulder. No response.

"Pereira. Get up here." Angelina looked forward around her seat and saw Elliott's limp body. She began to unfasten the buckles around her chest and crotch.

"What happened?"

"The general. He's out cold, Pat." Ormack disengaged the low-level autopilot and started a slow climb, leveling off at five thousand feet, reengaged the autopilot, unfastened his straps and leaned across to help Elliott.

Not until he was far enough over to Elliott to unfasten his chest straps did he smell it—the thick, cloying stench of dried blood. The overpowering scent forced his eyes down to Elliott's right leg. The general's fatigue pants from the knee down oozed a crusty red film. His boots stuck to the floor when Ormack tried to move the leg. The general's face made pale look healthy.

Ormack shouted the general's name, began to breathe again when he saw Elliott's eyes flutter open. Eyes that looked at the instrument panel and somehow found the radar altimeter indicator . . . "We're . . . we're too high, John . . ."

"Never mind that, General," Angelina crawled forward with some web straps cut from her walkaround oxygen bottle harness. "Lie back," she said, and turned to Ormack. "We're going to have to tie a tourniquet around that leg."

Ormack nodded. "General, lie still. We're going to lift your leg up so we can tie this around your knee."

"Won't hurt a bit, Angelina," Elliott said, smiling weakly at his gunnery specialist. "I haven't felt anything in this damn leg for three hours."

Ormack and Pereira carefully pulled Elliott's leg up and across the throttle quadrant. Angelina then wrapped the web strap around Elliott's leg beneath the knee and pulled it tight as she could. When she had finished Elliott's leg looked less than half its normal diameter.

"I should have been more realistic about the leg—"

"Don't apologize," Angelina said. "Sometime the pain just takes over, no matter how hard you try to fight it."

"You sound like you're speaking from experience."

"I'm no spring chicken either, General. I know there's some things you can't do a damn thing about."

The two looked at each other a moment, then Elliott struggled back into his seat. By the time he refastened his harness buckle, he was near total exhaustion.

Abruptly Ormack ordered Angelina back to her seat as he took a firm grip on the yoke and pushed the Old Dog down once again.

"On the double. We're under attack."

Angelina half-crawled, half-ran back down the narrow aisle to her seat and began strapping herself in. Wendy was studying her video-threat display. Every few moments she glanced at the counter-measures receiver set, waiting for the computer positively to identify the new signals and plot their direction from the *Megafortress.*

As Angelina plugged in her headset she heard Wendy report: "Golf-band search only."

"Position?"

"No clock position yet."

"High terrain, ten miles," from Luger. "Slight climb to clear it."

"Take fifteen degrees right," McLanahan directed, leaning over in his seat and studying Luger's tiny five-inch display. "Looks clear in that direction at this altitude. We can't afford to do any more climbs." Ormack turned the control yoke in a ten-degree-bank turn to the right.

"Clear of terrain for twenty miles," Luger said. "We can turn back to track at this altitude in five miles."

"Tork?"

"Signal strength increasing slightly but not as fast as I thought. Rough guess would be the MiG-25s or 31s out of Ossora Airfield. Probably converging on our tail at high altitude."

"It'll be the Foxbat-Es," Angelina said. "The 31s are their front-line fighters. They'll send the 25s with external tanks out to find us—or draw us out—then report our position and let the Foxhounds have us—"

"Wendy," McLanahan broke in, "can you tell if they find us?"

"I should be able to see a change in their—" She stopped abruptly, staring at the large video screen. The signals rapidly began to change. "*Missile alert.* One of the signals just went to tracking mode."

"But I thought you said—"

"They're too far away," Wendy said. "They *can't* be locked on. Their signal isn't strong enough." Confused by the sudden threat signals and the responding increase in thrust as Ormack pushed up the power, Wendy hurriedly rechecked her receivers and indicators. All self-tested normal.

"I don't understand . . ." A red MISSILE LAUNCH indicator blinked on her panel. At the same time a repeater warning light blinked on the front instrument panel in the cockpit.

"Missile *launch,*" Ormack announced. "Clear for evasive maneuvers?"

"Clear left and right, ten miles," Luger called out.

"C'mon, Tork, get with it," Ormack said. "Which way?"

"It can't be, they're . . . they're bluffing, wait . . ."

"Pereira." Ormack was over the edge. "Find those damn fighters."

Before Wendy could answer, Angelina had turned her tail *Scorpion* tracking radar to RADIATE. Since there was no azimuth information from

Wendy's receiver Angelina began a complete rear-hemisphere sweep behind the *Megafortress.*

"Nothing," Angelina reported after several sweeps. "No targets for thirty miles."

"They're bluffing," Wendy repeated, sounding surer of herself now. She reached across the defensive compartment and grabbed Angelina's denim jacket. Angelina was still searching her rectangular scope for the fighters.

"They *wanted* us to turn on our radars," Wendy said. "They couldn't find us down here so they're faking a lock-on. *Stop.*"

"Angelina, shut down," McLanahan said. "If you haven't seen them by now, shut down." Angelina put her radar to STANDBY.

"Damn . . ." Wendy whispered as she studied the video threat receiver. "Back to search radar . . . signal strength increasing—"

An inverted "V" airplane symbol appeared at the bottom of Wendy's countermeasure receiver scope. "Fighter at six o'clock!" A second "V" appeared. "Second fighter, both at six o'clock."

With Ormack having already throttled to military power, the roar of the eight turbofan engines was deafening . . . the sound was amplified as it vibrated off the mountains barely three hundred feet beneath them.

"He's still at extreme detection range," Wendy reported. "He can't shoot at us down here."

"*Scorpions* are ready," Angelina said.

"How far until the computer can start driving the autopilot?" Ormack asked.

"Still a hundred miles," McLanahan told him.

"We might not make it that long—"

"VHF transmissions," Wendy called out.

"Shut them down," Ormack told her. "They'll report our position." But Wendy was already adjusting her jammers, matching the frequency marker of the jammers with the wavy oscilioscope-like radio transmissions.

"Narrow-scan tracking signals," she said. "Sweeping around us . . . his computer can't find us so it looks like he's searching manually . . ."

"High terrain, twelve o'clock, seven miles," Luger reported.

"Pretty deep canyon on all sides," McLanahan added quickly. "Better climb over this one. Slow climb."

Ormack slowly pulled back on the yoke and began a gentle two hundred foot-per-minute climb.

"Clearing terrain on either side," Luger said. "Five degrees left." Ormack nudged the Old Dog to the left. "Looks like we'll be clear of terrain for thirty miles after this last ridge. Level off. This is a good altitude, ridge crossing in ten seconds."

"Signal strength decreasing," Wendy said. "He's still trying manual track but he's falling behind."

"Coming up on the ridge . . ."

"Looks like the fighter behind us lost us . . ."

"Cresting the ridge now . . ."

In the dim cockpit Ormack could just make out the snow-covered ridge line they had just crossed, the mountains dropping off sharply to a white-covered valley below. "Hey," he said, "it looks pretty flat out—"

A thunderous explosion echoed just outside Elliott's canopy. Ormack caught a glimpse of two dark streaks against the hazy stars. The shock wave hit the Old Dog's nose like a giant invisible hand.

"We nearly had a mid-air with two of them," Ormack said, and pushed the Old Dog's nose down to the snow-covered plain below, watching the radar altimeter and the canopy windows. He leveled the aircraft at two hundred feet. "Terrain-following autopilot reengaged, slaved to the radar altimeter. Set to two hundred feet."

"Clear of terrain for thirty miles," Luger reported.

"The two fighters are turning," Wendy said. "Infrared tracker has one of them . . . going high . . . stabilizing—"

A large red MLD light blinked rapidly on Ormack's threat repeater lights.

"Missile launch detection, infrared missile launch," Wendy broke in. "Break right . . ."

Ormach lurched the Old Dog into a furious dodge to the right, steered the huge bomber past the maximum thirty degrees of bank. The autopilot, slaved to the now failed radar altimeter, immediately commanded a two-G max climb. That climb command, with the Old Dog now in a forty degree bank to the right, increased the G load on the bomber and tightened the turn.

Simultaneously with the "break" call, Wendy popped two high-intensity flares from the *Megafortress'* left ejectors. The flares were shot a hundred yards from the bomber and burned hotter and moved slower than the Old Dog. They lowered themselves slowly to the snow-packed ground with tiny streamers as the *Megafortress* turned hard in the opposite direction.

The fury of the turn shook up Elliott, but he had the presence of mind to watch the altimeters before reaching for the ejection trigger in each armrest. He was scanning the engine instruments, making sure the roar echoing in his confused head was coming from all eight turbofans. Out of the front cockpit window he spotted two fiery streaks of light flashing past the windscreen and exploding in the valley below.

"Engine instruments okay, John," Elliott reported to Ormack who looked in amazement at the man, barely able to support his head upright, scanning the eight rows of instruments crowded on the forward panel.

"Fighters passing overhead," Wendy said, her report confirmed by the roar of turbojets in full afterburner skimming over the jet-black bomber. "But coming around for another pass."

"Like hell," McLanahan said, pressed the RADIATE button on his attack radar and slaved the azimuth-elevation controls to Wendy's threat receiver. The attack-radar's antenna immediately swung to the azimuth of the fighter and began a height-finding scan of the sky.

The radar reflection of the attacking fighter only a few miles away showed clear as a mountain on McLanahan's radar. He typed "TRACK 1" on his keyboard and a small circle cursor centered itself on the return. The LED azimuth and elevation readouts flickered as the antennas raced to keep up with the retreating fighter.

"Locked on, Angelina," McLanahan said. "Take over."

Angelina was ready. With pilot consent already given, she pressed the COMMIT button on the forward *Scorpion* missile pylons. In one-twenty-fifth of a second the fire-control computer selected a missile on the right pylon, gave it the initial elevation, azimuth and distance computations from the attack radar and ejected the air-to-air missile from the pylon down into the Old Dog's slipstream.

The advanced Medium-Range Air-to-Air Missile's gyros stabilized the ten-foot-long missile in the slipstream as if it were a sprinter feeling for a footing in the starting blocks. In the next three-hundredths of a second static ports on the missile's body sensed the slipstream around it and armed the *Scorpion*'s one-hundred-pound-high explosive warhead. The same sensor set the *Scorpion*'s large thirty-G rear fin to the proper angle, took one last look-around self-test, and fired its solid propellant motor.

Elliott and Ormack saw a blinding flash of light race a few hundred yards ahead of the Old Dog, then suddenly change direction up and over their heads. An instant later a huge fireball erupted just behind Elliott's side window, illuminating the entire upstairs crew compartment of the Old Dog with a red-yellow glare.

"A hit," Elliott said, shielding his eyes from the glare.

"I've got the second low-altitude fighter," Angelina said, confirming the fire-control computer's radar lock on the target. She held the safety levers of the *Stinger* airmine rockets down and fired twice.

"Second fighter decelerating," Angelina reported. "Sitting stable off our left rear quarter . . . slowing . . . we got him. I think we FODed him out."

"What?" Wendy asked.

"FODed him out. He sucked in an engineful of scrap metal."

Upstairs Wendy signaled a gloved okay to Angelina as the gunnery expert watched the range gate of the fighter rapidly increase as it fell behind. Wendy noted that her infrared tail-warning seeker had locked itself onto the disabled fighter, but she ignored the indication—Angelina had already tagged that one.

The Soviet pilot aboard the Mikoyan-Gureyvich E-266M "Foxbat-E" interceptor was preparing to abandon his aircraft. He was watching two hydraulic system failure-warning lights and two engine overspeed-warning lights, aware that although the flash of light was far behind him he had flown through a cloud of *something* . . . he could almost hear the flak rattling around in his engine's turbines, tearing through the hydraulic lines, ripping the compressor blades apart. The intruder, whatever it was, was invisible through the glare of the warning lights on his canopy.

But he did notice one more set of lights—the lock-on indication of two of his K-13A Atoll missiles tracking the intruder. Seconds before power drained from his interceptor, the pilot selected every last one of his remaining missiles, and with his other hand on his ejection ring, pressed the missile-launch trigger.

Ormack was checking his switches and asking General Elliott cross-cockpit how he was feeling. McLanahan had just put his attack radar to STANDBY and was leaning over to help Luger with terrain calls. Angelina had completed a quick scan of the rear hemisphere of the Old Dog before putting her radar to STANDBY. Wendy was readjusting a twisted parachute harness strap, trying to unwind a bit from her first real fighter engagement.

But the supercooled eye of the infrared seeker mounted on top of the short curved V-tail of the Old Dog wasn't relaxing. It was tracking the dimming heat signature of the fighter far behind them when it noticed the sudden increase in the heat-signature of the target as two heat-seeking missiles streaked toward the Old Dog's eight Pratt and Whitney TF33 turbofan engines. The increase quickly surpassed the delta-pK thermal threshold programmed into it months earlier by Wendy herself, and an MLD indicator flashed at both Tork's and Ormack's position. Simultaneously with the warning light, the decoy system ejected one bundle of chaff and one phosphorous flare from both left and right ejectors.

The automatic response to the infrared missile attack would have been successful—had anyone noticed the MLD warning indicators and initiated evasive action. The warning tone sounded in everyone's headsets at the same time the light illuminated, but both Ormack and Tork had to be watching for the target on the threat display and expecting the attack to escape the heat-seeking missiles. By the time Wendy noticed the blinking red Missile Launch Detection light, the Atoll missiles had accelerated to nearly Mach 2 and had closed the short distance between them in the blink of an eye.

Even so, the automatic system had its saving effect. The flares, shot two hundred yards away from the bomber's belly, caught the Atoll missiles' attention, providing a momentary distraction. But at less than a mile away the missiles could not ignore the huge globes of heat emanating from the Old Dog's turbofan engines.

One missile locked momentarily onto the right flare, then back onto the right engines. The sudden swing of the IR seeker head from one hot target to another—a sign that the seeker had picked up a decoy—triggered a proximity detonation signal to the sixty-pound warheads—the missile exploded less than twenty yards from the Old Dog's V-tail vertical stabilizer, blowing off the top nine feet of the Old Dog's right stabilator tail and leaving a short jagged stub of metal where the stabilator used to be.

The other missile took a sideways glance at the decoy flare and swung a few precious feet to the left toward the flare, but it wasn't enough to divert it. Driven by a solid propellant engine just approaching full thrust, it plunged into the exhaust port of the number one engine and detonated. That explosion immediately turned the number one engine into a blob of molten metal and blew what remained of the already damaged left wingtip into a shower of fire.

The Old Dog, pushed by an exploding missile on one side and pulled by one lost engine, skidded violently to the left. Ormack was able to keep the bomber a few knots above the stall only because all eight engines were already at maximum thrust. Stomping on the right rudder, he turned the control wheel full to the right. The lights flickered in the crew compartment and the interphone began to squeal.

"We're hit," Ormack reported, and pushed the right rudder hard all the way to the floor. The Old Dog slowly, slowly began to straighten its sideways slide. As it did, Ormack scanned the caution lights and engine instruments, but it was Elliott who noticed the engine instruments while Ormack fought for aircraft control.

"Fire on number one," he called out. Ormack glanced quickly at number one's engine instruments to confirm the call, then pulled the number one throttle CLOSED. Elliott, his handle on the fire-shutoff switch, pulled the T-handle when he saw Ormack's hand reaching for it. He then began reciting the emergency checklist: "Starter switch off."

Ormack checked the switch. "Off."

"Electrical panel."

"Checking," Ormack said, scanning the a-c and d-c electrical panel on his right instrument panel. "Crew, we've shut down number one engine.

Shut off all unnecessary equipment or we'll lose another generator." He checked the generator panel and confirmed total loss number-one generator. "All other generators are on high load but they're okay so far."

"Bleed selector switch, normal left hand inboard," Elliott continued, now reading from the emergency checklist displayed on the cockpit computer monitor.

"Normal."

Elliott painfully hauled himself forward out of his seat and strained to look out the cockpit window.

"Can't see the nacelle, don't see any fire out there . . ."

"Fire light has gone out," Ormack confirmed, then began a check of the fuel panel. "I think we have a leak in the number one wing tank, but it doesn't look too serious." He reached down to a large knob on the center aisle control stand and cranked in full right-rudder trim. "General, check the rudder hydraulics. We might have a problem with the rudder now."

Elliott checked the warning lights on his left instrument panel. "All the lights are out."

"Well, we got rudder problems, too," Ormack said. "I'm retarding engines seven and eight to help keep straight. Number two engine has to stay in military."

Ormack started a slow climb to four thousand feet and carefully engaged the low-level autopilot. He waited a few moments to be sure that the autopilot could hold the *Megafortress* straight and level. "All right, we've got control of the aircraft. Pereira, McLanahan, check for fighters before we get too involved in damage assessment."

Angelina and Patrick went to RADIATE on their radars and took careful but fast full hemisphere sweeps of the sky. With both radars operating, they could scan almost three thousand cubic miles of air-space in a few seconds.

"Clear," McLanahan reported.

"No pursuit," Angelina said.

"Scope's clear," from Wendy. "A few extremely low-powered search signals. The power fluctuation put some of my jammers into STANDBY but they should reset in a few minutes."

"Clear of terrain for thirty miles," Luger said.

"All right." Ormack relaxed his grip on the control yoke. "We're level at four thousand feet. We've lost number one engine and its generator. We can't visually confirm it but I think we lost the rest of the left wingtip. There's a slight leak in the number one wing-tank supplying the number two engine but I don't think it's fatal. Something's also gone haywire with the rudder, it's hard to keep her straight . . ."

"I feel a pretty good shudder in the airmine turret-controls," Angelina said. "Need to check out the cannon steering." She activated the *Stinger* airmine rocket cannon controls and began a self-test of her system.

"The navigation system went to STANDBY for a few seconds," Luger reported, "but the battery kept everything from dumping. We're reloading the mission data now from the 'game' cartridge."

In a few moments Angelina was back on the interphone. "Colonel Ormack, I think we lost the whole damn tail. My infrared scanner is dead. Everything's faulted. We won't have any more automatic IR detection from the tail anymore."

"Well," Luger said, "can't the threat-receiver—"

"The threat-receiver only detects fighters when they use their radar," Angelina told him. "If they get a visual or infrared lock-on they can launch missiles at us all day and we can't see them. They can drive in as close as they want and get a point-blank kill."

"The *Scorpions,*" Ormack said. "What about them?"

"I'm getting a flickering low-pressure warning light on the rotary launcher," Angelina said, checking a set of gauges on her right control panel. "Still in the green, but that last attack might have done some missile damage."

"High terrain, thirty miles," Luger reported.

"Any way around it?" Ormack asked.

"Solid ridge line. No other way."

Ormack cursed and nudged the Old Dog skyward. They were almost back at their pre-established five thousand foot safe-clearance altitude before Luger finally reported clear of terrain.

"Goddamn," Ormack said, "over four thousand feet above the ground—"

"But we may belly-flop that ridge line when we cross it," McLanahan reminded him. "We should be able to engage the auto terrain-following computer any second—"

"Airborne interceptors at twelve o'clock," Wendy interrupted. "At extreme detection range but closing rapidly. Multiple indications."

"And we're stuck up here," Ormack said. "No other way around it. Pereira, McLanahan, engage at long range. We'll have to blast our way out of here."

No one offered any alternative. McLanahan reactivated his *Scorpion* attack radar and tuned it immediately to fifty-mile range. Slaved to Wendy Tork's threat receiver, the radar immediately pinpointed the aggressors ahead.

"Locked onto one," McLanahan called out. Just as he designated the first target he heard the *whoosh* of a *Scorpion* missile leaving the left pylon.

"Locked onto a second one—"

"Fighter at six o'clock high," from Angelina. Instantly she activated her own radar and locked onto the fighter. A moment later she gave a look of surprise and reached for the airmine triggers. "Range decreasing rapidly," she said. "He's diving at us . . ."

"Radar's gone down," Wendy said. "And we don't have an infrared scanner to pick up—"

"It's an IR attack," Angelina announced. "Pilot, break right."

Ormack threw the Old Dog into a hard-banking turn to the right. The bomber, already without several thousand pounds of thrust from the number one engine, rumbled in protest, hovering just above a stall. Wendy punched out two flares from the left ejector while Angelina tried to locate the attacker on her radar.

"I got him, I got him on radar," she said, hit the green TRACK button, watched the circle cursor surround the fighter's radar reflection and squeezed the *Stinger* airmine rocket triggers.

But the attacking fighter had the advantage. Following a vector to the intruder from his low-patrol mates—both of whom he had lost contact with soon afterward—he had spotted the intruder on radar long enough to point his MiG-25's infrared search-and-track seeker at the penetrator. Once the seeker had locked onto the target, he had no need for the look-down radar and turned it off. His AA-7 missile immediately locked onto the two engines on the left inboard nacelle of the Old Dog, and he hit the launch button just as he noticed a short burst of flame from below him.

Angelina's right break had been perfectly timed. The AA-7 missile's IR seeker lost the engines in the break and locked onto the flares, but the change was too quick and the proximity and decoy-detection fuse exploded the missile.

Saved from destruction, the Old Dog was nonetheless naked . . . the missile's high-explosive detonation, together with the one-thousand-degree-Fahrenheit parachute-equipped flares and the low wide burst of an airmine rocket, perfectly outlined the Old Dog against the snow-covered mountains.

The MiG pilot attacking from above and behind the *Megafortress* had watched his missile streak toward the target. Then suddenly he saw a dark silhouette of incredible size. He blinked, not able to believe it as the outline of the massive aircraft materialized below him. A low-altitude warning horn sounded in his helmet, and he managed to pull out of his dive only a few hundred feet above the ground and force his fighter skyward.

Although the long sleek nose confused him, there was no misidentifying the rest of the plane. An American B-52 bomber. He had always thought that if he was called on to defend Kavaznya against attack, it would be against an FB-111, a B-1 or even the American Navy's F-18 or F-14. Never, never an aging dinosaur like the B-52.

Straining to keep the antediluvian bomber in view as he pulled on his control stick and crawled for altitude, he frantically keyed his microphone.

"*Aspana.* Danger. American B-52 bomber. *Paftariti.* American B-52 visually identified."

Another warning beep sounded in his helmet. He recognized the stall-warning buzzer, applied maximum afterburner and leveled off to wait for his airspeed to increase. He repeated his warning over the radio, including the bomber's direction and estimated speed.

Could the B-52 possibly have destroyed the other fighters? The MiG pilot had seen what he thought were gunblasts from the puny .50 caliber guns in the tail, but none of the pilots at Ossora would be stupid enough to fly that close to the intruder. . . .

Angelina had to haul herself upright by the armrests of her ejection seat to regain her balance. The sudden turn and the abrupt roll-out had her head spinning and she fought to refocus her eyes on her scope. When she did she was surprised to see the target still locked within her circle cursor. She grasped the triggers and fired twice at the almost stationary fighter.

The last thing the MiG pilot saw was the glass around him seeming to melt like cellophane. His canopy disintegrated as twenty pounds of metal chips from both *Stinger* rockets sheared through the plastic-laminated canopy, shredding everything in its path. His fighter flew on for several minutes, its pilot sightless and bleeding, before crashing into the low mountains.

"Angelina! Twelve o'clock high! Another MiG coming in fast . . ."

Bathed in the bright sunburst of the descending flares, the MiG-25 attacking from the nose had a solid visual contact on the intruder. The Old Dog was approaching a high ridge line, very close to the ridge but well above the snow-covered valley behind, and the attacking MiG was well above the bomber, which was perfectly highlighted. The Russian pilot had to strain, but even after the flare plunged the sky back into darkness the bomber was still visible.

He refocused his eyes on the heads-up display for a few seconds, rapidly checking his instruments to see if he could establish a more reliable shot on the bomber below him. The infrared seeker had not locked on—that would have been difficult unless he was behind the B-52. His tracking radar was randomly locking onto hundreds of targets all over the scope—completely jammed. Useless. A B-52, he knew, carried more jamming power than ten MiG-25s combined. He shut the radar off, banked hard to the left and began to dive at the bomber, fighting to keep it in sight as he approached the ridge . . .

"He's closing fast," McLanahan called out. "Ten miles."

Angelina had to take a few precious seconds to select a *Scorpion* missile and align it with McLanahan's steering signals, then launched the Mach three missile within six seconds of McLanahan's second warning. Still, in that time the MiG had halved the distance between them.

The MiG's warning receivers immediately detected the missile launch and the pilot quickly switched hands on the stick, activated the forward deception jammers with his right hand, switched hands again and hit the chaff-dispenser on his control stick.

A B-52 launching an air-to-air missile! It was worse than he ever imagined. He could easily see the fiery plume behind the missile below him, pointed his fighter directly at the missile, showing the missile only his smallest radar profile.

The glare from the missile spoiled his night vision some, but the bomber was still in sight. The MiG pilot saw a slight shift in the shape of the missile's plume—instead of a round dot, it was a bit more oblong. He smiled and relaxed his grip on the control stick. The American missile had locked onto one of the false targets his jammers had created. Instantly he released another bundle of chaff and pulled right and up on his stick. The missile's egg-shaped ball of fire became a long, orange line as it harmlessly passed underneath his MiG.

The pilot, who had his eyes squinted against the explosion he had feared as he watched the missile streak past, now opened his eyes—the huge B-52 was centered in his gunsights.

Even so he felt he was a heartbeat too late—he should have been firing his cannon before the B-52 entered his sights. He shoved the stick down now to lead the target more, but the snow-covered ridge line popped into view ahead of the bomber. He had only an instant left. His finger closed on the trigger and held it until trees began to show on the edge of the ridge, then released the trigger and hauled back on the stick with all his strength . . .

"The missile missed," Ormack answered as he watched the *Scorpion* disappear into the night.

"*Break right,*" McLanahan told him, watching the radar target grow to horrifying size.

The split-second the Soviet pilot had wasted realizing he was too late for a real kill had saved the Old Dog's life. Twenty-millimeter shells plowed into the leading edge of the Old Dog's left wing where Elliott's cockpit windows had been an instant before. The shells ripped into the left *Scorpion* missile pylon, destroying half of the remaining missiles. The explosions would have ripped the wing apart, but one ricocheting shell fired a jettison squib in the pylon and the entire burning pylon exploded into space. The pylon missed the remaining fragments of the Old Dog's V-tail and the *Stinger* airmine rocket cannon.

The MiG's strafing track continued through the wing and fuselage, piercing the number-two main center wing and forward body-fuel tanks, but the shells created no deadly spark and dissipated most of their heat in the fibersteel skin of the *Megafortress*.

Elliott could see sparks flying from the hardpoint where the *Scorpion* pylon used to be. "Angelina, the left missile pylon's hit."

McLanahan glanced up and checked the selective jettison board on his weapons-monitoring panel. "We lost the whole damned pylon," he called out, deselecting jettison power from the pylon circuitry.

Angelina immediately reached to her overhead circuit breaker panel and pulled a group of circuit breakers. "Pylon deactivated."

"That left wing must be getting awful light." McLanahan tried for a bit of grim humor.

It was wasted on Wendy, who called out, "Fighter at six o'clock."

"Here he comes again."

"I see him," Angelina said as she steered the circle-cursor on the radar return and hit the TRACK button, then began aligning a weapons-bay *Scorpion* for launch.

The Soviet pilot saw the missile lock-on indication on his threat receiver and immediately activated his own electronic countermeasures.

Angelina depressed the TRACK button once again. The green light stayed on but the circle-cursor kept on walking away from the return.

"He's jamming me," she said. "Switching to manual track." She deselected radar-track, grabbed the steering handles and carefully tried to position the circle-cursor on the fighter.

The Soviet pilot noted the persistent missile-alert signal even though his jammers were breaking the radar lock. He promptly began a series of random S-turns, rapidly closing the distance between them, trying to push his MiG-25 closer to the bomber's altitude.

***

The Old Dog cleared the ridge line by a scant forty feet, the wingtip vortices snapping fir trees like straw as it skimmed the ridge. Rooster-tails of snow and dirt were blasted dozens of feet in the air.

Suddenly, a large green TERRAIN DATA PROCESS and TERRAIN DATA GOOD readout flashed across McLanahan's computer monitor. "Computer terrain-following is active," McLanahan said. "Clear to engage."

Elliott and Ormack quickly engaged the terrain-following-pitch autopilot to the navigation computers. Now the computer, which already knew the elevation of all the terrain around them for thousands of square miles and had the accuracy of the satellite navigator for positioning, would put the Old Dog at the lowest possible altitude but climb her in anticipation of terrain ahead.

Through the MiG-25's windscreen the B-52 could be seen diving sharply toward the rocks below and disappearing. From radar, infrared, visual, everything. The pilot searched. No sign. The huge bomber had disappeared. Swearing into his mask, he throttled back and climbed to begin a search.

"I can't find him," Angelina said. "I can't lock onto him. His jamming is too powerful. We can try a home-on jam launch but we don't have the missiles to waste."

"He's back there, waiting for us to pop up into him," Luger said, staring at the radar altimeter readout on his computer screen. "He's not going to drive into our laps." He sucked in his breath as the readout dipped to thirty feet before climbing again to a hundred feet above the ground.

"We've got to suck him in," McLanahan said. "Draw him in, then chop the power."

"He'll blow us out of the sky," Ormack said. "We're staying down here."

"He's also vectoring in his buddies," McLanahan said. "If he doesn't get us in the next few minutes he's gonna have lots of help."

"We've got a dozen missiles left," Ormack said.

"Great, but we can't take on all of them." McLanahan shook his head.

Ormack was about to answer when Elliott put a hand on his wrist. "We have no choice, John."

"If we can't find him, General," Ormack yelled over the roar of the turbofans, "if we lose him . . . if he shoots first . . ."

"We've got to be the hunter, not the hunted," Elliott said. The two pilots looked at each other. Then Elliott took the throttles from Ormack, placed a tight grip on the yoke and gave it a shake.

"I've got the aircraft."

Ormack looked at the exhausted general as a wave of turbulence rumbled through the bomber. "We're taking a big gamble, General."

"Now's the time for one, John."

Ormack nodded. "You've got the aircraft, General."

"Thanks, John. Stand by on airbrakes and gear."

Ormack reached across the throttle quadrant and put his hand on the gear lever.

"Wendy? Angelina?"

Angelina nodded at Wendy, who reported, "Ready, General."

"Landing and taxi light-switches off. Setting two thousand feet." Elliott twisted the clearance plane knob from COLA to 2000, and the Old Dog's SST nose angled skyward.

The Soviet pilot was busy cursing himself and his low-powered radar when the American B-52 suddenly appeared from nowhere just off to the right of his MiG's nose. The radar range gate immediately set, azimuth locked on and his last AA-3 radar missile aligned and reported ready for launch.

"He's right *behind* us," Angelina called out.

"Missile alert," Wendy followed, and hit the right chaff ejector. "Jink left."

Elliott put the Old Dog in a sharp turn to the left just as the MISSILE ALERT indication changed to a MISSILE LAUNCH.

"Missile launch, break left!" Wendy punched out eight bundles of chaff from the right ejector as Elliott threw the bomber from a twenty to a forty-five degree bank to the left.

The MiG pilot watched in frustration as another huge radar target appeared on his scope. The aiming reticle moved across to the bigger, brighter, unmoving blob just as he thumbed the LAUNCH button . . . and watched as his last missile disappeared into empty space.

Immediately he shoved the throttles of his twin Turmansky engines to maximum afterburner and swerved to the left to get into cannon-firing position . . .

"Range decreasing rapidly," Angelina said. "Still no automatic lock-on. I'm setting the detonation range for the airmines manually."

"Range decreasing," Wendy reported. "Stand by for a break to the right."

"If we have our gear and airbrakes hanging out," Ormack said, "and then break to evade a missile we'll stall for sure. We may not have enough altitude to recover."

"Three miles and closing fast," Angelina said.

"If he was going to launch one, he'd do it now," Wendy said. "Two miles." She was staring hard at the threat video. The bat-wing interceptor threat symbol hovered behind them, inching closer and closer. "Approaching one mile . . . *now. Hit* it."

"Gear. Airbrakes six," Elliott ordered. Ormack dropped the landing-gear handle and flipped the airbrake lever full up. The Old Dog pitched down, throwing everyone hard against his shoulder straps. Elliott brought the power back to eighty percent, then quickly back to full military thrust as the initial buffet to stall again rumbled through the bomber. He had lost a thousand feet before he was able to bring the Old Dog under control.

The Russian pilot wasn't caught unaware. He had just throttled back to cut his closure rate on the B-52 when he noticed the radar range gate rapidly decreasing.

He immediately disregarded the indication. He had no radar-guided missiles to launch anyway, and the B-52's jamming probably had broken the range lock. Catching glimpses of the huge bomber's outline against the snowy backdrop, he kept his power in minimum afterburner and rested his finger against the cannon trigger.

The range gate wound past one thousand meters—well inside firing range. He stepped on the right rudder to completely align himself, and took a deep breath.

He saw several bright flashes of flame from the rear of the bomber, instinctively rolled his fighter left to begin S-turning behind the B-52. The .50-caliber machine guns could never hit the bomber without reliable radar guidance, he thought, and his own twenty-millimeter shells had a greater range and reliability. He started a right roll and pressed the trigger.

The flashes of light suddenly grew into huge, pulsing shafts of color. Immediately he threw his fighter into ninety degrees of bank to the right and pulled on the stick, breaking hard away. He caught a glimpse of his airspeed indicator—in his attempt to match speed with the intruder he had allowed his airspeed to decrease drastically.

He rolled until the stall-warning horn came on again, then rolled out. His stick would not respond to his control. He was sinking fast, in the grip of a near-stall. His MiG-25 wasn't made for low-altitude intercepts, it was designed for fast high-altitude dogfighting. It was with huge relief that he saw his airspeed increasing steadily. *Ochin.* In a moment, he thought, he'd finish this *Amirikanskaya.*

He looked out the left side of his canopy just in time to see a colorful line of fireworks explode less than fifty meters outside his canopy, the blossoms of light reminding him of starburst fireworks he had once seen—

big and bright with thousands of tiny stars racing out from a red center.

A moment later those stars riddled the entire left side of his MiG-25. The canopy became one giant mass of holes and jagged cuts, yet somehow stayed intact, but the left engine flamed out immediately, then seized as the engine oil drained from a hundred punctures in the engine cowling.

The radar signature of the MiG blossomed momentarily as the Soviet pilot ejected from his stricken fighter, but neither Wendy nor Angelina noticed. Angelina was congratulating her partner, who was busy watching her frequency video display. One transmitter band at the top of her display began to show low-power, high-energy activity.

She watched it, studied it—and her sweat turned cold.

"Activity, Wendy?" Ormack asked amid the quiet jubilation of the Old Dog's crew.

"Search radar . . . twelve o'clock."

"Identification?"

Wendy answered, but the words were uttered too softly to be understood.

"Say again?"

"Kavaznya." Wendy's voice was flat now, emotionless. "Kavaznya. The laser. It's looking for us."

FIFTY MILES FROM KAVAZNYA

The throttles were at maximum—the right outboard engines had been pulled back to ninety percent to compensate for the destroyed number one engine but all the rest were at full military power.

General Elliott tightened the throttle friction lever on the center throttle quadrant—he wasn't going to move any one of those throttles unless he had to shut down another engine. The number two engine had been restarted for the target run, but the RPMs were erratic and the vibration from the engine pod threatened to shear what remained of the left wing loose from the fuselage.

"Bomb run checklist," Dave Luger announced.

McLanahan nodded, taking a quick glance at his partner. The navigator had one finger on the checklist page ready to read off each step, but his hands were a shade unsteady.

"You all right, buddy? You look a little nervous."

"Me? Nervous? Why should I be nervous? Just because we're about to send the Russians a candygram loaded with TNT? What's to be nervous about?"

"Think positive, the man said."

"I've been trying—"

McLanahan interrupted. "We're going to shove this one down their throats and get out of here quick like a bunny. Okay?"

"Yeah, right, like a bunny."

McLanahan turned back to his instrument panel.

"Weapons monitor select switch," Luger recited.

"Center forward."

"Low altitude calibrated mode selector."

"Automatic."

271

"Target coordinates, elevation, and ballistics."

"Set, displayed, checked, locked in," McLanahan then made a swift check of the coordinates. "Ballistics set for glide mode." His response was reflexive; he had no master printout to check the coordinates.

"Consent switches, pilot and radar," Luger answered.

General Elliott painfully reached back along his left side instrument panel and checked that the three gang-barred consent switches—the permission switches for the forward and rear-firing *Scorpion* missiles and the *Striker* glide-bomb and bomb decoys—were in the full UP position.

"Pilot's switches are—"

A warning tone sounded in the crew's headsets, and the Old Dog pitched violently skyward, its pointy nose at a high, unnatural angle.

Ormack hit the AUTOPILOT DISCONNECT button on his control yoke and pushed the nose back toward the ground. "*Flyup.* Nav, clear terrain for me and get us back down. Radar, what happened?

McLanahan was already investigating. "The terrain-data computer dropped off the line." He looked over at Luger. "Dave, clear terrain for him. I'm going to reset the computer and reload the data."

"High terrain, three miles," Luger called out. "I'm starting to paint over it. Don't descend yet."

McLanahan's gloved fingers flew over the switches. "Computer's back on-line." He flipped the cartridge lever from LOCK to READ. "It'll take a few moments more."

"The Kavaznya radar is getting stronger," Wendy reported. "Well above detection threshold now."

"Clear of terrain for twenty miles," Luger said. "Start a slight descent. Possible high terrain in ten miles."

"Fighter radars have all gone down," Wendy said. "The Kavaznya radar has blotted them all out—or the fighters are now getting their vectors from that big radar . . ."

McLanahan glanced at the radar altimeter readout as the LOADING DATA indication appeared on his screen. The Old Dog's fail-safe flyup maneuver, designed to protect the aircraft in case of a failure of any of the components of the terrain-following computer, had zoomed the huge bomber to over two thousand feet above the terrain. The engines were at full military thrust, holding the bomber in the sky.

"Altitude's still increasing," McLanahan warned.

"Dammit, I know," Ormack said. He leaned on the yoke, helping Elliott force the SST nose of the Old Dog toward the protection of the rough Kamchatka hills. The Old Dog crested the flyup at twenty-three hundred feet above the ground before Ormack and Elliott together finally had it descending again.

"Fighters at seven o'clock," Angelina called out. "Maneuvering to intercept . . ." She steered the circle cursor of the airmine rocket tracker over one of the attackers but an electronic quiver in the scope sent a shower of interference waves through the display, sending the tracking cursor spinning off the radar return. "Something's screwing up my radar."

"Terrain-data computer is back on-line," McLanahan reported. Or-mack immediately reengaged the autopilot to the computer, and the Old Dog nosed earthward.

"First HARM missile programmed and ready," Wendy reported to Angelina. "Bay door coming open."

Wendy hit the LAUNCH button. The aft bomb-bay doors snapped open and the hydraulic launcher rotated to position one of the High-speed Anti-Radar Missiles on the bottom launch position. Wendy had already entered the radar's frequency range into the missile's sensor. Powerful ejectors pushed the missile into the slipstream, its rocket motor ignited and the launcher immediately rotated to put another HARM missile into launch position.

Wendy monitored the HARM TRACK light on her missile status panel, indicating that the missile had found the source of the prepro-grammed frequency transmissions and was heading straight for it. Sud-denly Wendy's entire threat panel and missile status board flickered. The HARM TRACK light illuminated again for a moment, then disappeared.

"It's the Kavaznya radar," Wendy said. "It's creating the interference in my equipment. The HARM missile won't track . . ."

Luger held his breath as a stream of ridgelines rushed toward them, their shadows speeding toward the edge of his wedge-shaped radar scope. As the Old Dog climbed over them, he stared transfixed—

"Dave! We got the computer back," McLanahan said as he finished recycling the computer. "Let's finish the checklist." He reached across to his left instrument panel and flipped a red-guarded switch up. "Radar's consent switch on."

Luger had to tear his eyes away from the scope to read the checklist. "Weapon and decoy power."

"On and checked," McLanahan said, and moved the tracking handle once more to check that the *Striker*'s seeker-head was still activated.

"Bomb-release lights."

Elliott sat forward and pressed-to-test his indicator lights. "Off and checked.

"Off and checked down here too," McLanahan replied.

"Release configuration check," Luger read. "Special weapons lock."

Suddenly the Old Dog threw itself skyward once more. Ormack swore, punched off the autopilot once again. Immediately Luger's full attention was riveted on the narrow wedge-radar display. "High terrain, five miles."

"Reset the computer," Ormack ordered, but McLanahan was already resetting the computer power-switches. He tried the circuit reset-switch. It corrected the fault but only for a few seconds, and then the computer faulted once again. He tried several more quick resets. "Something's wrong, it's not resetting. I'll have to recycle it. Maintain heading . . . goddamn, the inertial navigation computer died. We've lost navigation information. I'll try to reset . . ."

"Just *do* it," Ormack said. "Nav . . ."

"Clear to descent," Luger told him. "*Slowly.* Small ridge three miles, but we should clear it okay—"

"Fighters are closing," from Angelina. "It's hard to keep tracking them, my radar keeps spooking out."

"It's Kavaznya," Wendy told her. "The radar is interfering with *all* our equipment."

"We'll be flying right *over* that thing," Elliott said.

"Pilot, turn right! Fighter swinging over to eight o'clock on a left quartering attack—"

"McLanahan, can I turn?"

"We'll get shot down if you don't. *Do* it." The Old Dog banked to the right and moments later the muffled puffs of three airmine rockets rumbled through the bomber.

"Can't tell if I got them . . ." Angelina said.

"I've got nothing to jam," Wendy said, pounding in frustration on her ejection seat armrests. Her threat display was now a solid sheet of white— every frequency band that was possible to be displayed was filled with endless waves of energy. A jamming package put up against the energy transmitted by the nuclear-powered Kavaznya radar was lost in the spillover created by Kavaznya radar's sheer power.

"Clear of terrain for thirty miles." Luger double-checked his radar. They had cleared the last of the high coastal mountain ranges surrounding Kavaznya. At the edge of the scope was blackness—the Bering Sea, he suddenly realized. Only a few hundred miles further on was home— friendly territory. Right now, though, it seemed like a million miles away.

At the very edge of the sea was a huge, compact blob of radar returns. He got two sweeps of the radar on the Kavaznya complex itself before the ground-map scope blanked out.

"Just lost my radar, Kavaznya's at twelve o'clock, thirty miles."

McLanahan heard the warning and glanced over at Luger's blank five-inch radar scope, but he was concentrated on recovering the navigation and terrain-data computers. The first computer recycle failed, so he began the second.

"Try recycling your radar, Dave," McLanahan told him. Luger furiously switched the radar controls from STBY to TRANSMIT. The radar scope would paint a picture for only a few sweeps, then blank out again.

"It's not working, we're blind down here."

"You said we were clear of terrain—the pilots should be able to see enough out the cockpit windows to keep us from hitting the ground. We'll use the radar as much as we can later on. Keep the radar down until we make our escape turn."

"Two fighters at six o'clock," from Angelina; then, "My radar's failed, I can't see them anymore . . ."

McLanahan shook his head, then slapped his hands excitedly as a green NAV light illuminated on the computer monitor at his workstation. "Nav computer's back on-line. Pilot, center up on the target and try like hell to hold your airspeed steady. Dave, get a groundspeed and mileage to the target and start a watch. We might have to start the glide-bomb and decoys with a dead-reckoning position."

Luger immediately wrote down the mileage to the Kavaznya target and the groundspeed and started the timer on his wristwatch. When he rechecked it a moment later he found that his electronic LCD watch, like the three radar scopes on the Old Dog, had failed. He started the tiny forty-year-old wind-up ship's clock on his front panel and made a mental note to compensate for the extra twenty seconds lost.

"Reloading terrain data," McLanahan said, but before he could move the cartridge lever from LOCK to LOAD the navigation computer failed again.

"Four minutes to go," Luger announced.

"It's not going to come back up," McLanahan said. "The Kavaznya radar's interference is just too strong."

Ormack and Elliott had managed to get the Old Dog's nose down after the flyup, but after flying with a terrain-following computer for so long they weren't ready to fly at the same low altitudes. Ormack trimmed the bomber for level flight at about a thousand feet altitude and rechecked his instruments before the actual weapon release. Unfortunately the effect of the change to higher altitude was to make the Old Dog an all-too-easy target for the two Soviet fighters chasing it.

Taking vectors from interceptor radar operators at Ossora Airfield near the laser complex, the MiG-29 *Fulcrum* interceptor pilots didn't need their sophisticated look-down shoot-down equipment to launch their missiles. The controller gave the pilots range and azimuth information to ideal launch positions. Once they visually acquired the huge bomber, they maneuvered around it to stay away from its deadly tail and turn their missile's seeker-heads away from the glare and heat of the city beyond it.

"We can't drive into the target like this," Wendy said. "Colonel, I need you to make random maneuvers all the way toward the target—"

"We've got to program the weapons in a DR position," Luger interrupted. "We can't—"

"She's right, Dave," McLanahan said. "We'll get hosed if we drive straight and level all this way. Clear to maneuver."

"Random jinks," Wendy said. "Not left and right . . . left twice, right once, random all the way. I'll eject chaff just before each reversal."

Ormack nodded and began the first jink to the left. "Now we sound like a fighting—"

Suddenly a blinding flash erupted from just beyond Ormack's right cockpit window. Ormack, who was staring out the front windscreen, with the cockpit lights turned down so the pilots could start visually picking out terrain, caught the flash's full intensity.

"I'm blind . . ."

"Easy, John," Elliott said, took a firm grip on the yoke and trimmed it for level flight about five hundred feet above ground.

"We just had a missile explode off our right wing," Elliott said over the interphone. "The co-pilot got flashblinded. But the engines look okay . . ."

"Three minutes to go," Luger said, flicked his radar into TRANSMIT and took a fast range, azimuth and terrain check before the scope went blank again. "Four degrees right. Clear of terrain, General. You can descend, slowly."

"The radar altimeter should be good for terrain clearance now that we're clear of the mountains," McLanahan said.

"How can they still be shooting at us?" Luger said, puzzled. "If Kavaznya's radar blotted out our radar—they should've taken out the fighter's radars too."

"Infrared search-and-track system," Wendy told him. "They use an airborne IR tracker for azimuth and elevation data and the Kavaznya radar for range data. They can take shots at us all night like that."

"Well, we're running out of time, Dave," McLanahan said. He punched in range, elevation and azimuth data into the *Striker* glide-bomb's initial vector catalog. "We'll launch the bomb at maximum range—twelve miles, ninety seconds to go. I've set the initial steering data for twelve miles at twelve o'clock. Give me a countdown to the two minute point."

"Roger," Luger said.

"Amplitude shift in the Kavaznya radar signal," Wendy suddenly announced. "Looks like . . . looks like a target-tracking mode. The *laser* . . . it's locked onto us . . ."

McLanahan reacted as if he had been rehearsing the action, although he never had. In one fluid motion he moved the Weapons Monitor and Release Switch from the *Striker*'s forward center position to forward left, the weapon-rack position of one of the weapon decoys; moved the bay door control switch to MANUAL, hit the DOOR OPEN switch and reached down to his left knee and hit the recessed black button on the manual release "pickle" switch.

"Bay doors are open," Elliott announced as a large yellow BOMB DOORS OPEN light flared on the forward instrument panel. A moment later a similar light marked WEAPON RELEASE flicked on—then off.

"What the hell?"

"The decoys," McLanahan told Elliott. "We can't jam the laser's radar, but the decoys should draw it away long enough for us to get within range."

A moment later Elliott flinched as an object resembling a huge blue-orange meteor burst to life and flew diagonally away from the Old Dog. The mass of fire spit tiny, blinding balls of light from its flaming body, and streams of gleaming tinsel—radar-decoy chaff—poured from behind the drone. The glare from the decoy was almost blinding, but Elliott squinted anyway and watched the decoy fly earthward, jinking left and right as it burned away.

The next instant McLanahan moved the weapon-select switch to forward right and punched out the second decoy. Elliott noticed the WEAPON RELEASE button light once again; then, as the second decoy ignited and flew away to the right, Elliott's gaze was drawn to the right cockpit window.

The launch of the second decoy, and Elliott's attempt to spot it, saved the general's eyesight—and the life of the crew.

Although the tiny *Quail* decoy—an improved version of an old bomber defensive drone used on SAC bombers for years—was many times smaller than its parent B-52 bomber, its design made its radar, infrared and radiation signature more than ten-times larger than the Old Dog. Its refrigerator-size body had dozens of radar-reflecting nodules surrounding it, and even the design of the wings and tail, as well as the fifty pounds of chaff-bundles it ejected in regular intervals, enhanced its radar reflectivity. Its shape alone made it a more appealing target than the quarter-million pound bomber.

But there was much more packed into the tiny drone. It automatically broadcast a wide spectrum of radio transmissions to attract anti-radiation and home-on-jam missiles. To heat-seeking missiles and infrared trackers the phosphorus flares and burning jelly oozing along its surface made it appear as hot as a nuclear reactor.

***

The Kavaznya radar, even with its solid nuclear-powered lock-on, was drawn off its intended target. The first *Quail* bloomed like an electromagnetic stain across the target-tracking radar scope of the Russian laser weapons officer. The tracking computer quickly locked onto the larger return, and the target officer did not override the shift. There was nothing, he thought, bigger than a B-52 so close to the complex. He insured the new target lock-on, searching and not finding any malfunctions and signaled clear for laser firing. Just as Elliott's attention was drawn to the right cockpit window to watch the launch of the second *Quail* decoy, a thick beam of red-orange light split the darkness and lit up the interior of the Old Dog like a thousand spotlights turned up full-blast. The very atmosphere around the huge B-52 *Megafortress* seemed humid, almost tropical.

The vaporized air around the laser blast created a tiny vacuum around itself, sucking thousands of cubic acres of air into the shaft of light. The turbulence and lower-density, superheated air caused the Old Dog to sink, and only Elliott's fast reactions and the screaming thrust of the seven remaining turbofan engines kept the Old Dog from crashing into the rugged Kamchatkan shoreline.

The tiny *Quail* decoy was not merely destroyed by the laser blast—it was vaporized. There was no time, no fuel remaining, even to form a secondary explosion or a puff of smoke. The tiny drone simply ceased to exist.

Elliott felt as if he had been violently sunburned. He pulled on the yoke, fighting to arrest the sudden descent and gale-force turbulence. The MASTER CAUTION light snapped on, as did other warning lights, but Elliott had his hands full trying to control the bucking mountain of metal beneath him.

Dave Luger was thrown against his right instrument panel as the Old Dog swung sharply left into the vacuum, his outburst lost in the groaning metal of the *Megafortress* and the protesting roar of its engines. Still, he and the Old Dog made out better than some others. A MiG-29 had just closed into ideal IR missile-firing range and had not heard the call to clear the area when the laser beam sliced through the subzero Siberian air.

The gale-force wind-blast created by the mini-nuclear explosion within the krypton-fluoride laser beam, which had thrown the four-hundred-thousand-pound B-52 bomber around the sky like a paper airplane, reached up and swatted the thirty-thousand-pound *Fulcrum* fighter into the ground like an insect. The pilot of a second Russian fighter was too busy fighting for control of his own machine to notice.

"What the hell was *that?*" Angelina said. All of her equipment went blank—the airmine rocket system, the *Scorpion* missile system, her radar, all of it. She glanced at Wendy Tork alongside her, switching her equipment into STANDBY in an attempt to reset it.

"The laser," Elliott said. "They shot the laser at us. Two generators dropped off the line." He scanned the instruments quickly. "Engines appear okay. John, can you get the number two and three generators back on-line?"

"I can try," Ormack said. He wiped his eyes and felt carefully along his right generator panel for the proper switches . . . The power interruption had blanked out everything in the downstairs navigator's compartment, but Ormack's practiced fingers were able to reset the generators and get them back on-line. Trouble was, the only things that reactivated after power was applied were the downstairs lights.

"Dave, how much time?" McLanahan asked.

Luger was fumbling around his workdesk with a tiny battery flashlight, shining the weak beam on the few pieces of equipment on the right side. "We have to get out of here," he said. "We have to go back . . ."

"Easy, man, easy," McLanahan shook his partner's shoulders. Luger finally stopped his flailing and stared at McLanahan. "It's over, Pat."

"No it's *not.* Now give me a time to the twelve-mile point, dammit." McLanahan was just about to push Luger out of the way and check himself, but Luger finally relaxed enough to check his ship's clock.

"Two minutes ten seconds."

"All right. Switch all your stuff to STANDBY. It'll come back up by launch time. If it doesn't we'll slick the bomb, fly over that laser and drop it like a regular bomb." He rechecked the DCU-239 weapon-arming panel. "We might have another problem."

"Such as?" from Elliott.

"The generator-fluctuation knocked out DC power to the arming panel," McLanahan told him. "I've got no weapon indications at all."

"It should still be good—"

"I don't know what the bomb will do," McLanahan said quietly. Everyone on board heard the muted statement, even over the roar of the turbofans.

"You mean it won't explode?" Wendy said. "We've come all this way, and it won't *work?*"

"I mean I don't know its status. It may or may not be armed, it may be armed but be a dud . . . I just don't know."

"All this way . . . all this sacrifice . . . for nothing?"

"One minute to launch point," Luger said.

"I'll try to rearm the weapon," McLanahan said, and began to run the pre-arming checklists again. "Nothing," he muttered finally. "Battery power . . . recycling . . . sensor power . . . nothing. I've still got uplink power, so the thing will fly, but I still don't know what it will do."

The crew of the Old Dog grew very quiet.

"I've got my threat receivers back," Wendy announced. "Signal from Kavaznya . . . beginning to shift again."

"All the decoys are gone," McLanahan said. "I launched them just before the laser fired—"

"Power won't be back on the anti-radiation missiles for two minutes," Angela said. "That was our last hope."

"Angelina . . . preparation for ejection checklist," Elliott ordered, face tight.

Luger looked at McLanahan, who stared straight ahead, clenching and unclenching his fists.

"Wendy, try to give us some warning before the laser fires," Elliott told her.

Wendy clicked her microphone in response, said nothing. She could barely see the subtle frequency shifts through the interference, and even if she did spot the radar lock-on she knew they wouldn't be able to eject before the laser beam blew them into atoms.

"I'll trim it for a slight climb," Elliott said. "Maybe this beast will stall right over their heads, the sonsofbitches. Crew, our mission was to destroy that laser complex. I'll give the command to eject, wait until everyone is out, then crash the plane into the complex. Prepare for—"

"Wait," McLanahan said. "You can't do that. We'll still drop the damn bomb—"

"You said it wouldn't explode."

"I said I don't know its status. My job is to drop it on the target. Your job, *sir,* is to get us out of here."

"We can't risk it. If the bomb doesn't go off we've failed and we'll take the heat for nothing—"

"We can't just *quit* . . ."

"McLanahan, this is an order. *Prepare for ejection.* "

Luger began to tighten the straps of his parachute harness. He zipped his jacket up all the way, looked over at his partner. "Pat, you'd better—"

"How much time, Dave?"

"Pat . . ."

"Dave, *how much time?*"

"Thirty seconds. But—"

"Close enough." McLanahan hit the AUTOFIX button on his control keyboard, which entered a present-position update into the *Striker* glide-bomb's computer. He then opened the bay doors with the mechanical handles on the overhead panel and pulled a yellow-painted handle next to it marked SPECIAL WEAPONS ALTERNATE RELEASE.

"Bomb away, General, now please get us out of here."

Elliott had been adjusting his straps when he saw the BOMB DOORS OPEN and WEAPON RELEASE lights snap on. "We're too far, we won't have time to—"

"We're not bombing that laser with *this* plane," McLanahan challenged. "Break left, get us out of here . . ."

After that everything seemed to happen in slow motion. It was like watching a slide show, the frames clicking off one by one, the sound turned off . . .

Elliott stood the Old Dog on its left wingtip, whipping it to forty-five degrees of bank. The stall-warning horn blared but no one paid attention to it, if they could hear it. The general could *feel* the Old Dog slipping sideways—which was *downward* at forty-five degrees of bank—as it changed heading in its rudderless turn. Remarkably, it didn't hit the frozen ground . . .

Wendy released her grip on her ejection seat's triggers, held her finger on the CHAFF SALVO button, ejecting fifty bundles of chaff in one massive cloud just as the Old Dog began its turn. She would have kept ejecting chaff if the force of the turn hadn't pushed her finger off the button . . .

Ormack, unable to help out in any other way, tried by "seat-of-the-pants" to hold in enough back-pressure on the yoke to keep the turn going without forcing the *Megafortress* into a stall. To his surprise, he found that his and Elliott's efforts were in almost total coordination . . .

In spite of the hard break McLanahan managed to stay focused on the flight path of the *Striker* glide-bomb as it dropped from the Old Dog's bomb bay, saw the *Striker*'s TV monitor flare to life as the glide-bomb cleared the weapons bay.

McLanahan's hand-entered DR position was almost perfect. The center of the Kavaznya laser complex was dead in the center of the low-light TV screen. When a message printed out on the monitor stating that a visual low-light sensor lock-on was available, he pressed the LOCK switch to insure that the bomb would make it to the target. Even if the Old Dog didn't survive the bomb would now fly itself to the target . . .

"Radar switching to target-tracking mode," from Wendy.

"Prepare for ejection, crew," from Elliott. "Blinking light coming on." He reached down to the center console and flicked on the ejection-warning switch. The large red light between the two navigators began to blink furiously.

"Steady light is the order to eject—"

"*No.* Continue the break. If you do a complete one-eighty, do another one to the right. Don't give up now—"

"If they let go with that laser there won't be time to eject—"

"You'll be murdering this crew if you order us to eject," McLanahan said.

"But the bomb . . ."

McLanahan now acted on his own. He switched to the infrared display—the picture was near simulator-perfect. He could make out the "warm" town above the "hot" laser complex, and the "cold" Bering Sea beyond. He shifted the tracking handle slightly to the left, centering the aiming reticle onto the hottest infrared return in the complex. The *Striker's* steering uplink system was working perfectly. The strap-on mini-rocket engine had not yet fired—it was flying over a thousand feet higher than programmed, and the extra altitude meant a longer unassisted gliding ability.

The infrared orange laser site slowly began to enlarge as it got closer— the *Striker* was locked onto a huge power substation. McLanahan was just about to switch to narrow field-of-view and begin precise aiming when he noticed another "hot" object in the upper left corner of the infrared display, far above the main reactor complex in the valley.

He had only moments to study it before it went out of view, but he could make out a huge complex . . . only the base was "hot," four-fifths of the structure was "cold." Just before it went out of view he switched back to low-light visual display.

In this visual mode there was no mistaking it. The dome, large as a stadium, was clearly visible, with a large rectangular slot open and pointing directly at the Old Dog. McLanahan remembered back to Elliott's first briefing on the Kavaznya site, when he passed around early reconnaissance photographs of the complex.

The mirror building.

McLanahan's reaction was instantaneous. He moved the tracking handle left and aft all the way to the stops to get the dome back on the screen.

Luger was watching his own monitor in shock. "Pat . . . what are you—?"

"The mirror," McLanahan said. "It's the mirror building . . ."

"But the substation . . ."

McLanahan said nothing as he watched while a yellow SRB IGNITE appeared on the screen, indicating that the glide-bomb's strap-on rocket booster had fired in response to new steering commands. The substation slowly moved out of view.

"The substation . . ." Luger said again.

"I'm gonna punch a hole in the mirror building. Even if the bomb doesn't go off it should do enough damage to put this place out of commission."

The visual scene began to grow darker as the rugged hills above the Kavaznya complex and the town rushed just below the visual display. McLanahan had to hold the tracking handle full-back as the rocky ridgelines grew closer and closer.

Luger yelled, *"It's going to crash."*

But a moment later the last rock-covered ridgeline disappeared from view and the huge mirror-housing dome filled the TV monitor. McLanahan pushed the tracking handle down and centered the aiming reticle on the top of the dome's pedestal. Both navigators watched in fascination as the dome rushed forward right into the TV screen.

The six-inch glass eye of the *Striker* somehow stayed intact through the one-inch-thick fiberglas panels of the dome, so the two navigators were able to eavesdrop on the *Striker*'s exact impact point—the steel girders and counterbalances supporting the massive mirror.

The robot eye passed precisely through two support arms, and the bomb came to rest on the very base of the mirror support-structure. Instantly Russian technicians and security guards could be seen running around the weapon.

"It didn't go off," Luger said. "It's a dud, it didn't go off—"

"Radar locked onto us," Wendy broke through. "Solid lock-on, they've got us . . ."

McLanahan had tuned out the hubub of noise inside the Old Dog and was staring, transfixed, at the *Striker*'s TV screen. More soldiers surrounded the *Striker* as it lay inside the mirror building.

"Crew, eject light coming on . . . get ready . . ."

Ormack was rigid in his seat, his ejection levers raised, his control column stowed, ready for ejection. Elliott had just reached down to the center console and was about to flick the eject signal from WARNING to EJECT when something exploded off the Old Dog's right wing and a ball of flame hundreds of feet in diameter arched skyward, lighting up the entire coastline, the blast easily heard over the roar of the engines.

"What was *that?*" Ormack shouted, holding onto his seat as the shock wave rolled over the *Megafortress*. "The reactor?"

"We got the mirror building, Patrick got the mirror. The thing went off. It *wasn't* a dud," Luger reported, voice rising.

"The radar's down," Wendy said, "no tracking signals from Kavaznya."

Elliott began to pick out the ridgelines looming toward them, and slowly lifted the Old Dog's nose above the ridgelines, desperately trying to trade some slowly building airspeed for life-saving altitude. He noticed that most of the lights in the town above the laser complex were out . . . "The explosion must have knocked out power to the area. Check your equipment . . ."

McLanahan quickly scanned his instruments. "Computers are back on-line." He quickly synchronized the navigation satellites to his computers, and the green NAV light snapped on. Moments later the terrain data was reloaded from the "game" cartridges. "Terrain computers back up," he told Elliott who reengaged the pitch autopilot to the terrain-data computers, selected COLA on the terrain clearance-plane selector and watched as the long pointed nose again faithfully dipped earthward.

"Jesus," Ormack said. "We actually did it."

"Threat receivers and all jammers back up," Wendy reported.

"My radar's back up," Angelina said, as though back from the dead.

"Station check, crew," Elliott ordered, switched the ejection warning light off, pulled the firefighter's oxygen mask to his face and breathed deeply. "The ride's not over yet," he reminded them after his hit of oxygen. "Those fighters will be after us any minute."

McLanahan lay awkwardly in his seat, supported by his parachute harness straps that he never had time to tighten. "True, General, but there's no denying that it's Miller time."

"You're cleared to the potty, radar," Elliott said, helping Ormack put on the oxygen mask. "That's all. After that get back on watch. We're coming up on Ossora. Kavaznya may be down, but I repeat, four squadrons of MiGs will be after our butts."

McLanahan looked down at the warm stain between his legs. "It seems I don't need the john."

Dave Luger managed an exhausted chuckle. "Sorry for falling apart back there, partner. You can count on me from here on out—"

"Search radar at two o'clock. It's Ossora airfield," Wendy announced suddenly.

The two navs exchanged looks. "Back to work," McLanahan said, switching his attack radar to target-tracking mode.

"**R**adar contact is lost, Element Seven," Yuri Papendreyov heard the Soviet radar controller say over his command radio. "Report your position immediately." As if in reply, a large red LOW ALTITUDE WARNING light came onto the control panel of Papendreyov's advanced MiG-29 *Fulcrum* fighter.

He muttered unhappily to no one in particular and started a shallow climb away from the inky blackness around him. Suddenly the earth was his enemy, as much an enemy as the American warplane he was chasing. He held his heading steady and switched on his pulse-Doppler attack radar and nose infrared sensor pod.

He had been receiving steering signals from the radar site at Kavaznya to the attacking American B-52 bomber, signals that fed a stream of missile-launch data to his missile fire control system and provided range and bearing data to intercept the B-52. With the Kavaznya radar operating he didn't need his *Fulcrum*'s radar for hunting, a big advantage of the advanced Russian interceptor. Nothing could jam the Kavaznya radar, and without the *Fulcrum*'s onboard radar acting like a locating beacon the fighter could sneak up behind the American B-52 without being detected.

All that was gone now. Somehow the Kavaznya radar was off and he was forced to use his own narrow-beamed radar to search thousands of square miles of sky for the bomber, diverting his attention away from flying his *Fulcrum* and avoiding the rugged Kamchatka mountains.

The young PVO-Strany interceptor pilot activated his command radio and reported in a tight voice, "Element Seven has lost vectors to intruder—

"Wait, no, *still* chasing." A huge radar return appeared at the very left edge of his on-board radar, then disappeared. He began a thirty-degree bank turn to the left, quickly but futilely scanning for terrain to his left.

"Element Seven has possible radar contact . . ." he radioed, but he was too busy to report his position.

"Element Seven, repeat. Element Seven, report your position."

Which was when he saw it out of the corner of his eye—the fire was so big and bright that despite his training and discipline he took several precious seconds to study the destruction. Debris from the massive mirror dome in the hills above the Kavaznya research complex was spread out for at least a kilometer in all directions, and a huge twisted mass of metal sprawled awkwardly in the center of what used to be the mirror building. The blast must also have done some collateral damage, he figured, cut power to the complex . . .

Papendreyov throttled back to ninety-five percent power on the screaming Tumansky R-33D turbofan engines and divided his attention between the radar and the infrared detector while continuing his shallow turn. He made a quick scan for his wingman—nothing. They had been separated long before when the laser had fired and the incredible turbulence and windblast nearly wrecked him, and he assumed the worst—that either the laser had inadvertently hit him or that the American had gotten him.

This flying at night without radar monitoring was suicide, the pilot thought to himself. The Soviet ground radar controller was usually responsible for everything—terrain clearance, vectoring toward the intruder, closure, firing position—he did everything but pull the trigger. Now Papendreyov was completely blind, relying on an easily jammed nose radar and a range-limited infrared detector that wasn't worth—

A diamond symbol appeared in the lower right corner of his heads-up display—the infrared detector had found the B-52. Strange that the radar had not. He tried to get a radar range to the target but it still was not locking onto anything. He swung right, centered the diamond up in azimuth on his display and waited for a radar lock-on. Still nothing. The infrared scanner told him only elevation and azimuth, not range. One of his two AA-8 heat-seeker missiles could lock onto the bastard but they were close-range missiles and worked best under eight kilometers range.

He hesitated to drop the nose through the horizon until he found where he was and checked terrain elevation. Papendreyov throttled back to ninety percent and waited. No sense in driving blindly into the B-52's guns, he thought. The twenty-seven-year-old Soviet PVO-Strany Air Defense pilot then realized he hadn't talked to anyone, hadn't gotten permission to do anything, hadn't received one word of direction. He was still two years from being qualified to perform autonomous intercepts—going out to hunt down enemy planes without direction from ground controll-ers—but he was performing one now. It was easy, painfully easy—sui-cidal, but very easy. Easy to kill oneself.

He checked his engine instruments and fuel. If he stayed out of after-burner he could stay and track this intruder for another half-hour. He still had four missiles—two radar-guided missiles and two heat-seekers. Enough to get the job done?

"Airborne radar contact," Wendy Tork announced into the interphone. "Seven o'clock. Looks like . . . like . . . a *Fulcrum.* Pulse-Doppler attack radar."

At the same time Wendy sounded her warning the computer-drawn terrain trace zipped across General Elliott's video monitor. He grunted in relieved satisfaction and reached for the clearance plane knob.

"Terrain-avoidance computer back on-line, General," McLanahan said, but Elliott had already selected COLA on the clearance knob—the computer-generated lowest altitude, which meant a harrowing ride no higher than a hundred feet above the now-rapidly rising terrain. His lips were dry, but he felt clammy inside. "Get that strike message out, An-gelina?" he asked, rechecking his switch position.

"Repeated it twice, General." She reset her fire control radar to clear the faults created by the interference of the powerful Kavaznya radar, then switched it to SEARCH and the radar instantly found the fighter behind them.

"My gear's working again. Radar contact, seven o'clock high, twelve miles," Angelina reported. She watched it for a moment. "Hold-ing steady . . ."

She hit the TRACK button on her console and a green TRACK light illuminated. She lowered the safety handles on the twin turret handgrips, put a finger on the *Stinger* airmine trigger and watched the range count-down. When it reached five miles she gently squeezed the trigger, and fired once . . .

The *Fulcrum* pilot heard a warbling ALERT tone in his headset, quickly jammed his throttles to maximum afterburner and yanked his fighter into a risky ninety-degree, twenty-degree climb to evade a possible missile launch. He leveled off a thousand feet above his initial pursuit altitude and searched the horizon out his left cockpit window for the source of the missile alert.

"A fighter launching a missile at me?" Yuri Papendreyov asked himself, eyes searching the blackness. *"An enemy fighter over Russia?"*

Luck had followed the young Soviet pilot into that wild evasive snap-roll. The tiny *Stinger* rocket, with its small directional fins, could not keep up with the Soviet fighter and its half-scared, half-genius pilot. The *Stinger* did a lazy turn, trying to follow the steering signals from Angelina's radar, but its turn radius was twice the *Fulcrum's*. Suddenly it was behind and to the right of the *Fulcrum,* and there was no way the tiny solid-fuel rocket could catch the fighter. It tracked behind the *Fulcrum's* wake, its propellant almost exhausted. Not receiving a detonation signal, and realizing its fuel had run out, the tiny rocket issued its own detonation signal.

Papendreyov's attention was immediately directed to his right, where a huge fiery flower blossomed out of the grayness all around him. He could almost feel the sparks, the myriad bits of metal, flying out toward him, seeking him. Instinctively he tried to jam his throttles to maximum afterburner, then realized they were already there and began a shallow climb, watching the flower of death disappear behind him.

His breath was coming out in rapid, shallow heaves. Sweat trickled down his heavy glass faceplates. Thanking the stars and the shades of comrades Mikoyan and Gureyvich, the designers of his beautiful jet, he banked left and began to reaquire his quarry.

"AI at five o'clock," Wendy called out again.

Angelina was already shaking her head in disappointment. "This guy is good," she said. "He jinked just in time."

"Well, he's coming for us again," Wendy said.

Luger was watching his five-inch terrain scope, now clear and operating normally after their unwieldly three-thousand-pound *Striker* glide-bomb leveled the Kavaznya mirror building and, at least temporarily, took the radar site with it. "We'll get to the mountains in twelve miles."

"He's staying up high," Angelina said, glancing at the elevation and azimuth readouts on her console. "He's good but he's not ready to mix it up in the dirt yet."

"Can he still get an IR shot at us?" Ormack asked.

"He can track us, but unless he's ready to descend to within a few hundred feet of us we have a chance." Just then, the elevation readouts began to steadily decrease. Angelina swallowed hard.

"He's descending, crew. Get ready."

Yuri Papendreyov had finally gotten a reliable navigation beacon lock-on and found himself on his cardboard chart. He nodded to himself. At this present speed—over eight hundred kilometers per hour—he could descend another thousand meters and spend almost two precious minutes acquiring the B-52 bomber before the threat of the frozen peaks of the Koryakskiy Khrebet began to loom outside his cockpit—all completely invisible to him. He nudged his *Fulcrum* down, set the altimeter reminder bug on three thousand two hundred meters and maneuvered his fighter to center the IR TRACK diamond in his heads-up display.

That few hundred meters of altitude did the trick. The pulse-Doppler attack radar signaled lock-on, and firing information was instantly fed to the AA-7 radar-guided missile.

Yuri smiled. A solid infrared and radar lock-on, with four missiles ready to go. The range continued to click down. The memory of that fiery missile explosion snapped back to him, and his decision was made. He throttled back, holding the range at fourteen kilometers, selected the two AA-7 radar-guided missiles, fired.

A MISSILE ALERT warning generated by the pulse-Doppler attack radar focusing on the low-flying Old Dog had put the crew in a state of tense readiness. When Yuri Papendreyov selected the AA-7 missiles for firing his attack-radar switched to missile-guidance mode. The continuous-wave radar signal that guided and steered the AA-7 missiles triggered a MISSILE LAUNCH indication on Wendy Tork's threat panel, which was heard over ship-wide interphone and repeated up in the cockpit.

Wendy immediately ejected eight bundles of chaff from the left ejectors and ordered an immediate right break. Elliott and Ormack, having already accelerated to maximum thrust, threw the Old Dog into a coordinated hard turn to the right. Simultaneously Wendy found the continuous-wave missile steering signal from the Russian fighter and began to set a jamming package against it.

From directly on the stern the Old Dog's radar signature was miniscule. When Elliott and Ormack hauled the bomber into forty degrees of bank, however, that radar signature bloomed several times its original size . . . it was like seeing a book edge-on, then turning it so the whole cover could be seen. There was no mistaking it for ground clutter now.

The right AA-7 missile was distracted by the chaff, but that distraction added up to scarcely seven feet. The missile passed directly over the center of the Old Dog's fuselage and just in front of the leading edge of the right wing. When the seeker head snapped over to try to follow the steering signal, its eighty-nine-pound warhead detonated.

Dave Luger felt nothing. It was simply as if his entire right side instrument console, his computer keyboard and parts of his radar had freed themselves from their secured places on the aircraft and ended up in his lap and in his face all at once. The concussion would have knocked him clear out of his seat and across the *Megafortress'* tiny offensive compartment, but his shoulder and lap belts held him securely in his seat and subjected his upper body to the entire force of the blast that penetrated the fibersteel skin.

He felt hands across his shoulders and chest, but still no pain. He fought to focus his eyes and finally gave up on that. Air sucked out of his chest, debris from everywhere flew around him.

"Dave." McLanahan reached across the narrow aisle between their two downward ejection seats and propped Luger upright, straining against the weight of the two-G turn that Elliott and Ormack were still executing. "Dave's hit!"

"Yer crazy, radar," Luger muttered, but as McLanahan moved him upright his head dropped against the headrest on his ejection seat and rocked uncontrollably as the pilots fought for control of the crippled bomber.

Luger could feel his head jolted from side to side but was unable to convince his neck muscles to do anything about it . . . "I'm fine, I'm fine," he said. "Hey, my scope is out . . ." "Out" was a considerable understatement—it was as if a giant metal-eating monster had bitten off half the million-dollar cathode-ray tube. McLanahan reached down and locked Luger's inertial reel on his ejection seat, which helped his partner stay upright in the seat. "How are the computers, Patrick?"

"Screw the computers for now," McLanahan replied, unstrapping himself.

"Stay strapped in, Pat—"

"Just *shut up* for a second, Dave," McLanahan said quietly. He reached for the first aid kit secured to the bulkhead behind his seat, glancing at the computer displays as he opened it . . . they were still working, no faults or interruptions.

"The computers are fine, Dave." He braced himself against the sliding nav's table and examined his partner. "Oh, God . . ."

"I'm fine, I told you," Luger mumbled again. McLanahan held up a large gauze square from the first aid kid but was unsure about what to do first. He had never seen bone before, clean, white bone, except on a T-bone steak . . . the thought made him gag, but he forced the thought away . . .

"Put a bandage on whatever's wrong there, Pat," Luger said, "and let's get back to work." Luger raised a finger to wipe moisture out of his right eye. When he looked at it his entire hand was covered in glistening red blood.

"Ohhh . . ."

"Sit still," was all McLanahan could say as he covered the right side of Luger's face with a thick pad of gauze and taped it secure. Luger sat through it all as if he were getting a haircut.

McLanahan checked Luger's neck and chest, brushing away fragments of glass and fibersteel. The flight jacket and flightsuit had protected Luger's upper body, it seemed.

"I'm all right," Luger said, his voice now muffled slightly through the gauze. "I twisted my leg a little, that's all, forget it . . . but turn the heat up, will ya? It's gettin' cold in here . . ."

"Let me take a—"

"I said forget it."

But McLanahan had already ducked under the table to investigate. He stayed out of view for a few moments, came up to retrieve the first aid kit, then emerged again a few moments later.

Luger had felt nothing but a few tugs on his right leg. "See? I told you, mom."

McLanahan returned to his seat, his body jerking from side to side from the turbulence as the Old Dog crested another ridgeline in the mountains of the Kamchatka. He stared silently down at his worktable.

"All done playing Florence Nightingale?" Luger said as he reached down to his right thigh, touched, felt nothing. But when he brought his hand up he found it covered with sticky, darkening blood.

He finally met McLanahan's eyes. "Strong like a bull." He readjusted his headset, lowered the microphone to his lips. "Nav's up and okay," he said over the interphone.

General Elliott began, "David . . . ?"

"Lost my radar, sir," Luger said, forcing iron back into his voice. He tried to punch up a systems-diagnostic routine on his terminal but only a few buttons were left on his keyboard. He strained across the worktable to use McLanahan's terminal. "Looks like we're still talking to the *Scorpion* missiles through our controls but I've no search video. All the terrain-following computers look okay, all the weapons controls are out but that's a moot point now . . ."

"All right," Elliott said, trying to steady his voice. "Crew we've lost cabin pressurization. Wendy, Angelina, can you see that guy out there?"

"I've got his search radar shut down," Wendy replied. "I lost him right after he launched . . ." It was, of course, no longer just "a launch"—the Russian had hit one of their own, hurt him . . .

"Wendy, I'm okay," Luger said quickly, as though sensing her thoughts. "You . . . you ladies nail him . . ."

"My scope's clear," Angelina said. "We'll get him."

"Sure . . . they've taken their best shot and they couldn't flame us. Sure . . ."

***

Yuri Papendreyov angrily switched frequencies on his attack radar. The heavy jamming from the American B-52 attacker had begun precisely when he hit the missile-launch button on his control stick. The missile left the rail with a good steady TRACK indication but he lost it soon afterward. He saw no primary or secondary explosions, saw no crash indications and the jamming was continuing harder than ever. So he had to assume his AA-7s had missed, and that he had to start all over again—but this time closer to the mountains, at least three hundred meters above the bomber with no radar and with three thousand kilograms less fuel.

He leveled off at the minimal sector altitude, throttled back to ninety percent and began a slow roll to the left to try to reacquire the B-52. The auto-frequency shift mode of his attack radar, which randomly changed frequencies to try to defeat the B-52's jamming, was all but useless. The shift was too little, too late, and it always seemed to shift right into a jammed band. Yuri changed the frequency all the way to the lower end of the scale and swept the area for the bomber.

Who would have believed it? he thought. A B-52 in the middle of restricted Soviet airspace. A lone B-52, at that. No escort, no wave of cruise missiles preceding it, no mutual defenses, no B-1, no FB-111 raid like the one on Libya and Syria two years before. *One B-52.*

Well, why not, Yuri said to himself as he began to search another twenty-degree quadrant. The plan was working very damn well so far. The B-52 had obviously flown several thousand kilometers, drove right up the Kamchatka, *and* dropped a bomb on just about the most important piece of land in the Soviet Union next to Red Square itself.

There . . . at the very bottom of his radar . . . just before another wave of interference flooded his scope, a cross with a circle around it appeared, then disappeared. Hostile radar emissions. The B-52's own radar, the one that obviously was used to steer whatever weapon they had launched against him, had given them away.

He rolled further left on an intercept course. Switching the attack radar to STANDBY to avoid giving himself away—it was useless, anyway, with the heavy jamming—he maneuvered to parallel the B-52's course. The radar emission from the B-52 was sporadic—they were looking for him, he was sure, but being careful not to transmit too long. Not careful enough, though. They transmitted on their radar long enough for him to compute their track.

He set the infrared search-and-track seeker to maximum depression and waited for the supercooled eye of the seeker to find the B-52—there was, he knew, the possibility of the seeker locking onto a warm building with the angle so low, but eight jet engines should be brighter than anything else in the sky or on the ground right now. He was already at the minimum safe altitude for the sector he was in, and without solid visual contact on the terrain, descending any lower would be suicide. He increased throttle to ninety-five percent and waited. Soon, he was sure, the range would decrease to the point where the seeker would lock-on, and then he'd stay high and pick off the intruder . . .

When a few minutes later the infrared seeker locked onto a hot target there was no mistaking the size or intensity of the target. The infrared seeker had a longer range than the AA-6 missile, so, he realized, he would need to close in on the B-52 a bit more.

Yuri thought about using the attack radar once more to get a range-only estimate on the B-52, but that would give him away. If he was in range of a surveillance-radar site they could give him a range to the B-52, but for some reason he couldn't hear the station at Korf or Ossora. Probably too low, too close to the mountains . . . if he couldn't hear them on the radio they surely couldn't see him on radar.

Yuri's track had been fairly constant for the last few moments, meaning that the B-52 was making no evasive maneuvers. He relaxed his grip on his control stick and throttles . . . maybe they didn't know he was behind them. The B-52's tail radar hadn't been activated for several minutes. He had to launch before they spotted him on that tail radar—

Suddenly he felt it—a slight shudder through the titanium body of his *Fulcrum* fighter. He scanned his engine instruments for a malfunction, but already suspected the cause—wake turbulence from the B-52's engines, he was closing quickly. He stared as hard as he could out the canopy of his *Fulcrum* but couldn't see it.

But that too was unnecessary. A moment later a green light spewed on his weapon-control panel . . . his selected AA-6 heat-seeking missiles were tracking the target.

He released the safeties on the launch button on his control stick and—

A scratchy, faded message blared on both of his command radios. "For all Ossora and Korf units, code yellow. Repeat, code yellow. Acknowledge immediately and comply."

His fingers didn't move from the missile launch button, but neither did it squeeze. A general forces recall . . .

"All Ossora units, code yellow. Acknowledge and comply."

He tried to force himself to make a decision. He had the B-52 in his sights, but if he transmitted on his radio, so close to the B-52, they might hear or detect his transmission and evade or reattack. The Korf interceptor units had all responded immediately to the recall instructions. All of the Ossora units had probably responded as well—all but him. His career was probably already in jeopardy. A young pilot commanding a long-range fighter, capable of reaching Japan or Alaska, who didn't respond immediately to recall instructions could easily end up attacking vegetables in a warehouse in some isolated Siberian base. Or worse.

"Vawl." Papendreyov swore aloud, maintained track on the target, activated his command radio and said, "Element seven acknowledges. Triangulate position immediately. Stand by. Closing on intruder."

"Element seven, comply immediately with instructions," came the voice once again. His number had been called this time—he was indeed the last one to rejoin at the navigation beacon over Ossora. His ticket to Ust-Melechenskiy three hundred miles north of the Arctic Circle was probably already being processed . . .

Fat hare-brained dogs, Yuri let loose, this time to himself. Enraged, he pressed the missile-launch button and began a climbing left turn toward Ossora . . . before realizing that the green IR TRACK light had long extinguished. The two hundred thousand ruble missiles vanished into the darkness.

Yuri proceeded to curse all his superiors, the flight commander, the ground controllers, the command post officers and everyone else he could think of on his way back to the rendezvous point. He wasn't worried about that icy base in Siberia—he was worried about exactly how he'd wring the neck of the first person unlucky enough to get in his way.

General Elliott and Lt. Col. Ormack, acting in unison, forced the Old Dog lower and lower into the mountains. The terrain-following computer was already set to COLA, the lowest setting possible in the automatic mode, but with the threat of a Soviet fighter on their tail, even a hundred feet above the ground was like ten thousand. There were constant warning beeps as the automatic-climb commands were overridden by the two pilots, and the bomber's radar altimeter, measuring the exact distance between the bomber's belly and the ground, occasionally entered the double-digit area.

Dave Luger's one good eye, and both of Patrick McLanahan's, were on the ground-mapping display of McLanahan's ten-inch scope. The two navigators carefully called out even the smallest peaks and ridges that could pose a threat. Elliott and Ormack reacted in sync—one man forcing the bomber lower, the other scanning the instruments and nudging it higher in response to the warnings from the terrain-following computer and what he heard over the interphone.

"He was so close," Wendy said, "his radio signal was so strong I swear I heard him over interphone." She swallowed, studying her video displays. "His signal is decreasing . . . I think he's leaving . . ."

"My scope's clear," Angelina reported, shivering for a moment. "I saw him for a second, but he's gone."

Elliott relaxed his grip on the yoke and let the terrain-following computer control the Old Dog again. "Well, that was close. I saw the missiles hit out there . . . they were so damned close, and we didn't even know he was out there. We didn't even know . . ."

Yuri Papendreyov stood at attention before his squadron leader's desk in the PVO-Strany Interceptor Squadron ready-room at Ossora Airfield. The squadron leader, a thin, aged naval commander named Vasholtov, still on active duty from the Great Patriotic War, paced behind his desk. Not a word had been spoken yet, even though Papendreyov had been standing at attention for two minutes.

He had to chew this young Papendreyov cub out a few minutes longer, the squadron leader thought to himself—although that didn't always mean a verbal tirade. The squadron—and his superiors—expected a good five to ten minutes of closed-door time, perhaps a slammed door, a curse or two, then an administrative reprimand. It would go no farther than the squadron records—good pilots who didn't drink on the job were hard to find in the cold, barren Kamchatka—and the reprimand would disappear after a month or two. How he hated these chewing-out sessions. But it had to be done to maintain the discipline and integrity of his unit.

"You have disappointed your entire squadron, Papendreyov," the old squadron leader finally said, glancing at the young *Fulcrum* pilot. "Failure immediately to acknowledge a recall instruction is almost as serious as treason. Or desertion." The youngster didn't blink. Didn't move a muscle—most young pilots would be melting at the mention of the word "treason."

Vashaltov studied the youngster for a moment. Papendreyov could have been from Berlin or even further west—Copenhagen or Britain. He was of average height but broad-shouldered with close-shaved blond curls and narrow blue eyes caged straight ahead. His boots were polished to a high gloss, every zipper was closed and every patch on his flight suit was perfectly aligned. Five years from now this young pilot would probably be a flight commander . . . The new breed, Valshaltov thought, but just now this "new breed" needed a tongue-lashing. Valsholtov knew how fast unrest, boredom, lack of discipline and insubordination grew in a unit where the men, especially the young ones, thought the commander didn't care. Might as well get it over with . . .

"I suppose you will now tell me that your radio was malfunctioning."

"There was nothing wrong with my radio, sir."

"Silence, Papendreyov. Silence or I will have your wings here and now." The squadron leader circled the young pilot a few times like a shark circling in for the kill. Papendreyov remained at rigid attention.

"Ice-and-snow-removal detail for forty-eight hours for that outburst, Flight Captain. Perhaps a few nights in the Siberian winds will cool down your hot-headedness. Pray I don't put you on that detail permanently."

Papendreyov blurted out, "I had the intruder, Squadron Leader. I saw the American B-52. I took a missile shot at it."

"You what . . . ?"

Papendreyov still stood firmly at attention. "I found the B-52 at three hundred meters above the ground, squadron leader. I pursued him down to seventy meters—"

"*Seventy* meters? You took your interceptor to seventy meters? Without authorization? Without—"

"I found him. I found him on radar but his jamming was too strong. So I locked onto him on the infrared search-and-track system. I closed to within three kilometers of him."

Vasholtov stifled his annoyance at the interruption. "Go on."

"I was then ordered back to base. I waited as long as I could. I fired just before obeying the order to return but I had lost track by then. They must have detected my radio trans—"

"You *fired* on the B-52?" In forty years he had never heard of any man under his command actually firing on anything or anyone except target drones. "Did you . . . hit it?"

"My first radar shot . . . yes, I believe I hit him," Papendreyov said, wishing he hadn't sounded so unsure, so hesitant—now it sounded like he was lying.

"You could have been killed," Vasholtov said. "You could have crashed at any time. Flying at seventy meters at night in the mountains with the flight director radar down . . . you risked too much. This will have to be reported—"

"Let me go after him," Papendreyov interrupted once again. "I can find him again. He is using a tail-mounted radar that can be detected for forty kilometers. He is only traveling five hundred, perhaps six hundred kilometers an hour . . . I can catch him. I can stay low enough for the infrared system to lock onto him. He cannot detect a fighter closing on him if radar is not used."

"Not use radar . . . ?" Valsholtov was almost too flabbergasted to reply. Papendreyov had been down in the Kamchatka mountain range at night—he had only recently been certified for night duty—at seventy meters, about a thousand meters lower than he should have been, without using his radar. He had broken more rules in one hour than the entire squadron had done in months. The Defense Force Commander would retire him for sure when they saw this report.

"You are lucky, very lucky," Vasholtov said, "to be alive. Very, very lucky. The rules of engagement exist to protect stupid young hotheads like you. You broke at least four of them—not including the crime of ignoring a unit recall-order. You are very close to a flight tribunal, flight captain. Very close."

"Punish me, then," Papendreyov said defiantly. "Send me to Ust-Meryna or Gorky. Take my wings. Just let me take one more crack at the Americans—"

"*Enough.*" Vasholtov's tobacco-singed throat throbbed from all his yelling. "You will report to the intelligence branch and give them a complete debriefing on your supposed contact with the American B-52. Then you will immediately report to your barracks. I'll have to decide what to do with you—give you to a flight tribunal or a criminal board."

"Please, *tovarisch,*" Papendreyov said, his sharp blue eyes now round and soft. "I deserve punishment, squadron leader, severe punishment, but I also deserve to shoot down this intruder. I know where to find him and how to take him. Please . . ."

"Get out," Vasholtov ordered, dropping into his rough wooden chair before he collapsed into it. "Get out before I have your insubordinate hide arrested."

Papendreyov's round eyes hardened and narrowed. He snapped to unbending attention, saluted, spun on a heel and left the office.

Papendreyov quickly returned to his barracks room as ordered—without stopping at the flight intelligence branch. He turned on the light to his desk and fished out a pen and paper. As he wrote he picked up the telephone and dialed.

"Alert maintenance, crew sergeant speaking."

"Starshiy Serzhant Bloiaki, this is Flight Captain Papendreyov. I am calling from the ready room. Is one-seven-one combat ready?"

"One-seven-one, sir? Your plane? The one you just returned—"

"Of course, my plane, sergeant. Is it ready?"

"Sir . . . we . . . it has been towed to recovery area B, sir, but it hasn't—"

"Starshiy Serzhant Bloiaki, this is not like you," Papendreyov said. "This is the worst time not to get the orders. My plane was to be immediately reconfigured with one four hundred decaliter centerline drop tank and four infrared missiles. It was to be ready on the hour." He paused, then said quietly, "I'll have to tell squadron leader Vasholtov that my sortie will be delayed—"

"That won't be necessary," Bloiaki said quickly. "One drop tank and four infrared missiles . . . they will be ready in fifteen minutes, sir."

Papendreyov checked his watch. "It will be ready in ten minutes or we will both have a chat with Squadron Commander Vasholtov. I must refile my flight plan once more," he said, finishing his hurried scribbling. "I'll be out there right away."

He hung up the phone and went to his bureau, took one last long loving gaze at the photo of his wife and infant daughter, then opened the top drawer. As he studied his wife's dark chestnut hair and his daughter's blonde curly locks he began stuffing his pockets with packets of freeze-dried survival food and dried beef. He quickly unzipped his flight suit and put on a second thermal shirt over his flame-proof underwear, and replaced his lightweight flight boots with insulated flying boots. He touched the picture of his wife, then put on his flight jacket, gloves and fur hat and hurried toward the flightline.

He had left the hastily written note and last will and testament unsigned; there was no longer time even for that. No matter. His career was over the minute he stepped foot on the flightline. His life—period—would have been over as he taxied onto the main runway except that on account of the air emergency declared over the entire eastern air-defense region the air traffic controllers allowed him to take off without a fully verified flight plan. In an emergency, better to have the fighters airborne first, question their procedures later. Papendreyov had known this, of course, and was airborne again within thirty minutes of landing from his first sortie.

It had only been an hour and a half since he had broken off the attack with the American B-52. The B-52, obviously wounded, was flying slow —at the most, he figured, it had only gone some seven hundred fifty kilometers from Ossora Airfield since he had fired his last missiles. His MiG-29 *Fulcrum* fighter could chase after it easily at three times the B-52's speed with fuel from the drop tank only, then spend two, three hours searching for the intruder.

Papendreyov gave his call sign to Ossora Intercept Control, which questioned him briefly about his absent flight-tasking code but quickly gave him vectors to the bomber's last known position, nearly five hundred kilometers ahead. The young *Fulcrum* pilot kept the throttles at max afterburner and began a ten-degree climb at seven hundred kilometers per hour. Within minutes he was at twenty thousand meters, screaming northeast at seventeen hundred kilometers per hour, almost twice the speed of sound.

Quickly he was handed off to Korf Intercept Control, which had few updates on the bomber's position, but Papendreyov made his own estimate where the American B-52 would be. The fuel in his centerline drop tank having exhausted itself less than ten minutes after his takeoff, he made another calculation, then jettisoned the tank, not having the luxury of considering who or what might be underneath . . . he was high over the mountains, but they were still sparsely populated. He continued at maximum afterburner for five more minutes, then pulled his throttles to cruise power and set his autopilot.

He had fifty thousand liters of fuel remaining to find the American, and he was wasting two thousand liters per hour just hoping to catch up. But Papendreyov wasn't worried. He knew, thanks to his subtle course corrections, that the nose of his *Fulcrum* was pointed right at the American's heart.

"We aren't going to make it," Ormack felt obliged to report. "We've got thirty minutes of fuel tops."

General Bradley Elliott double-checked the autopilot and flight control annunciators while Ormack went over his fuel calculations. They had been flying for well over an hour at ten thousand feet, forced to that altitude by the damage to the pressurized crew compartment.

"Fuel flow?"

"Pretty steady," Ormack said, "but the fuel curve is getting worse. Looks like a major leak from wing and body tanks. I've pumped all the fuel out of the body tanks but I can't do anything about the mains . . . I've got the minimum in them to keep the engines going as it is. We've had low-pressure lights on for a long time—"

"Can we make it to the ocean?" Elliott asked, scanning his engine instruments and checking them by moving the throttles. "Put it down on an ice floe or punch out near the coastline?"

"Punch out?" Angelina Pereira said. "You mean *eject?*"

"We'd have to cross high mountain ridges to get to the coast," Luger said, warming his hands on an overhead air vent. "It would be real close."

"Now's the time to decide," Elliott said. "Patrick, give me a heading toward the ocean, away from any active Russian fighter bases. Crew, prepare for—"

"Hold on," McLanahan broke in. "General, what does WXO near an airfield mean?"

"WXO? Warm-weather operations only. They close the place during winter because it's too expensive and too difficult to maintain. Why?"

"I found one," McLanahan said, putting a finger on his high-altitude navigation chart and checking the satellite navigation system's present-position counters. "Straight ahead, fifteen minutes."

"Fifteen minutes?" Ormack said. "You're crazy. That's in Russia."

"They got a long runway at the very least," McLanahan said. "Maybe they'll have gas and oil for the number two engine. If it's abandoned or vacant we could—"

"They're not abandoned," Elliott said. "At least *our* Alaskan warm-weather bases aren't. We usually have caretakers, mostly locals, that look after the place. Maybe some minimal security, National Guard or Reserve deployments."

Ormack stared at Elliott. "General, you're not seriously considering . . . You're both crazy. Maybe you ought to go back on oxygen." He looked hard at Elliott, expecting him to turn and shrug off McLanahan's notion. Some last-minute humor . . .

"General . . ."

"We're armed . . ."

"We've got your automatic and two lousy thirty-eight revolvers in the survival kits," Ormack said. "They're more of a hazard to us than they'd be to anyone else. They could have been stowed on this plane for years."

"We could do the refueling . . ." Elliott said, talking more to himself than anyone else.

"I've done that, lots of times," McLanahan put in, excitement rising in his voice. Luger was staring at McLanahan pretty much the way Ormack was looking at Elliott—in disbelief. "Global Shield missions. Remember, Dave? Simulated post-strike recovery at an emergency airfield. Keep the number two nacelle running, pump gas into the right outboard, right external, or right drop tank, then transfer gas to the rest of the plane. I once hand-pumped ten thousand pounds of—"

"The Russians aren't going to just let us take their gas," Luger said. "It's crazy."

"We'd end up captured," Angelina said. "I'd rather take my chances in the mountains than be captured by them—especially after this mission."

"No, you don't want to go down in the mountains," Elliott said. "Even if you come out of the ejection unhurt your chances are at best fifty-fifty even with the global survival kits we've got. And we can't ditch the Old Dog. She wouldn't withstand the impact."

"I still think those odds are better than landing at a Russian airfield—"

"Do you, John?" Elliott said. "How long do you think we could survive out there in those mountains?"

"If we made it to the coast we'd have a chance."

Elliott ignored that, asked his navigators for the distance to the coast-line.

"One hundred miles is the closest," Luger said. "But we cross two ranges, each about nine or ten thousand feet, and we're within radar range of Trebleski airfield the whole way. After we cross the mountains we can cut away from Trebleski to the northeast."

"We can stay near the mountains," Wendy offered. "Get as much distance as possible from Trebeski and hide in the ground clutter."

"Can we go around Trebleski at all?"

"Not on the coastal side of the mountains," Luger told him, rubbing his one uncovered eye, "unless we turn around."

"So it's unlikely we'd make it to the coast," Elliott said. "And that means we get out over the mountains in the dead of winter, hundreds of miles from any kind of friendly forces. We could try to evade but I wouldn't give us much of a chance of making it to the coast, much less into Alaska."

"General, are you saying that landing at a Russian military airfield, abandoned or not, is a better option?" Ormack said. "We'd be surrender-ing. We'd be handing ourselves and this plane over to them. And I sure as hell wouldn't give us a snowball's chance in hell of making it out of a Soviet prison alive."

Elliott kept silent for a long moment, then: "Distance to that airfield, Patrick."

McLanahan already had the geographic coordinates of the field typed into his navigation computer. "Anadyr is eighty miles, five degrees left."

"Any radar circles around it?"

"Yes," McLanahan said, studying his civil-aviation chart. "Can't tell what they are but they've got something there."

"Wendy, any activity?"

Wendy Tork had been carefully studying her threat displays ever since McLanahan had first made his wild suggestion. "Clear scope ever since Ossora airfield."

"I've got no terrain on my scope for a hundred miles," McLanahan said, tuning his ten-inch radar scope in one-hundred-nautical-mile range. "If there were any threat signals they're not being blocked by terrain. I can't make out the base, though."

"Okay," Elliott said, "you've all heard the arguments. There's no guar-antee that we'll get gas, oil or anything but our asses in a sling if we land at Anadyr. On the other hand it's possible that we could land this beast and walk away from it uninjured, steal a truck and have a better than even chance of evading toward the Bering Strait, where our chances of getting rescued significantly increase. If you're a wild dreamer like Patrick you'll actually believe there's an outside chance of pumping this aircraft full of gas, restarting the number two engine and running it enough to lift off again, *and,* maybe, making it back to Alaska."

"Crazy," Ormack muttered. "If the base is occupied we won't have any chance of taking off again—we'd flame out long before liftoff. If we can't find gas we're stuck three hundred miles from friendly territory on a Russian military base. The Russians would get the Old Dog and we'd be stuck trying to evade all the way back to Alaska. Fat chance."

"Well, I can't have this crew bail out over the mountains," Elliott said. "Chances of surviving the ejection itself are low. If we did survive we'd be faced with a three-hundred-mile trek across Siberia with the Red Army chasing us. I say we take our chances on solid ground, in one piece. At least we'll be alive to fight or run."

"I'm for it," Luger said. "Hell, that base will be the last place on this earth they'd look for us, except downtown Moscow."

"All right, General," Wendy said, closing her eyes in a silent prayer, "let's try to land it."

Angelina shrugged. "Check. I don't know if I could eject myself out of this damn thing anyway."

"I'm giving a crash course, anyway," McLanahan told her. "You may still have to do it. General, I'm clearing off to go upstairs. Dave, watch my scope for me."

Ormack agreed they really didn't have much choice, pulled out the emergency landing checklists as McLanahan went upstairs and knelt between Wendy and Angelina. He plugged his headset into the defense instructor's station and told the two women to switch their interphones to the "private" position, which allowed them to talk without bothering the rest of the crew.

"How are you warriors doing?"

Angelina nodded but looked almost as bad as Luger. Because of the damage to the downstairs crew compartment McLanahan had been forced to transfer most of the available heat downstairs to keep Luger from going back into shock. Even with Wendy's borrowed jacket and thermal top, without the protection the rest of the crew had, Angelina was losing to the cold. Her lips were purple, her eyelids drooped as if she were struggling to stay awake. Her hands, in stiff, metallic firefighting gloves, were shoved deep inside her jacket for warmth.

Bomber defense was almost out of the question, McLanahan thought. It would be difficult if not impossible for Angelina to try to operate her equipment under these conditions. Landing was absolutely the only option.

"Hang in, Angie," he said.

"I'll be all right . . ."

McLanahan turned to Wendy. "How you doing?"

"Holding up. I could use a drink."

"Champagne when we get home . . . okay, you were taught this months ago, but let's go over it again. If we get attacked while trying to land, or if the pilots can't land this thing, we've got no choice but to eject. Listen carefully, watch the warning light and don't panic—but don't hesitate eighter. There's a simple three-step system for using upward seats—just remember, ready, aim, fire.

"The ready is to pull the safety pin out of the handle on your armrests, trip the handle release lever and rotate the handle upward. Grab the front of the handle, not the middle or inside. There's no hurry, do it smooth and easy. This equipment is old and it needs some care. The aim is like align. You shove your fannies deep into the back of your seat, press your back into the seat and push your head back into the headrest. After that lower your chin to your chest. Think about a nice straight spine the whole time. Put your feet flat on the deck, knees together. Put your elbows inside the armrests and brace your arms against the back. The fire is easy—grab both triggers inside the ejection handle and squeeze. Next thing you know, you'll be on the ground."

"What happens if it doesn't fire?" Angelina asked between shivers. "Can you go over the emergency ejection sequence?"

"Don't worry about it. If necessary I'll pop your manual catapult initiator pull-out pins for you."

"You?" Wendy said, looking up at McLanahan. "How?"

"The chances of navigators surviving a downward ejection at less than two thousand feet is fifty percent. If we go below one thousand feet . . . never mind what the book says . . . our chances are about zero."

"But—"

"Dave doesn't have an ejection seat," McLanahan told them. "After the decision was made to get a second navigator I requested that another ejection seat be installed. But there was so much pressure to complete the testing that it somehow got overlooked." He tried a smile and flunked. "I'll make sure the cross-hairs are on the runway so that the bombing computers help the pilots land the Dog, get Dave strapped in, then come back upstairs and strap in right here. I'll see to it that you two get out if it's necessary to eject—"

"Patrick, you can't—"

"Can and will. End of discussion—"

"Pat, we're fifty miles from Anadyr," Luger reported. He waited a few moments. "Pat?"

Wendy was shaking her head. He figured he should say something else but the words wouldn't come. He groped for the interphone wafer switch. "What?"

"Fifty miles," Luger said. "You okay?"

"Great."

"Strap in," Elliott called back. "Everyone back on watch."

McLanahan made his way slowly down the ladder, leaned over Luger's shoulder. Luger was now in the left-hand radar navigator's ejection seat, studying the ten-inch radar scope.

"See it yet, buddy?" McLanahan asked. Luger had switched the radar scope to fifty-mile terrain-mapping display and was adjusting the video and receiver gain controls near his left knee, tuning the terrain returns on the scope in and out to search for the runway.

"Nope," he said, moving his uncovered left eye closer to the scope. "Nothing under the crosshairs. I get a blank scope when I tune out terrain."

"Assume the computers are bad. You should be able to break out a runway within thirty miles. Just keep tuning." He stopped down, checked Luger's straps and harnesses. "All snug?"

"I still don't want to do this," Luger said.

"It's my fault you're even on this plane," McLanahan said quickly. "It's my fault you got hurt. At least I want you to have a chance to get out of it if something goes wrong."

"Thanks, buddy, but I'd like to think my so-called professionalism helped get me a ticket on this ride. I wouldn't have missed it for anything. Well, almost anything."

"Check. I'll buy you a beer back at my place," McLanahan said. "Or a vodka. I guess that would be more appropriate."

McLanahan thumped his long-time partner on the back, grabbed Luger's tactical chart and made his way upstairs, where he strapped himself into a spare parachute and fastened his seatbelt.

"Forty miles," Luger announced. "Clear of terrain for fifty miles."

"We'll have enough gas for one low approach," Ormack said. "We've got fuel low-pressure lights on all four mains. One pass clean, then a left turn into a visual overhead for landing."

"Crew, listen up," Elliott said. "If we pick up ground fire we'll break out of the pattern and climb out as fast as we can. We'll level off at fifteen thousand and go straight ahead until we flame out. Jump out on my command, but if you see the red light don't wait for my command. After you land use your survival radios on the discrete channel and we'll try to locate everyone and form up."

"Thirty miles," Luger reported. "High terrain at two o'clock. Shouldn't be a factor. Looks reasonably clear for a left-hand traffic pattern."

"We're setting up on a sort of extended base leg, Luger," Ormack said. "That airfield will be moving off to your left."

"Rog."

"Descent and penetration checklist, crew," Ormack called out. "We've got twenty thousand pounds of fuel, nav. Approach speed and emergency landing data?"

Luger called up the landing data on a computer terminal in the downstairs compartment. "Two engines out on one side—approach speed is less than minimum maneuvering speed, so min maneuvering speed takes precedence," Luger read. "Min maneuvering speed is one-twenty-eight with full flaps, plus twenty-five with less than full rudder authority. One hundred and fifty-eight knots. Go-around EPR setting, three point zero, military power on symmetric engines only. Touchdown speed one-forty-eight. Brake energy limited one-fifty to the bottom of the danger zone, one-thirty to the bottom of the caution zone. Max drag chute speed one-thirty-five."

"There may not be a go-around," Ormack said, checking the fuel gauges. He continued the lengthy series of checklists, letting the Old Dog's on-board computer display each checklist on Ormack's display in the cockpit. It seemed the Old Dog was one huge emergency procedure. Ormack reviewed checklists for fuel leaks on landing, double engine-out, engine fire, drag chute failure, hydraulic failure, overrunning the runway, landing on ice and snow, strange field procedures, ejection and emergency aircraft evacuation. When he finished, Luger announced that they were less than twenty miles from the Anadyr Far East Fighter-Inceptor Airbase.

Elliott and Ormack began a gradual descent to fifteen hundred feet above the field's elevation.

"Clear of terrain for thirty miles," Luger said. "Still nothing on radar."

McLanahan had already double-checked that Angelina and Wendy were secure in their ejection seats. Now he made his way forward to the cockpit and slipped into the steel instructor-pilot's jumpseat. "Need an extra set of eyes?" he asked Elliott.

"What the hell are you doing up here?"

"Dave's got the left seat downstairs. I'll help you look for the runway, then I'll go aft and help Wendy and Angelina with their seats in case . . ."

"Patrick, that's suicide. Get your butt back to your seat."

"Dave doesn't have an ejection seat, sir," McLanahan said quietly. "One of the details we never got around to."

"I didn't know . . ."

"Forget it. Dave's as good on the radar as I am. If something goes wrong I'll try to make sure Wendy and Angelina get out. Meanwhile I'll help find that runway."

"This whole deal is still crazy . . ." Ormack muttered.

"Maintain the element of surprise," McLanahan said. "We've kept the whole Russian air force off our backs by confusing 'em. This is just the next step." And over the interphone he asked, "Dave? Anything?"

"It all looks the same," Luger told him, increasingly frustrated.

"Keep tuning, you'll find it. Remember, we're setting up for a base-leg, not a straight-in. Don't just rely on the nav computers—check shorter ranges."

"Rog," Luger said, retuning the scope once more.

"We'll stay unconfigured at two hundred and fifty knots until we see the runway," Elliott said. "We'll turn final and check the runway and base and make a decision to land. Then we'll turn onto the downwind, configure and—"

"I've *got* it," Luger suddenly announced. "Six miles, eleven o'clock."

"Six miles?" Ormack said.

"The navigation computer must be way off," McLanahan told him. All three heads in the cockpit swung to the left. Elliott found it immediately. "Got it," he said. "We're right on top of it . . . we'll never get configured fast enough. Let's go on straight ahead, check out the base from the end of the runway, then make a turn into a right downwind for landing."

"Roger," Ormack said. "I've got the airplane. You check out the base." He turned the cockpit lights down to bare minimum to make it easier to see the runway.

Elliott muttered unhappily as the runway moved to his left window. "That runway looks like the rest of the tundra. Some of those snow drifts out there must be ten feet high."

"No signals," Wendy reported. "Still a clear threat-scope. Not even any radio transmissions."

It was a small, almost obscure base in a mountain valley that reminded McLanahan of Hill Air Force Base in Utah, with snowy mountain peaks peering down from the sky. The most noticeable feature of the base was the "Christmas tree"-alert parking area at the end of the runway—two rows of six parking areas for Russian fighters, staggered on each side so that all twelve fighters could move at once and line up on the runway. Fortunately the parking areas were empty—more than empty, they appeared not to have been plowed out for quite a while. Some of the Quonset hut fighter shelters were partially dismantled, with snow piled in deep drifts everywhere.

A big problem was the tiny village nearby, which McLanahan could see out Ormack's right cockpit window. It was about ten miles from the base, but a B-52 made a lot of racket and would attract attention. What the villagers would do about the noise was another question. Did people in Russia complain about military planes waking them up at night? McLanahan prayed they didn't.

"The base isn't completely deserted," Elliott said as the runway moved out of view. "I saw some trucks parked out in front of a building near the main taxiway. They looked military."

The crew was suddenly quiet. Ormack started a slow, wide turn to the right to parallel the runway.

Wendy said, "If it's not deserted, they could have troops there . . ."

"Fifteen minutes of fuel left," Ormack said. "I guess we can make it back above ten thousand feet for ejection, but that's all."

"If they had a military force there, there'd be more than just a couple of trucks," McLanahan said, liking his logic but not altogether believing it.

"Agreed," Elliott said quickly. "Besides, the runway looked closed and the buildings looked deserted. *And,* we don't have any choice." He turned to Ormack. "Let's do it. I'll take the airplane. Run the landing checklists."

McLanahan patted Elliott on the shoulder. "Good luck, see you guys in Russia," he said, and made his way back to the defense instructor's seat and strapped in. "Next stop, ladies, beautiful downtown Anadyr."

"Can they land the plane on all that snow?" Angelina asked McLanahan cross-cockpit.

"Not recommended, but this is a tough bird and those are two tough pilots . . ." Big brave talk, he told himself.

"Airbrakes zero," Elliott said as Ormack read from the computerized checklist on his screen. "Ready for the gear and flaps, here they come." He lowered the gear handle, Ormack moved the flap switch to its first-stage position, Elliott started a slow right turn to put them perpendicular to the snow-covered runway.

"Left-tip gear shows unsafe," Ormack said, watching the gauges. "All other wheels down. Flaps twenty-five percent."

Elliott moved the throttles forward to regain speed as the huge flaps, large as barn doors, lowered into the slipstream, allowing the bomber to fly increasingly slower on final approach.

"Fuel danger lights on for all mains," Ormack announced.

"Okay, crew, this is it," Elliott said, forcing his voice to sound calmer than he felt. "The fuel's run out. We either land or eject. Dave, I'll make sure you get a few hundred feet altitude, but don't delay pulling the trigger."

"Nav . . . copies . . ." Luger was not as successful in controlling his voice. His shoulder harness was already locked, his back and neck stiff and straight, his hands rested lightly on the trigger-ring between his legs.

"Patrick . . ." he whispered, fighting off the pain in his leg. McLanahan didn't have a chance. He would need several thousand feet to even attempt manual bailout, much less survive it.

Elliott started a slow turn to the right again to align the Old Dog onto the runway.

"Flaps fifty," Ormack said. "Starters on. Fuel panel is set. Running on fumes now . . ."

"Lower the nose," Elliott said. Ormack flipped a switch and the long, pointed SST-style nose slid down beneath the windscreen.

"Landing lights," Elliott ordered, and the four-thousand-watt lights on the landing gear struts snapped on and the Russian runway leapt into view. A massive snowdrift at least thirty feet high blocked the approach end of the runway. Elliott shoved the power forward.

"Flaps *full,*" he called out.

The howl of the engines obliterated all sound. Luger had his eyes on the bailout warning light on his front console, waiting for the command to eject, his fingers closing around the trigger ring. Wendy and Angelina tensed.

The right-front landing-gear truck plowed into the small mountain of ice, the Old Dog heeled sharply to the right and plummeted down, its nose rushing toward the frozen runway. Elliott stomped on the left rudder before realizing that their rudder was useless, shot away long ago. He jammed the yoke full-back and full-left to try to counteract the headlong tumble, but the Old Dog was a freight train out of control.

McLanahan folded his arms across his chest, waited. He felt the impact on the ice, felt the plane lurch to the right at an angle so steep and so sudden he thought the plane had flipped upside down. The right wing stayed down, and he found himself wondering what the crash would look like from outside, a hundred tons of B-52 cartwheeling around on the frozen ground.

He closed his eyes and waited for everything to grow dark and the sound to stop . . .

For the first time since he began his chase Yuri Papendreyov was beginning to feel he had made a mistake.

Despite stealing his MiG-29 *Fulcrum,* he had been receiving assistance from ground and air forces in trying to locate the B-52 intruder. But so far he hadn't found it. The climb to twenty-six thousand meters, almost eighty thousand feet, was necessary to receive reports from the elements of the Far East Air Defense Force searching for the B-52 . . . at lower altitudes the mountains would block out reports from coastal or partially terrain-obscured stations. All had reported negative contact . . .

Yuri had taken his *Fulcrum* nine hundred kilometers along the Korakskoje Mountains toward Trebleski and Beringovskiy, the main coastal air-defense base and radar installation north of Ossora. He was sure the B-52 would stay along the Korakskoje, hiding in the rugged mountain peaks, then destroy or jam the Beringovskiy radar and head out across the Gulf of Anadyr toward Alaska. With the powerful Beringovskiy radar down, the inferior MiG-23s of the Trebleski Air Reserve Forces, although very heavily armed, would not be able to spot the low-flying B-52 or engage it.

Papendreyov checked his fuel. He would already be in emergency fuel status if he had not taken along the largest external fuel tank available, but now he was again very low on fuel. Only his long idle glide from high altitude left him with enough to make some decisions . . . Trebleski was the most obvious choice for a quick-turn refueling, but Anadyr, a small limited-operations base, was available and within gliding range. He had been briefed, though, not to use Anadyr or other such warm-weather bases except in an emergency.

He had no choice—Trebleski it had to be. He switched his radios to Trebleski Command Post, requested permission for landing and a "hot" refueling, a battlefield-quick refueling technique where a high-pressure tank truck pumped fuel while the aircraft engines were still running.

"Ossora one-seven-one, Trebleski copies your request. Stand by."

"Standing by," Papendreyov replied. Then: "Trebleski, say latest reports on intruder aircraft."

"One-seven-one, intruder last reported by Ossora radar bearing two-eight-two true, range twenty-one kilometers, heading three-four-one true."

"That report is hours old, Control. Any other reports? Has Beringovskiy reported contact?"

"No reports by Beringovskiy radar, one-seven-one. You are cleared for approach to Trebleski Airfield, descend and maintain two thousand meters. Your request for hot refueling has been delayed. Expect cold refueling support in bunker seventeen on landing."

"Control, I am a priority air-defense aircraft. Request priority hot refueling."

"Copy your request, one-seven-one," the Trebleski controller replied.

"Priority request is being delayed by your headquarters. Stand by for confirmation of your flight-tasking. Reset transponder to one-one-one-seven for positive identification. Stand by this frequency."

Papanedreyov swore into his face mask. So that was the reason for the delay . . . by requesting priority refueling he'd forced Trebleski to run a check on his flight-tasking order—which, of course, Yuri didn't have. If he'd just accepted a normal bunker refueling he would have gotten a fast turnaround because of the air-defense emergency and Trebleski wouldn't have double-checked. Now Ossora would know exactly where he'd taken his fighter on its unauthorized chase. No doubt they'd order him arrested after landing.

Yuri checked his chart, saw he was now actually closer to Anadyr than Trebleski. Anadyr would have fuel, might even be set up for a hot refueling. He could wait at Anadyr and monitor the interceptor frequency for any sign of the B-52, then chase it down and destroy it. If the B-52 didn't show—but that was impossible—he could refuel, cruise back to Ossora and try to talk his way out of a court-martial or a firing squad.

He ignored the request to set a new identification code and pointed his MiG-29 *Fulcrum* toward Anadyr, switching radio frequencies to Anadyr's command post. He would be in radio range of the base in half an hour, and he would still have almost an hour's worth of fuel once over Anadyr . . .

Sergei Serbientlov was indulging in one of his few delights—Chinese food. It wasn't exactly a popular dish in this remote corner of the Soviet Union but perhaps that was one of the reasons why he enjoyed cooking and eating Chinese food—it set him apart. Unfortunately it was that sort of anti-Soviet thinking—and eating—that got him stuck in Anadyr in the first place, but everyone had to be somewhere.

Besides, it wasn't so bad. It wasn't a state of exile being here in the very northeastern tip of the Soviet Union; it was more like an unscheduled, involuntary reassignment. He had free housing, free food, vehicles at his disposal and a few hundred rubles extra every month being sent back to his family in Irkutsk.

Plus, he had responsibility and a lot of autonomy. During the preceding two months and for the next two, he had been and would be the chief custodian of a Far East Defense Force Fighter-Interceptor Base. It didn't matter that there were no fighters here—he was in charge of the base. He was the chief policeman, firefighter, banker, lawyer, janitor and mayor of millions of rubles of equipment and buildings. During the long dark winter months he was the richest and most powerful man in this province of fishermen, trappers, and loggers.

Sergei now deftly manipulated a hand-whittled pair of chopsticks to pick up a mass of noodles and fish. He had grown the seasonings and herbs himself in a greenhouse on the base, and he frequently traded with the villagers and nearby fishermen for the fish and flour to make the noodles. The area seemed to have everything, and Sergei was sure that the fishermen took their boats out into the wild Anadyrskij Zaliv across to Saint Lawrence Island or even Nome to trade with the Americans.

He passed his nose over the noodles and spiced fish. It was a strange concoction for breakfast, but his only other option was some four-month-old *ryepa*—turnips—from some old witch in town. No thank you.

He brought the savory, heavily spiced noodles to his lips and was about to take a bite when the double-doors leading to the outer hallway burst open and two figures rushed into the tiny office and half-stumbled, half-ran up to the chest-high counter that extended the length of the room.

The taller of the two was dragging his right leg, which was covered with blackened blood from toe to hip. He had an arm over the shoulder of his companion, who was wrapped in a coarse green blanket.

"*Gdye poonkt skoray pomashchi!*" the injured man screamed in thick monotone Russian. "My leg! Where's the hospital?"

Sergei nearly dropped his noodles in his lap. "What?"

"Where is the *hospital?* My leg—"

"There is no hospital. What happened to your leg?" Sergei came quickly from behind the long counter to the two men. Except on closer inspection he found that the man in the blanket was a *woman*. She had long, salt-and-pepper gray hair and deep, dark eyes—she could have been Oriental herself, Sergei guessed, or Latin. Her lips chattered in the cold as she looked quickly at Sergei, then averted her eyes to her injured companion.

The man dragged himself over to a rough wooden bench in a far corner of the office and dropped onto it. He was tall and ruggedly built, perhaps an old military man. He looked frozen as well, and his skin was gray and sunken—probably from loss of blood, Sergei thought.

"*Gyde polizei?*" the man said. His accent was strange, obviously not from the local area, although very few locals *were* from this obscure corner of the world.

"Why do you want the police?" Sergei bent to examine the man's leg. He couldn't see the wound itself but the blood loss was obviously great. "There are no police here. The village constables won't come to the base. I will help you all I can, but only if you tell me—"

"*Nyet, spasiba.*" Suddenly Sergei was looking into the barrel of a very big, very ugly blue-black automatic pistol. As the muzzle touched his nose, Sergei slowly rose and backed away.

The woman threw off her blanket and helped the injured man to his feet. Her clothing made Sergei forget about the pistol. She was wearing a short, rough blue jacket—*denim*. She was wearing *denim*. And then Sergei noticed her blue jeans and fancy leather boots.

". . . blue jeans?" Sergei said, one of the few foreign phrases he knew. "*Gdye mozhna koopit* blue jeans?"

The woman turned to her companion. "What did he say, General?"

"I didn't catch it all, but the man likes your blue jeans," Elliott said. He turned toward the double doors. "Patrick!"

Crouching low, McLanahan rushed through the doors, a .38 caliber survival revolver clutched in his hand. He ran over to the Russian and pointed his revolver at the man's temple. Sergei closed his eyes.

"Search him," Elliott ordered. McLanahan quickly pat-searched Sergei, keeping his revolver aimed at his head. Elliott then turned Sergei around and backed him into the bench, forcing him to sit. With both his own and McLanahan's guns still pointed, Elliott took Sergei's hands and put each one on top of his head. Sergei sat on the wooden bench, eyes tight shut.

"*Vi gavariti pahangliyski?*" Elliott was asking if he spoke English. Sergei opened his eyes, forced himself to look at each of the strangers.

"*Nyet.* Please don't kill me . . ."

"*Pazhaloosta, gavariti myedlinna,*" Elliott said, telling him to speak slowly. The man looked less terrified now, though very confused. "*Kagda polizei virnyotsa?*" Elliott asked when the police would be back.

"No police," Sergei replied. He kept his hands up, but his shoulders visibly relaxed. Slowly he said in Russian, "Police . . . do not come . . . to base."

"I understood the *no,*" McLanahan said, taking a double-handed grip on the pistol.

"I think he's saying there are no police," Elliott said. "This is going to be rough—I can understand about every fifth word." He leaned forward, still aiming his pistol at Sergei's forehead. "*Binzuh, binzuh.* Gasoline. *Binzuhkalonka?*"

Sergei looked relieved. "*Pazhaloosta!*" Sergei said. "Don't worry, *tovarisch.* Put down your gun, I won't turn you in, I know the routine . . ."

"Whatever you said, General," Angelina said, "the man looks happy now. What'd he say?"

"Hell if I know. I just asked him for gasoline. I'm his comrade now, that's all I understood."

They were speaking English, Sergei said to himself. Obviously only the old man knew any Russian at all—the younger ones still wore blank expressions.

Sergei winked and tried to stand. McLanahan pushed him back down. Sergei looked at the strangers with a mixture of surprise and humor.

"*Yest li oo vas riba?*" Sergei asked. "Sir? *Kooritsa?* I will trade. No problem."

"Fish? Cheese? Chicken?" Elliott said to himself. "He's asking if we have fish? I don't . . ." Then he did. He nodded at the Russian, who nodded in return. Elliott pulled him up off the bench and allowed him to lower his hands.

McLanahan didn't lower his revolver. "What's the story, General?"

"Black market," Elliott said, smiling. The Russian smiled back. "This gentleman runs some kind of black market out here. If my guess is right, he trades fish, meat, cheese, and stuff for gasoline."

Sergei let out a sigh of relief when the younger man finally lowered his revolver—his eyes had looked scared, but his hand didn't waver and Sergei had no doubt he would have pulled the trigger in an instant. Followed by the younger man, Sergei went to a locker behind his desk and pulled out his hat, mittens and coat. As he pulled them on he had a chance to examine the young man's coat. It was thick, dark gray, and it didn't look like cotton or leather.

Slowly, carefully, he reached over to the man's collar and touched it. It looked like cloth but felt like plastic. A plastic coat? It had pockets on the front and arms that fastened with strange zipperless fasteners. Who were these men? And why were they wearing plastic and warm while their woman wore rare expensive cotton denim but was freezing to death?

Elliott saw the fur-lined coat the Russian wore and glanced at the shivering Angelina. *"Mnye noozhnuh adyezhda,"* Elliott said. He pointed at the fur billowing out from the Russian's collar. *"Baranina."*

Sergei nodded, reached into his locker and took out his severe-weather coat, a long, heavy sealskin greatcoat with wolf-fur lining the hood, then went over to the woman and held it out to her. Angelina, noticing the man's obvious interest in her denim jacket, slipped it off and held it out to him.

The Russian acted as if she had just given him the crown jewels. Sergei examined every seam and stitch in the jacket, muttering the strange English words he found on the steel buttons, then carefully folded it and hid it far back on the top shelf of his locker.

"I can make a fortune here," Angelina said as she pulled the coat over her shivering shoulders. "I've got a whole closet full of those old beat-up jackets." Her face brightened as, for the first time in hours, she felt her body warming up.

"Come," Sergei said in Russian. "Back to business." He led the group outside. They climbed into a waiting Zadiv panel truck and drove down the flightline.

Over the clatter of the truck's ancient heater, which stubbornly refused to emit any heat despite the racket, Elliott said, "Keep an eye out for a fuel truck or fuel pumps."

"What do they say on them?" McLanahan asked, keeping his hand on the Smith and Wesson revolver in his pocket.

"I don't know." Elliott breathed on the side window of the truck, which instantly froze. Against the rumble and crunching motion of the truck he drew five Cyrillic characters—an "O" with a flag on top of it, and "E," a backward "N," a curly backward "E," and an "O." *"Binzuh,"* Elliott said. "That means gasoline."

Sergei nodded and smiled . . . the old man was giving the youngsters a lesson in Russian. *"Da,"* Sergei said in Russian, "we are going to get you gasoline."

"Look," Angelina said, pointing to the right. There, surrounded by a tall barbed-wire fence, was a white steel cylinder twenty feet high and about thirty feet in diameter. A lone white tanker truck was parked beside it.

"Binzuh?" Elliott asked the Russian, pointing to the tank. The Russian glanced at the tank but continued driving.

"Nyet," Sergei said, pointing ahead. "Not gasoline. Kerosene." Elliott showed his puzzlement, not understanding the words. Sergei kept on driving.

"Pahvirniti napravah," Elliott said. "Turn right." He pointed at the tank once again. Sergei shook his head.

McLanahan pulled out his revolver and held it to the Russian's temple. "Do as the man says, *tovarisch.*" Sergei stiffened. Elliott nodded and pointed to the tank.

Sergei turned toward Elliott, clearly puzzled. What did they want? "Does your boat use kerosene?" Sergei said in Russian. "That will do you no good."

"Boat?" Elliott said, trying to decipher the words. "I understood boat but nothing else."

Sergei was pointing more emphatically toward a road nearby that headed east. "Diesel," Sergei said in Russian, pointing. "This way. Don't worry. I won't cheat you."

McLanahan pressed the revolver's muzzle against Sergei's head.

"Pazhaloosta," Sergei said, holding up his hands. "All right." With a shrug of his shoulders he bullied the old truck into a right turn and headed for the tank. A few minutes later, with McLanahan holding his revolver in sight but not aimed at him, Sergei had opened the gate to the tank compound and led the group inside.

Now he opened a belly valve on the tank truck parked next to the large above-ground tank and a few gallons of liquid spilled onto the snow. Angelina bent down and sniffed.

"It smells like kerosene," she said. "It's not jet fuel or gasoline. What do we do?"

"We may have lucked out," Elliott said, reaching into an inner pocket and taking out a yellow hand-held survival radio. Depressing a black button in the center, he turned a channel select switch to an unmarked frequency position and pushed the transmit button.

"John, how do you read?" Elliott spoke into the radio.

Aboard the Old Dog, John Ormack pulled the boom microphone of his headset closer to his lips and raised his voice over the noise of the number four engine idling in the background. "Loud and clear, General. Where are you? Any luck?"

"We're good. We may have what we need. Double-check section five of the tech order. Check on the use of alternate fuels. We might have enough kerosene here . . ."

"Stand by." Ormack reached behind his seat and pulled out the Old Dog's technical order, the plane's instruction manual, found the listing and keyed his microphone.

"Got it, General. Kerosene is an approved alternate fuel. We may have trouble with it if it has no anti-icing additive, but we can fly with it. How much do you have?"

"We got a tank truck that looks like it holds ten thousand gallons. That's sixty thousand pounds."

"Should do it," Ormack said. "Dave figured a minimum of fifty thousand to get us to Nome."

"We'll call you back when we're headed toward you."

"A B-52 can use kerosene for fuel?" Angelina asked doubtfully.

"The books says it can," Elliott told her. He turned to the Russian. He was no longer smiling and jovial.

"*Kak vasha imya? Atkooda vi?*" the Russian said sternly. "Who are you? Where are you from? You are not fishermen."

"*Sputniks,*" Elliott said, getting the bare gist of the questions. "Travelers." Sergei was still looking suspicious. Suddenly he snatched at the yellow survival radio, and before Elliott could grab it back Sergei had read U.S. AIR FORCE on a back instruction plate. McLanahan quickly raised the revolver to Sergei's head.

"I think we lost our buddy here, troops," Elliott said. He pointed at the truck. "Patrick, check out that tank truck. See how much kerosene it has."

McLanahan gave his revolver to Angelina, who pointed it with some expertise at the Russian. McLanahan found a dipstick in the truck's cab, climbed on top of the truck and checked the amount of fuel inside through a cap. "Probably one-quarter full," he said.

"Not enough. Okay, *tovarisch,*" Elliott said in Russian. "I want gasoline in truck. *Mnye noozhna binzuh . . .*" he tapped on the truck. Sergei did not move, unsure.

"I'll convince him, General," Angelina said. She prodded the Russian around to the side of the truck where McLanahan was busy lifting a high-pressure hose. McLanahan fastened one end of the hose onto the truck, the other to one of the valves rising from the ground. Angelina motioned to the truck with her revolver.

"Help him," she said. The Russian looked at McLanahan lugging the heavy hose, then blankly back at Angelina. Angelina cocked the revolver and held it to the Russian's forehead. *"Now."*

Sergei held up his hands and nodded, walked to McLanahan and gestured for him to reattach the hose at another valve, then removed and replaced the end of the hose at the truck. When the hose was fully attached Sergei opened the valves and kerosene began rushing from the tank to the truck. Minutes later the truck was full.

"Patrick, you drive the panel truck," Elliott said. "Angelina, go with him. I'll ride with our buddy here in the tanker."

McLanahan ran over to the Zadiv, started it up and waited for Elliott and the Russian to get in the tanker.

"Pazhaloosta," Elliott said when he and Sergei had climbed inside the icebox-like cab of the tanker. He gestured at the truck outside the fence, then pointed his pistol at the Russian. *"V etam napravlyenil.* Please. This way."

Sergei watched the muzzle of the .45. When Elliott inadvertently swung it too high he reached out with his right hand and tried to grab it away. He'd been a clown too long . . .

A shot rang out, and the windshield of the tanker truck exploded, showering them with shards of glass. Sergei leapt out of the truck, running back around the fence. No longer a hero.

McLanahan and Angelina caught a glimpse of him just as he disappeared down a line of trees that paralleled the flight line road, and Angelina took a shot at him but the bullet ricocheted harmlessly away.

McLanahan ran for the tanker and jumped into the cab. "You all right, General?"

"Yes, dammit, but things are going to get tense here real quick." He turend to Angelina as she came to the right side of the tanker. "Take the panel truck to the plane. Patrick and I will take the tanker. Sure as hell he's going to call for help, we won't have much time."

It took a few moments for McLanahan to figure out how to get the fuel truck moving, but soon the two trucks pulled up to where they had half-hidden the Old Dog in a wide parking area between two hangars. Ormack came running out, the second survival revolver in hand. He saw the smashed windshield, looked to Elliott. "What . . . ?"

"We had a comrade but he bugged out on us. We've got to work fast before he calls in the Marines. John, you'll be up in the cockpit on the fuel panel. I think I can figure out how to work the pump on the tank truck so I'll be outside." He called over to Angelina in the panel truck. "Pull the truck over to the right wingtip. Patrick, climb up on the right wing, open one of the fuel filler ports and we'll fill it from there. Angelina will help with the hose. Where's Wendy and Dave?"

"I've got Dave in the cockpit monitoring the engines," Ormack said. "Wendy is on the radios calling for help."

"Any luck?"

"Not yet. I'm not sure what anyone can do for us anyway, unless we lift off out of here."

Ormack then began unreeling the refueling hose from the truck while McLanahan climbed on the Old Dog's right wing, a screwdriver in his teeth.

"The main-wing tanks have dozens of holes in them," Ormack told Elliott as the general began to decipher and operate the truck's pump controls. "The forward body tank has a few leaks too. McLanahan will pump fuel into the center tank. I'll plan on keeping the fuel in the center, aft and mid-body tanks, but once we get up to engine start and takeoff we'll have to put fuel in the mains. We'll be losing fuel like crazy after that—"

"Nothing we can do about it," Elliott said, "unless you've enough chewing gum to plug the holes." Elliott started the truck's fuel pumps and waved to McLanahan, who had a filler cap off the center-wing fuel tank and was dragging the hose across the wing and over to the fuselage. "Ready anytime, Patrick."

Huddled against the biting wind, McLanahan inserted the fuel nozzle into the open fuel port on the fuselage between the two huge wings and began pumping fuel. Below him, Ormack ran inside the Old Dog and took Luger's place at the controls.

Luger, right leg heavily taped and bandaged, limped downstairs and out to the fuel truck, carrying several quart cans taped together. "I found the spare oil downstairs near the survival rations. I'll fill up the number two engine with oil. At least we should be able to use it for takeoff before it disintegrates."

"Good, Dave . . . how you doing?"

"Great," Luger said, dropping the case of oil on the truck's fender to spell himself. "I have a blinding headache, I'm freezing cold and my right leg looks like Swiss cheese. How are you, sir?"

"Got you beat, Dave, but if I talk too much I'm afraid I'll pass out."

"Let me handle the pump, General. You get inside."

"No, put the oil in, then see what you can do about ripping loose some of the metal and that broken tip gear off the wings. It's all drag—we can do without it. Especially for a seven-engine takeoff."

"You got it, sir . . . you know, I still don't believe we're doing this. I mean, actually stealing gas from a Russian fighter base—"

"We may be pumping water into our tanks, for all we know. There just wasn't time to keep on looking . . ." And so saying, Elliott seemed to be drifting off, falling asleep, the rush of adrenaline wearing off . . .

Chief Constable Vjarelskiv, the regional militia commander, grimmaced as he took a sip of what he was told was *kofye,* a thick liquid of grain and coffee. He took a bite of *khlyep* to take the dusty taste away, glaring all the time at Serbientlov, who was standing wringing his hat in his hands in front of Vjarelskiv's desk.

"This is nonsense, Serbientlov," the constable said. "You bring me tales of armed attackers at the base—two men and a woman . . . What did they steal? Your precious Chinese chopsticks? Are you sure you didn't dream up the whole story?"

"This is no joke, *tovarisch,*" Sergei said. "If we don't hurry they'll get away."

"With *what?* A snow plow? Your noodles?"

"They commandeered a fuel truck, and . . . and they had explosives. They threatened to blow up everything. The whole base. You have to do something—"

"Your story gets taller every moment, Serbientlov," the constable said. He leaned back into his chair, fixing Sergie with an icy stare. "Are you sure this is not a . . . shall we say, a falling-out of thieves?"

Sergei fidgeted uncomfortably but managed to sound indignant. "Thieves? You are not accusing *me, tovarisch?* The only thieves here are the ones out—"

"Stop it, Serbientlov. The little empire you've built at the base is well-known, at least to the citizens in the area. You use more diesel in four months than the whole Soviet navy uses in a year, supposedly for your fleet of plows but the streets and runways are always clogged with snow and you feed your fat gut with Chinese noodles and real coffee." Vjarelskiy threw his grain beverage into a garbage can. "Now I'm busy, so if you'll—"

"Chief Constable, I *demand* that you send a unit out to investigate. That's your job. You convinced the Far East Defense Force that for a price you could handle any security problems at the base during the winter. They wouldn't be too happy to learn that fifty thousand liters of fuel that *you* are supposed to be protecting have vanished—"

The constable stood and grabbed Servientlov by the collar. "You maggot. You dare to threaten *me?* I'll throw your pig body into one of your snowdrifts where they won't find it until summer . . ."

But as he watched the caretaker wilt under his tirade the chief constable also knew that the old man had already destroyed his own career and could take his along with him. "All right, I'll send a patrol out—"

"An armed unit," Serbientlov said. "I want—"

"What *you* want is irrelevant. I won't have my men mixed up in a fight with your pirates. Now get out of my sight." He pushed Serbientlov toward the door, watched him scramble away, then turned to his intercom. "Sergeant, take a patrol—wait, take a squad with the halftrack out with Serbientlov to the base. Have him show you where he saw his so-called thieves. If you find anyone, bring him back to me. If you don't find any evidence of robbery, bring Serbientlov back to me—*in handcuffs.*"

"God, it's freezing up there," McLanahan said as he ran over to Elliott near the cab of the tanker truck, trying to warm his hands. He'd been obliged to switch places with Angelina on top of the Old Dog . . . after almost an hour of pumping kerosene in the bitter Siberian cold he had lost feeling in his hands and feet. "Fifty thousand liters of fuel—kerosene or not . . . should be enough to make it."

"I'll feel better when we're . . ." Elliott's voice came out in weak, barely audible grunts. Instantly McLanahan forgot his own cold, reached into Elliott's pockets and extracted the survival radio. "Ormack, this is McLanahan. General Elliott is almost unconscious out here."

"Copy," Ormack said. "We got enough—all body tanks are full. I've started putting fuel into the leaking mains. Get the general inside, then start wrapping things up down there."

"Roger." McLanahan shoved the radio into his own pocket, then took hold of Elliott's jacket and started to pull him out of the tanker. "Let's go, General." McLanahan half-walked, half-carried him to the belly hatch, then called up to Wendy, who ran down and helped Elliott up the ladder to the upper deck, then over to his seat in the cockpit.

"Wendy, push in all the vent-control knobs at the left side station downstairs," McLanahan said. "It'll pump all the heat to the upper deck. I'll get Angelina and Dave."

McLanahan ran back outside. Angelina called to him, "I'm not getting anymore."

"We're packing up," he said over the whine of the idling number-four engine. "I'll help you button up in a minute." He searched and found

Luger near the left wingtip. He had just wrestled a big piece of hanging fibersteel skin off what remained of the left wingtip.

"Dave, we're done refueling. Let's *go.* "

Two local militiamen in long, gray-green greatcoats, black fur caps and carrying forty-year-old bolt-action rifles came into the caretaker's office, made a quick check of the small flightline building, hurried outside.

The squad leader called out to the halftrack. Sergeant Gazetti waved them back inside and turned on Serbientlov. "There is no one here, caretaker. I would not like to be in your shoes when Comrade Chief Constable Vjarelskiv gets his hands on you."

Sweat broke out on Serbientlov's face despite the bitter cold of the early morning. "They were here . . . I swear—"

"Show me this fuel tank and the truck, caretaker," Gazetii said. The halftrack rumbled down the road paralleling the deserted, snow-choked flightline and taxiway. A few minutes later they had pulled to a stop outside the fence surrounding the large white tank.

"This is the tank?" Gazetti said emerging from the steel interior of the armored halftrack. "A tank of heating oil? What would your terrorists want with a tank full of heating oil?"

"I don't know," Serbientlov said in exasperation. "But they forced me at gunpoint to fill the tank truck. I narrowly escaped with my life. They had three guards on me and . . . and machine guns, but I escaped—"

"Comrade Sergeant." One of the militiamen pointed to tracks in the deep snow. Gazetii studied them carefully.

"Fairly fresh . . ." And then, he heard it . . . the diffused roar of a jet aircraft engine in the distance. He turned on Serbientlov. "Is that an aircraft? I didn't know you had aircraft here this time of year?"

Serbientlov listened, then blanched. "But we don't have any aircraft here. It . . . it must be the terrorists . . . the English terrorists."

Gazetii waved his men back into the halftrack and directed them down the flightline toward the noise.

Angelina had just slipped off the Old Dog's right wingtip onto the roof of the Zadiv panel truck. McLanahan was back on top of the Old Dog's fuselage just behind the ejection-hatch covers, scraping snow and dirt off the center-wing-tank fuel cap and replacing the cap. Luger, half-dragging his right leg, was pulling the fuel hose back toward the tanker truck.

Wendy had jumped out the belly hatch of the Old Dog to look for her fellow-crewmembers when she saw a large, squat vehicle roll to a stop just around the end of one of the hangars surrounding their parking spot. Her heart stopped. It was a Russian armored vehicle, with a Russian soldier sitting behind a shielded gun-mount.

"Patrick . . ." Wendy pointed her finger at the vehicle. "Over there . . ."

"*Yanimnogah simye,*" Gazetii swore as the halftrack driver stomped on the brakes. "*Shto etah?*" What he and the others saw in the dim three-month-long twilight was a huge, black unearthly winged creature with a long pointed nose and large ungainly wings.

"*Etaht samalyot?*" one of the militiamen said. "I've never seen a plane like *that* before."

"It has no markings, no insignia," another said. "It must be some kind of experimental aircraft . . ."

"That's *it,*" Serbientlov insisted. "That's their plane, that's the plane that . . . that the terrorists almost forced me into. You've got to stop them. Destroy it—"

"Control yourself, Serbientlov." Gazetii jumped out of the half-track. "What if it's one of our experimental aircraft? We have them, you know. Corporal, contact Chief Constable Vjareiskiy. Tell him we have an unidentified aircraft parked on the center parking ramp on the base. I am going to talk to the crew. Everyone else stay here."

Luger tossed the hose as far as he could away from the Old Dog's wheels. "Pat, Angelina. We've got us some company."

Angelina had already heard Wendy's warning and spotted the half-track. She quickly climbed down off the Zadiv and sprinted for the Old Dog's belly-hatch. McLanahan screwed the tank cap closed, then slid down the fuselage to the right wing. When he saw a Russian soldier emerging from the half track he slid across the wing to the leading edge between the two engine nacelles, shimmied over the edge and dropped to the snow.

Hearing Wendy's warning, Ormack stopped strapping the nearly unconscious Elliott into an upper-deck crash-seat, jumped into the left seat, looked out the left cockpit window and saw the halftrack.

"*Goddamn,*" he shouted over his shoulder, hoping his voice would carry. "Wendy, get everyone on board." He then slapped the wing flap switch to full DOWN and double-checked the fuel panel, opening the fuel supply from the fuselage tanks to the engines. He moved the number-four engine throttle to ninety percent power, leaned across the co-pilot's seat and put the engine number-five starter-switch to START, using engine bleed-air from the running number-four engine to spin the turbine on the number-five engine. When that engine's RPMs moved to fifteen percent he jammed its throttle to eighty-five percent to begin pumping fuel into the engine's ignition-chamber.

A thunderous *bang* reverberated through the Old Dog, and the right wing shuddered. Ormack scrambled over to the right cockpit window. The entire number-five engine was engulfed in smoke. He checked the engine instruments. The RPMs of that engine were slowly increasing but wondrously there was no indication of fire. Another loud *bang* and the engine RPMs stopped at forty percent.

The HATCH NOT CLOSED AND LOCKED light on the front-instrument panel snapped off, and a moment later Wendy reported everyone was aboard.

"Get Patrick up here," Ormack called out, and McLanahan came scrambling up to the cockpit to see General Elliott limp in his emergency web seat, forehead and face dripping from sweat, head lolling back with fever.

"He's out of it," Ormack said. "Get up here. I'll fly the plane from the left seat. You get in the co-pilot's seat and monitor the instruments." McLanahan hesitated—

"McLanahan!"

Patrick shook himself, stepped carefully around Elliott. Just before climbing into the co-pilot's seat he reached down and retrieved Elliott's .45 caliber automatic from his holster. "Can we start the rest of the engines?" he said, looking at the gauges.

"Not yet. When number five reaches forty-five percent shut off its starter and switch on three, six, seven and eight. Move throttles up to IDLE when each engine RPM reaches fifteen percent. Watch the fire lights—that kerosene has been giving us some hard ignitions." McLanahan nodded and watched the number five RPM gauge, a finger on the starter switch.

Ormack opened the left-cockpit window. The Russian soldier was now advancing on the Old Dog, more cautiously than before the engines were started. He did not hear Ormack open the sliding window.

"He's still coming," Ormack said. McLanahan pulled the automatic from his jacket pocket and tapped Ormack's shoulder with it. Ormack turned, saw the gun. "If we start a firefight here . . ."

"We may not have any choice."

Ormack nodded, took the gun, keeping it out of view. McLanahan pointed at the number five RPM gauge. "RPMs are up to forty-five. Number five starter off. Starting three, six, seven and eight."

The Russian militiaman walked right up to within fifteen yards of the Old Dog, toward the left cockpit window, his pistol holster in clear view on his waist but his weapon still in it. When he heard the number three engine start to spool up he drew his right index finger across his throat.

"He wants us to shut down," Ormack said. He shook his head at the soldier. The militiaman drew his finger across his throat several more times.

"Patrick, we're running out of time . . ."

There were several loud *bangs* on both wings this time, and the Old Dog began to buck and rumble as if its insides had been seized by a coughing fit. The Russian soldier backed away several feet as a cloud of blue-black smoke from the number three engine hit him.

"Continue the start," Ormack yelled. Clouds of smoke began to enter the cockpit through the open window. "Move the generator switch on number five engine from RESET to RUN." When he next saw the Russian soldier he was back beside his halftrack shouting orders inside. Suddenly another soldier appeared at the machine-gun mount on top of the half-track. A moment later he was handed a large machine gun, which he began bolting into its armor-plated mount.

Ormack saw it and called out a warning.

"Number three's not starting," McLanahan said. "Number six started."

"We're set to taxi," Ormack answered. "Continue the start. Hang on." He tapped the toe brakes to release the parking brake, scanned the engines, took hold of number four, five and six throttles and jammed them to almost full military thrust.

The Old Dog rumbled mightily but refused to move.

"She's not taxiing, we need all available engines," Ormack told McLanahan.

McLanahan kept a hand on the number seven throttle. As Ormack spoke he advanced that throttle to IDLE power. "Seven started, three's coming up." Three engines now running at almost full power, along with three sputtering and exploding.

Ormack jammed the number-seven throttle to military, but the Old Dog still would not move.

"*C'mon,* you sonofabitch."

Ormack looked at the Russian halftrack, could see the first Russian soldier pressing one hand to his ear, giving the "cut-engines" sign with his other, then slapping it back over his uncovered ear.

"Three's started," McLanahan said. "Eight coming up."

"Get the generators on-line for the running engines," Ormack told him, keeping an eye on the Russian at the halftrack's gun-mount. "Anti-icing switch on. Manifold switch closed. Hydraulic switches on. Stabilizer trim set—" Ormack looked up from his checklists in time to see the gunner on top of the halftrack point his gun just over the Old Dog's fuselage and fire.

Ormack instinctively ducked, pulling McLanahan down. The roar of the engines drowned out the chatter of the heavy-caliber gun and the bullets whizzing a few feet above them. McLanahan went on with the engine start, advanced the throttle on number eight to IDLE. Both men looked up over the instrument-panel glare-shield. The lead Russian soldier was again giving them the cut-engine sign, and this time the gunner had his weapon pointed directly at the cockpit.

Ormack did not look at McLanahan as he pulled on his headset. Over interphone he called, "Everyone on interphone? Report by compartment."

He then brought all engine throttles to IDLE. "Crew, we've got a Russian armored vehicle about a hundred yards off our left wing. They've got a machine gun. They've ordered us to cut our engines—"

The HATCH NOT CLOSED AND LATCHED light on the forward instrument panel snapped on then and before either Ormack or McLanahan could react it popped out.

"What was *that?*"

"I don't . . . Dave, did you open the hatch?" No reply. "Luger. Report." McLanahan was about to unbuckle his safety belt and go downstairs but stopped when Ormack called out, "Luger, *no.*"

McLanahan turned and looked outside. Wearing only his flight suit and boots, Luger was hobbling toward the fuel truck parked near the Old Dog's left wingtip. He was carrying one of the .38 caliber survival revolvers.

Nobody could speak, only watch, horrified, as Luger stumbled, right leg flopping in the air, then quickly rolled back up to his feet and half-crawled to the fuel truck as the gunner swung his machine gun directly at Luger.

Ormack came alive, stuck the .45 caliber automatic out his left cockpit window and fired, the slug creating a bright blue spark as it ricocheted off the gun mount's armored shield. The gunner whirled his gun toward the cockpit, which provided an opening to his right side. Luger had reached the truck, now steadied his arm on the hood and emptied the revolver at the gunner. One of the slugs found its target.

"*Luger.* Get back here . . ."

Luger heard Ormack, started back for the Old Dog. But another soldier appeared from behind the halftrack, lifted a rifle with a long, curved cartridge clip, fired. Luger clutched his left thigh and pitched forward.

Ormack could only fire his pistol again, forcing the Russian at the back of the halftrack to retreat, but he did not notice another soldier sliding into the machine gun mount on the halftrack.

He took aim on the Old Dog, fired.

The twenty-millimeter shells plowed through the Old Dog's left side, showering the cockpit with glass. Ormack was thrown over to the center console, where he tried to shield his face from flying glass. Pain clutched his left shoulder.

"Get down," McLanahan yelled back to Wendy and Angelina.

Another fusillade of bullets erupted inside the Old Dog, sparks flying as the left load central circuit breaker panel was hit. Lights flickered, exploded. One of the engines faltered. Wendy unfastened her parachute straps and flattened herself on the deck as bullets hit her defensive-systems jammers and threat-receivers.

Abrupt dead silence. Aft, McLanahan saw the two women crawling on the upper deck beside the unconscious General Elliott.

"You two all right?"

"Yes," Wendy said, "Oh, God . . . Colonel Ormack . . ." McLanahan turned, saw Ormack slumped against the center console and throttle quadrant, bleeding heavily, hands covered with blood. McLanahan pulled him back into his seat, searched out the window for his partner. And then he understood why they had stopped shooting at the Old Dog. Luger was no longer lying in the snow. Somehow he had managed to crawl back to the fuel truck, had started it up and was now barreling toward the armored halftrack, whose gunner had turned the machine gun muzzle on the cab of the truck.

"Dave, *noo* . . ."

The halftrack's gunner had gotten off a half-second burst at the truck, and McLanahan watched what was left of the truck's windshield explode. A moment later the truck smashed into the halftrack.

"Dave . . ."

The tank truck's remaining fifty gallons of unusable fuel and three thousand cubic feet of kerosene fumes ignited and ripped it apart like an overinflated balloon. The halftrack did some lazy cartwheels and landed upside-down eighty yards from the blast, scattering metal and men across the parking ramp.

The noise of the six running engines seemed a purr next to the force of the blast. When McLanahan looked outside where the truck used to be, he saw a blackened crater, a smoking hunk of metal on the other side of the ramp, smoldering mounds of human flesh in the snow.

No sign of Luger.

McLanahan couldn't, wouldn't accept it. "He can't be dead, can't be . . ."

"We've got to get out of here," Ormack said, hauling himself straight in the pilot's seat. "Patrick, you've got to make the takeoff, I can't do it—"

"But Dave . . . we can't leave—"

"Patrick. Dave . . . gave us our chance. We've got to take it . . ."

McLanahan shook his head. "I . . . I can't take off, never done it before . . ."

Ormack climbed out of the left seat. "Climb in. You're up, buddy. Do it."

"Anadyr Control, this is Ossora one-seven-one, Element Seven. Requesting landing clearance. Over."

No answer. Yuri Papendreyov scanned his navigation instruments. There was no error; he was only thirty miles from Anadyr Far East Fighter-Interceptor Base. Although the base was not active *someone* should still be there.

Papendreyov switched his radio to the Fleet Common frequency, the backup frequency for all Soviet air defense forces. "This is Ossora one-seven-one on Fleet Common Alpha. One-seven-one is making an emergency approach and landing at Anadyr Airfield. Over."

No answer on Fleet Common. He set his transponder to a special emergency code, activated it. Any air-defense forces, he *hoped,* would see his beacon before they started shooting . . . with an Air Defense Emergency declared for the region he'd be lucky to get near the base without finding himself under attack from his own people.

Yuri flipped his checklist cards over to the approach-and-landing section, began to set up for landing. One more ridge line to cross and Anadyr should be within visual range.

With only a half-hour of fuel left he decided to wait until just a few kilometers from the base before lowering his gear and configuring for landing. He would make one pass over the runway to check it over—and hope to get someone's attention—then pitch out, enter the visual pattern and land. He had to save his fuel in case he had to orbit the field to wait for the runway to be plowed off enough to make it safe to land.

Damn the luck, he was positive—still positive—that the American intruder was nearby, still a threat. He checked his chronometer . . . it had only been an hour and forty minutes since he last saw the B-52 near Ossora. Flying in the Korakskoje Nagorje mountain range at six hundred kilometers an hour maximum, the B-52 could not have gone farther than Uel-Kal or Egvekinot on the Anadyrskij Zaliv, only two hundred kilometers from Anadyr. But none of those coastal bases had picked up the B-52 on radar, so it must still be hiding in the mountains around Anadyr, trying to pick its way around the defenses.

If the intruder had tried to dodge north and west of the Kamchatka peninsula instead of toward Alaska, it would have fallen right into the waiting arms of two squadrons of MiG-29s from the regional defense force headquarters at Magadan. But no one had reported spotting the bomber there either. No. It was nearby. It *had* to be.

After refueling he was determined to find the B-52. Its tail radar was going to give it away, and its hot engines would, literally, be its downfall. With twilight Yuri figured he wouldn't need his pulse-Doppler radar to find the American plane. Using the infrared spotting scope and passive electronic scanners he could prowl about at will, virtually undetectable, until the B-52 gave itself away or was spotted by Beringovskiy radar.

He thought once, very briefly, about his wife and family, safe and warm in his Kiev apartment while he chased over thousands of kilometers of Siberia looking for an intruder that might have already crashed. He also thought about consequences . . . His expertise, his zeal might get him through the inquiry that followed his unauthorized chase for the B-52, the old Squadron Commander might give him a year's worth of runway snow removal duty or a demotion. An Air Defense Emergency could forgive a lot of things, he told himself. Anyway, he didn't believe he'd actually face a firing squad or exile.

But only one thing could guarantee him a satisfactory return to his family—a promotion, a full pardon. As Anadyr Airfield popped into view, still thirty-six kilometers away, he knew that the only thing that would earn him that result was gun-camera film of the B-52 going down in flames after being shot apart by his GSh-23 twin-barrel guns or by one of his newer AA-8 heat-seeking missiles.

Yes. The B-52 had to be destroyed.

The Old Dog seemed more like a hospital ship than a strategic bomber as it taxied down the narrow, snow-covered taxiways of Anadyr Airbase.

In command as it limped down the taxiway was Patrick McLanahan. As the most experienced and now physically able crewman, he had taken the pilot's left seat. Icy wind blasted his face from the dozens of holes on the left side of the cockpit and from a completely blown-out glass panel just behind his ejection seat. He was trying to do too much at once—but most important was to keep the Old Dog roughly in the center of the taxiway.

Ormack, blood all over his left shoulder, barely strong enough to move a switch, had taken his copilot's seat again. He continued to read the pre-takeoff checklists and give McLanahan a running last-minute lecture on how to accomplish a takeoff.

Angelina remained at her gunner's position, checking and rechecking her equipment. She had two *Scorpion* missiles on the right external pylon, three *Scorpions* on the bomb-bay launcher, two HARM anti-radar missiles on the interior launcher and twenty *Stinger* air-mine rockets in the tail cannon—and no way in the world to guide any of them . . . the target-acquisition radar-scope had been damaged in the attack at the airbase. The Old Dog might be still an adversary to be considered, its *Scorpions* and HARMs could be self-guided to their targets—but their effectiveness was greatly reduced.

Wendy was back in her electronic warfare officer's seat beside Angelina. Using computer-displayed instructions she had restarted the ring-laser gyro and satellite navigation system in the freezing cold navigator's station below. There was little else downstairs—McLanahan's ten-inch radar scope had been destroyed by the Russian machine gun attack. The attack had also destroyed or damaged most of Wendy's electronic-warfare gear.

While she had been in the lower compartment she had looked over Dave Luger's notes and doodles, even picked up his headphone . . . wanting to offer it to him when he emerged from the aft bulkhead door, smiling and laughing and gabbing with his impossible Texas accent . . . she imagined she heard a knock on the belly hatch, and there he would be . . . except, of course, he would not. Face it . . .

He was gone.

She had given Luger's coat to General Elliott, who was strapped into an emergency crash web chair on the upper deck between the cockpit and the defense crew's station, caught between a severe fever and the onset of deep shock.

Ormack continued with the checklists as they scrolled onto the computer monitor. "Flight instruments checked, pilot and copilot."

"Mine are gone," McLanahan said. "Adjust your ADI. I can hardly see it but it's the only reliable one we have." He watched as Ormack adjusted the artificial horizon. "That's it. Standby altimeters are good. Standby turn-and-slip indicators are good."

"Electrical panel." Ormack strained to read the tiny gauges. "One and two are zero. All the rest are okay." He advanced the computerized checklist. "Crosswing crab."

"Zeroed. Next."

"Pitot heat."

It took McLanahan a moment, interrupted with a few small turns to stay on hard pavement, to find the switch. "On."

"Stability augmentation system."

"On."

"Stabilizer trim."

"That's this big wheel here, right?" McLanahan asked. "We don't have time to compute the right setting so I'm setting it to one-half unit nose up. Set. Next."

"Airbrake lever."

"Off."

"Flaps."

"One hundred percent down, lever down."

"Fuel panel. I think I have it set up right," Ormack said, wincing from a stab of pain that shot through the area around his neck. "Check it for me. We've got minimum fuel in the main tanks because of the damage, so those pumps right . . . there should be on, and those . . . there should be to OPEN. Checked. Next."

"Starter switches."

"Okay, we're almost ready to go." Using the rudder pedals, McLanahan nudged the Old Dog around a tight corner and turned onto the end of the Russian runway, then stepped on the tops of the pedals to engage the brakes.

"Angelina, Wendy, ready to go back there?"

"Ready," Angelina said over the interphone.

"Ready," Wendy said. "Good luck."

"Thanks." McLanahan gripped the control yoke. "I'm gonna need it."

"All right," Ormack said, "we're going to start the number two engine. Ready?"

"Ready."

McLanahan moved the number-four engine-throttle to ninety percent. "Go!" Ormack moved the starter to START. Slowly, the RPMs on the number two engine began to increase. McLanahan pointed to a yellow light on the forward panel.

"What's that?" Ormack said over the interphone. "I can't see . . ."

"A low oil-pressure light," McLanahan told him over the roar of the engines. "We've got to hope it'll give us enough thrust for takeoff before it seizes . . ."

There was a tremendous *bang* on the left engine as the Old Dog bucked and rumbled so that no one could read the instruments.

"That's the bad gas," McLanahan said, "it should work okay, though . . ." Anxious moments later the RPMs on the number-two engine went to idle settings, and McLanahan pulled the power back on the number-four engine.

"Okay, starter on number two is in FLIGHT position, generator on number two is on," Ormack said. "Takeoff data."

McLanahan gave it over the interphone. "We roll until just before we run out of runway, then I pull back on the stick. If we fly, we fly. If we don't, we eject. Next."

"Arming lever safety pins."

"All right, everyone," McLanahan told them, "get your seats ready for ejection. And don't hesitate. If you see the red bailout warning light, eject. Immediately."

"Couldn't have made a better takeoff briefing myself, McLanahan," Ormack said, trying to smile. "Takeoff checklist. Steering ratio selector lever."

McLanahan took a deep breath and tried not to think of Luger. Concentrate, he told himself. Get the job done. Everybody was counting on him . . . including himself. He moved a lever on the center console. "TAKE-OFF LAND. Set."

"Air conditioning master switch."

"RAM."

"Throttles."

"Here we go." McLanahan took hold of the seven active throttles and moved them slowly forward to full military power. Because of the dead number-one engine the Old Dog slid to the left on the snow-covered runway. McLanahan stomped on the right stabilator pedal to correct, then, realizing the dual rudders had been destroyed, slowly pulled back the number-eight engine throttle until he was able to straighten out the Old Dog along the runway, then slowly pushed it back almost to full power.

"Good." Ormack strained to be heard over the roar of the engine. "No stabilators . . . do whatever you need to do to keep her on the runway." He put his hands on the yoke but could not help. "Keep an eye on the distance-remaining markers if you can . . . they'll be labeled in hundreds of meters. Lift off with about a thousand meters remaining—"

"I can't *see* them," McLanahan shouted. "They're going by too damn fast—wait . . . sixteen, fifteen, fourteen . . ." The wild rumbling and vibrations made it tough to refocus his eyes on the instruments.

When McLanahan swung the control yoke to the right to correct the violent left skid, it seemed the Old Dog was sliding sideways down the runway. He scanned the instruments. A caution light was lit but he couldn't make out which one.

"Hold it steady, Patrick—"

"I can't, it's skidding too hard—"

"Easy . . . you can do it. *Easy* . . ."

McLanahan realized with a surge of fear that the one-thousand-meter sign had just whizzed by. At the nine-hundred meter he pulled back on the control yoke, wrestled it back, back, back until it was touching his chest. Still the Old Dog's nose refused to leave the ground.

"C'mon, baby, lift off, dammit."

"Add some nose-up trim," Ormack yelled. "The big wheel by your knee. *Gently.* Keep the back pressure in but get ready to release it when the nose comes up."

"It's not lifting off . . ." The shaking, the turbulence almost made him lose his grip on the wheel . . . Now he could see the end of the runway, a tall wall of drifting snow and ice . . .

"Four . . . three . . . two . . . oh God, there's a snow drift out there, we're not—"

With its nose still pointing downward the Old Dog left the ground less than three feet above the peak of ice at the end of the runway. Buoyed then by "ground effect," the swirl of air generated by the wings that bounced off the ground and back up at the plane, the Old Dog skittered only twenty feet above the snowy surface, the air pounding on the bomber's huge wings adding to the turbulence.

Like a blessing, the pounding began to decrease, and as the airspeed slowly increased, the Old Dog's nose lifted skyward, McLanahan at times swinging the control yoke all the way to its limit to control the swaying as the huge bomber lifted into the Siberian sky.

Carefully now, McLanahan, reached down to the gear-control lever and moved it up, also checking the main-gear indicator-lights. "Gear up, Colonel, keep an eye on the—"

He was interrupted by a blur of motion outside the cockpit window. Ormack spotted it first but was too shocked to speak. All he could do was point as the light gray MiG-29 *Fulcrum* fighter flew just ahead and above the Old Dog, then banked erratically to the left and out of sight, its twin afterburners lighting up the sky.

It was impossible.

Yuri Papendreyov had been busy with landing checklists, configuring his MiG-29 *Fulcrum* fighter for the penetration and descent into Anadyr and following the navigation beacon and instrument-land-system beam. He had been taught not to rely on visual cues for landing until very close to the runway, especially during long winter twilight conditions.

The young fighter pilot was less than two miles from touchdown when he finally had his *Fulcrum* configured and ready. It was then that he studied the runway. Since the first pass was going to be a visual inspection and flyover, he was moving almost twice as fast as usual. The landing gear was up, but he had flaps and leading-edge slats deployed to make the relatively slow, low-altitude pass safer. He was flying his advanced fighter at a high angle-of-attack, which meant keeping the fighter's nose higher than normal during the pass.

In the dusky conditions Papendreyov didn't see the massive billows of smoke rising from the airfield and the sudden huge, black shape against the white snow-covered runway. When he did look out the cockpit windscreen, the huge ebony aircraft had left the runway, blending in with the rugged terrain and dark horizon.

Yuri made his pass, looking right toward the tower, the base-operation building and aircraft-parking ramp. All empty. He was thinking he might be forced to pump his own gas, when he shifted his attention forward. His windscreen was filled with dark smoke. He jammed the throttles forward, igniting the twin Turmansky afterburners as a wave of turbulence shook his *Fulcrum* fighter.

And then, he saw it. He was close enough to touch it, close enough to see the pilot straining to lift his aircraft skyward.

The American B-52—lifting off from Anadyr! Yuri reacted instinctively, flicked the arming switch to his GSh-23 twin twenty-three-millimeter nose cannon, and fired.

The shots went wide as another giant wave of turbulence from the B-52 swatted at his *Fulcrum* fighter, and Yuri was forced to roll hard left to keep from plowing into the bomber's tail. As he passed to its left, he noticed with satisfaction that the huge gun on its tail did not follow him . . .

Marveling at his good fortune, he continued his left turn, retracting flaps and slats and selecting two AA-8 heat-seeking missiles . . . The initial shock of seeing the elusive American bomber *here,* of all the possible places to find him, dissolved back into the hard concentration of the hunt.

He had searched eleven thousand square kilometers, risked everything to hunt it down.

Now he had found it.

The radar altimeter showed only a few hundred feet above the ground, but he couldn't wait . . . McLanahan reached down and began to raise the flaps.

"Flaps coming up, Colonel. SST nose retracting. I don't believe it, but a Russian fighter just went past us . . . do you see him?"

Ormack looked out the right cockpit windows. "No."

"Keep watching for him." McLanahan watched the flap-indicator as the huge wing high-lift panels rose out of the slipstream. With the flaps retracting, the Old Dog's lift began to erode and she began to sink. McLanahan took the number-eight throttle and jammed it to full military thrust, then fought the control yoke like it was a bucking horse as the differential thrust threatened to flip the bomber over and send it crashing to the mountain below. Using what was left of the lateral trim controls, he struggled to keep the bomber level . . .

"Flaps up," he called out. Suddenly a blinking yellow light on the upper-eyebrow instrument panel caught his attention—the number two engine. Its oil pressure had dropped below the minimum. He pulled the number-two throttle to CUTOFF, shutting down the engine before the lack of oil pressure caused it to seize and explode. Now, because of the two missing engines on the left side, McLanahan again had no choice but to decrease power on the number-eight engine—without full rudder he couldn't hold the nose straight with such a difference in thrust.

"Number two engine shut down," he said over the interphone. "Number eight pulled back to compensate. Angelina, try to get your system working—"

"I've tried, the pylon, bomb bay and *Stinger* airmine missiles are working but I've no radar guidance. I can release the missiles but I can't guide them."

McLanahan leveled the Old Dog at about a thousand feet, pressed the PAGE ADVANCE button on the computerized checklist calling up the automatic terrain-avoidance procedures. "We're going into auto-terrain-avoidance, everybody. Wendy, go downstairs and try to reload terrain data into the avoidance computers."

Behind the cockpit in the defense section Wendy Tork quickly unbuckled her parachute harness straps, gingerly climbed out of the electronic-warfare officer's ejection seat, grabbed onto the "firepole" above the ladder, half-slid half-climbed downstairs, then plugged her headset into the radar navigator's station below.

"Patrick, I'm downstairs," she radioed to the cockpit. "Now what?"

"Okay, good . . . hit the checklist button and enter TA on the keyboard. The terrain-avoidance checklist will come up. Page ahead to the data-reload section. That has the steps."

The computerized checklist readout, and the unpopular Colonel Anderson's insistence that everyone know about everyone else's duties aboard the Old Dog, now paid off. Wendy moved the terrain-data cartridge reader lever from LOCK to READ. "Reloading terrain data, Patrick."

McLanahan had quickly read the terrain-avoidance checklist as it scrolled onto Ormack's computer screen. He activated the autopilot, and the computer-drawn terrain-trace zipped across his video monitor. He found the auto-terrain-avoidance switch and threw it, setting the clearance altitude to two hundred feet.

And the crippled Old Dog began to respond.

***

As Yuri's *Fulcrum* fighter rolled out behind the B-52, the huge bomber nosed over and Yuri was positive the American intruder was going to crash. But at the last possible moment the plane somehow leveled off, skimming so close to the earth the rocks and jagged peaks seemed to be scraping the bomber's black belly as they rushed underneath in a blur . . .

McLanahan kept the engines screaming at full throttle. Using the number eight engine's throttle, he made a hard left turn, searching out his cockpit window.

Ormack, gripping the glare-shield for support in the tight turn, called to McLanahan that "we need to head east, we're heading the wrong way—"

"We also need to get back in the mountains," McLanahan said. He rolled the wings level on a southwesterly heading back down the Korakskoje Mountains, aiming the Old Dog toward a low row of rugged, snow-covered peaks. "If we get over the water with that fighter on our tail he'll nail us for sure."

"But our fuel—"

"We should have enough, but there's no alternative . . . Angelina, can you steer your rocket turret at all?"

She activated the double handgrips on the *Stinger* airmine rocket turret. "The radar's working. I can move my controls. But I don't know if the cannon is moving, I've lost all my position indicators."

"Will the rockets still detonate?"

"Yes, I can set the detonation range manually, or they'll detonate themselves just before their propellant runs out."

"Okay, if we spot the fighter we'll call out its position. Set the airmines for different ranges and—"

"*I see him, he's right behind us—*"

An explosion rocked the bomber—like a wrecking ball had crashed into the Old Dog's midsection. McLanahan felt as if he were riding an elevator that had just dropped twenty floors in an instant. The Old Dog seemed to hover in midair, its six working engines straining against the impact of a Soviet AA-8 missile slamming into its fuselage.

Yuri Papendreyov, flying slightly high and to the right of his quarry, clenched a fist and allowed a smile. One of his heat-seeking missiles had missed, but the second had hit the American bomber in the mid-body, just forward of the wing's leading edge. Clouds of smoke erupted from the hole he'd created. The bomber's tail sank down, the nose shot up.

Yet somehow it was still flying. Well, those Americans might lead charmed lives, but their luck had run out. He still had two AA-8 heat-seekers and five hundred rounds of ammunition, and the bomber was badly crippled.

In his tight right-hand turn to set up for another attack, he checked his navigation instruments and saw he was only forty kilometers from Anadyr . . .

There was no greater prize than the B-52, he told himself, no greater victory . . . He widened his right turn and smiled broadly, seeing his destiny unfolding.

Choking and coughing from the thick clouds of black smoke, Wendy aimed a fire extinguisher out the open aft bulkhead door leading to the bomb bay catwalk and squeezed the trigger. She was bleeding from a gash in her forehead sustained when she was thrown against the forward instrument panel after the missile hit. A moment later Angelina was beside her, carrying the firefighting mask and another extinguisher bottle. While Wendy put on the mask and plugged it into the instructor-nav's oxygen panel, Angelina moved as far as she could toward the fire on the catwalk and fired her extinguisher.

The flames had intensified the instant Wendy had opened the bulkhead door, but the blast of air racing from the breaks in the cockpit through the open door sucked the smoke and flames aft and gave her a clear and effective shot at the fire in the electronic countermeasures transformers and control boxes.

Wendy dropped back into the radar nav's seat, her forehead dripping blood, her arms and legs throbbing. She pulled off the firefighting mask, gasped over the interphone: "Fire's out, Patrick. Big hole in the fuselage and fire in the ECM boxes, but it looked like it missed the landing gear."

"We're blind up here," Ormack said. "We can't see him, we can't see when he shoots at us . . ."

McLanahan had already put the computer-controlled clearance plane setting to COLA so the Old Dog would seek its own lowest possible altitude. But because of the reduction in thrust and the severe damage, the terrain-climbing capability of the Old Dog was reduced. And as the terrain became more rugged, the altitude slowly crept higher, exposing the bomber more and more to the Soviet fighter.

"All right, everyone, check your areas for damage," McLanahan said, his grip on the control wheel so tight his hands began to cramp.

"We've got a leak in the aft fuel tank," Ormack said, blowing on his hands and scanning the fuel panel. "I'm opening valve twenty-eight, closing twenty-nine. Also pumping all fuel out of the aft body tank before it leaks out—"

A sudden motion out of the left-cockpit windscreen drew his attention outside. "Patrick, *look* . . ."

McLanahan spun around to a sight that made him go rigid . . . The gray MiG-29 *Fulcrum* fighter was directly beside the Old Dog, just ahead of the cockpit, slightly above them and no more than a hundred feet away. McLanahan could clearly see the pilot's right shoulder and head out his bubble canopy, along with a sleek air-to-air missile on its wing hardpoint.

The MiG was amazingly small and compact, resembling a twin-tailed American F-16 fighter. The Russian pilot apparently had little trouble flying beside the B-52, even at its low altitude, perfectly matching each of the Old Dog's computer-commanded altitude adjustments.

"Angelina, he's on our left side, ten o'clock, about a hundred feet. Can we get him with the *Scorpions* on our right pylon?"

"He's too close. The missile wouldn't have time to lock on."

The MiG pilot glanced over at McLanahan, rocked his *Fulcrum's* wings up and down three times. He stopped, then made one last rock to the right.

"Why is he doing that . . . ?"

Ormack's jaw tightened. "It's the interception signal. He wants us to follow him."

"Follow him?" McLanahan said, stomach tightening. "No way, we can't—"

"Patrick, we've got nowhere to run. He can knock us out of the sky anytime—"

The MiG rocked up its left wing once more, very emphatically, as if underscoring Ormack's words. To back up his message the MiG pilot fired a one-second burst from his belly guns, the bright phosphorous-tipped tracer shells knifing off into the twilight like deadly shooting stars.

"If we don't follow he comes back around and tags us," Ormack said. "We've got no chance—"

"We can still fight," McLanahan said. "As long as we got missiles we can't give up."

Ormack grabbed his arm. "If we try to run he'll just come around again and shoot us down." He lowered his voice. "You did a great job, Pat, but it's over. It's—"

McLanahan shrugged his arm free. The MiG had dropped back a few feet, his bubble-canopy now directly beside the Old Dog's narrow, slanted cockpit. The Russian pilot pointed down three times.

McLanahan turned and looked directly at the MiG pilot, flying in unison with the fighter at a distance of fifty feet. To Ormack's surprise, he nodded to the Russian, and the MiG pilot pointed to McLanahan's right, indicating a right turn.

Ormack looked away, not wanting to see what he had insisted was necessary for their survival. The pain he felt was from more than his blood-soaked shoulder.

McLanahan nodded one more time to the MiG pilot. "Stand by to turn, crew," he said, gripping the wheel tight.

Yuri Papendreyov was flushed with pride. He had done it. The American was surrendering. Of course, he could hardly do anything else—with its mangled left wingtip, the destroyed far left engine, the B-52 was flying slower and slower, without the extreme dives and climbs Yuri had seen before as it hugged the ground. Yuri also noted the small-caliber bullet holes all over the B-52's left side from the nose to the wings, and figured the AA-8 missile he'd shot into their fuselage had been the final blow.

The B-52 began its very slow right turn, and Yuri had just begun applying pressure on his control stick to follow—suddenly the entire right side of the canopy was filled with the dark, menacing form of the American bomber . . . Instead of turning right toward Anadyr the insane pilot had turned *left*—directly *into* Yuri's MiG-29.

Yuri yanked his control stick hard to the left, rolling up into ninety, one hundred degrees of bank. A moment later his world exploded in a crunch of metal as the two aircraft, traveling almost twelve kilometers a minute, collided. With both aircraft in a hard left turn, the top of the B-52 had plowed into the bottom of Yuri's fighter.

Somehow Yuri managed to continue his hard turn, standing his MiG on its left wingtip and pulling back on the stick to increase the roll rate. The B-52 seemed to be turning right with him, even pushing him on, dragging him to the earth. The fighter was now at ninety-degrees bank, and the terrifying crushing and grinding sounds underneath him continued. Yuri could see rocks and trees out of the *top* of his canopy. His controls refused to respond . . .

He ignited his twin afterburners, and like a snapping rubberband his MiG was flung away from the B-52. In the process Yuri found himself inverted, then in a wild tumble. The roar of the B-52 was everywhere, he expected another impact any moment . . .

But the spin slowed and he managed to level his wings. He was barely at twenty meters. Rocks and trees were all around him—he was staring *up* at a huge ridge line encrusted with jagged snow-covered boulders. But his airspeed at last began to build and he felt the ground rushing away beneath him.

Quickly he checked around for the B-52 . . . *nothing. Gone.* Shaking his head, Yuri started a slow right turn to check behind him . . .

***

Numb from the midair collision he had contrived, McLanahan watched transfixed as the gray MiG continued its spin down, heading for the rocks, reaching the point where McLanahan thought the pilot could never recover.

But he did. He must have been close enough to the rocks to get one in his boot, but his spin stopped and the MiG sped away from the earth, gaining breathtaking speed in seconds, and now McLanahan was fighting for control of his own plane. The stall-warning buzzer sounded, and the Old Dog seemed to be floating straight *down* instead of flying forward.

"Get the nose down, we're in a stall," Ormack was yelling at him. McLanahan shoved the yoke forward, fighting the initial-stall buffet that shook the entire hundred-ton bomber.

The buzzer stopped. McLanahan found he had control, leveled the nose until the airspeed came up, but he had to force himself to stop looking at the rugged ground that whizzed so close to the Old Dog's groaning wings.

"There he is, here he comes . . ." Ormack shouted, pointing straight ahead.

He was coming, all right. Directly in front of them. "Angie," McLanahan called over the interphone. "Pylon missile . . . *fire.*"

The MiG was in a thirty-degree right bank directly off the Old Dog's nose at a range of perhaps three to four miles when the missile left the right pylon rail. It ignited in a bright plume of fire, sped away toward the wide bubble canopy of the MiG.

But the *Scorpion* that left the Old Dog's rail was an unguided bullet, not a sophisticated air-to-air missile. Without radar tracking and uplink from the Old Dog to guide it, the *Scorpion* relied on either an infrared signature or an anti-radar jamming signal to home in on. It had neither. The MiG had kept its radar and jammers off, presenting no heat signature at all so long as it was in its right turn.

The *Scorpion* streaked forward, passing a hundred feet in front of the MiG. Ten seconds after it automatically armed its warhead after launch, the *Scorpion*'s computer asked itself if it was tracking a target. The reply was no, and the *Scorpion* harmlessly detonated its warhead almost two miles past the MiG-29.

Papendreyov saw the American bomber and the missile at the same time. There was no time to turn, to dive, or accelerate—not even time for him to close his eyes and brace for the impact—

And then, just as quickly, the missile was gone. Yuri watched for a second missile—a B-52 bomber launching *missiles?*—but there was none.

He continued his wide right-climbing turn, keeping a close watch on the

B-52, which now was a serious adversary, not just a helpless whale resigned to its fate.

He watched it far below him, making a left turn, heading east. With his own speed regained, it looked to Papendreyov as if the B-52 was almost hanging suspended in midair. Not dead, but an inviting target.

He maneuvered behind it, stalking it, closing slowly for the kill. Noting the tail cannon sweeping back and forth in a rectangular pattern, he rolled out high and to the right of the bomber. The cannon continued its erratic box-pattern sweep, occasionally seeming to be altogether out of control and useless . . . yes, it could launch missiles, but it had no way of guiding them.

Yuri armed his GSh-23 cannon and maneuvered behind and slightly above the B-52, slowly closing the distance. He no longer considered trying to force the bomber to land—his gun's cameras would record his victory over the intruder.

He edged closer to the bomber, then began his strafing run . . .

"We lost him." Ormack was searching his side cockpit windows.

"He's out there," McLanahan said, reengaging the terrain-avoidance autopilot. "He can find us easy. We've got to find him before he gets a shot off . . ."

Angelina watched her rocket-turret-position indicators as they oscillated in random sputters and jerks. The radar was locking onto ghosts, starting and stopping, breaking lock. Frustrated, she turned the radar to STANDBY, waited a few moments, then turned it back to TRANSMIT . . .

A large bright blip appeared on the upper left corner of her radarscope. She waited for it to disappear, just like all the rest of the electronic ghosts, but this one stayed.

She stomped her foot on the interphone button. "Bandit five o'clock high, break right!"

McLanahan swung the control yoke hard right.

Ormack's head banged against the right cockpit window but he pulled himself upright and scanned as far behind the bomber as he could . . . "Pereira, five o'clock, one and a half miles, twenty degrees high and comin' down. Nail him."

Yuri had the shot lined up perfectly, a textbook gun-pass. He had just squeezed the trigger on his control stick, squeezed off a hundred precious rounds, before realizing that the B-52 wasn't in his sights. It had *moved*. He tried to rudder-drag his sight around to the right but it wasn't enough and he was forced to yank off power and roll with the B-52 to reacquire it.

He was almost aligned again when a sharp white flash popped off his left side not a hundred meters away. He yanked his MiG into a hard right turn and accelerated away, saw another white flash and a cloud of sparkling shards of metal exploding above him. The B-52 was *shooting* at him, and that was no machine-gun round—the intruder had tail-firing rockets . . .

Yuri expertly rolled out of his turn, perpendicular to the bomber's flight path and out of range of the strange flak missiles.

A blinking warning light caught his attention. He was now on emergency fuel—less than ten minutes time left and with no reserve. He didn't even have the time to set up another gun pass. He rearmed his last two remaining AA-8 missiles, rechecked his infrared spotting scope and checked the location of the bomber.

Time for one last pass, and it had to be perfect. At least his AA-8s had to have greater range than those tiny missiles. He would roll back in directly behind the B-52 and fire at maximum range when the AA-8s locked onto the bomber's engine-exhaust.

He made a diving left-turn, staying about twelve kilometers behind the bomber. His infrared target-spotting scope with its large supercooled eye locked onto the B-52 immediately and sent aiming information to the AA-8 missiles. The B-52 was making no evasive maneuvers. Slowly, the distance decreased.

The American bomber, Yuri noted, had maneuvered itself onto a flat plateau just above Anadyr Airbase, heading east toward the Bering Strait. It had nowhere to hide, nowhere to evade. Yuri hoped it wouldn't smash into Anadyr. On the other hand, what better place to deposit the evidence of his victory? His vindication?

The range continued to decrease. Yuri could see the B-52's tail now, and the missile-firing cannon, still pointing up and to the right, jammed in position. Yuri put his finger on the launch trigger, ready . . .

A high-pitched beep sounded in his helmet—the AA-8's seeker heads had locked onto the B-52. Yuri checked his target once more, waited a few more seconds to close the distance—fired. The green LOCK light stayed on STEADY as the two Mach-two missiles streaked from their rails . . .

Ormack searched the skies from the cockpit window. "I can't see him, I lost him."

"Angie, can you see him?"

"No, my radar's jammed. I can't see anything."

The plateau dropped away into a wide frozen plain, Anadyr Airbase centered within the snow-covered valley. McLanahan did not wait for the terrain-avoidance system to take the Old Dog down. He grabbed onto the yoke and pushed the Old Dog's nose down, then shoved all six operating engine-throttles to full power.

The Old Dog had only dropped about a hundred feet down into the valley when McLanahan suddenly realized the implications of what he was doing and used every ounce of strength left to pull back on the control column.

"Patrick, what the hell are you doing?" Ormack shouted.

"He's *behind* us," McLanahan told him. "He's gotta be behind us. If we dive into that valley we're dead meat."

Shattered fibersteel from the Old Dog's damaged fuselage screamed in protest but somehow stayed together. The stall-warning horn blared, but McLanahan still held the yoke back, forcing the Old Dog's nose skyward at a drastic angle.

The AA-8 missiles, only a few hundred meters from impact, lost their lock-on to the engine's hot exhaust when the Old Dog nosed upward. The missiles then immediately reacquired a warm heat-source and readjusted to a target—the base-operations building and the vehicles parked near it at Anadyr Airbase, which was now manned by several squads of the Anadyr constabulary. Surrounded by a meter of unplowed snow in all directions, the halftracks and jeeps were the hottest objects for miles.

Chief Constable Vjarelskiy, who had run from the hangar area to the flightline to watch the chase unfolding in the skies above Anadyr Airbase, now watched in horror as the two missiles screamed directly at him.

Before he could shout a warning, the missiles hit—one plowing into the wooden base operations building, the other finding an unoccupied truck with its hood open because of an overheated radiator. The twin explosions scattered troops in all directions.

Properly enraged, Vjarelskiy pulled his nine-millimeter pistol from his holster and raised it toward the American B-52, then stopped, realizing how absurd he must look.

Yuri had expected the American bomber to try to duck into the valley. Well, it would do him no good—actually it would improve the intruder's heat-signature.

What he never expected was a *climb* . . . the B-52 had appeared out of nowhere from behind the ridge, streaking skyward, its nose pointed straight up in the air.

No missile, not even the new AA-8s, could follow that. Yuri flicked on his cannon and managed a half-second burst, but his overtake speed was too great and he was forced to climb over the B-52.

The huge black bomber had disappeared beneath him. Yuri could only keep his throttles at max afterburner, try to loop around and align himself once more for another cannon pass before his fuel ran out . . .

McLanahan was now fiercely pushing the control column, fighting the lumbering Old Dog. Its airspeed had bled off well below two hundred knots. Over the blare of the stall-warning horn Ormack shouted to him that they had stalled and to get the nose down . . .

McLanahan somehow did it. He had just leveled the Old Dog's nose on the horizon when a blur and a roar erupted just outside his left window.

The fighter had rushed past, its twin afterburners glowing. It was so close McLanahan felt the heat of its engines through the broken glass and bullet holes. Then it began a shallow climb, arcing gracefully up and to the left.

Ignoring the blaring stall-warning horn, McLanahan pulled back on the control column and pointed the Old Dog's nose skyward once again.

But with the number-eight throttle at full power, the Old Dog began to slide to the left, its nose reaching a forty-degree angle, knifing skyward.

"Patrick, release the controls, *now* . . ."

McLanahan ignored Ormack's order, waited, bone-tired, wrestling with a hundred tons of near-uncontrollable machine. Then seconds before the MiG disappeared from sight, he ordered: "Angie, right pylon missile— *FIRE.*"

It took a few seconds, but with a screech and a long plume of fire the *Scorpion* missile sped free of its pylon rail . . . and in the cold semidarkness of the long Siberian night, with two bright turbofans in full afterburner dead-ahead, there was only one possible target.

The missile plunged into the fighter, detonating as the hot afterburner exhaust hit the propellant. The entire aft section of the twin-tailed MiG broke apart, shredding the nearly empty fuel tanks and adding thousands of cubic feet of fumes to the fury of the explosion.

McLanahan watched the fireball fly on for several moments in a wide bright arc, before plunging into the snowy peaks of the Korakskoje Mountains below.

Silence. No cheers. No gloating. And then the Old Dog turned eastward toward the Bering Straits—and home.

The hospital rooms were small and cold, the beds hard and narrow, and the food was just edible—but for the past week the crew of the Old Dog had felt like they had died and gone to heaven.

For the first time since their arrival, and by accident, they were all together. When she was notified by a nurse that General Elliott was accepting visitors, Angelina Pereira, the only one of the crew not seriously injured, walked through the frozen streets of the Nome Airport to the Air National Guard infirmary and General Elliott's guarded room.

The entire crew was assembled.

"Well, hello," she said, surprised but pleased. They were all there— John Ormack, sitting at a desk beside Elliott, his head and shoulder heavily bandaged; Patrick McLanahan, frostbite on his ears, hands and face; Wendy Tork, bandages over parts of her face and forehead; and General Elliott. Angelina went over to his bedside.

"How you doing, Angie?"

"Fine, sir . . . I'm . . . I'm sorry about your leg. I'm truly—"

"Forget it, Angie," Elliott said, glancing at the folds of bedspread where his right leg would have been. "Some team of doctors out at Bethesda already has me on the slate for a new mechanical job, so I'll be up and making trouble before you know it. I'm not trying to be brave, I'm just damn glad to be alive . . . actually I'm the one who should be making the apologies." He was thinking especially of Dave Luger.

Angelina said: "I was proud to serve with you, sir, and proud of what we accomplished. I think I speak for everybody."

Elliott looked at his assembled crew. "Thank you, I'm damn grateful to all of you." He cleared his throat. "I think you'll be glad to know that I spoke with the President this morning. He congratulated everyone of you. He also said that a new agreement has been reached . . . the Soviets have agreed *not* to rebuild the Kavaznya facility, and in return we've agreed not to launch another *Ice Fortress.*

"He told me something else that will interest you. Our suspicions about a breach of security were on target. It seems a certain aide in CIA Director Kenneth Mitchell's office was passing information to the Soviets. I don't know if it was a birds-of-a-feather sort of thing, or money, or both. Whatever, if we hadn't faked that crash over Seattle, my guess is that the Russians would have been waiting for us with every fighter they could put in the air. As it was, we had our hands full . . ."

No one argued with that.

Elliott motioned to Wendy, who had gotten a smuggled bottle of wine from the general's closet. She and Angelina poured for everyone as Elliott went on.

"Of course the destruction of the Kavaznya laser and our new agreement doesn't nail down the lid on laser technology. It's probably only a matter of time before we develop laser systems equivalent to the Soviet's. What we've got to hope is that they'll neutralize each other . . ."

Elliott raised his glass. "Well, to right now, and to the crew of the Old Dog. You guys broke the mold."

Angelina raised her glass. "And to Lewis Campos."

McLanahan forced his voice to be steady. "To Dave Luger . . ."

"To Dave Luger," Wendy added. "The one who really brought us home."

They finished their wine in a strained silence. It was Angelina who finally spoke.

"What will happen to the Old Dog, General?"

"Well, as a matter of fact, it may be back in action—although I still think John here suffered a crack in the head he's not telling us about."

Ormack shrugged. "With what it's been through, it doesn't seem right to let it be cut up for scrap metal. I'll supervise some repairs and fly it back to Dreamland."

McLanahan said, "I'm probably out of my mind, but I volunteered to go back with him."

"Patrick seems to like the idea of hanging around with an old coot like me," Elliott said, smiling. "He's accepted a job working with me at Dreamland."

Elliott nodded at Ormack, who reached into a duffel bag. "I saved this one for you, McLanahan," Ormack said, and presented him with the pilot's control wheel. "It popped right off the Old Dog's left control column. I didn't have it cut off or anything. I guess the beast *wanted* you to have it."

***

Wendy hung up the telephone at the nurse's station, turned to Patrick McLanahan sitting beside her.

"Everything okay at home?" McLanahan asked.

"Fine. They were relieved to hear from me. They hadn't been able to get word-one out of the Air Force for the last two months."

"My Mom was worried too," McLanahan said. "I had a good excuse, though. Told her I was busy bombing Russia."

"You didn't—"

"Sure, why not? She didn't believe a word I said."

Wendy smiled, then turned serious. "Pat . . . that girl, Catherine, you told me about. Did you call her too?"

"Yes. We had a long talk. Very long. I told her the truth. I told her I used to worry I wasn't making a difference being in the Air Force, that what I was doing wasn't adding up to anything. I said I didn't feel that way anymore, that I was going to stay in. I think she understood. She wished me luck."

"Oh, well, that's good . . . I guess . . . And now you're off to Dreamland next month." She fidgeted with her hands. "I'm sure you'll do . . . I'm glad things have worked out for you . . ."

He stood up and looked down at her, into her eyes that raised to meet his. "Hey, it's just a thought, but . . . well, you know, Elliott could use a good electronic warfare officer at Dreamland. And I'd like it if . . . oh, to hell with it," and he put his arms around her and drew her to him.

"I want you to come with me. I want us to be together. How about it?"

Her arms tightened around him, and the kiss that followed gave him all the answer he needed.

no date(no cards 5-5-98
c 3

Bro   Brown, Dale
          Flight of the
          old dog

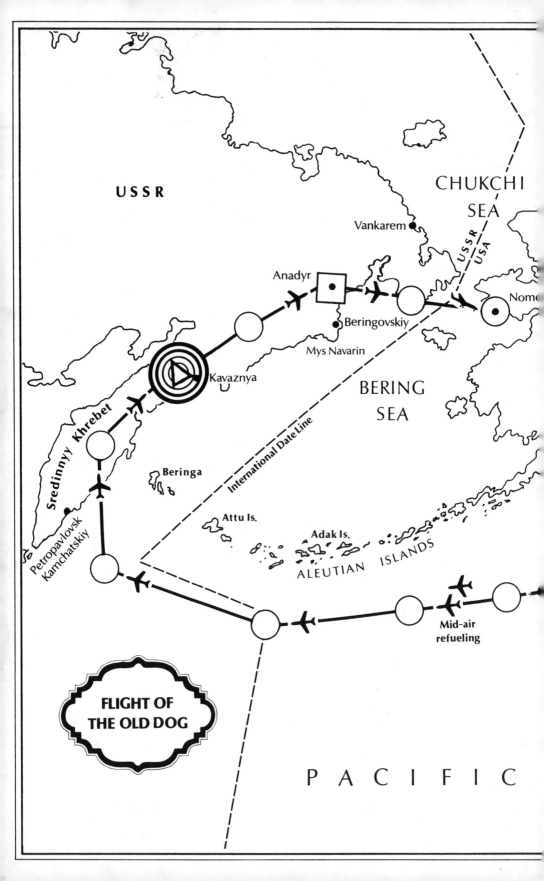